s bo

loa
the

solitude creek

JEFFERY DEAVER

solitude creek

**HODDER &
STOUGHTON**

First published in the United States of America in 2015 by
Grand Central Publishing

First published in Great Britain in 2015 by Hodder & Stoughton
An Hachette UK company

1

A CIP catalogue record for this title is available from the British Library

Hardback ISBN 978 1 444 75739 2
Trade paperback ISBN 978 1 444 75740 8
Ebook ISBN 978 1 444 75741 5

Typeset in Sabon MT by Palimpsest Book Production Limited,
Falkirk, Stirlingshire

Printed and bound by Clays Ltd, St Ives plc

Hodder & Stoughton policy is to use papers that are natural,
renewable and recyclable products and made from wood grown in
sustainable forests. The logging and manufacturing processes are
expected to conform to the environmental regulations of the
country of origin.

Hodder & Stoughton Ltd
Carmelite House
50 Victoria Embankment
London EC4Y 0DZ

www.hodder.co.uk

To Libraries and Librarians everywhere . . .

Fear is the mind-killer.

– Frank Herbert, *Dune*

FRENZY

TUESDAY, APRIL 4

CHAPTER 1

The roadhouse was comfortable, friendly, inexpensive. All good.

Safe, too. Better.

You always thought about that when you took your teenage daughter out for a night of music.

Michelle Cooper did, in any event. Safe when it came to the band and their music, the customers, the wait staff.

The club itself, too, the parking lot – well lit – and the fire doors and sprinklers.

Michelle always checked these. The teenage-daughter part again.

Solitude Creek attracted a varied clientele, young and old, male and female, white and Latino and Asian, a few African Americans, a mirror of the Monterey Bay area. Now, just after seven thirty, she looked around, noting the hundreds of patrons who'd come from this and surrounding counties, all in buoyant mood, looking forward to seeing a band on the rise. If they brought with them any cares, those troubles were tucked tightly away at the prospect of beer, whimsical cocktails, chicken wings and music.

The group had flown in from LA, a garage band turned backup turned roadhouse headliner, thanks to Twitter and YouTube and Vidster. Word of mouth, and talent, sold groups nowadays, and the six boys in Lizard Annie worked as hard on their phones as onstage. They weren't O.A.R. or Linkin Park but were soon to be, with a bit of luck.

They certainly had Michelle and Trish's support. In fact, the cute boy band had a pretty solid mom-daughter fan base, judging by a look around the room tonight: other parents and their teenagers – the lyrics were rated PG at the raunchiest. For this evening's show the ages of those in the audience ranged from sixteen to forty, give or take. Okay, Michelle admitted, maybe mid-forties.

She noted the Samsung in her daughter's grip and said, 'Text later. Not now.'

'Mom.'

'Who is it?'

'Cho.'

A nice girl from Trish's music class.

'Two minutes.'

The club was filling up. Solitude Creek was a forty-year-old, single-story building featuring a small, rectangular dance floor of scuffed oak, ringed with high-top tables and stools. The stage, three feet high, was at the north end; the bar was opposite. A kitchen, east, served full menus, which eliminated the age barrier of attendance: only liquor-serving venues that offered food were permitted to seat children. Three fire-exit doors were against the west wall.

On the dark-wood paneling there were posters and during-the-show photos, complete with real and fake autographs, of many of the groups that had appeared at the legendary Monterey Pop Festival in June of 1967: Jefferson Airplane, Jimi Hendrix, Janis Joplin, Ravi Shankar, Al Kooper, Country Joe. Dozens of others. In a grimy Plexiglas case there was a fragment of an electric guitar, reportedly one destroyed by Pete Townshend of The Who after the group's performance at the event.

The tables at Solitude Creek were first come, first claimed, and all were filled – the show was only twenty minutes away now. Presently servers circulated with last-minute orders, plates of hefty burgers and wings and drinks on trays hovering atop their stable, splayed palms. From behind the stage, a miaow of tuning guitar strings and an arpeggio chord from a sax, a chunky A from a bass. Anticipation now. Those exciting moments before the music begins to seize and seduce.

The voices were loud, words indistinct, as the untabled patrons jockeyed for the best position in the standing-room area. Since the stage wasn't high and the floor was flat, it was sometimes hard to get a good view of the acts. A bit of jostling but few hard words.

That was the Solitude Creek club. No hostility.

Safe . . .

However, there was one thing that Michelle Cooper didn't care for. The claustrophobia. The ceilings in the club were low and that accentuated the closeness. The dim room was not particularly spacious, the ventilation not the best; a mix of body scent, aftershave and perfume clung, stronger even than grill and fry-tank aromas, adding to the sense of confinement. The sense that you were packed in tight as canned fish. No, *that* never sat well with Michelle Cooper.

She brushed absently at her frosted blonde hair, looked again at the exit doors – not far away – and felt reassured.

Another sip of wine.

She noted Trish checking out a boy at a table nearby. Floppy hair, narrow face, skinny hips. Good looks to kill for. He was drinking a beer so Mother vetoed Trish's inclination instantly, if silently. Not the alcohol, the age: the drink meant he was over twenty-one and therefore completely out of bounds for her seventeen-year-old.

Then she thought wryly: At least I can try.

A glance at her diamond Rolex. Five minutes.

Michelle asked, 'Was it "Escape", the one that was nominated for the Grammy?'

'Yeah.'

'Focus on *me*, child.'

The girl grimaced. 'Mom.' She looked away from the Boy with the Beer.

Michelle hoped Lizard Annie would do the song tonight. 'Escape' was not only catchy but brought back good memories. She'd been listening to it after a recent first date with a lawyer from Salinas. In the six years since a vicious divorce, Michelle had had plenty of awkward dinners and movies, but the evening with Ross had been fun. They'd laughed. They'd dueled about the best *Veep* and *Homeland* episodes. And there'd been no pressure – for anything. So very rare for a first date.

Mother and daughter ate a bit more artichoke dip and Michelle had a little more wine. Driving, she allowed herself two glasses before getting behind the wheel, no more.

The girl adjusted her pink floral headband and sipped a Diet Coke. She was in black jeans, not too tight – yay! – and a white sweater. Michelle was in blue jeans, tighter than her daughter's, though that was a symptom of exercise failure, and a red silk blouse.

'Mom. San Francisco this weekend? Please. I need that jacket.'

'We'll go to Carmel.' Michelle spent plenty of her real-estate commissions shopping in the classy stores of the picturesque and excessively cute village.

'Jeez, Mom, I'm not thirty.' Meaning ancient. Trish was simply stating the more or less accurate fact that shopping for cool teen clothes wasn't easy on the Peninsula, which had been called, with only some exaggeration, a place for the newly wed and nearly dead.

'Okay. We'll work it out.'

Trish hugged her and Michelle's world glowed.

She and her daughter had had their hard times. A seemingly good marriage had crashed, thanks to cheating. Everything torn apart. Frederick (never *Fred*) moving out when the girl was eleven – what a tough time for a break-up to happen. But Michelle had worked hard to create a good life for her daughter, to give her what had been yanked away by betrayal and the subsequent divorce.

And now it was working. Now the girl seemed happy. She looked at her daughter with moon eyes and the girl noticed.

'Mom, like what?'

'Nothing.'

Lights down.

PA announcements about shutting off phones, fire exits and so on were made by the owner of the club himself, the venerable Sam Cohen, an icon in the Monterey Bay area. Everybody knew Sam. Everybody loved Sam.

Cohen's voice continued, 'And now, ladies and gentlemen, Solitude Creek, the premier roadhouse on the west coast . . .'

Applause.

'. . . is pleased to welcome, direct from the City of Angels . . . Lizard Annie!'

Frantic clapping now. Hooting.

Out came the boys. Guitars were plugged in. The seat behind the drum set occupied. Ditto the keyboard.

The lead singer tossed his mass of hair aside and lifted an outstretched palm to the audience. The group's trademark gesture. 'Are we ready to get down?'

Howling.

'Well, are we?'

The guitar riffs started. Yes! The song *was* 'Escape'. Michelle and her daughter began to clap, along with the hundreds of others in the small space. The heat had increased, the humidity, the embracing scent of bodies. Claustrophobia notched up a bit. Still, Michelle smiled and laughed.

The pounding beat continued, bass, drum and the flesh of palms.

But then Michelle stopped clapping. Frowning, she looked around, cocking her head. What was that? The club, like everywhere in California, was supposed to be non-smoking. But somebody, she was sure, had lit up. She definitely smelled smoke.

She looked around but saw no one with a cigarette in their mouth.

'What?' Trish called, seeing her mother's troubled expression.

'Nothing,' the woman replied, and began clapping out the rhythm once again.

CHAPTER 2

At the third word into the second song – it happened to be 'love' – Michelle Cooper knew something was wrong.

She smelled the smoke more strongly. And it wasn't cigarette smoke. Smoke from burning wood or paper.

Or the old, dry walls or flooring of a very congested roadhouse.

'Mom?' Trish was frowning, looking around too. Her pert nose twitched. 'Is that . . .'

'I smell it too,' Michelle whispered. She couldn't see any fumes but the smell was unmistakable and growing stronger. 'We're leaving. Now.' Michelle stood fast.

'Hey, lady,' a man called, catching the stool and righting it. 'You okay?' Then he frowned. 'Jesus. Is that smoke?'

Others were looking around, smelling the same.

No one else in the venue, none of the two hundred or so others – employees or patrons or musicians – existed. Michelle Cooper was getting her daughter out of there. She steered Trish toward the nearest fire-exit door.

'My purse,' Trish said over the music. The Brighton bag, a present from Michelle, was hidden on the floor beneath the table – just to be safe. The girl broke away to retrieve the heart-embossed bag.

'Forget it, let's go!' her mother commanded.

'I'll just be . . .' the girl began and bent down.

'Trish! No! Leave it.'

By now, a dozen people nearby, who'd seen Michelle's abrupt rise and lurch toward the exit, had stopped paying attention to the music and were looking around. One by one they were also rising. Curious and troubled expressions on their faces. Smiles becoming frowns. Eyes narrowing. Something predatory, feral about the gazes.

Five or six oozed between Michelle and her daughter, who was still rummaging for the purse. Michelle stepped forward fast and went for the girl's shoulder to pull her up. Hand gripped sweater. It stretched.

'Mom!' Trish pulled away.

It was then that a brilliant light came on, focused on the exit doors.

The music stopped abruptly. The lead singer called into the microphone, 'Hey, uhm, guys, I don't know . . . Look, don't panic.'

'Jesus, what's—' somebody beside Michelle shouted.

The screams began. Wails filled the venue, loud, nearly loud enough to shatter eardrums.

Michelle struggled to get to Trish but more patrons surged between them. The two were pushed in different directions.

An announcement on the PA: '*Ladies and gentlemen, there's a fire. Evacuate! Evacuate now! Do not use the kitchen or stage exit – that's where the fire is! Use the emergency doors.*'

Howling screams now.

Patrons rose and stools fell, drinks scattered. Two high-top tables tipped over and crashed to the floor. People began moving toward the exit doors – their glowing red signs were still obvious; the smell of smoke was strong but visibility was good.

'Trish! Over here!' Michelle screamed. Now two dozen people were between them. Why the hell had she gone back for the damn purse? 'Let's get out!'

Her daughter started toward her through the crowd. But the tide of people surging for the exit doors lifted Michelle off her feet and tugged her away, while Trish was enveloped in another group.

'Honey!'

'Mom!'

Michelle, being dragged toward the doors, used every muscle in her body to turn toward her daughter but she was helpless, crushed between two patrons: a heavy-set man in a T-shirt, which was already savagely torn, his skin red, bearing scratch marks from fingernails, and a woman, whose fake breasts pressed painfully into Michelle's side.

'Trish, Trish, Trish!'

She might have been mute. The patrons' screams and wailing – from fear and from pain – were numbing. All she could see was the head of the man in front of her and the exit sign they surged toward. Michelle pounded her fists on shoulders, on arms, on necks, on faces, just as she, too, was pounded by other patrons.

'I have to get my daughter! Go back, go back, go back!'

But there was no stopping the tide streaming for the exits. Michelle Cooper could breathe only an ounce or two of air at a time. And the pain – in her chest, her side, her gut. Terrible! Her arms were pinned, feet suspended above the floor.

The house lights were on, bright. Michelle turned slightly – not her doing – and saw the faces of the patrons near her: eyes coin-wide in panic, crimson streaks from mouths. Had people bitten their tongues out of fear? Or was the crush snapping ribs and piercing lungs? One man, in his forties, was unconscious, skin gray. Had he fainted? Or died of a heart attack? He was still upright, though, wedged into the moving crowd.

The smell of smoke was stronger now and it was hard to breathe – maybe the fire was sucking the oxygen from the room, though she could still see no flames. Perhaps the patrons, in their panic, were depleting the air. The pressure of bodies against her chest, too.

'Trish! Honey!' she called, but the words were whispers. No air in, no air out.

Where was her baby? Was someone helping her escape? Not likely. Nobody, not a single soul, seemed to be helping anyone else. This was an animal frenzy. Every person was out for himself. It was pure survival.

Please . . .

The group of patrons she was welded to stumbled over something.

Oh, God . . .

Glancing down, Michelle could just make out a slim young Latina in a red-and-black dress, lying on her side, her face registering pure terror and agony. Her right arm was broken, bent backward. Her other hand was reaching up, fingers gripping a man's pants pocket.

Helpless. She couldn't rise; no one paid the least attention to her even as she cried out with every shuffled foot that trampled her body.

Michelle was looking right into the woman's eyes when a booted foot stepped onto her throat. The man tried to avoid it, crying, 'No, move back, move back,' to those around him. But, like everyone else, he had no control of his direction, his motion, his footfalls.

Under the pressure of the weight on her throat, the woman's head twisted even farther sideways and she began to shake fiercely. By the time Michelle had moved on, the Latina's eyes were glazed and her tongue protruded slightly from her bright red lips.

Michelle Cooper had just seen someone die.

More PA announcements. Michelle couldn't hear them. Not that it mattered. She had absolutely no control over anything.

Trish, she prayed, stay on your feet. Don't fall. Please . . .

As the mass surrounding her stumbled closer to the fire doors, the crowd began to shift to the right and soon Michelle could see the rest of the club.

There! Yes, there was her daughter! Trish was still on her feet, though she too was pinned in a mass of bodies. 'Trish, Trish!'

But no sound at all came from her now.

Mother and daughter were moving in opposite directions.

Michelle blinked tears and sweat from her eyes. Her group was only feet away from the exits. She'd be out in a few seconds. Trish was still near the kitchen – where somebody had just said the fire was raging.

'Trish! This way!'

Pointless.

And then she saw a man beside her daughter lose control completely – he began pounding the face of the man next to him and started to climb on top of the crowd, as if, in his madness, he believed he could claw his way through the ceiling. He was large and one of the people he used as a launching pad was Trish, who weighed a hundred pounds less than he did. Michelle saw her daughter open her mouth to scream and then, under the man's massive weight, vanish beneath the sea of madness.

BASELINE

WEDNESDAY, APRIL 5

CHAPTER 3

The two people sitting at the long conference table looked her over with varying degrees of curiosity.

Anything else? she wondered. Suspicion, dislike, jealousy?

Kathryn Dance, a kinesics (body language) expert, got paid to read people but law enforcers were typically hard to parse so at the moment she wasn't sure what was flitting through their minds.

Also present was her boss, Charles Overby, though he wasn't at the table but hovering in the doorway, engrossed in his Droid. He'd just arrived.

The four were in an interrogation-observation room on the ground floor of the California Bureau of Investigation's West Central Division, off Route 68 in Monterey, near the airport. One of those dim, pungent chambers separated from the interrogation room by a see-through mirror that nobody, even the most naïve or stoned perps, believed was for straightening your tie or coiffing.

A no-nonsense crowd, fashion-wise. The man at the table – he'd commandeered the head spot – was Steve Foster, wearing a draping black suit and white shirt. He was the head of special investigations with the California Bureau of Investigation's Criminal Division. He was based in Sacramento. Dance, five six and about a hundred twenty pounds, didn't know exactly when to describe somebody as 'hulking' but Foster had to figure close. Broad, an impressive silver mane, and a droopy moustache that could have been waxed into a handlebar, had it been horizontal and not staple-shaped, he looked like an Old West marshal.

Perpendicular to Foster was Carol Allerton, in a bulky gray pants suit. Short hair frosted silver, black and gray, Carol Allerton was a senior DEA agent operating out of Oakland. The stocky woman had a dozen serious collars to her credit. Not legend, but respectable. She'd had the opportunity to be fast-tracked to Sacramento or even Washington but she'd declined.

Kathryn Dance was in a black skirt and white blouse of thick cotton, under a dark brown jacket, cut to obscure if not wholly hide her Glock. The only color in her ensemble was a blue band that secured the end of her dark blonde French braid. Her daughter had bound it this morning on the way to school.

'That's done.' Hovering around fifty, Charles Overby looked up from his phone, on which he might've been arranging a tennis date or reading an email from the governor, though, given their meeting now, it was probably halfway between. The athletic if pear-shaped man said, 'Okay, all task-forced up? Let's get this thing done.' He sat and opened a manila folder.

His ingratiating words were greeted with the same non-negotiable stares that had surveilled Dance a moment ago. It was pretty well known in law-enforcement circles that Overby's main skill was, and had always been, administration, while those present were hard-core line investigators. None of whom would use the verb he just had.

Mumbles and nods of greeting.

The 'thing' he was referring to was an operation that was part of a statewide push to address a recent trend in gang activity. You could find organized crime everywhere in California but the main centers for gang activity were two: north and south. Oakland was the headquarters of the former, LA the latter. But rather than being rivals, the polar crews had decided to start working together, guns moving south from the Bay Area and drugs moving north. At any given moment, there would be dozens of illicit shipments coursing along Interstate-5, the 101 and the dusty, slow-moving 99.

To make it harder to track and stop these shipments, the senior bangers had hit on an idea: they'd taken to using break-bulk and way stations, where the cargo was transferred from the original tractor-trailers to dozens of smaller trucks and vans. Two hours south of Oakland and five north of LA, Salinas, with its active gang population, was perfect as a hub. Hundreds of warehouses, thousands of vehicles and produce trucks. Police interdiction nearly ground to a halt and illicit business surged. This year alone the statistics cops reported that revenue in the gun/drug operation had risen nearly a half-billion dollars.

Six months ago the CBI, FBI, DEA and local law-enforcement agencies had formed Operation Pipeline to try to stop the transportation network but had had paltry success. The bangers were so connected, smart and brazen that they constantly remained one step ahead of the good guys, who managed to bust only low-level dealers or mules with mere ounces taped to their crotches, hardly worth the bytes to process into the system. Worse, informants were ID'd, tortured and killed before any leads could be developed.

As part of Pipeline, Kathryn Dance was running what she'd dubbed the Guzman Connection and had put together a task force that included Foster, Allerton and two other officers, presently in the field. The eponymous Guzman was a massive, borderline psychotic gang-banger, who reportedly knew at least half of the transfer points in and around Salinas. As near a perfect prize as you could find in the crazy business of law enforcement.

After a lot of preliminary work, just last night Dance had texted the task force that they had their first lead to Guzman and to assemble here, now, for a briefing.

'So, tell us about this asshole you're going to be talking to today, the one you think's going to give up Guzman. What's his name? Serrano?' From Steve Foster.

Dance replied, 'Okay. Joaquin Serrano. He's an innocent – what all the intel shows. No record. Thirty-two. We heard about him from a CI we've been running—'

'Who's been running?' Foster asked bluntly. The man was adept at interruption, Dance had learned. Also, it was true that law enforcers were quite sensitive about their colleague's attempts to poach confidential informants.

'Our office.'

Foster grunted. Maybe he was irritated he hadn't been informed. His flick of a finger said, Go on.

'Serrano can link Guzman to the killing of Sad Eyes.'

The victim, actually Hector Mendoza (droopy lids had led to the nic), was a banger who knew higher-ups in both the north and south operations. That is, a perfect witness – had he remained alive.

Even cynical, sour Foster seemed content at the possibility of hanging the Sad Eyes killing on Guzman.

Overby, often good at stating the obvious, said, 'Guzman falls, the other Pipeline crews could go like dominos.' Then he didn't seem to like his metaphor.

'This witness, Serrano. Tell us more about him.' Allerton fiddled with a yellow pad of foolscap, then seemed to realize she was doing so. She aligned the edges and set it free.

'He's a landscaper, works for one of the big companies in Monterey. Documented. Probably trustworthy.'

'Probably,' Foster said.

'He's here now?' Allerton asked.

'Outside,' Overby replied.

Foster said, 'Why's he going to want to talk to us? I mean, let's be transparent. He knows what Guzman'll do, he finds out.'

Allerton: 'Maybe he wants money – maybe he's got somebody in the system he wants us to help.'

Dance said, 'Or maybe he wants to do the right thing.' Drawing a laugh from Foster. She, too, gave a faint grin. 'I'm told it happens occasionally.'

'He came in voluntarily?' Allerton wondered aloud.

'He did. I just called him up. He said yes.'

'So,' Overby inquired, 'we're relying on his good graces to help us?'

'More or less.' The phone against the wall hummed. Dance rose and answered it. 'Yes?'

'Hey, boss.'

The caller was a thirtyish CBI agent in the West Central Division. He was Dance's junior associate, though that was not an official job description. TJ Scanlon, a dependable, hard-working agent and, best put, atypical for the conservative CBI.

TJ said, 'He's here. Ready to go.'

'Okay, bring him up.' Dance dropped the phone into the cradle and said to the room. 'Serrano's coming in now.'

Through the mirror window, they watched the door to the interview room open. In walked TJ, slim, his curly hair more unruly than usual. He was in a plaid sports coat and red pants, which approached bell-bottoms. His T-shirt was tie-dyed, yellow and orange.

Atypical . . .

Following him was a tall Latino with thick, short-cut dark hair. He walked in and looked around. His jeans were slim-cut and dark blue. New. He wore a gray hoodie with 'UCSC' on the front.

'Yeah,' Foster grumbled. 'He graduated from Santa Cruz. Right.'

Dance said stiffly, 'Not graduated. Took courses.'

'Hmm.'

The Latino's right hand was inked, though it didn't seem to be a gang sign, and on his left forearm, near the sweat jacket, you could just make out the start of a tat. His face was untroubled.

Over the speaker, they heard the young agent say, 'There you go. There. Take a seat. You want some water?'

The somber man said, 'No.'

'Somebody'll be in in a minute.'

The man nodded. He sat down in a chair facing the one-way mirror. He glanced at it once, then pulled out his cell phone and read the screen.

Foster shifted slightly. Dance didn't need any body-language skills to understand his thoughts. She said, 'He's just a witness, remember. We don't have a warrant to intercept. He hasn't done anything wrong.'

'Oh, he's done something wrong,' Foster said. 'We just don't know what yet.'

She glanced at him.

'I can smell it.'

Dance rose, slipped her Glock out of its holster and set it on the table. She picked up her pen and a pad of yellow paper.

Time to go to work and uncover the truth.

CHAPTER 4

'She works miracles, does she?' Foster asked. 'This kinesics stuff?'

'Kathryn's good, yes.' Overby had taken a dislike to Foster, who was the sort to snatch credit and press time away from those who'd done much of the legwork. He had to be careful, though. Foster was roughly on Overby's level, pay-grade wise, but higher up, in the sense that he was based in Sacramento and had an office no more than thirty feet from the head of the CBI. He was also within lobbing distance of the legislature.

Allerton adjusted her notebook, empty at the moment. She drew '1'.

Overby continued, 'Funny. When you know what she does – that body-language stuff – then go out to lunch with her, you watch what you're doing, where you're looking. Like you're waiting for her to say, "So, you had a fight with your wife this morning, hmm? Over bills, I'd think."'

'Sherlock Holmes,' Allerton said. She added, 'I like that British one. With the guy with the funny name. Like "cummerbund".'

Overby, staring into the interrogation room, said absently, 'That's not how kinesics works.'

'No?' Foster.

Overby said nothing more. As the others turned to the glass, he in turn examined the two members of the Guzman Connection task force present at the moment. Foster, Allerton. Then Dance walked into the interview room. And Overby's attention, too, turned that way.

'Mr Serrano. I'm Agent Dance.' Her voice crackled through the overhead speaker in the observation room.

'"Mister",' Foster muttered.

The Latino's eyes narrowed as he looked her over carefully. 'Good to meet you.' There was nothing nervous about his expression or posture, Overby noted.

She sat across from him. 'Appreciate your coming in.'

A nod. Agreeable.

'Now, please understand, you're not under investigation. I want to make that clear. We're talking to dozens of people, maybe hundreds. We're looking into gang-related crimes here on the Peninsula. And hope you can help us.'

'So, I no need a lawyer.'

She smiled. 'No, no. And you can leave anytime you want. Or choose not to answer.'

'But then I look kind of suspicious, don't I?'

'I could ask how you liked your wife's roast last night. You might not want to answer that one.'

Allerton laughed. Foster looked impatient.

'I couldn't answer that anyway.'

'You don't have a wife?'

'No, but even if I did I'd do the cooking. I pretty good in the kitchen.' Then a frown. 'But I want to help. Terrible, some of the things that happen, the gangs.' He closed his eyes momentarily. 'Disgusting.'

'You've lived in the area for a while?'

'Ten years.'

'You're not married. But you have family here?'

'No, they in Bakersfield.'

Foster: 'Shouldn't she have looked all this up?'

Overby said, 'Oh, she knows it. She knows everything about him. Well, what she could learn in the past eight hours since she got his name.'

He'd observed plenty of Dance's interrogations and listened to her lecture on the topic; he was able to give the task force a brief overview. 'Kinesics is all about looking for stress indicators. When people lie they feel stress, can't help it. Some suspects can cover it up well so it's really hard to see. But most of us give away indications that we're stressed. What Kathryn's doing is talking to Serrano for a while, nothing about gang activity, nothing about crime – the weather, growing up, restaurants, life on the Peninsula. She gets his baseline body language.'

'Baseline.'

'That's the key. It tells her how he behaves when he's answering truthfully. When I said earlier that kinesics doesn't work that way? I meant it doesn't work in a vacuum. It's almost impossible to meet somebody and instantly read them. You have to do what Kathryn's doing – getting that baseline. After that she'll start asking about gang activities he might've heard of, then about Guzman.'

Allerton said, 'So she compares his behavior then to his baseline, when she knows he's telling the truth.'

'That's it,' Overby replied. 'If there's any variation it'll be because he's feeling stress.'

'And that's because he's lying,' Foster said.

'Possibly. Of course, there's lying because you just machine-gunned somebody to death. And there's lying because you don't want to *get* machine-gunned. His deception'll be that there's a point past which he won't want to cooperate. Kathryn'll have to make sure he does.'

'Cooperation,' Foster said. The word seemed to take on extra syllables as it trickled from a cynical mouth.

Overby noted that Foster was or had been a smoker – slight discoloration of his index and middle finger. The teeth were yellowish.

Sherlock.

In front of them, in the small, sterile room, Kathryn Dance continued to ask questions, chat, share observations.

Fifteen minutes rolled past.

Dance asked, 'You enjoy landscaping?'

'I do, *sí*. It's . . . I don't know . . . I like to work with my hands. I think maybe I'd be an artist if I had some, you know, skill. But I don't. Gardening? Now that's something I can do.'

Overby noted his nails were dark crescents.

'Here's what we're looking into. A week ago a man named Hector Mendoza was killed. Shot. His nickname was Sad Eyes. He was coming out of a restaurant in New Monterey. On Lighthouse.'

'Sad Eyes. Yeah, yeah. On the news. Near Baskin-Robbins, right?'

'That's it.'

'Was— I no remember. Was a drive-by?'

'That's right.'

'Was anybody else hurt?' He frowned. 'I hate it when children, bystanders are hurt. Those gang people, they don't care who they hurt or don't hurt.'

Dance nodded, on her face a pleasant expression. 'Now, Mr Serrano, the reason I'm asking you this is that your name came up in the investigation.'

'Mine?' He seemed curious but not shocked. His dark face folded into a frown for a moment.

'The day this man I mentioned, Mendoza, was killed, I believe you were working at the house of Rodrigo Guzman. It was March twenty-first. Now, while you were working for Mr Guzman, did you see a black BMW? A large one. This would be the afternoon of March twenty-first, I was saying, around three p.m.'

'There were some cars there, I saw. Maybe some black ones but I no think so. And no BMW. Definitely.' He added wistfully, 'I always wanted one. I recognize a car like that, I would have gone to look at it.'

'How long were you there?'

'Oh, much of the day. I get to the job early, as early as the customers will have me. Señor Guzman, he has a lot of property. And there is always much to do. I was there at seven thirty. Took a lunch break maybe eleven thirty but only for thirty minutes. But, please, I am working for someone involved in the gangs? You are saying that?' The frown deepened. 'He a very nice man. Are you saying he involved in this death of . . . Men- . . .'

'Mendoza. Hector Mendoza.'

'Sí. Señor Guzman, he the nicest guy. Never hurt nobody.'

'Again, Mr Serrano, we're merely trying to get the facts.'

'I can't tell how he's reacting,' Allerton said. 'He's shifting in his chair, looking away, looking at her. I don't know what it means.'

'That's *Kathryn*'s job,' Overby said.

'I think he's a prick,' Foster said. 'I don't care about body language. He's sounding *too* innocent.'

Overby: 'He's just learned one of his company's big money-makers might be a banger and he's not very happy about it. That's how I'd act.'

'Would you?' Foster said.

Overby bristled but said nothing in response to the condescension. Allerton cast a sharp glance Foster's way. He said, 'I'm just saying. I don't trust him.'

Dance: 'Again, Mr Serrano, there are many questions, things we don't know. We have had reports that the man who shot Mr Mendoza met with Mr Guzman just before he drove to New Monterey. But they're just reports. You can see how we have to check it out.'

'Sure. Yeah.'

'So you're telling me you're certain there was no BMW at his house that morning?'

'That's right, Agent Dancer – no, Dance, right? Agent Dance. And I'm almost just as sure there were no black cars. And at that time I was in the front of the property, near the driveway. I would have seen. I was planting hydrangeas. He likes the blue ones.'

'Well, thanks for that. Now, one more thing. If I showed you a few pictures of some men, could you tell me if any of them came to Mr Guzman's house while you were there? Ideally on the twenty-first, but if not, some other time.'

'I try.'

Dance opened her notebook and extracted three pictures.

'Hard to see. They're taken with, what, a spy camera or something?'

'That's right, a surveillance camera.'

The young man was sitting forward, pulling the pictures closer. He seemed to notice his dirty nails and looked embarrassed. Once he'd positioned the pictures he slipped his hands into his lap.

He studied them for a long time.

Allerton said, 'Looks like he's giving it a real shot. Fingers crossed.'

But then the young man sat back. 'No, I'm sure I never seen

them. Though' – he tapped one – '*he* look like that outfielder for the As.'

Dance smiled.

'Who is that?' Foster asked. 'I can't see.'

Allerton said, 'I think it's Contino.'

'Now there's a prick and a half,' Foster snapped.

A triggerman for one of the Oakland crews.

Dance gathered the pictures. She put them away and said, 'I think that's it, Mr Serrano.'

He shook his head. 'I wish I could help you, Agent Dance. I hate the gangs as much as you do, no, probably more.' His voice grew firm. 'It is *our* teenagers and children getting killed. In *our* streets.'

Now Dance was leaning forward and she spoke in a soft voice: 'If you *did* happen to see anything at Mr Guzman's house and tell me, we'd make sure you're protected. You and your family.'

Now the young man looked away once more. This time it was a moment before he spoke. 'I no think so. I think I no be working there any longer. I'll tell my boss to give me other jobs. Even if I make less.'

Allerton said, 'Boy doesn't have the *cojones* to snitch.'

Foster muttered, 'She didn't offer him anything. Why would he—'

'You know, Mr Serrano, we have a budget for people who help us eliminate the gang threats. It's cash, so nobody knows.'

The young man rose, smiling. 'There only one problem with what you said. "Eliminate". If you could eliminate the gangs, then maybe I think about it. But what you mean is, you put a few of them in jail. That leave plenty of others to come pay me and my girlfriend and her family a visit. I gotta say no.'

She held out her hand. 'Thank you for coming in.'

'I'm sorry. Not so clean.' He showed his palms, though not the nails.

'That's all right.'

They gripped hands and he walked out of the room. Dance flipped the lights off.

CHAPTER 5

Dance stepped into the observation room and swung the door shut behind her. She walked to the table, set her notes down. She hit the button that shut off the recorder. Clicked her Glock back in its holster.

'Well?' Steve Foster asked. 'Did something wonderful happen that I missed?'

'What's your assessment, Kathryn?' Overby asked.

'Very few variations from the baseline. I think he's telling the truth,' Dance announced. 'He doesn't know anything.' She went on to explain that some people were masters of deception and could manipulate their behaviors – like the yoga experts who could slow their heart rate nearly to stopping – but Serrano didn't strike her as that skilled.

'Oh, I think he's got a few skeletons. But nothing related to the CI or the gangs or Guzman. I'd guess he boosted a car when he was a kid or scores some weed from time to time. Got a ripple of evasion when we were talking about life on the Peninsula, never in trouble with the law. But it was small-time.'

'You read that?' Allerton said.

'I inferred it. I think it's accurate. But nothing we can use.'

'Hell,' Overby muttered. 'Our one chance to nail Guzman.'

Dance corrected, 'A chance. That didn't pan out. That's all. There'll be others.'

'Well, I don't *see* a lot of others,' Foster pointed out.

Carol Allerton said, 'We've got that delivery boy. *He* knows something.'

Foster muttered, 'The pizza kid? That's a non-lead. It's a dead lead. It's a pushing-up-daisies lead.' His face tightened. 'There's something about that asshole Serrano. I don't like him. He was too slick. You learn anything in body-language school about slick?'

Dance didn't answer.

Allerton: 'It's a pepper.'

'What?' Overby asked.

'Serrano's a pepper. Just saying.'

Foster read texts. Sent some.

Allerton thought for a moment, said, 'I think we should try again – to turn him, I mean. Offer him more money.'

'No interest,' Dance said. 'Serrano's a dead end. I say we put better surveillance on Guzman. Get a team in place.'

'What, Kathryn, twenty-four/seven? You know what that costs? Try the pizza boy, try the domestic staff in Guzman's. Keep following up on the other leads.' Overby looked at his watch. 'I'll leave it to you guys and gals to work it out.' His body language suggested that he regretted using the second G-word. Political correctness, Dance reflected, could be so tedious. Overby rose and walked to the door.

And nearly got decked as TJ Scanlon pushed inside. He looked past them and into the observation room. Eyes wide. 'Where's Serrano?'

'He just left,' Dance told him.

The agent's brow was furrowed. 'Shit.'

'What's up, TJ?' Overby asked sharply.

'He's gone?' the young agent exclaimed.

Foster snapped, '*What?*'

'Just got a call from Amy Grabe.' FBI special agent in charge of the San Francisco office. 'They busted this guy in Salinas for possession, major. He gave up Serrano.'

'Gave him up?' Foster's brow furrowed deeply.

TJ nodded. 'Boss, Serrano's on Guzman's *payroll*.'

'*What?*' Dance gasped.

'He's a shooter. *He* was the triggerman took out Sad Eyes. Serrano picked up the BMW at Guzman's that afternoon, popped Sad, then went back and finished his shift planting daisies or pansies or whatever. He's taken out four witnesses for Guzman in the last six months.'

'Fucking hell,' Foster raged. His eyes on Dance. 'Outfielder for the As?'

'Is it confirmed?'

'They found the piece Serrano used. Ballistics check out. And it's got Serrano's prints all over it.'

'No,' Dance whispered harshly. She flung the door open and began sprinting down the hall.

He grabbed her before she got three feet into the parking lot behind CBI.

The tackle took Dance down hard and she sprawled on the concrete. She got her Glock out of her holster but, fast as a striking snake, he pulled the gun from her hand. He didn't turn it her way, though. He saw that she was lying stunned on the ground and fled, a pounding sprint.

'Serrano!' she called. 'Stop!'

He glanced at his car, realized he couldn't get to it in time. He looked around and spotted, nearby, a slim redheaded woman in a black pantsuit – an employee of the CBI business office. She was climbing out of her Altima, which she'd just parked between two SUVs. He sprinted directly toward her, flung her to the ground. And ripped the keys from her hands. He leaped inside the SUV, started the engine and floored the accelerator.

The sounds of the squealing, smoking tires and the engine were loud. But they didn't cover the next sound: a sickening crunch from the wheels. The woman's screams stopped abruptly.

'No!' Dance muttered. 'Oh, no.' She rose to her feet, gripping her sore wrist, which had slammed into the concrete when he tackled her.

The others in the Guzman Connection task force ran to Dance.

'I've called an ambulance and Sheriff's Office,' TJ Scanlon said, and raced to where the redhead was lying in the parking space.

Foster raised his Glock, aiming toward the vanishing Altima.

'No!' Dance said, and put a hand on his arm.

'The fuck're you doing, Agent?'

It was Overby who said, 'Across the highway? There? On the other side of those trees. It's a daycare center.'

Foster lowered the weapon reluctantly, as if insulted they'd questioned his shooting skill. He reholstered his Glock as the stolen car vanished from sight. Foster glanced toward Dance and, though he didn't fling her words of the young man's innocence back in her face, his body language clearly did.

CHAPTER 6

What would the next few hours, next few days bring?

Kathryn Dance sat in Charles Overby's office, alone. Her eyes slipped from pictures of the man with his family to those of him in tennis whites and in an outlandish plaid golf outfit to those with local officials and business executives. Overby, rumor was, had his eye on political office. The Peninsula or possibly, at a stretch, San Francisco. Not Sacramento: he'd never set his sights very high. There was also the issue that you could get to fairway or tennis court all year round here on the coast.

Two hours had passed since the incident in the parking lot.

She wondered again: And a few hours from now?

And days and weeks?

Noise outside the doorway. Overby and Steve Foster, the senior CBI agents here, continued their conversation as they walked inside.

'. . . got surveillance on the feeders to Fresno, then the One-o-one and the Five, if he's moving fast. CHP's got Ninety-nine covered. And we've got One roadblocked.'

Foster said, 'I'd go to Salinas, the One-oh-one, I was him. Then north. He'll get, you know, safe passage in a lettuce truck. All the way to San Jose. The G-Forty-sevens'd pick him up there and he disappears into Oakland.'

Overby seemed to be considering this. 'More chance to get lost in LA. But harder to get to, roadblocks and all. Think you're right, Steve. I'll tell Alameda and San Jose. Oh, Kathryn. Didn't see you.'

Even though he'd asked her – no, *told* her – to come to his office ten minutes ago.

She nodded to them both but didn't rise. A woman in law enforcement is constantly aware of the gossamer thread she negotiates in the job with her bosses and fellow officers. Excessive deference can derail respect, as can too little. 'Charles, Steve.'

Foster sat beside her and the chair groaned.

'What's the latest?'

'Not good, looks like.'

Overby said, 'MSCO found the Altima in a residential part of Carmel, near the Barnyard.'

An old outdoor shopping center, with a number of lots for parking cars.

And for hijacking or stealing them too.

Overby said, 'But if he's got new wheels, nobody's reported anything missing.'

'Which may mean the person who *could* do the reporting's dead and in the trunk,' Foster offered. Implicitly blaming Dance for a potential death-to-be.

'We're just debating, would he go north or south? What do you think, Kathryn?'

'What we know now, he's associated with the Jacinto crew. They've got stronger ties south.'

'Like I was saying,' Foster reminded, speaking exclusively to Overby, 'south is three hundred miles of relatively few roads and highways, versus north, with a lot more feeders. We can't watch 'em all. And he can be in Oakland in two hours.'

Dance said, 'Steve, airplanes. He flies to a private strip in LA, out in the county, and he's in South Central in no time.'

'Airplane? He's not cartel level, Kathryn,' Foster fired back. 'He's I'm-hiding-in-a-lettuce-truck level.'

Overby put on his consideration face. Then: 'We can't look everywhere and I think Steve's is the more, you know, logical assessment.'

'All right. North, then. I'll talk to Amy Grabe. She'll get eyes going in Oakland, the docks, the East Bay. And—'

'Whoa, whoa, Kathryn.' Overby's face registered surprise, as if she'd just said, 'I think I'll swim to Santa Cruz.'

She looked at him with a critical furrow of brow. There had been a lacing of condescension in his tone.

She glanced at Foster, who had lost interest in her and was

studying a golden golf ball on Overby's desk, some award. He didn't want to be seen gloating when she heard what she knew was coming. Better to look at small-time awards made of plastic masquerading as precious metal.

Overby said, 'I've just been on the phone with Sacramento. With Peter.'

The director of the CBI. The boss of bosses.

'We talked, I explained . . .'

'What's the bottom line, Charles?'

'I did everything I could, Kathryn. I went to bat for you.'

'I'm suspended.'

'Not suspended, no, no, not at all.' He beamed, as if she'd won a Caribbean cruise in a state fair draw. 'Not completely. You lost your weapon, Kathryn. He's got it now. That's . . . Well, you know. It *is* leave-of-absence-without-pay suspendable. They're not going to go there. But they want you in Civil Division for the time being.'

Civ Div would correspond to a traffic division in the city police department. No weapon and with all the power of anybody else to make a citizen's arrest. It was the entry level into the Bureau of Investigation and involved such tasks as compiling information on non-criminal violations by citizens and corporations, like failure to follow building or revenue-collection regulations, improper signage in the workplace and even failure to remit soda-bottle deposits promptly. Agents tended to endure the overwhelming paperwork and crushing boredom for only so long. If they weren't promoted out into Crim Div, they usually quit cold.

'I'm sorry, Kathryn. I didn't have a choice. I tried. I really did.'

Going to bat for her . . .

Foster now regarded Overby with a neutral gaze that Dance, however, read as contempt for her boss's backpedaling.

'I told him body language isn't an exact science. You did the best you could with Serrano. I saw you. We all did. It looked to me like he was telling the truth. Right, Steve? Who could tell?'

Dance could see that Foster was thinking, But it's not *our* area of expertise to sit across from a perp and pick apart the entrails of his words, poses and gestures to get to the truth.

Overby continued, 'But no one was hurt. Not badly. No weapons were discharged.'

The redhead in the parking lot had not been run over after all. She'd rolled out of the way, under an SUV, as the Altima had sped out of the parking space. Her Dell computer and her lunch had not survived; their loss was what the horrific-sounding crunch had signaled.

'Charles, Serrano is High Mach. I missed it, I admit. But you see those one in every hundred cases.'

'What's that? High what?' Foster asked.

'A category of liars' personalities. The most ruthless and, yeah, slick —' she threw the word back at Foster '— are the "High Machiavellians". High Machs love to lie. They lie with impunity. They see nothing wrong with it. They use deceit like a smartphone or search engine, a tool to get what they want. Whether it's in love, business, politics — or crime.' She added that there were other types, which included social liars, who lied to entertain, and adaptors, who were insecure people lying to make a positive impression. Another common type was the 'actor', someone for whom control was an important issue. 'They don't lie regularly, only when necessary. But Serrano, he just didn't present like any of them. Sure not a High Mach. All I picked up was what I said, some small evasions. Social lies.'

'Social?'

'Everybody lies.' The statistics were that every human being lied at least once or twice a day. Dance shot a glance to Foster. 'When did you lie last?'

He rolled his eyes. She thought, Maybe when he said, 'Good to see you,' this morning.

She continued, 'But I was getting to know him. I'm the only one here, or in any other agency, who's spent time with him. And now we know he could be a key to the whole operation. I don't need to lead it. Just don't take me off the case.'

Overby ran a hand through his thinning hair. 'Kathryn, you want to make it right. I understand. Sure you do. But I don't know what to tell you. It's been decided. Peter's already signed off on the reassignment.'

'Already.'

Foster: 'More efficient, when you think about it. We didn't really need two agents from this office. Jimmy Gomez is good. Don't you agree, Kathryn?'

A junior agent at the CBI, one of the two others on the Guzman Connection task force. Yes, he was good. That wasn't the point. She ignored Foster. She stood and, to Overby, said, 'So?'

He looked at her with one raised eyebrow.

Her shoulders rose and fell impatiently. 'I'm not suspended. I'm Civ Div. So, what's on my roster?'

He looked blank for a moment. Then scoured his desk. He noted a Post-it, bright yellow, glaring as a rectangle of sun fell on it. 'Here's something. Got a memo on the wire from MCFD a little while ago. About that Solitude Creek incident?'

'The fire at the roadhouse.'

'That's right. The county's investigating but somebody from the state is supposed to make sure the club's tax and insurance certificates're up to date.'

'Tax? Insurance?'

'CHP didn't want to handle it.'

Who would? Dance thought.

Foster's absence of gloat was the biggest gloat she had ever seen.

'Take care of that. Then I'll see what else needs doing.'

With Dance 'tasked' to take on the fine print of California insurance regulations and tacitly dismissed, Overby turned to Steve Foster to discuss the manhunt for Joaquin Serrano.

CHAPTER 7

'First, this is interesting – there was no fire.'

'No fire?' Dance asked. She was standing in front of the Solitude Creek club, which was encircled with yellow police tape. The man in front of her was stocky, forties, with an odd patch on his face; it looked like a birthmark but, she knew, was a scar from a blaze years ago that had attacked the newly commissioned firefighter before he snuffed it dead.

She'd worked with Monterey County fire marshal Robert Holly several times and found him low-key, smart, reasonable.

He continued, 'Well, there *was*, technically. Only it was outside. The club itself was never on fire. There, that oil drum.'

Dance noted the rusty fifty-five-gallon vessel, the sort used to collect trash in parking lots and behind stores and restaurants. It rested near the club's air-conditioning unit.

'We ran a prelim. Discarded cigarette in the drum, along with some rags soaked in motor oil and gasoline. That was all it took.'

'Accelerant, then,' Dance said. 'The oil and gas.'

'That was the effect, though there's no evidence it was intentional.'

'So people thought there was a fire. Smelled smoke.'

'And headed to the fire exits. And that was the problem. They were blocked.'

'Locked? The doors were *locked*?'

'No, *blocked*. The truck?'

He pointed to a large tractor-trailer parked against the west side of the club. It, too, was encircled with yellow tape. 'It's owned by that company there. Henderson Jobbing and Warehouse.' Dance regarded the one-story sprawling structure. There were a half-dozen similar tractor-trailers sitting at the loading dock and nearby. Several men and women, in work clothes, a few in suits, stood on the dock or in front of the office and looked over at the club, as if staring at a beached whale.

'The driver parked it there?'

'Claims he didn't. But what's he going to say? There've been other incidents of trucks blocking the roadhouse parking lot. Never a fire exit.'

'Is he here today?'

'He'll be in soon. I called him at home. He's pretty upset. But he agreed to come in.'

'Why would he park there, though? Anybody can see the signs: "No Parking, Fire Exit". Tell me the scenario. What happened exactly?'

'Come on inside.'

Dance followed the burly man into the club. The place had apparently not been straightened up after the tragedy. Chairs and tables – low- and high-tops – were scattered everywhere, broken glasses, bottles, scraps of cloth, snapped bracelets, shoes. Musical instruments lay on the stage. One acoustic guitar was in pieces. A Martin D-28, Dance observed. An old one. Two thousand dollars' worth of former resonance.

There were many smears of old blood on the floor, brown footsteps too.

Dance had been there dozens of times. Everybody on the Peninsula knew Solitude Creek. The club was owned by a balding, earringed restaurateur and former hippie from (where else?) Haight-Ashbury named Sam Cohen, who had been to the Monterey Pop Festival in '67 and reportedly not slept for three days. So moved by the show had the young man been that he had devoted his early life to promoting rock concerts, not so successfully, then given up and opened a steakhouse near the Presidio. He'd sold it for a profit and pocketed enough to buy an abandoned seafood restaurant on the small tributary that had become the club's name.

Solitude Creek was a vein of gray-brown water running to the nearby Salinas River. It was navigable by any vessel with a draft no deeper than two or three feet, which left it mostly for small boats, though there wasn't much reason to sail that way. The club squatted in a large parking lot between the creek and the trucking company, north of Monterey, off Highway One, the same route that wound through majestic Big Sur; the views were very different, there and here.

'How many deaths?'

'Three. Two female, one male. Compressive asphyxia in two cases – crushed to death. One had her throat closed up. Somebody stepped on it. Dozens of badly injured. Bone breaks, ribs piercing lungs. Like people were stuck in a huge vise.'

Dance couldn't imagine the pain and panic and horror.

Holly said, 'The club was pretty full but it was under the limit. We checked, first thing. Occupancy is two hundred, most owners pretend that means two-twenty. But Sam's always been buttoned up about that. Doesn't fool around. Everything looked in order, all the county documentation – that's the safety issues. I saw the tax- and insurance-compliance certs on file in the office. They're current too. That's what Charles said you were here about.'

'That's right. I'll need copies.'

'Sure.' Holly continued, 'Fire inspector gave him a clean bill of health last month and Sam's own insurance company inspected the place a couple of days ago and gave it an A-plus. Extinguishers, sprinklers, lights, alarms and exits.'

Except the exits hadn't opened.

'So, crowded but up to code.'

'Right,' Holly said. 'Just after the show started – eight, little after – the fire broke out in the oil drum. The smoke got sucked into the HVAC system and spread throughout the club. Wasn't real thick but you could smell it. Wood and oil smoke, you know, that's particularly scary. People went for the closest doors – most, of course, for the exits along the east wall. They opened a little – you can see the truck's about a foot away so nobody could fit through. Worse, some people reached out through the opening. Their arms or hands got stuck and . . . well, the crowd kept moving. Three or four arms and shoulders were shattered. Two arms had to be amputated.' His voice grew distant. 'Then there was this young woman, nineteen or so. It more or less got torn off. Her arm.' He was looking down. 'I heard later she was studying classical piano. Really talented. God.'

'What happened when they realized the doors wouldn't open?'

'Everybody in the front was pressed against the doors, screaming for the people behind them to turn around. But nobody heard. Or if they did they didn't listen. Panic. Pure panic. They should've gone back toward the other exits, the front, the stage door. Hell, the kitchen had a double door. But for some reason everybody ran the other way – toward the fire doors, the blocked ones. I guess they saw the exit signs and just headed for them.'

'Not much smoke, you said. But visibility?'

'Somebody hit the house lights and people could see everything fine.'

Sam Cohen appeared in the doorway. In his sixties, dressed in filthy jeans and a torn work shirt, blue. His remaining curly gray hair was a mess, and he had not slept that night, Dance estimated. He walked through the club slowly, picking up items from the floor, putting them into a battered cardboard box.

'Mr Cohen.'

The owner of Solitude Creek made his way unsteadily toward Dance and Holly. His eyes were red: he'd been crying. He walked up, noting a smear of blood on the floor; cruelly, it was in the shape of a heart.

'I'm Kathryn Dance, Bureau of Investigation.'

Cohen looked at, without seeing, the ID card. She slipped it away. He said to no one, 'I just called the hospital again. They've released three. The critical ones – there were four of those – are unchanged. One's in a coma. They'll probably live. But the hospitals, the doctors don't tell you much. The nurses never do. Why's that a rule? It doesn't make any sense.'

'Can I ask you a few questions, Mr Cohen?'

'Bureau of Investigation? FBI?' '

'California.'

'Oh. You said that. Is this . . . I mean, is it a crime?'

Holly said, 'We're still doing the preliminary, Sam.'

Dance said, 'I'm not a criminal investigator. I'm in the Civil Division.'

Cohen looked around, breathing heavily. His shoulders sagged. 'Everything . . .' he said, in a whisper.

Dance had no idea what he'd been about to say. She was looking at a face marred by indelible sorrow. 'Could you tell me what you recall about last night, sir?' She asked this automatically. Then, remembering the fire marshal was in charge, 'Okay with you, Bob?'

'You can help me out anytime you want, Kathryn.'

She wondered why she was even asking these questions. This wasn't her job. But sometimes you just can't leash yourself.

Cohen didn't answer.

'Mr Cohen?' She repeated the question.

'Sorry.' Whispering. 'I was at the front door, checking receipts. I heard the music start. I smelled smoke, pretty strong, and I freaked out. The band stopped in the middle of a tune. Just then I got a call. Somebody was in the parking lot and they said there was a fire in the kitchen. Or backstage. They weren't sure. They must've seen the smoke and thought it was worse than it was. I didn't check. I just thought, Get everybody out. So I made the announcement. Then I could hear voices. Swelling. The voices, I mean, getting louder and louder. Then a scream. And I smelled more smoke. I thought, No, no, not a fire. I was thinking of the Station in Rhode Island a few years ago. They had fireworks. Illegal ones. But in, like, six minutes the entire club was engulfed. A hundred people died.'

Choking. Tears. 'I went into the club itself. I couldn't believe it, I couldn't believe what I saw. It was like they weren't people at all – it was just one big creature, staggering around, squeezing toward the doors. But they weren't opening. And there were no flames. Anywhere. Not even very thick smoke. Like in the fall, when I was growing up. People burning leaves. Where I grew up. New York.'

Dance had spotted a security camera. 'Was there video? Security video?'

'Nothing outside. Inside, yes, there's a camera.'

'Could I see it, please?

This was her Crim-Div mind working.

Sometimes you can't leash yourself . . .

Cohen cast a last look around the room, then stepped into the lobby, clutching the box of survivors' tokens he'd collected. He held it gingerly, as if a tight grip would mean bad luck for the hospitalized owners. She saw wallets, keys, shoes, a business card in his grasp.

Dance followed, Holly behind. Cohen's office was decorated with posters about the appearances of obscure performers – and many from the Monterey Pop Festival – and was cluttered with the flotsam of a small entertaining venue: crates of beer, stacks of invoices, souvenirs (T-shirts, cowboy hats, boots, a stuffed rattlesnake, dozens of mugs given away by radio stations). So many items. The accumulation set Dance's nerves vibrating.

Cohen went to the computer and sat down. He stared at the desk for a moment, a piece of paper; she couldn't see what was written on it. She positioned herself in front of the monitor. She steeled herself. In her job as investigator with the CBI, most of her work was backroom. She talked to suspects after the deeds had been done. She was rarely in the field and never tactical. Yes, one could analyze the posture of a dead body and derive forensic insights but Dance had rarely been called on to do so. Most of her work involved the living. She wondered what her reaction to the video would be.

It wasn't good.

The quality of the tape was so-so and a pillar obscured a portion of the image. She recalled the camera and thought it had been positioned differently but apparently not. At first she was looking at a wide-angle slice of tables and chairs and patrons, servers with trays. Then the lights dimmed, though there was still enough light to see the room.

There was no sound. Dance was grateful for that.

At 8:11:11 on the time stamp, people began to move. Standing up, looking around. Pulling out phones. At that point the majority of the patrons were concerned, that was obvious, but their facial expressions and body language revealed only that. No panic.

But at 8:11:17, everything changed. Merely six seconds later. As if they'd all been programed to act at the same instant, the patrons surged *en masse* toward the doors. Dance couldn't see the exits: they were behind the camera, out of the frame. She could, however, see people slamming against each other and the wall, desperate to escape from the unspeakable fate of burning to death. Pressing against each other, harder, harder, in a twisting mass, spiraling like a slow-moving hurricane. Dance understood: those at the front were struggling to move clockwise to get away from the people behind them. But there was no place to go.

'My,' Bob Holly, the fire marshal, whispered.

Then, to Dance's surprise, the frenzy ended fast. It seemed that sanity returned, as if a spell had been sloughed off. The masses broke up and patrons headed for the accessible exits – this would be the front lobby, the stage and the kitchen.

Two bodies were visible on the floor, people huddled over them. Trying pathetically ineffective revival techniques. You can hardly use CPR to save someone whose chest has been crushed, their heart and lungs pierced.

Dance noted the time stamp.

8:18:29.

Seven minutes. Start to finish. Life to death.

Then a figure stumbled back into view.

'That's her,' Bob Holly whispered. 'The music student.'

A young woman, blonde and extraordinarily beautiful, gripped her right arm, which ended at her elbow. She staggered back toward one of the partially open doors, perhaps looking for the severed limb. She got about ten feet into view, then dropped to her knees. A couple ran to her, the man pulling his belt off, and together they improvised a tourniquet.

Without a word, Sam Cohen stood and walked back to the doorway of his office. He paused there. Looked out over the debris-strewn club, realized he was holding a Hello Kitty phone and put it in his pocket. He said, to no one, 'It's over with, you know. My life's over. It's gone. Everything . . . You never recover from something like this. Ever.'

CHAPTER 8

Outside the club, Dance slipped the copies of the up-to-date tax- and insurance-compliance certificates into her purse, effectively ending her assignment there.

Time to leave. Get back to the office.

But she chose not to.

Unleashed . . .

Kathryn Dance decided to stick around Solitude Creek and ask some questions of her own.

She made the rounds of the three dozen people there, about half of whom had been patrons that night, she learned. They'd returned to leave flowers, to leave cards. And to get answers. Most asked her more questions than she did them.

'How the hell did it happen?'

'Where did the smoke come from?'

'Was it a terrorist?'

'Who parked the truck there?'

'Has anybody been arrested?'

Some of those people were edgy, suspicious. Some were raggedly hostile.

As always, Dance deferred responding, saying it was an ongoing investigation. This group – the survivors and relatives, rather than the merely curious, at least – seemed aggressively dissatisfied with her words. One blonde, bandaged on the face, said her fiancé was in critical care. 'You know where he got injured? His balls. Somebody trampled him, trying to get out. They're saying we may never have kids now!'

Dance offered genuine sympathy and asked her few questions. The woman was in no mood to answer.

She spotted a couple of men in suits circulating, one white, one Latino, each chatting away with people from their respective language pools, handing out business cards. Nothing she could do about it. First Amendment – if that was the law that protected the right of scummy lawyers to solicit clients. A glare to the chubby white man, dusty suit, was returned with a slick smile. As if he'd given her the finger.

Everything that those who'd returned here told her echoed what she'd learned from Holly and Cohen. It was the same story from different angles, the constant being how shockingly fast a group of relaxed folks in a concert snapped and turned into wild animals, their minds possessed by panic.

She examined the oil drum where the fire had started. It was about twenty feet from the back of the roadhouse, near the air-conditioning unit. Inside, as Holly had described, were ash and bits of half-burned trash.

Dance then turned to what would be the crux of the county's investigation: the truck blocking the doors. The cab was a red Peterbilt, an older model, battered and decorated with bug dots, white and yellow and green. The trailer it hauled was about thirty feet long and, with the tractor, it effectively blocked all three emergency-exit doors. The right front fender rested an inch from the wall of the Solitude Creek club; the rear right end of the trailer was about ten inches away. The angle allowed two exit doors to open a bit but not enough for anyone to get out. On the ground beside one door Dance could see smears of blood. Perhaps that was where the pretty girl's arm had been sheared off.

She tried to get an idea of how the truck had ended up there. The club and the warehouse shared a parking lot, though signs clearly marked which areas were for patrons of Solitude Creek and which for the trucks and employees of Henderson Jobbing. Red signs warned about 'towing at owner's expense' but seemed a lethargic threat, so faded and rusty were they.

No, it didn't make any sense for the driver to leave the truck there. The portion of the parking space where the tractors and trailers rested was half full; there was plenty of room for the driver to park the rig anywhere in that area. Why here?

More likely the vehicle had rolled and come to rest where it had;

the warehouse, to the south of the club, was a higher elevation and the lot sloped downward to here, where it leveled out. The heavy truck had got as far as the side wall and slowed to a stop.

Dance walked to the warehouse now, a hundred feet away, where the office door was marked with a handmade sign: 'Closed'. The people she'd seen moments ago were now gone.

She gripped the knob and pulled. Locked – though lights were visible inside through a tear in a window shade, and she could see movement.

A loud rap on the glass. 'Bureau of Investigation. Please open the door.'

Nothing.

Another rap, harder.

The shade moved aside; a middle-aged man, unruly brown hair, glared at her. His eyes scanned her ID and he let her in.

The lobby was what one would expect of a mid-size transport company squatting off a secondary highway. Scuffed, functional, filled with Sears and Office Depot furniture, black and chrome and gray. Scheduling boards, posted government regulations. Lots of paper. The smell of diesel fumes or grease was prominent.

Dance introduced herself. The man, Henderson, was the owner. A woman, who appeared to be an assistant or secretary, and two other men, in work clothing, gazed at her uneasily. Bob Holly had said the truck's driver was coming in: was he one of these men?

She asked but was told, no, Billy hadn't arrived yet. She then asked if the warehouse had been open at the time of the incident.

The owner said quickly, 'We have rules. You can see them there.'

A sign on the wall nearby reminded, with the inexplicable capitalization of corporate culture:

Remember your Passports for International trips!

The sign he was referring to was beneath it:

Set your Brake and leave your Rig in gear!

Interrogators are always alert to subjects answering questions they haven't been asked. Nothing illustrates what's been going on in their minds better than that.

She'd get to the matter of brakes and gears in a moment. 'Yessir, but about the hours?'

'We close at five. We're open seven to five.'

'But trucks arrive later, right? Sometimes?'

'That rig came in at seven.' He looked at a sheet of paper – which of course he'd found and memorized the minute he'd heard about the tragedy. 'Seven ten. Empty from Fresno.'

'And the driver parked in a usual space?'

'Any space that's free,' the worker piped up. 'The top of the hill.' He bore a resemblance to Henderson. Nephew, son, Dance guessed. Noting he'd mentioned the incline. They'd already discussed scapegoating the driver and had planned his public crucifixion.

'Would the driver have parked the truck there intentionally, beside the club?' Dance asked.

This caught them off guard. 'Well, no. That wouldn't make sense.' The hesitation told her that they wished they'd thought about this scenario. But they'd already decided to sell the driver out by implying he hadn't set the brake.

The top of the hill . . .

The third man, brawny, soiled hands, realized his cue. 'These rigs're heavy. But they'll roll.'

Dance asked, 'Where was it parked before it ended up beside the club?'

'One of the spots,' Henderson Lite offered.

'Gathered that. Which one?'

'Do I need a lawyer?' the owner asked.

'I'm just trying to find out what happened. This isn't a criminal investigation.' And she added, as she knew she should: 'At this point.'

'Do I have to talk to you?' Henderson asked the tax- and insurance-certification lady.

She said evenly, as if concerned for him, 'It will be a lot better for you if you cooperate.'

Henderson gave a calculated shrug and directed her outside, then pointed to the spot that was, not surprisingly, directly uphill from the club. The truck seemed to have rolled in almost a straight line to where it rested. A slight bevel of the asphalt would have accounted for the vehicle's angle with respect to the building: it had veered slightly to the left.

Henderson: 'So we don't know what happened.'

Meaning: Take the driver. Fuck him. It's his fault, not ours. We posted the rules.

Dance looked around. 'How does it work? A driver comes in after hours, he leaves the key somewhere here or he keeps it?'

'Leaves it.' Henderson pointed. A drop-box.

A white pickup pulled into the lot and approached them and squealed to a stop nearby. A slim man of about thirty-five, jeans and an AC/DC T-shirt stepped out of it. He pulled on a leather jacket, straightened his slicked-back blond hair, fringy at the ends. His face was etched with parentheses around his mouth, his brow permanently furrowed. He was white but his skin was leather-tanned.

'Well,' Henderson said, 'here he is now.'

The sheepish man stepped up to his boss. 'Mr Henderson.'

'Billy,' the owner said. 'This's . . .'

'I'm Kathryn Dance, CBI.' Her ID rose.

'Billy Culp,' the young man said absently, staring at her ID. Eyes wide, perhaps seeing an opening door to a jail cell.

She ushered him away from the others.

The owner sighed, hitched up his belt, gave it a moment more, then vanished inside. His blood kin joined him.

'Could you tell me about parking the truck here last night?'

The young man's eyes shifted to the club. 'I came back this morning to help. I was thinking maybe I could do something. But there wasn't anything.' A faint smile, a hollow smile. 'I wanted to help.'

'Mr Culp?'

'Sure, sure. I had a run to Fresno, came in empty about seven. Parked there. Spot ten. You can't see clear. The paint's gone mostly. Wrote down the mileage and diesel level on my log and slipped it through the slot in the door, put the keys in the drop-box, there. Call me "Billy". "Mr Culp", I start looking for my father.'

Dance smiled. 'You parked there and set the brake and put the truck in gear.'

'I always do, ma'am. The brake, the gears.' Then he swallowed. 'But, fact is, I was tired. I admit. Real tired. Bakersfield, Fresno, here.' His voice was unsteady. He'd been debating about coming clean. 'I'm *pretty* sure I took care of things. But to swear a hundred percent? I don't know.'

'Thanks for being honest, Billy.'

He sighed. 'I'll lose my job, whatever happens. Will I go to jail?'

'We're just investigating at this point.' He wore a wedding band. She guessed children too. He was of that age. 'You ever forgotten? Gears and brake?'

'Forgotten to lock up once. Lost my CB. My radio, you know. But, no.' A shake of his head. 'Always set the brake. Never drive my personal car I've had a single beer. Don't cruise through yellow lights. I'm not really smart and I'm not really talented at a lot of stuff. I'm a good driver, though, Officer Dance. No cita-tions, no accidents were my fault.' He shrugged. 'But, truth is, yes, I was tired, ma'am. Officer.'

'Jesus, look out!' Henderson shouted, calling through the open office door.

Billy and Dance glanced back and ducked as something zipped over their heads. The rock bounded over the asphalt and whacked the tire of another rig.

'You fucking son of a bitch!' the man who'd thrown the projec-tile shouted.

A group of a dozen people – mostly men – were walking fast up the incline from the direction of the club. Another flung a second rock. Dance and Billy dodged. The throw was wide but if it had hit it would have cracked a skull. She was surprised to note that these were people who were well dressed. They seemed middle class. Not bikers or thugs. But their expressions were chilling: they were out for blood.

'Get him!'

'Fucker!'

'You're the fucking driver, aren't you?'

'Look! Over there! It's the driver!'

'Police,' Dance said, holding up her ID, not bothering with specific authentication. 'Stop right there.'

Nobody paid the least attention to her.

'You asshole! Killer.'

'No,' Billy said, his voice choking. 'I didn't do anything.'

Suddenly the group was joined by others striding fast from the impromptu memorial site near the roadhouse. Some started running. Pointing. They numbered about twenty now. Faces red with anger, shouting. Dance had her mobile out and was dialing 911. Dispatch would have taken too long.

She heard: 'Police and fire emergen—'

Dance gasped as a tire iron spiraled straight for her face.

CHAPTER 9

Billy tackled Dance as the metal rod zipped past.

They both collapsed onto the ground. Then he yanked her to her feet and together they hurried toward the company's office door. She completed her call, officer needs assistance, and twisted back, shouting to the approaching mob, 'This is a police investigation! Disperse now. You will be arrested!'

And was greeted with another missile – a rock again. This one connected, though obliquely, with her left forearm, not far from the watch, which had shattered in the CBI parking lot. She cried out in pain.

'Arrest him!' called the burly blonde woman, whose fiancé had been so badly injured.

'Arrest him? Fuck him up!'

Now the crowd caught up with them. Several of the men pushed Dance aside and shoved Billy backward, their palms slamming into his chest.

'You are committing a felony! There are police on their way.'

One man sprinted up and got right in their faces. Livid, he stuck a finger in Billy's chest and raged, 'You parked there to take a crap or something! Ran off. Fuck you, Officer! Why isn't he under arrest?'

'No, no, I didn't do anything. Please!' Billy was shaking his head and she saw tears in his eyes. He rubbed his chest from one of the blows a moment ago.

Others were swarming around them now. Dance held her shield up and this resulted in a momentary stay of the madness.

Dance whispered, 'This's going to blow up. We've got to get out of here now. Back to the office.'

She and Billy pushed around those immediately in front of them and kept walking toward the door. The crowd followed behind them, a hostile escort. She told herself: Don't run. She knew if they did the crowd would attack once again.

And though it was impossibly hard, she kept a slow, steady pace.

Somebody else growled, 'Give me five minutes with him. I'll get a confession.'

'Fuck him up, I keep saying!'

'You killed my daughter!'

They were now thirty feet from the office door. The crowd had grown and were shouting insults. At least no more projectiles.

Then one short, stocky man in jeans and a plaid shirt ran up to his prey and slugged Billy in the side of the head. He cried out.

Dance displayed her shield. 'You. Give me your name. Now!'

He laughed cruelly, grabbed the badge and flung it away. 'Fuck you, bitch.'

She doubted that even a weapon brandished would have slowed them down. In any event she had no Glock to draw.

'Fuck him up! Get him!'

'Kill him.'

'Her too, bitch!'

These people were insane. Animals. Mad dogs.

'Listen to me,' Dance shouted. 'You're committing a felony! You will be arrested if you—'

It was then that their control broke. 'Get him. Now!'

She glanced back to see several picking up rocks. One gripped another tire iron.

Jesus.

She ducked as a large stone zipped past her ear. She didn't see who'd thrown it. She stumbled and ended up on her knees. The crowd surged forward.

Billy yanked her to her feet and, hands over their heads, they sprinted for the office door. It was now closed. If Henderson had locked it, hell, they could very well be dead in a few minutes.

Dance felt the full-on panic, an antelope hearing the rhythm of the lion's paws moving closer and closer.

The door . . .

Please . . .

Just as they arrived it swung open. Billy turned and this time a rock hit its target square. It slammed into the man's jaw and he gave a sharp cry. Blood poured and it was obvious he'd lost a tooth or two and possibly a bone had broken.

He stumbled inside and collapsed on the floor, gripping his mouth. Dance leapt in too. The door slammed shut and Henderson locked it.

'I called nine one one,' the office manager said.

'I did too,' Dance muttered, looking at Billy's gash. 'They should be here soon.'

She peered out of the window, her hands shaking, heart pounding audibly.

Panic . . .

The crowd had ganged at the door. Their faces were possessed. She thought of the time when a crazed Doberman, off its leash, had charged her and her German shepherd, Dylan, on a walk. Only pepper spray had stopped it.

No reasoning, no escaping.

Dance grimaced, noting that Henderson was holding a revolver, a Smith & Wesson, short-barrel .38 Special. Gripped uneasily in his hand.

'Put that away.'

'But—'

'Now,' she snapped.

He set the weapon back in its drawer.

A rock smashed into the side of the office, a huge sound, thanks to the metal walls. Others. Two windows broke, though no one tried to climb in. More shouts.

Dance looked at Billy, whose eyes were closed from the pain. He held a towel, filled with ice, against his swollen face. Henderson's relative had brought it. It appeared that the jawbone was shattered.

Looking out through a broken window Dance could see flashing blue-and-white lights.

And, just like in the Solitude Creek video of last night, the madness vanished. The mob who'd been ready to lynch Billy and

break Dance's skull turned and were walking away, making for
their own cars, as if nothing had happened.

Fast, so fast. As quickly as they'd become enraged they'd
calmed. The possession was over with. She noted several of them
drop the rocks they held; it seemed some of them hadn't even
realized they were holding the weapons.

Squad cars from the MCSO eased to a stop in front of
Henderson Jobbing. Two sheriff's deputies from the vehicle
closest to the office surveyed the scene around them and walked
inside.

'Kathryn,' said the woman deputy, a tall, striking Latina. The
other, a squat African American, nodded to her. She knew both
of them well.

'Kit, John.'

'The hell happened?' Kit asked.

Dance explained about the mob. She added, 'You could probably get a few collars for assault and battery.' A nod toward Billy
and she showed her own rock-bruised arm. 'I'll leave that up to
you. I'm not processing criminal cases.'

Kit Sanchez lifted an eyebrow.

'Long story. I'll witness, you need it.'

John Lanners, the other deputy, looked over Billy Culp's shattered face and asked if he wanted to press charges against anyone
in the mob. Billy's mumbled words: 'I didn't see anyone.'

He was lying, Dance could see. She understood, of course,
that it was simply that he didn't want any more publicity as the
man responsible for the Solitude Creek disaster. And his wife
and children . . . They, too, would be targeted.

Dance shook her head. 'You decide.'

'Who's running this? CBI or us?' Lanners asked, nodding back
to the roadhouse.

Sanchez said, 'We don't care. Just, you know . . .'

'Bob Holly's here, for the county, so I guess you are.' Dance
added, 'I came to check some licenses.' She shrugged. 'But I
decided to stay. Ask some questions.'

Lanners wiped sweat – he was quite heavy – and said to Billy,
'We'll call in some medical help.'

The driver didn't seem to care, though he was in significant pain. He wiped tears.

Lanners pulled his radio off his belt and made a call for the EMS bus. The dispatcher reported they'd have one there in ten minutes. Dance asked Lanners, 'Can you go with him?' She added, in a whisper, 'It's like there's a price on his head.'

'Sure,' he said. 'And we'll give his family a call.' The deputy, too, had spotted the wedding band.

Dance swiped at her own injury.

Kit asked, 'You all right, Kathryn?'

'It's . . .'

Then Dance's eyes focused past the deputy to another sign on the wall. She pointed. 'Is that true?'

Henderson squinted and followed her gaze. 'That? Yeah. Saved us a lot of money over the years.'

'All the trucks?'

'Every single one.'

Kathryn Dance smiled.

CHAPTER 10

The man Ray Henderson was going to sell out, the man the crowd ten minutes ago was ready to lynch, was innocent.

It took only five minutes to learn that Billy Culp was not responsible for the tragedy at Solitude Creek.

The sign Dance'd seen on the wall of Henderson Jobbing, not far from where the driver sat, miserable in his heart and hurting in his jaw, read:

> *WE know you Drive safely.*
> *Remember: Our GPS does too!*
> *Obey the posted speed limits.*

All the Henderson Jobbing trucks, it seems, were equipped with sat nav, not only to give the drivers directions but to tell the boss exactly where they were and how fast they'd been going. (Henderson explained that this was to protect them in the case of hijacking or theft; Dance suspected he was also tired of paying speeding tickets or shelling out more than he needed to for diesel fuel.)

Dance got permission from Bob Holly and the county deputies to extract the GPS device from Billy's truck and take it into the Henderson office. Once it was hooked up via a USB cord, she and the deputies looked over the data.

At 8:10 last night the GPS unit came to life. It registered movement northward – toward the roadhouse – of about one hundred feet, then it stopped and shut off.

'So,' Kit Sanchez said, 'somebody drove it into position intentionally.'

Yep,' Dance said. 'Somebody broke into the drop-box. Got the key. Drove the truck into position to block the club doors, shut the engine off and returned the key.'

'I was home then!' Billy said. 'When it happened, eight o'clock, I was home. I've got witnesses!'

Henderson and his perhaps-nephew diligently avoided looking at either Dance or Billy, now knowing that the man they had wanted to throw under the . . . well, truck was innocent.

'Security cameras?' Dance asked.

'In the warehouse. Nothing outside.'

Too bad, that.

'And the key to the truck?' she asked.

'I've got it.' He reached for a drawer.

'No, don't touch it,' Dance said.

Fingerprints. Forensics didn't much interest Kathryn Dance but you had to treat physical evidence with consummate reverence.

'Shit. I've already picked it up.'

John Lanners, the MCSO deputy: 'There'll be plenty of prints on it, I'd imagine, but we'll sort it out. Take yours for samples. Find the ones that don't match Billy's or the other drivers'.'

In gloved hands, Kit Sanchez collected the key fob from the offending truck and put it in an evidence bag. Dance knew in her heart, however, that there was no way there would be any prints from the man who'd intentionally blocked the club's doors. She knew instinctively he would be meticulous.

Ironically, just after Dance had been shifted from criminal mode to civil, the administrative matter she'd come here about, taxation and insurance certificates, had just turned into a crime. A felony. Murder. Perhaps even a terrorist attack.

She said to Sanchez and Lanners, 'Can you declare this a homicide? I can't.' A wry smile. 'That's the long-story part. And secure the scene. The drop-box, the truck, the oil drum, the club. Better go for the parking lot too.'

'Sure,' Lanners said. 'I'll call Crime Scene. Secure everything.'

With a dribble of a siren, a county ambulance pulled up and parked in front of the office. Two techs, large white men, appeared in the doorway and nodded. They spotted Billy and walked over to him to assess damage and mobility.

'Is it broke, my jaw?' Billy asked.

One tech lifted off the icy and bloody towel. 'Got to take X-rays first and then only a doctor can tell you after he looks over the film. But, yah, it's broke. Totally fucking broke. You can walk?'

'I'll walk. Is anybody out there?'

'How do you mean?'

Dance glanced out of the window. 'It's clear.'

The four of them stepped outside and helped the scrawny driver into the ambulance. He reached out and took Dance's hand in both of his. His eyes were moist and not, Dance believed, from the pain. 'You saved my life, Agent Dance. More ways than just one. God bless you.' Then he frowned. 'But you be careful. Those people, those animals, they wanted to kill you just as much as me. And you didn't do a lick wrong.'

'Feel better, Billy.'

Dance found her shield, dusted it off and slipped it into her pocket. She then returned to the roadhouse. She'd tell Bob Holly what she'd discovered but keep the news from Charles Overby until she'd done some more canvassing.

She needed as much ammunition as she could garner.

As she approached the gathered press and spectators, she glanced toward a pretty woman TV reporter, in a precise suit, interviewing a Monterey County firefighter, a solid, sunburned man with a tight crew-cut and massive arms. She'd seen him at several other fire and mass-disaster scenes over the past year or so.

The reporter said to the camera, 'I'm talking here with Brad C. Dannon, a Monterey County fireman. Brad, you were the first on the scene last night at Solitude Creek?'

'Just happened I wasn't too far away when we got the call, that's right.'

'So you saw a scene of panic? Could you describe it?'

'Panic, yeah. Everybody. Trying to get out, just throwing themselves against the door, like animals. I've been a firefighter for five years and I've never . . .'

CHAPTER 11

'. . . seen anything like this.'

'Five years, really, Brad? Now tell me, it looks like the doors, the fire doors, were unlocked but they were all blocked by a truck that had parked there. A tractor-trailer. We can see . . . there.'

Antioch March lifted his eyes from his present gaze – the pillow-case of fine-weave cotton, six inches from his face – and glanced at the TV screen, across the bedroom in the sumptuous Cedar Hills Inn in Pebble Beach. The camera from the crew outside the Solitude Creek roadhouse panned to Henderson Jobbing and Warehouse, which was all of ten miles from where March now lay.

A mouth beside his ear: 'Yes, yes!' A moist whisper.

On TV, the anchor, blonde as toffee, came back into high-definition view. 'Brad, a number of victims and relatives of victims are accusing the driver of the truck of negligently blocking the doors, accusing him of parking there to go to the bathroom, or maybe even sneaking in to see the show last night. Do you think that's a possibility?'

'It's too early to speculate,' the firefighter replied.

It's *never* wise to speculate, March corrected Brad, early or late. The bodybuilding firefighter, not quite as buff as March, looked smug. Wouldn't trust him to rescue *me* from a smoke-filled building.

Much less a stampede in a roadhouse. Brad did, however, go on to offer graphic descriptions of the 'horror' last night. They were quite accurate. Helped by Brad and the images he was describing, March turned his attention back to the task at hand, lowered his head back to the pillow and pulsed away.

Calista gripped his earlobe between two perfectly shaped teeth. March felt the pressure of the incisors. Felt her studded nose against his smooth cheek. Felt himself deep inside her.

She grunted rhythmically. Maybe he did too.

Calista whispered, 'You're so fucking handsome . . .'

He wished she wouldn't talk. Besides, he didn't know what to do with that sentence. Maybe she was hoping for this to be more than a couple-days thing. But he also knew that people said all sorts of things for all sorts of reasons at moments like this and he didn't sweat it.

Just wished she wouldn't talk. He wanted to hear. Wanted to see. Wanted to imagine.

Her heels banged against his tailbone, her bright crimson fingernails – the color of arterial blood – assaulted his back.

And he replayed what people often replayed at moments like now: earlier times. The Solitude Creek incident. But then, going way back: Serena, of course. He often returned to Serena, the way a top eventually spins to stillness.

Serena. She helped move him along.

Jessica he thought of too.

And, of course, Todd. Never Serena and Jessica without Todd.

He was moving more quickly now.

Again she was gasping, 'Yes, yes, yes . . .'

As she lay under him Calista's hands now eased up his spine and gripped his shoulders hard. Those GMC-finish nails pressed into his skin. He reciprocated, digging into her pale flesh. Her moaning was partly pain; the rest of the damp gusts from her lungs were from his two hundred plus pounds, little fat. Pounding.

Compressing.

Sort of like the people last night.

'Oh . . .' She stiffened.

He backed off at that. There was a balance between his pleasure and her pain. Tricky. He didn't really need her to cry at the moment. He had all he needed.

'Again, if you're just joining us . . .'

'Oh, yeah,' Calista whispered, and it wasn't an act. She was gone, lost in the moment.

His left hand slid out from under the bony spine and then was twining the strawberry mane of hair in his blunt fingers, pulling her head back. Her throat – smooth for cutting. Though that wasn't on the agenda. Still, the image socketed itself into his thoughts. That helped him too.

March gauged rhythm and sped up slightly. Then a rich inhale and those luminous pearls of teeth went against his neck – many women were into the vampire thing, Calista too, apparently. A shudder and she hissed, 'Yesssss,' not as an act or a prod for him to finish: it was involuntary. Genuine. He was moderately pleased.

Now, his turn. He gripped her more tightly yet. Chest and breasts, thigh and thigh, sliding unsteadily; the room was hot, the sweat abundant.

'I'm speaking to Brad Dannon, Monterey County firefighter and first on the scene at the Solitude Creek tragedy last night. Brad is credited with saving at least two victims, who were bleeding severely. Have you talked to them today, Brad?'

'Yes, ma'am. They'd lost a lot of blood but I was able to keep them going till our wonderful EMS got there. They're the true heroes. Not me.'

'You're very modest, Brad. Now—'

Click.

He realized that the impressive nails of one hand had vanished from his back. She'd found the remote and shut off the TV.

No matter. With a flash of Serena's beautiful face, combined with Brad's comment, *a lot of blood*, he was done.

He gasped and let his full weight sag down upon her. He was thinking: It had been good. Good *enough*.

It would distract for a while.

Then he was aware of her squirming slightly. Her breath labored.

He thought again: Compressive asphyxia.

And stayed where he was. Ten seconds passed.

Twenty. Then thirty. He could kill her by simply not moving.

'Uhm,' she gasped. 'Could you . . .'

He felt her chest heaving.

March rolled off. 'Sorry. You totally tuckered me out.'

Calista caught her breath. She sat up slightly and tugged the sheets across her body. Why, afterward, did women grow modest?

He pulled off a pillow case and used it as a towel, then glanced casually at his nails. No blood. He was disappointed.

She turned back to him, faintly smiling, and put her head on the pillow.

March stretched. As always, moments like this, just after, he remained silent, since you could never trust yourself, even someone as controlled as he was. He'd learned that.

She, however, spoke. 'Andy?'

He preferred the nickname. 'Antioch' drew attention. 'Yes?'

'That was terrible, what happened.'

'What's that?'

'The stampede or crush. It was on the news. Just a minute ago.'

'Oh, I wasn't listening.'

Was this a test? He didn't know. He'd provided the good answer, though. She put a hand, tipped in red, on his arm. He supposed he shouldn't even have had the set on – not wise to be too interested in Solitude Creek. But when she'd arrived forty minutes ago, the first thing he'd done was pour some Chardonnay for her and start talking away, so she wouldn't think to shut off the unfolding news reports.

March stretched again, the luxurious inn's mattress not rocking a quarter-inch. He thought of the endlessly moving Pacific Ocean, which you could hear, if not see, from the cranked-open window to his left.

'You work out a lot,' she said.

'I do.' He had to. His line of work. Well, one of his lines of work. March got in at least an hour every day. Exercise was easy for him – he was twenty-nine, naturally strong and well built. And he enjoyed the effort. It was comforting. It was distracting.

With unslit throat and her non-compressed lungs, Calista eased from the sheets and, like an A-list actress, kept her back to the camera as she rose.

'Don't look.'

He didn't look. March tugged off the condom, which he dropped onto the floor, the opposite side of the bed. Out of her view.

Looked at the remote. Decided not to.

He thought she was going to the bathroom but she diverted

to the closet, flung it open, looking through his hanging clothes. 'You have a robe I can borrow? You're not looking?'

'No. The bathroom, the hook on the door.'

She got it and returned, enwrapped. 'Nice.' Stroking the fine cotton.

The inn was one of the best on the Monterey Peninsula, and this area, he'd learned in the past few days, was a place with many fine inns. The establishment was happy for guests to take its robes home with them as lovely souvenirs of their stay – for the oddly random price of $232.

This, he reflected, defined Cedar Hills. Not an even $250, which would have been outrageous but logical. Not $100, which would be the actual retail price and made more sense.

Two hundred thirty-two pretentious dollars.

Something to do with human nature, he guessed.

Calista Sommers fetched her purse and rummaged, collected from it some of the contents.

He smelled wine, from the glasses nearby. But that had been for her. He sipped his pineapple juice, with ice cubes whose edges had melted to dull.

She tugged aside a curtain. 'View's amazing.'

True. Pebble Beach golf course not far away, contortionist pine trees, crimson bird-of-paradise flowers, sculpture, fountains. Deer wandered past, ears twitchy and legs both comical and elegant.

Her mind seemed to wander. Maybe she was thinking of her meeting. Maybe of her ill mother. Calista, a twenty-five-year-old bookkeeper, wasn't from here. She'd taken two weeks off from work and driven to California from her small town in northern Washington State to look for areas where her mother, in assisted living because of Alzheimer's, might relocate, a place where the weather was better. She'd tried Marin, Napa, San Francisco and was now checking out the Monterey Bay area. This seemed to be the front-runner.

She walked into the bathroom and the shower began to pulse. March lay back, listening to the water. He believed she was humming.

He thought again about the remote. No. Too eager.

Eyes closed, he replayed the incident at Solitude Creek once more.

Ten minutes later she emerged. 'You bad boy!' she said, with a devilish smile, but chiding too. 'You scratched me.'

Hiking the robe up. A very, very nice ass. Red scratch marks. The image of them hit him low in the torso. 'Sorry.' Not a *Fifty Shades of Grey* girl, it seemed.

She forgot her complaint. 'You look like somebody, an actor.'

Channing Tatum was the default. March was slimmer, about the same height, over six feet.

'I don't know.'

Didn't matter, of course. Her point was to apologize for the jab about the scratches.

Accepted.

She dug into her purse for a brush and makeup, began reassembling. 'The other night you didn't really tell me much about your job. Some non-profit. A website? You do good things. I like that.'

'Right. We raise awareness – and money – to benefit people in crises. Wars, natural disasters, famine, that sort of thing.'

'You must be busy. There's so much terrible stuff going on.'

'I'm on the road six days a week.'

'What's the site?'

'It's called Hand to Heart.' He rolled from the bed. Though not feeling particularly modest, he didn't want to walk around naked. He pulled on jeans and a polo shirt. Flipped open his computer and went to the home page.

Hand to Heart

Devoted to raising awareness of
humanitarian tragedies
around the world

How you can help . . .

'We don't take money ourselves. We just make people aware of needs for humanitarian aid, then they can click on a link to, say, tsunami relief or the nuclear disaster in Japan or gas victims in Syria. Make donations. My job is I travel around and meet with non-profit groups, get press material and pictures of the disaster to put on our site. I vet the groups too. Some are scams.'

'No!'

'Happens, yep.'

'People can be such shits.' She closed the laptop. 'Not a bad job. You do good things for a living. And you get to stay in places like this.'

'Sometimes.' In fact, he wasn't comfortable in 'places like this'. Hyatt was good enough for him or even more modest motels. But his boss liked it here; Chris liked all the best places so this was where March was put. Just like the clothes and accessories scattered about the room. The Canali suit, the Louis Vuitton shoes, the Coach briefcase, the Tiffany cufflinks weren't his choice. His boss didn't get that some people did this job for reasons other than money.

Calista vanished into the bathroom to dress – the modesty bump was growing – and she emerged. Her hair was still damp but she'd rented a convertible from Hertz and he supposed that, with the top down, the strands would be blow-dried by the time she got to whatever retirement home she was headed for. March's own sculpted brown hair, thick as pelt, irritatingly took ten minutes to bring to attention.

Calista kissed him, brief but not too brief; they both knew the rules. Lunchtime delight.

'You'll still be around for a couple of days, Mr Humanitarian?'

'I will,' March said.

'Good.' This was delivered perky. Then she asked, genuinely curious, 'So you having a successful trip?'

'Real successful, yeah.'

Then, moving breezily, Calista was out of the door.

The moment it shut, March reached over and snagged the remote. Clicked the TV back on, thinking maybe national news had picked up Solitude Creek, and wondered what the big boys and girls were saying about the tragedy.

But on the screen was a commercial for fabric softener.

He put on his workout clothes, shorts and a sleeveless T, rolled to the floor and began the second batch of the five hundred push-ups for today. After, crunches. Then squats. Later he'd go for a run along Seventeen Mile Drive.

On TV: acid-reflux remedies and insurance ads.

Please . . .

'And now an update on the Solitude Creek tragedy in Central California. With me is James Harcourt, our national disaster correspondent.'

Seriously? That was a job title?

'It didn't take much at all for the panic to set in.'

No, March reflected. A little smoke. Then a phone call to whoever was on duty in the lobby: 'I'm outside. Your kitchen's on fire! Back stage too! I've called the fire department, but evacuate. Get everybody out now.'

He'd wondered if he would have to do more to get the horror started. But, nope, that was all it took. People could erase a hundred thousand years of evolution in seconds.

Back to the workout, enjoying the occasional images of the interior of the club.

After thirty minutes, sweating, Antioch March rose, opened his locked briefcase and pulled out a map of the area. He was inspired by something the national disaster correspondent had said. He went online and did some more research. He scrawled some notes. Good. Yes, thank you, he thought to the newscaster. Then he paused, replaying Calista's breathy voice.

'*So you having a successful trip?*'

'*Real successful, yeah.*'

Soon to be even more so.

CHAPTER 12

The politicos had started to arrive at Solitude Creek.

Always happened at incidents like this. The bigwigs appearing, those in office or those aspiring, or those, like her boss, Charles Overby, who simply wanted a few minutes in the limelight because they enjoyed a few minutes in the limelight. They'd show up and talk to the press and be seen by the mourners or the spectators.

That is, by the voters and the public.

And, yes, occasionally they really would step up and help out. Occasionally. Sometimes. Possibly. (A state government employee, Kathryn Dance struggled constantly against cynicism.)

There were more news crews than grandstanders here at the moment, so the biggest networks were targeting the most newsworthy subjects, like sportsmen on a party boat in Monterey Bay going for the fattest salmon.

Networks. Nets. Fish. Dance liked the metaphor.

The US Congressman representing the district Solitude Creek fell within was Daniel Nashima, a third- or fourth-generation Japanese American who'd held office for several terms. In his mid-forties, he was accompanied by an aide, a tall, vigilant young man, resembling the actor Josh Brolin, in an unimpeachable if anachronistic three-piece suit.

Nashima was wealthy, family business, but he usually dressed down. Today, typical: chino slacks and a blue dress shirt, sleeves rolled up – an outfit you'd wear to a Kiwanis fundraiser pancake breakfast. Nashima, a handsome man with tempered Asian features – his mother was white – looked over the exterior of the Solitude Creek club with dismay. Dance wasn't surprised. He had a reputation for being responsive to natural disasters, like the earthquake that had struck Santa Cruz not long ago. He'd arrived at that one at three a.m. and helped lift rubble off survivors and search for the dead.

The anchor from CNN, a striking blonde, was on Nashima in a San Francisco instant. The Congressman said, 'My heart goes out to the victims of this terrible tragedy.' He promised that he would work with his colleague to make sure a full investigation got to the root of it. If there had been any negligence at all on the part of the club and its owner he would make sure that criminal charges were brought.

The mayor of Monterey happened to arrive a few moments later. No limo. The tall Latino stepped from his personal vehicle – a nice one, a Range Rover – and made it ten steps toward the spectators/mourners/victims before he, too, was approached by the media. Only a few local reporters, though. He glanced toward Nashima and managed, just, to keep a don't-care visage, downplaying that he'd been upstaged by the Congressman; the folks from Atlanta – and a woman with such perfect hair – knew their priorities.

Dance heard that the California state representative for this area – and a rumored competitor for the US Senate seat Nashima was considering next year – was out of town and not making the trip back from Vegas for a sympathy call. This would be an oops for his career.

Nashima politely but firmly ended the interview he was giving and walked away, refusing other media requests. He was studying the scene and walking up to people who were leaving flowers or praying or simply standing in mournful poses. He spoke to them with head down, embraced them. Dance believed once or twice he wiped tears from his cheek. That wasn't for the camera. He was pointedly turned away from the media.

About thirty such grievers and spectators were present. With Bob Holly's blessing, Dance made the rounds of them now, flashed her badge, as shiny and official in its Civ-Div mode as when she was a criminal investigator, and asked questions about the truck, about the fire in the oil drum, about anyone skulking about outside the club last night.

Negatives, all around.

She tried to identify anyone who'd been in the mob that morning but couldn't. True, most had probably vanished. Still, she knew from her work that at harrowing times our powers of observation and retention fail us completely.

She noticed a car pulling into the lot and easing slowly to the police line, near where the impromptu memorial of flowers and stuffed animals was growing. The car was a fancy one, a new-model two-door Lexus, sleek, black.

There were two occupants, and, though Dance couldn't see them clearly, they were having a serious discussion. Even in silhouette, the body radiates intent and mood. The driver, a man in his forties, climbed out, bent down, said a few more words through the car's open door, then flipped the seat forward and extracted a bouquet from the back. He said something else to the other occupant, in the front passenger seat, whose response must have been negative because the man shrugged and continued on his own to the memorial.

Dance walked up to him, showed her ID. 'I'm Kathryn Dance. CBI.'

Distracted, the handsome man nodded.

'I assume you lost someone last night.'

'We did, yes.'

'I'm sorry.'

We . . .

A nod back to the Lexus. There was a glare . . . and the Japanese engineers were quite adept, it seemed, at tinting glass but Dance could see that the person occupying the passenger seat had long hair. A woman. His wife, probably. But no ring on his finger. An ex-wife, perhaps. And she realized with a shock. *My God.* They'd lost a child here.

His name was Frederick Martin and he explained that, yes, his ex-wife, Michelle, had brought their daughter here last night.

She'd been right. Their child, probably a teen. How sad. And, given the flowers resting on the memorial, she hadn't been merely injured. She'd died.

Dance's worst horror. Every mother's.

That had been the tension in the car. Ex-spouses, forced together at a time like this. Probably on the way to a funeral home to make arrangements. Dance's heart went out to them both.

'We're investigating the incident,' she said, a version of the truth. 'I have a few questions.'

'Well, I don't know anything. I wasn't here.' Martin was edgy. He wanted to leave.

'No, no. I understand. But if I could have a few words with your ex-wife.'

'What?' he said, frowning broadly.

Then a voice behind them, a girl's voice. Nearly a whisper. 'She's gone.'

Dance turned to see a teenager. Pretty, but with a face distorted and puffy from crying. Her hair had been carelessly herded into place with fingers, not a brush.

'Mommy's gone.'

Oh. The ex was the fatality.

'Trish, go back to the car.'

Staring at the club. 'She was trapped. Against the door. I saw her. I can't – we looked at each other and then I fell. This big man, he was crying like a baby, he climbed on my back and I went down. I thought I was going to die but I got picked up by somebody. Then the people I was with went through another door, not the fire exits. The crowd she was in—'

'Trish, honey, no. I told you this was a bad idea. Let's go. We've got your grandparents to meet at the airport. We've got plans to make.'

Martin took his daughter's arm. She pulled away. He grimaced.

To the girl: 'Trish, I'm Kathryn Dance, California Bureau of Investigation. I'd like to ask you a few questions, if you don't mind.'

'We do,' Martin said. 'We do mind.'

Crying now, softly, the girl stared at the roadhouse. 'It was hell in there. They talk about hell, in movies and things, but, no, *that* was hell.'

'Here's my card.' Dance offered it to Frederick Martin.

He shook his head. 'We don't want it. There's nothing she can tell you. Leave us alone.'

'I'm sorry for your loss.'

He got a firmer grip on his daughter and, though she stiffened, maneuvered her back to the Lexus. When they were seated inside, he reached over and clicked on her belt. Then they sped from the lot before Dance could note the license plate.

Not that it mattered, she supposed. If the girl and her mother had been inside during the panic, they wouldn't have seen what really interested Dance: the person who'd parked the truck in front of the doors and lit the fire.

Besides, she could hardly blame the man for being protective. Dance supposed that the father had now been catapulted into a tough, alien role; she imagined that the mother had had a higher percentage of custody, maybe full.

The Solitude Creek incident had changed many lives in many different ways.

A gull strafed and Dance instinctively lifted her arm. The big bird landed clumsily near a scrap of cardboard, thinking it was food. It seemed angry the prize held aroma only and catapulted off into the sky once more, heading toward the bay.

Dance returned to the club and had a second difficult conversation with Sam Cohen, still bordering on comatose, then spoke with other employees. No one could come up with any patrons or former club workers who might have had gripes with Cohen or anyone there. Nor did competitors seem behind the incident – anyone who might want to drive the man out of business or get revenge for something Cohen had done professionally in the past.

Heading back outside, Dance pulled her iPhone from her pocket and phoned Jon Boling, asking if he could pick up the children at school.

'Sure,' he replied. She enjoyed hearing his calm voice. 'How's your Civ Div going?'

He knew about the Serrano situation.

'Awkward,' she said, eyes on Bob Holly, interviewing some of the same people she just had. 'I'm at Solitude Creek.'

A pause.

'Aren't you handling soda-bottle deposits?'

'Supposed to be.'

Boling said, 'It's terrible, on the news. They're saying a truck driver parked behind the club to smoke some dope. Then he panicked when the fire started and left the truck beside the doors. Nobody could get out.'

Reporters . . .

She looked at her iPhone for the time, now that her watch was out of commission. It was two thirty. 'I'll be another three, four hours, I'd guess. Mom and Dad are coming over tonight. Martine, Stephen . . .'

'The kids and I'll take care of dinner.'

'Would you? Oh, thanks.'

'See you soon.'

She disconnected. Her eyes did a sweep of the club, the jobbing company, then the parking lot.

Finally the bordering vegetation. At the eastern end of the lot was what seemed to be a tramped-down area leading through a line of scrub oak, Australian willow, pine, magnolia. She wandered that way and found herself beside Solitude Creek itself. The small dark tributary – thirty feet wide there – was framed by salt and dune grass, thistle and other sandy-soil plants whose identity she couldn't guess at.

She followed the path away from the parking lot, through a head-high tangle of brush and grass. Here, overgrown with vegetation and dusted with sand, were the remnants of old structures: concrete foundations, portions of rusting chain-link fences and a few columns. They had to be seventy-five years old, a hundred. Quite extensive. Maybe back then Solitude Creek was deeper and this was part of the seafood industry. The site was fifteen miles north of Cannery Row but back then fishing was big business all along this area of the coast.

Or possibly developers had started to build a project here – apartments or a hotel or restaurant. Still would be a good spot for an inn, she reflected: near the ocean, situated amid rolling, grassy hills. The creek itself was calming and the grayish water didn't necessarily mean bad fishing.

Continuing past the ruins, Dance looked around. She wondered if the killer had parked his car here – there were residences and surfaced roads nearby – and walked this same path. He could have gotten to the parking lot without being seen, then circled around to the jobbing company to get to the drop-box and trucks.

When she got to the pocket of homes – a half-dozen bungalows, one trailer – she realized that someone would be very visible parking there: basically the only place would be directly in front of a house. She doubted that the perp would have been that careless.

Still, you did what you could.

Three of the homes were dark and Dance left a card in the doorframes of each.

Two women, however, were home. Both white, large and toting infants, they reported they hadn't seen anyone and, as Dance had surmised, 'Anybody parking here, well, we would've noticed, and at night, Ernie would've been out to talk to him in a hare-lick.'

Dance moved on to the last place, the trailer, which was the only residence actually overlooking Solitude Creek.

Hmm. Had he used a boat to cruise up to the roadhouse and jobbing company?

She knocked on the door frame. A curtain shifted and Dance held up her ID for the woman to peruse. Three locks or deadbolts got snapped. A chain too. The person lives alone, Dance thought. Or she's a meth cooker.

Dance's hand dipped to where her gun used to be. She grimaced and tugged her jacket closed.

The woman who opened the door was slimmer than the others, about forty-five, long gray-brown hair. A thin braid, purple, ended in a feather at her shoulder. From what she wore and what was scattered around the cluttered living area, Dance saw that the woman's fashion choices favored macramé, tie-dye and fringe. She immediately thought of her associate TJ Scanlon, at the CBI, whose one regret in life was that he wasn't living in the late sixties.

'Help you?'

Dance identified herself and flashed her ID once more for a

closer examination The woman, Annette, didn't seem uneasy to be talking to a law enforcer. Dance detected only cigarette smoke and its residue, bitter and stale. Nothing illegal.

'Have you heard about the incident at Solitude Creek roadhouse?'

'Terrible. Are you here about that?'

'Just a couple of questions, you don't mind.'

'Not at all. You want to come in?'

'Thanks.' Dance joined her. Thousands of CDs and vinyl records sat on the shelves and were stacked against the walls. A lapsed musician and co-founder of a website devoted to music, Dance was impressed. 'You go to the roadhouse often?'

'Sometimes. Little pricey for me. Sam's got a pretty dear cover charge.'

'So you weren't there last night?'

'No, I'm talking once a year I go and only if it's somebody I really, really like.'

'Now, Annette, I'm wondering if people boat down Solitude Creek.'

'Boat? You *can*. I've seen a few kayakers and canoes. Some powerboats. Real small. It gets pretty shallow you go further east.' Her fingers, quite ruddy, played with her feathered rope of purple hair.

'Is there a place where anyone could park and kayak down to the club?'

A nod toward the road. 'No, this is the only place anybody could leave a car and Ernie—'

'Across the street?'

'Yeah, that Ernie. He's not going to let anybody park here he doesn't know.'

'Ernie's a big guy?'

'Not big. Just, you know.'

Hare-lick. Whatever that meant.

Dance noticed state-government envelopes, ripped open like picked-over road kill. Welfare. The woman lit a cigarette and blew the smoke away from Dance.

'So, last night, you didn't see anybody on the creek in a boat?'

'No one. And I could've seen. Look at the window. It looks over the water. Right there. That one.'

It did indeed, though it was so grimy with smoke residue that at dusk it would've been impossible to spot much through it.

Dance removed the small notebook she kept with her and flipped it open. Jotted a few notes. 'Are you married? Anyone else live here?'

'Nope. Just me. Solo. Not even a cat.' A smile. 'This,' Annette said, 'what you're asking, makes it sound like there was something going on. I mean, like you think somebody did something at the club on purpose.'

'Just routine investigation. We always do this.'

'Like *NCIS*.'

Now Dance smiled. 'Just like that. You can't see the club from here but would you have by any chance taken a walk last night, ended up near there?'

'No. You gotta be careful. We've had mountain lions.'

True. A woman had been killed not long ago, a jogger, banker from San Francisco.

'You were in all night?' Dance asked.

'Absolutely. Right here.'

'And anyone you didn't recognize in the neighborhood recently? Not just last night.'

'No, ma'am. I'd tell you if I did.'

Another note.

Dance reached into her purse and exchanged her pink-framed glasses for a pair that had black-metal frames.

Predator specs.

'Annette?'

'Yes, ma'am?'

'Could you tell me why you're lying?'

She expected denial, expected resistance. Expected anger.

She didn't expect the woman to drop to her knees, overcome with sobbing.

CHAPTER 13

'Kathryn, no. You can't be Civil half the time, Criminal the rest. It doesn't work that way. We've been through this.'

Charles Overby seemed just pissy. She was in his office, close to five p.m. She was surprised he was still there: there was still an hour of tennis light left.

She knew he was right but the fast dismissal – *It doesn't work that way* – was irritating. She asked, 'Who else is going to handle it? We're short-staffed.' The CBI had been hit with budget cutbacks, like every other agency in California, whose new nickname among government workers was the 'Bare State', a play on the grizzly on the flag.

'TJ. Rey. I'll assign one of them.'

They were two very competent agents but young. Neither they nor anyone else in the Bureau had Dance's skill at interrogation. And this case, she felt, had instances aplenty to get people into interview rooms. There were nearly a hundred victims, any one of whom might have a lead. Any one of whom might also be the perp. Stationed by the club door last night, where he could escape safely if it became too dangerous – maybe to enjoy his revenge for a real or imagined slight.

Or just because he wanted to watch people die.

'You shouldn't even be in the office. You should be home planting flowers or baking or something . . . All right, I'm just saying.'

Dance forwent the grimace. She said, 'How's this? Michael O'Neil.'

Chief of detectives of the Monterey County Sheriff's Office.

'What about him?'

'He'll run it.'

'I don't know.'

'Charles. It's not a Fire Department matter. The burn in the oil drum was secondary. Makes sense the MCSO would handle it.'

His eyes slipped away. 'You'll *brief* O'Neil, that's all.'

'Sure. I'd advise.'

Advising wasn't the same as briefing. Overby didn't protest but she sensed he might not have noted her verb.

'Nothing changes, Kathryn. No weapon. You're still Civ Div.'

'Sure,' Kathryn Dance said brightly. She was winning.

'You think he'll agree?' Overby said.

'We'll see. I think so.'

She knew this because she'd already texted him. And he *had* agreed.

But now Overby was troubled once more. 'Of course, if it becomes a county operation . . .'

Meaning he'd miss out on the credit – and press conferences – that went with closing a case.

'Tell you what. *You* can't do more than brief.'

Advise.

'But we can still get our oar in.'

She'd never understood that expression. 'How do you mean, Charles?'

'Let's involve the CBI folks we've got here, on the task force. Jimmy Gomez and Steve Foster.'

'What? Charles, no. They're on Serrano and Guzman . . . I need them focused on that.'

'No, no, this'll be good. Just to kick around some ideas with them.'

'With Foster? Kick ideas around with Steve Foster? He doesn't kick around ideas. He shoots them in the head.'

Overby was looking away. Perhaps her glare seared. 'Now that I think about it, makes sense to run it by them. Good on all counts. We have . . . considerations. Under the circumstances.'

'Charles, please, no.'

'Let's just go talk to them, that's all. Get Foster's thoughts. Jimmy's too. He's one of us.'

Whatever the consequences, he'd decided his office couldn't take a complete back seat to the Sheriff's.

Avoiding her eyes, he rose, slipped his jacket over his immaculate white shirt and strode out of the office. 'I think it's a brilliant idea. Come along, Kathryn. Let's have a chat with our friends.'

CHAPTER 14

The Guzman Connection task force was up to full strength.

In addition to blustery Steve Foster and staunch Carol Allerton, two others were present in the conference room dedicated to the operation.

'Kathryn, Charles.' This was from Steve Lu, the chief of detectives at the Salinas Police Department, a.k.a. Steve Two, since another, Foster, was on the team. Lu, an excessively skinny man – Dance's opinion – was a specialist in gangs. His younger brother had been in a crew and been busted on a few minor counts – though he was now out of the system and clean. Lu was persistent and no-nonsense, maybe trying harder to make up for his sibling's stumble. He was humorless, Dance had learned over several years of working with him, but he was not, as the other Steve was, bluntly contrary.

The fourth task-force member was Jimmy Gomez, the young CBI agent whose name had come up earlier. Dark-complexioned and sporting a moustache as brown as Foster's was light and elaborate, he stayed in shape by playing football – that is, soccer – every minute when he wasn't at work or attending to his family. He was assigned to this division of the CBI and his office was two doors down from Dance's. They were both co-workers and friends. (Just two weeks ago Dance, her children, Gomez, his wife and their three youngsters had done the Del Monte Cineplex thing, then gone to Lala's after, to discuss over dessert and coffee the brilliance of Pixar and which animated character they each would want to be; Dance had selected the hero from *Brave*, mostly because she envied the hair.)

The two Steves were at one table, Jimmy Gomez at another. Carol Allerton, in the corner, waved to the newcomers and returned to a serious mobile-phone conversation.

Overby announced, 'Some help, *s'il vous plaît?*'

Dance felt her jaw tighten and knew exactly what she was radiating kinesically. She wondered if anyone else in the room did. Her displeasure had to be obvious.

'You've probably heard about the incident at the roadhouse, Solitude Creek,' Overby said. 'I know *you* have, Jimmy.'

'That fire?' Foster asked. He seemed perpetually distracted.

'No, it was more than that.' Overby glanced at Dance.

She said, 'The club itself didn't burn. The perp started a fire outside near the HVAC system to get the smell of smoke into the club. He'd blocked the exit doors. Three dead, dozens injured. A stampede. It was pretty bad.'

'Intentional? People crushed to death,' Allerton whispered. 'Terrible.'

'Jesus,' Steve Lu muttered. 'So it's homicide.'

Homicide embraces everything from suicide to vehicular manslaughter to premeditated murder. It was into the last of those categories that the Solitude Creek incident probably fell.

Foster took the news less emotionally. 'Can't be insurance. Otherwise the owner would've torched the place empty. Wouldn't want any fatalities. Disgruntled workers, pissed-off customers got kicked out drunk?'

'Preliminary interviews don't turn up any obvious suspects but it's a possibility,' Dance said. 'We'll keep looking.'

Overby then said, 'Now. Kathryn's got a lead.'

'I was canvassing the area. I found a woman who lives about two hundred yards from the end of the club's parking lot. She told me she didn't see anything odd around the time of the incident, she wasn't near the club, but I knew she was lying.'

Foster continued to gaze at her, his eyes neutral but still managing to radiate criticism for her missing the clues during the interview earlier.

'How?' Steve Lu asked.

'I had a feeling she had a connection with the club. She's on welfare and poor but she loves music. I suspected she'd hike to the club and listen to the shows from the outside. I asked if she was there last night. She said no. But she was clearly lying.'

Foster looked over a pad containing his precise notes.

Dance continued, 'Generally, it's hard to tell if somebody's being deceptive without establishing their baseline behavior.'

'Charles was telling us,' Allerton said.

'But there're a few things that signal deception on their own. One is beginning to speak more slowly, since your mind is trying to craft the lie and make sure it'll be consistent with everything you've said before. The second is a slight increase in pitch – deception creates stress and stress tightens muscles, including the vocal cords. Those both registered deception when she was talking to me. I called her on it. She broke down and confessed she'd lied and she had been outside the club, from about seven thirty until the incident.'

'What'd she see?' Lu asked.

'White male, over six feet, in a dark green jacket with a logo, like a construction or other worker, black cap, yellow aviator sunglasses. Medium build. Brown hair. Probably under forty. Nobody at Henderson Jobbing wears that kind of outfit. This guy parked the truck beside the club, started a fire in the oil drum and walked back to the warehouse – to drop the keys off. That was it. She stayed until the stampede happened and she took off.'

'Afraid to come forward.'

'She said anybody who'd do that, if he found out about her, would come back and kill her in a minute.'

'Bring her in, grill her,' Foster said, still looking over his notes.

'She's told us everything she knows.'

His look said, Has she? He said, 'If she's afraid, maybe she was withholding.'

'She got unafraid when I told her we'd relocate her temporarily, get her into one of our safe houses.'

She saw Overby stiffen. She hadn't shared this with him. Keeping witnesses alive was expensive.

Budget issues . . .

Foster shrugged. 'Get the descrip out on the wire. ASAP.'

'It is,' Dance said. Every cop and government official on the Peninsula and in neighboring counties had the information the witness, Annette, had relayed. 'She had no facial description – the light was too dim and she was too far away.'

'Get it to the news too,' Foster said.

'No,' Dance said.

He looked up from beneath impressive brows.

Carol Allerton lifted an eyebrow, inquiring about the topic of conversation. Dance briefed her.

Foster reiterated, 'On the news. Go broad.'

Overby said, 'We were debating that.'

'What's to debate?' Foster asked.

Allerton said, 'He hears, he vanishes.'

Gomez offered, 'Yeah, what I'd do. He rabbits. He dyes his hair. Tosses the jacket, switches to pink Ray-Bans.'

Foster to Dance: 'Did the witness think he tipped to her?'

'No. The wit's positive he didn't see her.'

'So he's still walking around and probably still wearing the same clothes. The green jacket and all that. A thousand people could've seen him. Maybe the clerk in his hotel, or his dry cleaner, if he's local. It's standard operating procedure in my cases.'

Overby trod the tightrope. 'Pluses and minuses on both sides.'

'I'd vote no,' Gomez said. Allerton nodded her agreement.

Dance turned to Overby. Her gaze lasered him briefly.

After a moment, eyes on the well-examined linoleum floor, he said, 'We'll keep it private for the time being. No releasing the details to the media.'

Well, score one for us, Dance thought, and made an effort not to reveal her surprise.

CHAPTER 15

'Mom, Donnie's got a, you know, a question.'

Dance, thinking: *You know*. But she rarely corrected the children in front of anyone. She'd chide them gently later. She cocked her head to her son, lean and fair-haired. Nearly as tall as she. 'Sure. What?'

Donnie Verso, a dark-haired thirteen-year-old in Wes's class, looked her in the eye. 'Well, I'm not sure what to call you.'

Dusk was around the three of them as they stood on the expansive porch – known to friends and family as the 'Deck' – behind Dance's Victorian-style house, which was dark green with weathered gray railings, shutters and trim, in the north-western Pacific Grove. You could, if you chose to risk a tumble off the porch, catch a glimpse of ocean, about a half-mile away.

Wes filled in: 'He doesn't know whether he should call you Mrs Dance or Agent Dance.'

'Well, that's very polite of you to ask, Donnie. But since you're a friend of Wes's, you can call me Kathryn.'

'Oh, I'm not supposed to call people that. I mean adults. By their first name. My dad likes me to be respectful.'

'I can talk to him.'

'No, he just wouldn't like it.'

'Then call me Mrs Dance.' Wes readily shared with his friends that his father had died but Dance had learned that children rarely registered the niceties of Mrs versus Miss versus Ms.

'Cool.' His face brightened. 'Mrs Dance.'

With his curly hair and cherubic face, Donnie would be a girl magnet soon. Well, he probably already was, she thought. (And Wes? Handsome . . . and nice. A dangerous combination: already girls were starting to flutter. She was inclined to put the brakes on her own children's growing up but knew it'd be easier to stop the surf crashing on the sand at Spanish Bay.) Donnie lived not far away, biking distance, which Dance was grateful for – as a single mother, even with a good support net like hers, anything that reduced the task of chauffeuring was a blessing. She thought Donnie'd look better not wearing hoodies and baggy jeans . . . but valedictorians of middle-school classes and Christian pop singers all dressed like gangstas nowadays, so who was she to judge?

Arriving from work just now, Dance had not come through the front door but through the side yard and gate – to make sure it was locked – then ascended the steps to the Deck. Which meant she hadn't said hello to the four-legged residents of the household. They now came bounding forward for head rubs and, with any luck, a treat (alas, none today). Dylan, a German shepherd, named for the legendary singer-songwriter, and Patsy, a flat-coated retriever, in honor of Ms Cline, Dance's favorite C&W singer.

'Can Donnie stay for dinner?' Wes asked.

'If it's okay, Mrs Dance.'

'I'll call your mother.' Protocol.

'Sure. Thanks.'

The boys returned to a board game and dropped to the redwood decking, crunching some chips and drinking Honest Tea. Soda was not to be found in the Dance household.

Dance found the boy's home number and called. His mother said it was fine for him to stay for dinner but he should be home by nine.

She disconnected, then returned to the living room where her father, Stuart, and ten-year-old, Maggie, sat in front of the TV.

'Mom! You came in the back door!'

She didn't, of course, tell her that she'd been checking the perimeter and double-locking the gate. Two active cases, with a number of bad actors, who could, if they really wanted to, find her.

'Give me a hug, honey.'

Maggie complied happily. 'Wes and Donnie won't let me play their game.'

'It's a boys' game, I'm sure.'

A frown crossed Maggie's heart-shaped face. 'I don't know what that is. I don't think there should be boy games and girl games.'

Good point. If and when Dance ever remarried, Maggie had announced she was going to be 'best woman' – whatever her age. She had also learned of feminism in school and, returning home after social studies, had declared, to Dance's delight, that she wasn't a feminist. She was an equalist.

'Hi, Dad,' Dance said.

Stuart rose and hugged his daughter. He was seventy, and though his time outdoors as a marine biologist had taken a toll on the flesh, he looked younger than his years. He was tall, six two, wide-shouldered, with unruly, thick white hair. Dermatologists' scalpels and lasers had left their mark too and he now rarely went outside without a floppy hat. He was retired, yes, but when not babysitting the grandkids or puttering around the house in Carmel, he worked at the famed Monterey Bay Aquarium several days a week.

'Where's Mom?'

Staunch Edie Dance was a cardiac nurse at the Monterey Bay Hospital.

'Took the late shift, filling in. Just me tonight.'

Dance headed into the bedroom, washed and changed into black jeans, a silk T-shirt and burgundy wool sweater. The central coast, after sunset, could get downright cold and dinner tonight would be on the Deck.

As she walked down the stairs and into the hallway a man stepped through the front door. Jon Boling, forties, wasn't tall. A few inches above Dance but lean – thanks mostly to biking and occasional free weights (twenty-five-pounders at his place and a pair of twelves at hers). His straight hair, thinning, was a shade similar to Dance's, though a little darker than chestnut, and with none of her occasional gray strands (which coincidentally disappeared after a trip to Rite-Aid or Save Mart).

'Look, I'm bearing Greek gifts.' He held up two large bags from a Mediterranean restaurant in Pacific Grove.

They kissed and he followed her into the kitchen.

Boling was a professor at a college nearby, teaching the Literature of Science Fiction, as well as a class called Computers and Society. In the graduate school, Boling taught what he described as some boring technical courses. 'Sort of math, sort of engineering.' He also consulted for Silicon Valley firms. He was apparently a minor genius in the world of boxes – computers. She'd had to learn about this from the press and Wes's assessment of his skill in programming: modesty was hardwired into Boling's genes. He wrote code the way Richard Wilbur or Jim Tilley wrote poetry. Fluid, brilliant and captivating.

They'd been going out for a while now, ever since she'd hired him to assist on a case involving computers.

As he offloaded containers of moussaka, octopus, taramasalata and the rest, he noted her arm. 'What happened there?'

She frowned and followed his gaze. 'Oh.' Her watch, crystal shattered. 'The Serrano thing.' She explained about the run-in at CBI, when the young man had fled after the interview.

'You all right?' His gentle eyes narrowed.

'No danger. I just didn't fall as elegantly as I should have.'

She grimaced as she examined the broken glass. The watch had been a Christmas present from friends in New York, the famed criminalist Lincoln Rhyme and his partner, Amelia Sachs. She'd helped them out on a case a few years ago, involving a brilliant for-hire criminal known as the Watchmaker. She undid the dark-green leather strap and set the damaged watch on the mantel. She'd look into getting it repaired soon.

Boling called, 'Mags?'

Dance saw her daughter leap up and run to the doorway. The child wrinkled her brow. Then called, '*Geia!*'

Boling nodded. '*Kalos!*'

Dance laughed.

He said, 'Thought we should learn a little Greek in honor of dinner. Where's Wes?'

'Outside with Donnie.'

Boling did a fair amount of baby-sitting too; his teaching load was light, and as a consultant he could work here, there, anywhere. He knew as much about the children's schedule and friends as Dance did. 'Seems like a nice boy, Donnie. Year older, right?'

'Thirteen, yes.'

'His parents picked him up once. Mother's sweet. Dad doesn't say much.' Boling frowned. 'Was wondering. Whatever happened to Rashiv? He and Wes seemed pretty tight for a while. He was brilliant. Math, phew.'

'Don't know. Kids move on.' Wes, whom Dance had always thought mature for his age, had recently gravitated to Donnie and an older crowd. Rashiv, she recalled, was a year younger than her son. Maggie, who'd always been a bit of a loner, had started hanging out with a group of four girls in her grade school (to Dance's further surprise, the popular ones, two contestants in National American Miss pageants, one a would-be cheerleader).

Boling opened some wine and passed out glasses to the adults.

The doorbell.

'I'll get it!' Maggie charged forward.

'Hold on, Mags.' Boling knew that Dance was involved in several potentially dangerous cases and quickly walked there with the child. He peeked out, then let Maggie unlock the door.

The guests were dear family friends. Steven Cahill, about Boling's age, was wearing a poncho. His salt-and-pepper ponytail dangled and he'd recently grown a David Crosby droopy moustache. Beside him was Martine Christensen. Despite the name she had no Scandinavian blood. She was dark-complexioned and voluptuous, descended in part from the original inhabitants of the area: Ohlone Indian, the loose affiliation of tribelets hunting and gathering from Big Sur to San Francisco Bay.

Steve and Martine's children, twin boys a year younger than Maggie, followed them up the front steps, one toting his mother's guitar case, the other a batch of brownies. Maggie shepherded the twins and the two dogs down to the backyard, below the Deck. Dance smiled, noting she had shot a fast aside to her brother, undoubtedly about how wrong male-exclusive games were. The older boys ignored her.

The younger children and the canines struck up an impromptu and chaotic game of Frisbee football.

The adults congregated around the large picnic table on the Deck.

This was the social center of the house – indeed, of the lives of many people Dance knew, family and friends. The twenty-by-thirty-foot expanse, extending from the kitchen into the backyard, was populated by mismatched lawn chairs, loungers and tables. Christmas lights, some amber globes, up-lights, a sink and a large refrigerator were the main decorations. Some planters, too, though the flowers struggled. Beneath, in the backyard, you could find scrub oak and maple trees, grasses, monkey flowers, asters, lupins, potato vines and clover. Some veggies tried to survive but the slugs were merciless.

The Deck had been the site of hundreds of parties, big ones and small ones, and quiet family meals or cocoa nights, just the four of them. Then, more recently, the three. Her husband had proposed to her there, and Dance had eulogized him in virtually the same spot.

The evening was dank so Dance cranked up the propane heater, which exhaled cozy air. The adults sat around the table and had wine, juice or water and talked about . . . well, everything. That was one enduring quality of the Deck. Any topic was fair game. And it was here that all of the town's, state's, country's and world's problems were solved, over and over.

Martine asked, lowering her voice, 'You heard about Solitude Creek?'

'I'm working it,' Dance said.

'No!'

'Katie,' her father said, 'be careful.' As parents would do.

Steve said, 'The company'll be out of business, the trucking company. And the driver, he should get jail time, don't you think?'

Dance said, 'It's not for public consumption yet. Please don't say anything.' She didn't bother to wait for nods of agreement. 'It wasn't the truck driver. And it wasn't an accident.'

'How do you mean?' Martine asked.

'We're still looking into it, but somebody got into the truck and drove it against the doors to block them, then started a fire nearby to send everybody into a panic.' A glance to make sure the children were out of hearing. 'And everybody sure did. The injured and dead were trampled and crushed or suffocated. There was blood everywhere.'

'What's the motive?' Boling asked.

'That's a mystery. We find that out and we can track suspects. But so far, nothing.'

'Revenge?' Steven speculated.

'Always a good one. But no patrons, employees or competitors stand out.'

Martine said, 'I'm claustrophobic. I can't imagine what it would be like to be trapped in a crowd like that.'

Stuart Dance brushed a hand through his tempestuous hair. 'I don't think I ever told you, Katie, but I saw a stampede once. Human, I mean. It was terrible.'

'What?'

'You may have heard about it. Hillsborough, in Sheffield, England? Twenty-five years ago. I still have nightmares. Do you want to hear about it?'

Dance noted the children were out of earshot. 'Go ahead, Dad.'

CHAPTER 16

He was sure they'd die.

Some of them, at least.

Antioch March was on the turbulent shoreline in Pacific Grove, near Asilomar, the conference center. Off Sunset Drive.

He had been doing reconnaissance for tomorrow's 'event' and was driving back to his room at the Cedar Hills Inn when he'd spotted them.

Ah, yes . . .

He'd pulled over.

And then wandered to an outcropping of rock, from which he would have a good view of the unfolding tragedy.

Now he was eyeing the cluster of people nearby, surrounded by spray flying over the rocks from the impact of the roiling water. The sun was low. That 'special time', he'd heard it called by photographers. When light became your friend, something to help out with the pictures, not fight against. March had studied photography, in addition to more esoteric intellectual topics, and he was good. Many of the pictures on the Hand to Heart website were his.

They're dead, he reflected again.

The family he was watching was Asian. Chinese or Korean, probably. He knew the difference in facial structure – he'd been to both of those countries (Korea had been far more productive for his work). But here he was too far away to tell. And he certainly wasn't going to get much closer.

A wife and husband, two pre-teen children, and a mother-in-law: a bundled-up matriarch. Armed with a point-and-shoot, the husband was directing the kids as they posed on dark brown, red and dun rocks.

Spanish Bay, a tourist 'twofer', with beach *and* rugged shoreline, is a beautiful coastal preserve featuring everything one would want in scenic California. A mile of sand, surfers immune to the icy water, dolphins, pelicans, dunes, deer, rocks on which seals perch, busy tidal pools.

And sea otters, of course. Cute little fuzzy-faced critters that float easily on the turbulent surface, smashing shellfish open on rocks perched on their chests.

The area was idyllic.

And deadly.

In researching his plans for the Monterey Bay area, March had learned that every few months tourists wandered too far out onto these craggy rocks and, crash, a muscular arm of the Pacific Ocean lapped them indifferently out to sea. Those who didn't break their heads open on the rocks and drown died of hypothermia before the Coast Guard found them or breathed their last while tangled in the pernicious kelp. It was near here that the singer John Denver had died, his experimental plane falling from the sky.

The Asian family was now prowling the rocks, getting closer and closer to the end of the bulwark that stretched forty feet into the ocean, two yards above the agitated water. The rosy light from the low sun hit them full on.

Beautiful.

He slipped the Galaxy S5 mobile phone from his pocket and began shooting video of the scene around him. Just another tourist. Nothing odd about him, catching the beautiful, rugged scenery in high-def pixels.

A huge crash of water, and the spray must have tickled the children. They seemed to giggle. The father gestured them to go some feet closer to the end. He aimed his Nikon and shot.

Grandmother remained on the trail, some distance. Mother was about twenty feet behind her husband and children. March noticed she was calling. But the roar of the ocean on this windy evening was loud. The man probably couldn't hear.

Another huge wave, exploding on the gray-and-brown rocks. For a moment the children weren't visible. He glanced at the screen and saw a rainbow in the angled sunlight.

Then there were the children once more, oblivious, looking down at the water, as their father directed them closer yet to the terminus point of the rocks.

March now noted that out to sea a large wave was gaining strength.

The lens of his camera app was pointed their way but his concentration wasn't on the video he was taking. He was looking at the swelling wave.

Fifty yards, forty.

Water travels fast even though it is, of course, the largest moving thing on earth. And this behemoth began to race.

Closer, closer, come on . . .

March's palms sweated. His gut thudded, as he thought: Please, I want this . . .

Thirty yards.

*The wave beginning to sharpen into a peak at the crest, God's palm to slap the family to their deaths.

Twenty-five yards.

Twenty . . .

It was then that the mother had had enough. She charged forward, unsteady on the slippery rocks, and stepped in front of her husband, who gestured angrily with his hands.

Would he ignore her? Stand up to the bitch, March thought. Please.

Fifteen yards away, that huge swell of water.

His breathing was coming fast. Just thirty more seconds. That's all I need.

But the woman stepped stridently past her husband, her face dark, and strode up to her children.

Ten . . .

She took them by the hands and, raging at them too, dragged the bewildered youngsters back toward the trail. The husband followed, his face blank.

The wave struck the rocks and inundated the spot where the children had been standing seconds before. It had had plenty of energy to sweep father and children into the water. Even more frustrating, March judged from the angle, they would have been slammed into the rocks just in front of him, then sucked into a churning mass of ocean nearby.

He lowered the phone.

The parents and children, their backs turned to the rocks, hadn't seen the dramatic detonation of fiery water. Only the grandmother had. She said nothing but swiveled arthritically and followed her brood along the path.

March sighed. He was angry. One last glance at the foolish, oblivious family. He found his teeth jammed together.

The hollowness within him spread, like water melting salt.

Somebody's not happy . . .

He climbed into the car and started the engine. He'd return to the Cedar Hills Inn and continue his plans for the next event in the Monterey area. It would be even better than Solitude Creek. He had another task, too, of course. In this business you had to be beyond cautious. Part of that was learning who was hunting for you.

And figuring out how best to avoid them.

Or, even better, stop them before they grew into a full-blown threat. Whatever it took.

CHAPTER 17

None of those on Kathryn Dance's Deck had heard of the disaster in Sheffield, England.

Stuart Dance was now explaining: 'I was in London as a research fellow.'

Dance said, 'I remember. Mom and I came over to see you. I was seven or eight.'

'That's right. But this was before you got there. I was in Nottingham, lecturing, and the post-doc I was working with suggested we go to Sheffield to see a game at Hillsborough Stadium. You know football – soccer – fans can be pretty intense in Europe so they would host the association semi-finals in neutral venues to avoid fights. It was Nottingham – my associate's team, of course – versus Liverpool. We took the train up. My friend had some money – I think his father was a Sir Somebody or Another – and got good seats. What happened wasn't near us. But we could see it. Oh, my, we could see.'

Dance became alarmed as her father's face grew pale and his eyes darted toward the children, to confirm they weren't close. He seemed edgy, reflecting the horror he was experiencing at the memories.

'It seems that just as the game was about to start, Liverpool fans were clustering at the turnstiles and were agitated, afraid they wouldn't get in. Pushing forward. Someone opened an exit gate to relieve the pressure and fans surged inside and made their way to a standing-room pen. The crush was terrible. Ninety-five, ninety-six people died there.'

'God,' Steve muttered.

'Worst sports disaster in UK history.' Nearly whispering now. 'Horrible. Fans trying to climb on top of everyone else, people jumping over the wall. One minute alive, then snuffed out. I don't know how they died. I guess suffocation.'

'Compressive asphyxia, they call it,' Dance said.

Stuart nodded. 'It all happened so fast. Ridiculously fast. Kick-off was at three. At three-oh-six they stopped the game but almost everybody who died was dead at that point.'

Dance recalled that the deaths at the Solitude Creek roadhouse, though fewer, had taken about the same amount of time.

Stuart added, 'And you know what was the scariest? Together, all those people became something else. Not human.'

It was like they weren't people at all – it was just one big creature, staggering around, squeezing toward the doors . . .

Stuart continued, 'It reminded me of something else I saw. When I was on a job in Australia. I—'

'We're hungry!' Wes called, and he and Donnie charged to the table. Several of the adults jumped at the sudden intrusion, coming in the midst of the terrible story.

'Then let's eat,' Dance said, secretly relieved to change the subject. 'Get your sister and the twins.'

'Maggie!' Wes shouted.

'Wes. Go *get* your sister.'

'She heard. She's coming.'

A moment later the other youngsters arrived, accompanied by the dogs, ever optimistic at the possibility a klutzy human would drop a bit of dinner.

As Dance, Maggie and Boling set the table, she told those assembled that her friend, country crossover singer, Kayleigh Towne, who lived in Fresno, had sent her and the children tickets to the Neil Hartman concert taking place next weekend.

'No!' Martine hit her playfully on the arm. 'The new Dylan? It's been sold out for months.'

Probably not the new Dylan but a brilliant singer-songwriter, and ace musician too, with a talented backup band. The gig here in town had been scheduled before the young man's Grammy nomination. The small Monterey Performing Arts Center had sold out instantly after that.

Dance and Martine had a long history and music informed it. They'd met at a concert that was a direct descendant of the famed Monterey Folk Festival, where the 'original Dylan' – Bob – had made his west coast debut in '65. The women had become friends and formed a non-profit website to promote indigenous musical talent. Dance, a folklorist by hobby – song-catcher – would travel around the state, occasionally farther afield, with an expensive portable recorder, collect songs and tunes, sell them on the site, keeping only enough money to maintain the server and pay expenses, and remitting the profits to the performers.

The site was called American Tunes, a homage to the great Paul Simon song from the seventies.

Boling brought the food out, opened more wine. The kids sat at a table of their own, though right next to the adults' picnic bench. None of them asked to watch TV during the meal, which pleased Dance. Donnie was a natural comedian. He told joke after joke – all appropriate – keeping the younger kids in stitches.

Conversation reeled throughout dinner. When the meal wound down and Boling was serving Keurig coffee, decaf and cocoa, Martine cracked open her guitar and took out the beautiful old Martin 00-18. She and Dance sang a few songs – Richard Thompson, Kayleigh Towne, Rosanne Cash, Pete Seeger, Mary Chapin Carpenter and, of course, Dylan.

Martine called, 'Hey, Maggie, your mom told me you're singing "Let It Go" at your talent show.'

'Yeah.'

'You liked *Frozen*?'

'Uh-huh.'

'The twins loved it. Actually, *we* loved it too. Come on, sing it. I'll back you up.'

'Oh. No, that's okay.'

'Love to hear it, honey,' Stuart Dance encouraged his granddaughter.

Martine told everyone, 'She has a beautiful voice.'

But Maggie said, 'Yeah, it's that I don't remember the words yet.'

Boling said, 'Mags, you sang it all the way through today. A dozen times. I heard you in your room. And the lyric book was in the living room with me.'

A hesitation. 'Oh, I remember. The DVD was on and they had the, you know, the words at the bottom of the screen.'

She was lying, Dance could easily see. If she knew anything, it was her own children's kinesic baseline. What was this about? Dance recalled that Maggie had seemed more shy and moody in the past day or two. That morning, as she'd tipped her mother's braid with the colorful elastic tie, Dance had tried to draw her out. Her husband's death had seemed to hit Wes hardest at first but he seemed better, much better, about the loss; perhaps now Maggie was feeling the impact. But her daughter had denied it – denied, in fact, that anything was bothering her.

'Well, that's okay,' Martine said. 'Next time.' And she sang a few more folk tunes, then packed up the guitar.

Martine and Steven took some leftovers that Boling had bagged up for them. Everyone said goodbye, hugs and kisses, and headed out of the door, leaving Boling alone with Dance and the older boys. Wes and Donnie were now texting friends as they sat around their complicated board game, gazing at it intensely. At their phone screens too.

Ah, the enthusiasm of youth . . .

'Thanks for the food, everything,' Dance told him.

'You look tired,' Boling said. He was infinitely supportive but he lived in a very different world from hers and she was reluctant to share too much about her impossible line of work. Still, she owed him honesty. 'I am. It's a mess. Not Serrano so much as Solitude Creek. That somebody'd do that on purpose. It just doesn't make sense. It's not like any case I've ever worked. It's already exhausting.'

She hadn't told him about the run-in with the mob outside Henderson Jobbing. And chose not to now. She was still spooked – and sore – from the encounter. And, to be honest to herself, she just didn't want to relive it. She could still hear the rock shattering Billy Culp's jaw. And still see the animal eyes of the mob as it bore down on them.

Fuck you, bitch . . .

The doorbell rang.

Boling frowned.

Dance hesitated. Then: 'Oh, that'd be Michael. He's running

Solitude Creek with me. Didn't I tell you he was coming over?'

'I don't think so.'

'Been a crazy day, sorry.'

'No worries.'

She opened the door and Michael O'Neil walked in.

'Hey, Michael.'

'Jon.' The men shook hands.

'Have some food. Greek. Got plenty left.'

'No, thanks.'

'Come on,' Boling persisted. 'Kathryn can't eat moussaka for a week.'

She noted that he didn't say, 'We can't eat moussaka,' though he might have. But Boling wasn't a chest-thumping territory-staker.

O'Neil said, 'Sure, it's not too much trouble.'

'Wine?'

'Beer.'

'Done.'

Boling prepared a plate and passed him a Corona. O'Neil lifted the bottle in thanks, then hung his sports jacket on a hook. He rarely wore a uniform and tonight was in khaki slacks and a light gray shirt. He sat on a kitchen chair, adjusting his Glock.

Dance had known and worked with O'Neil for years. The chief deputy and senior detective for the Monterey County Sheriff's Office had been a mentor when Dance had joined the Bureau. Her background wasn't law enforcement: she'd been a for-hire kinesics expert, helping attorneys and prosecutors pick juries and providing expert testimony. After her husband's death – Bill Swenson had been an FBI agent – she'd decided to become a cop.

O'Neil had been with the MCSO for years and, with his intelligence and dogged nature (not to mention enviable arrest and conviction record), he could have gone anywhere but had chosen to stay local. O'Neil's home was the Monterey Peninsula and he had no desire to be anywhere else. Family kept him close and so did the Bay. He loved boats and fishing. He could easily have been a protagonist in a John Steinbeck novel: quiet, solid of build, strong arms, brown eyes beneath dipping lids. His hair was thick and cut short, brown with abundant gray.

He waved to Wes.

'Hey, Michael!'

Donnie, too, turned. The boy exhibited the fascination young-sters always did with the armament on the hip of a law officer. He whispered something to Wes, who nodded with a smile, and they turned their attention to the game.

O'Neil took the plate, ate some. 'Thanks. Okay, this is excellent.'

They tapped bottle and glasses. Dance wasn't hungry but gave in to a few bits of pita with tzatziki.

She said, 'I didn't know if you could make it tonight. With the kids.' O'Neil had two children from a prior marriage, Amanda and Tyler, nine and ten. They were good friends with Dance's youngsters – though Maggie more, because of the age proximity.

'Somebody's watching them,' he said.

'New sitter?'

'Sort of.'

Footsteps approached. It was Donnie. He nodded to O'Neil and said to Dance, 'Um, I really better be getting home. I didn't know it was this late.'

Boling said, 'I'll drive you.'

'The thing is I've got my bike. I can't leave it, you know.'

'I've got a rack on the back.'

'Excellent!' He looked relieved. Dance believed the bike was new, probably a present for his birthday a few weeks ago. 'Thanks, Mr Boling. Night, Mrs Dance.'

'Anytime, Donnie.'

Boling got his jacket and kissed Dance. She leaned into him, ever so slightly.

The boys bumped fists. 'Later,' Wes called, and headed for his room.

Boling shook O'Neil's hand. 'Night.'

'Take care.'

The door closed. Dance watched Boling and Donnie walk to the car. She believed Jon Boling looked back to see her wave but she couldn't tell for certain.

CHAPTER 18

After checking on the kids ('Teeth! No texting!'), Dance joined O'Neil on the Deck. He was finishing up the food. He glanced at her and said, 'All right. Solitude Creek. You're sure you want to handle it this way?'

She sat beside him. 'How do you mean?'

'You're Civ Div?'

'Right.'

'No weapon?'

'Nope. Busted down to rookie. I'd be, quote, "briefing" on the roadhouse case. I boosted that up to "advising", then I did an end run and—'

'And blustered your way into running it.'

She'd been smiling at her joke but, at his interruption, the smile faded. 'Well, with you.'

'Look, I'm happy to handle it solo.'

'No, I want it.'

A pause. O'Neil said, 'This unsub. I profile he's armed. Or could be. You think?'

It was fairly easy to do a preliminary profiling of an unknown subject. One of the easiest determinations was an affinity to commit a crime with a weapon.

'Probably. He's not going into a situation like this clean.'

He shrugged.

She said, 'You'll look out for me.'

O'Neil grimaced. He almost said something, which she suspected was, 'I can't babysit.'

Her level gaze told him, though, she wasn't going to be a spectator. She was going to run the case shoulder to shoulder with him. He nodded. 'Okay, then, that's the way it is.'

Dance asked, 'What do you have going on? Busy now?'

'A couple of cases is all. You hear about Otto Grant?'

'Sounds familiar.'

'Sixty-year-old farmer, Salinas Valley. The state took a big chunk of his property, eminent domain. The farm had been in his family for years and he had to sell off the rest for taxes. He was furious about it. He's gone missing.'

'That's right.' Dance recalled the 'Have You Seen This Man?' posters around town. There were two images. One of a man, smiling at the camera, sitting beside his Labrador retriever. The other showed him with hair askew, looking a bit of a crank. He resembled the great actor Bruce Dern in *Nebraska*. 'It's sad,' she said.

'Is, yes. He was writing these blogs trashing the state for what it did. But they stopped a few days ago and he's disappeared. His family thinks he's killed himself. I suppose that's it. No point in kidnapping a man who doesn't have any money. I've got a team out trying to find him. Or his body.'

O'Neil offered another grimace. 'Then there're the hate crimes. That's on my plate too.'

Dance knew this story. Everybody in town did. Over the past few weeks, vandals had defaced buildings associated with minorities. They'd tagged an African-American church with graffiti of the KKK and a burning cross. Then a gay couple's house had been tagged with 'Get Aids and Die'. Latinos had been targeted too.

'Who do you think? Neo-Nazis?'

Such groups were rare in the Monterey area. But not unheard of.

'Closest are some biker and redneck white social clubs in Salinas and Seaside. Fits their worldview but graffiti's not their MO. They tend to bust heads in bars. I've talked to a few of them. They were actually insulted I was accusing them.'

'Guess there are degrees of bigotry.'

'Amy Grabe's considering sending a team down. But for now it's mine.'

FBI. Sure. The crimes he was referring to would probably fall into the category of civil-rights violations, which meant the feds would be involved.

He continued, 'But no physical violence so it's not a top priority. I can work Solitude Creek okay.'

'I'm glad,' Dance said.

O'Neil let out a sigh and stretched. She was standing close enough to smell his aftershave or soap. A pleasant, complicated scent. Spicy. She eased away.

He explained, 'Crime Scene should have their report tomorrow from around the roadhouse and the jobbing company.'

She told him in detail exactly what had happened that day from the moment of her arrival at Solitude Creek. He took notes. Then she handed him the printouts of the interviews she'd conducted. He flipped through them.

'I'll read these tonight.'

She summarized: 'You might find something I didn't see. But there're no employees, former ones, or patrons who might have been motivated to organize the attack. No competitor wanting to take Sam out of commission.'

'Was wondering. Any pissed-off husband wanted to get even with somebody on a date at the club that night?'

'Or wife,' Dance pointed out. The second-most-popular motive for arson – after insurance fraud – was a woman burning down the house, apartment or hotel room with a cheating lover inside. 'That was in the battery of questions. No hints, though.'

He riffled the many pages. 'Been busy.'

'Wish I'd been *productive*.' She shook her head.

O'Neil finished his beer. Looked through the pictures again. 'One thing I don't get, though.'

'Why didn't he just burn the place?'

He gave a smile. 'Yep.'

'That's the key.'

O'Neil's phone hummed once. He looked at the text. 'Better be getting home.'

'Sure.'

They walked to the door.

'Night.'

Then he was going down the front steps of the porch, which creaked under his weight. He turned back and waved.

Dance checked the house, securing it, as always. She'd made enemies in her job over the years, and now, in particular, she could be in the sights of any of the gangs being targeted by Operation Pipeline. From Oakland to LA.

And by the Solitude Creek unsub too. A man who had used panic as a weapon to murder in a horrific way.

Then into and out of the bathroom quickly, change to PJs, then lugging her gun safe from floor to bedside table. A true Civ-Div officer, she couldn't pack on the job but in her own home nothing was going to stop her triple-tapping an intruder with her Glock 26.

She lay back in bed, lights out. Refusing to let the images of the crime scene affect her, though that was difficult. They returned on their own. The bloodstain in the shape of a heart. The brown pool outside the exit door where, perhaps, the girl had lost her arm.

Really talented . . .

Tough images reeling through her mind. Dance called this 'assault by memory'.

She listened to the wind and could just hear a whisper of the ocean.

Alone, tonight, Dance was thinking of the name of the rivulet near the roadhouse. Solitude Creek. She wondered why the name. Did it have a meaning other than the obvious, that the stream ran through an out-of-the-way part of the county, edged with secluding weeds and rushes and hidden by hills?

Solitude . . .

The word, its sound and meaning, spoke to her now. And yet how absurd was that? Solitude was not an aspect of her life. Hardly. She had the children, she had her parents, her friends, the Deck.

She had Jon Boling.

How could she be experiencing solitude?

Maybe, she thought wryly, because . . .

Because . . .

But then she told herself: Enough. Your mood's just churned up by these terrible deaths and injuries. That's all. Nothing more.

Solitude, solitude . . .

Finally, strength of will, she managed to fling the word away, just as the children would do with snowballs on those rare, rare occasions when the hills of Carmel Valley were blanketed white.

THE GET

THURSDAY, APRIL 6

CHAPTER 19

No. Oh, no . . . .

Having deposited the children at school and nursed a coffee in the car while having a good-morning chat with Jon Boling, Kathryn Dance was halfway to CBI headquarters when she heard the news.

'. . . authorities in Sacramento are now saying that the Solitude Creek roadhouse tragedy may have been carried out intentionally. They're searching for an unknown subject – that is, in police parlance, an unsub – who is a white male, under forty years of age, with brown hair. Medium build. Over six feet tall. He was last seen wearing a green jacket with a logo of some type.'

'Jesus, my Lord,' she muttered.

She grabbed her iPhone, fumbled it, lunged, but then decided against trying to retrieve the unit. This angry, she'd be endangering both her career and her life to text what she wanted to.

In ten minutes she was parking in the CBI lot – actually left skid marks, albeit modest ones, on the asphalt. A deep breath, thinking, thinking – there were a number of land mines to negotiate here – but then the anger lifted its head and she was out of the door and storming inside.

Past her own office.

'Hi, Kathryn. Something wrong?' This from Dance's administrative assistant, Maryellen Kresbach. The short, bustling woman, mother of three, wore complex, precarious high-heels, black and white, on her feet and impressive coifs on her head, a mass of curly brown hair, sprayed carefully into submission.

Dance smiled, just to let the world know that nobody in this portion of the building was in danger. Then onward. She strode to Overby's office, walked in without knocking and found him on a Skype call.

'Charles.'

'Ah. Well. Kathryn.'

She swallowed the planned invective and sat down.

On the screen was a swarthy, broad man in a dark suit and white shirt, striped tie, red and blue. He was looking slightly away from the webcam as he regarded his own computer screen.

Overby said, 'Kathryn. You remember Commissioner Ramón Santos, with the Federal Police in Chihuahua?'

'Commissioner.'

'Agent Dance, yes, hello.' The man was not smiling. Overby, too, was sitting stiffly in his chair. Apparently the conversation had not been felicitous thus far. The commissioner was one of the senior people in Mexico working on Operation Pipeline. Not everyone south of the border was in favor of the effort, of course: drugs and guns meant big money, even – especially – for the police down there.

'Now, I was telling Charles. It is a most unfortunate thing that has just happened. A big shipment. A load of one hundred M-Four machine-guns, some fifty eighteen-caliber H & Ks. Two thousand rounds.'

Overby asked, 'They were delivered through the—'

'Yes. Through the Salinas hub. They came from Oakland.'

'We didn't hear,' Overby said.

'No. No, you didn't. An informant down *here* told us. He had first-hand knowledge, obviously, to be that accurate.' Santos sighed. 'We found the truck but it was empty. Those weapons are on our streets now. And responsible for several deaths. This is very bad.'

She recalled that the commissioner was, of course, adamant to stop the cartels from shipping their heroin and cocaine north. But what upset him more was the flood of weapons into Mexico, a country where owning a gun was illegal under most circumstances although it had one of the highest death-by-gunshot rates in the world.

And virtually all those guns were smuggled in from the US.

'I'm sorry to hear that,' Overby said.

'I'm not convinced we're doing all we can.'

Except that the 'we' was not accurate. His meaning: '*You* aren't doing all you can.'

'Commissioner,' Overby said, 'we have forty officers from five agencies working on Operation Pipeline. We're making progress. Slow, yes, but it still *is* progress.'

'Slow,' the man said. Dance looked over the streaming video. His office was very similar to Overby's, though without the golf and tennis trophies. The pictures on his wall were of him standing beside Mexican politicians and, perhaps, celebs. The same category of poses as her boss's pix.

The commissioner asked, 'Agent Dance, what is your assessment?'

'I—'

'Agent Dance is temporarily assigned to another case.'

'Another case? I see.'

He had not been informed about the Serrano situation.

'Commissioner,' Dance pressed on, even under these circumstances not one to be shushed, 'we've interdicted four shipments in the past month—'

'And eleven got through, according to our intelligence officers. Including this particularly deadly one, the one I was mentioning.'

She said, 'Yes, I know about the others. They were small. Very little ammo.'

'Ah, but, Agent Dance, the size of the shipment probably is of no consequence to the family killed by a single machine-gun.'

'Of course,' she said. Nothing to argue about there.

'Yes, yes,' said Overby. 'Well, we'll look at the statistics, year end. See the trend.'

The commissioner stared at the webcam for a moment, perhaps wondering what on earth Overby was talking about. He said, 'I have a meeting now. I will look into the situation. And I will look forward to hearing next month about a *dozen* interdictions. At least. *Adios.*'

The screen went blank.

'Testy,' she said.

'Who can blame him? Over fifteen hundred people were murdered last year in his state alone.'

Then Dance's anger returned. 'You heard?'

'About what?'

'It was on the radio. The Solitude Creek unsub's description went out, after all. It's all over the press. Now he knows we're on to him.'

Overby was looking at the blank computer screen. 'Ah, well. Yes. I heard too.'

'How did it happen? I mean, did you release it?'

Overby loved any chance to chat with the press. But she doubted he'd directly undermine her, especially after he'd agreed to back her position – besides, if he'd done it, the story would have featured his name prominently.

'Me? Of course not. It was . . . I'm not sure but I think it was Steve Foster. It came from Sacramento. His turf.' He did seem genuinely upset, though hardly as livid as she.

But she understood he was troubled for a different reason. She was concerned about spooking the unsub. Overby had been out-politicked. He'd brought Foster in to make sure the CBI got some credit for running the case, since Dance had been sidelined. But Foster had taken it one step further and made sure the kudos would go to Headquarters, Sacramento. Not the West Central Division of CBI.

Why didn't that surprise her? 'Whose case is it?'

'Well, technically, Kathryn, it's not ours.'

'Oh, come on. We can play this fiction only so far. Foster's here on the Guzman Connection thing. He has nothing to do with my case.'

'O'Neil's case. MCSO's case. I—'

'Charles! Never mind. I'll go talk to him.'

'Do you think that's a good—'

But she was already walking down the hall. And into the Guzman Connection task-force room. Overby appeared a moment later.

'Hey,' Jimmy Gomez said.

'Steve.' Both men with that name turned but Dance's eyes were squarely on Foster.

'It was a misunderstanding,' the bulky man said, and looked back to his computer. Not even trying to deny it.

'We agreed we weren't going to release the description. We weren't even going to say it was a murder investigation.'

He grumbled, 'I should've been more specific when I was talking to my people in Sacramento. Should've told them not to speak to the press.'

'Who was it?' Dance asked.

'Oh, hard to say. I don't know what happened. It's a mystery. I'm sorry.'

Though he was no more perplexed by it than he was contrite.

'What's this all about?' asked stolid Carol Allerton, the DEA star. Dance reminded her of the debate about releasing the description of their perp. As she spoke, she kept her eyes on Foster.

'It made the news?' Carol Allerton asked. 'Ouch.' Indicating which way she would have voted.

'It made the news,' Overby said, with a wrinkly mouth.

To Foster, Dance said, 'Why would you even discuss it? With anybody in Sacramento? It's a West Central Division investigation. Our investigation.'

He wasn't used to being cross-examined.

'You mean a Monterey Sheriff's investigation.'

'I mean not Sacramento's.' Her lips tautened.

'Well, sorry about that. I told somebody, they talked to the press. I should've told 'em to keep the lid on. It was a fuck-up. But, bright side, I'll bet somebody's already spotted some could-bes. And'll call it in. Anytime now. You may have your boy before sundown, Kathryn.'

'This morning Michael and I had every mobile unit on the Peninsula to start making sweeps of venues that might make good locations for other attacks. All day long. Shopping mall, churches, movie theaters. I don't know what they're going to be looking for now. If our perp heard the same news show I did, there's not going to be any brown-haired man in a green jacket to spot.'

Foster wouldn't back down. 'That presupposes your unsub's going to try this again. Is there any evidence to that effect?'

'Not specifically. But my assessment is it's a strong possibility.' And she certainly wasn't going to take the chance that there'd be no other attack.

Foster didn't need to reiterate his opinion of Dance's ability to make assessment.

He said, 'It's probably moot. He's a thousand miles away by now.'

CHAPTER 20

Antioch March had changed majors four times in three years at two schools. Distraction, boredom and, truth be told, the Get kept him jumping from department to department (and finally drove him out of both Northwestern and Chicago altogether, without any degree, despite his near-perfect academic record).

Still, he'd picked up some insights in various classes. He was thinking of one now, recalling the neo-Gothic classroom overlooking the north shore of Lake Michigan. Psychology. March had been fascinated to learn that there are only five basic fears.

For instance, take the fear of sharks, one that particularly interested him. That's merely a sub-category of the fear of mutilation: having part of our body damaged or excised. More broadly, fear of injury.

The four other basic fears: of physical death, of ego death (embarrassment and shame), of separation (from Mommy, from the drugs we inhale so desperately, from our lover) and of loss of autonomy (claustrophobia on a physical level to being dominated by an abusive spouse).

March remembered the cold November day when he'd heard about them in a lecture. Truly mesmerizing.

And now he was about to put several to good use. Fear of physical death, of mutilation and loss of autonomy, all rolled into one. A movie theater would be his next target.

He had parked his car in a strip mall about a hundred yards from the Marina Hills Cineplex, just off Highway One in Marina. He was walking toward the theaters now.

Don't we love the comfort of the lights going down, the trailers coming to an end, the film starting? Waiting to be exhilarated, amused, thrilled – laughing or crying. Why is a theater so much better than Netflix or cable? Because the real world is gone.

Until the real world comes crashing in.

In the form of smoke or gunshots.

And then comfort becomes constriction.

Fear of physical death, fear of mutilation and, most deliciously, fear of loss of autonomy – when the crowd takes over. You become a helpless cell in a creature whose sole goal is to survive, yet in attempting to do so it will sacrifice some of itself: those cells trampled or suffocated or changed for ever, thanks to snapped spines or piercing ribs.

He now examined the Marina Hills Cineplex, regarding the parking lot, the entrance, the service doors. This was one of the older multiplexes in the area, dating to the seventies – it featured only four theaters, ranging from three hundred seats to six hundred. It showed first-run movies, along with an occasional art film, and competed with the big boy up at Del Monte Center by discounting tickets (if you were fifty-nine, you were a senior. How 'bout that?) and offering free cheese powder with the popcorn (which was still overpriced).

March knew this because after meeting with an Indonesian tsunami-relief charity for the Hand to Heart website he'd been to see a film here: *When She's Alone*, a slasher flick, which wasn't bad – like a lot of such films nowadays, in this age of inexpensive technology, the effects were good and the acting passable. Some clever motifs (stained glass, for instance: the colored shards turned out to be the killer's weapon of choice).

He'd also carefully examined the exits. Each theater had only two ways by which patrons could leave: the entrance, which led to a narrow hallway off the lobby, and the emergency exit in the back. The latter was a double door, wide enough to accommodate a crowd intent on escaping . . . if they weren't too unruly.

But tonight the back doors would not be in play.

Six hundred people speeding through the single door to the lobby.

Perfect.

He looked over the parking lot keenly, noting trash cans, lamp-posts and, more important, the feeble landscaping – excellent camouflage.

Okay, time to get to work.

He hiked his gym bag onto his shoulder and started toward the theater. The hour was early and the place was largely deserted at this time. A few employees' cars, parked, as ordered, in the back of the lot.

Another car happened to turn in and make its way to the back of the theater, not far from March. A tall, balding man got out and started toward the back service door, fishing keys from his pocket. He glanced at March and froze.

His eyes took in the green jacket, the utility logo, the dark slacks, the hat, sunglasses.

And those eyes explained everything.

Someone had seen him at Solitude Creek. He guessed his description had been on the news.

Hell. Antioch March had been positive that he hadn't been seen last night, circling the parking lot, stealing the truck and maneuvering it in front of the doors. Starting the fire near the club's HVAC system. He'd changed his clothes just afterward but there had been a twenty-minute window during which somebody could have spotted him in his worker's garb, which he wore now.

The man was fishing a phone from his pocket.

Leave, March told himself. Instantly.

He turned. And that was when he noticed something else. Parked in the shade on the lawn nearby was an unmarked police car. It was pointed directly at the theater. If March had walked twenty feet further, the officer inside would have seen him. And if the theater employee recognized March, certainly the police would have his description.

Luck. Pure luck had saved him.

As he walked slowly toward the mall where his car was parked, a hundred yards away, he noted that the police officer didn't look in his direction. There would be some delay, if not miscommunication, in transmitting to the officer the information that the suspect had been spotted there.

If either the employee or the officer followed he'd have to pull his Glock from the gym bag and use it. March walked a block before unzipping the bag, gripping the gun and turning.

No. No one was following.

Now March stripped off the green jacket, stuffed it into the bag and began to sprint. He leaped into the gray Honda Accord, pressing the start button before the door was closed. The gym bag, heavy with his tools of the trade, was on the passenger seat and it set off the warning ding about neglecting to put on the seatbelt. As he headed out the driveway slowly, he eased it to the floor. He had to be very careful of the contents. The dinging stopped.

He felt a wave of anger that the theater had been denied him as a perfect place for the second attack, which had been inspired by the 'national disaster correspondent' he'd listened to on TV after sex with Calista: *What this man did was akin to the classic situation of yelling 'Fire' in a crowded movie theater.*

Angry, yes. But as he cruised through traffic he glanced into the rear-view mirror and noticed something. He decided that there might just be a silver lining to the debacle.

He circled around and pulled into a space not far from the theater he'd just left; it was perfect for his purpose. And, it turned out, good for another as well: who doesn't love a nice, salty Egg McMuffin and some steaming coffee this time of the morning?

CHAPTER 21

Kathryn Dance walked into the Gals' Wing.

This was an area of the CBI's West Central Division that, purely coincidentally, housed the four women who worked there: Dance, Connie Ramirez, the most decorated CBI agent in the office, Grace Yuan, the office administrator, and Maryellen Kresbach.

The name of the wing came from a male agent who, trying to impress a date on a tour of his workplace, had referred to the area as such. It probably wasn't the recurring vandalism of his office, including feminine hygiene products, that had driven him out of the CBI but Dance liked to think that that had helped.

Though, ironically, the women had decided unanimously to keep the designation. A badge of pride.

A warning too.

She accepted the coffee Maryellen offered, thanked her and, palming one of the woman's incredible cookies, headed into her office.

'Nice shoes. Okay. Excellent.' Maryellen was eyeing Dance's Stuart Weitzman Filigree sandals, brown leather (and, Dance was proud to say, bought at less than half price). They matched her long coffee-colored linen skirt. Her sweater today was a ribbed off-white, the sports coat black. Today's concession to color was a bright elastic tie Maggie had twined at the end of her mother's French braid. Red.

She acknowledged the compliment – Maryellen was a woman who knew wicked shoes when she saw them.

In her office she dropped into her desk chair, thinking she'd have to tame the squeak, then, as always, forgetting about it.

She had just returned from the Marina Hills Cineplex, where there'd been a sighting of a man suspected of being the Solitude

Creek unsub. The manager of the theater had spotted someone wearing the same clothes as the witness had described, about the same build. The suspect noted that he'd been recognized and fled, pretty much confirming that he was their perp.

Dance and the others had conducted a canvass but had found no other witnesses who'd seen the man. No vehicles and no further description. She'd been troubled to learn that one of the police cars on the lookout for the unsub had been stationed in front of the theater; she wondered if, because of Steve Foster's 'accidental' release of the perp's description, the manager had spooked him away before he got into view of the cop.

Sometimes, she reflected, your colleagues' mistakes and carelessness – as well as your own – can be as much of an adversary as the perps you're pursuing.

The miss was, of course, frustrating enough. But far more troubling was that he'd apparently been planning another attack. Not, Steve Number One, a thousand miles away at all. Perhaps, since he knew he'd been spotted, he'd now flee the area. Certainly he was going to change his appearance or at least ditch the clothes. But was he still determined to strike again? She sent out a second memo to all local law enforcers to alert managers of venues that she'd confirmed their unsub had attempted a second attack.

Reaching for the phone to call Michael O'Neil, she was interrupted by TJ Scanlon. He was in a T-shirt that bore the name Beck (not, like you'd think, the Grateful Dead). He was in jeans too. And a sport coat, striped. It was of the Summer of Love era and might actually have come from the 1960s; TJ stocked his hippie house in Carmel Valley with counterculture artifacts from an era and way of life that had ended long before he was born.

He dropped into the chair across from her.

'Oh-oh, boss. Oh-oh and a *half*. Something wrong?'

'You didn't hear? Our friend from Sacramento leaked the description of the unsub.'

'Oh, man. Foster?'

'Yep.' She added, 'And somebody spotted the perp.'

'Good news but then, given your expression, I guess it isn't.'

'He spotted the spotter and vanished.'

'Hell. So he's left town.'

'Or become a quick-change artist – who knows? Platform shoes. Dyed his hair. New clothes. And,' she added grimly, 'maybe he's still going forward, targeting someplace else. Right now. Before we can regroup.'

She told him about the movie theater, where the unsub had apparently been planning a new attack.

The young man nodded. 'Right up his alley. Crowded multiplex.'

Dance glanced at the folder in the agent's hand.

TJ said, 'Something helpful, maybe. I tracked down that girl. Trish.'

Dance had given him the job of finding the teenager she'd met at the Solitude Creek crime scene.

'Michelle Cooper – the mother who died. Her daughter's Trish Martin. Her father's name.'

Like Maggie and Wes were Swenson.

'The girl's seventeen. Don't have her mobile but here's the mother's home number.' He added, 'It's on Seventeen Mile Drive.'

Dance could see the scenario. Husband cheats on wife, she catches him, he pays through the nose and foots the bill for a house in the poshest neighborhood of Pebble Beach. 'You have the father's address and number? Mr Friendly. She'd be staying with him now, I'd guess.'

'Sorry, didn't get it. Want me to check?'

'I'll try her mother's first.'

As it turned out, though, there wouldn't be any conversations of any kind.

'Hello?' A man's voice. Abrupt. Hell, she knew who it was.

'I'm calling for Trish Martin.'

'Who is this?'

Unfortunately, you had to play the game honestly. 'Agent Kathryn Dance, the California Bureau of Investigation. Is this Mr Martin? I—'

'Yeah, I met you. I remember. How did you know I was here?'

Odd question.

'I didn't. I was calling for Trish. It's important that I talk to her. I'm hoping—'

'Why?'

'There's been a development in the investigation. The doors at Solitude Creek were blocked intentionally. Your ex-wife's death, the others, they were homicides, not accidental.'

A pause. 'I heard. It was on the news. Some guy they're looking for. A workman or something.'

'That's right. And we're canvassing to see if anybody might've seen him. Your daughter seems intelligent, perceptive. I'm hoping—'

'She's too upset.'

'I understand it's a difficult time for her, for your whole family. But it's important that we understand exactly what happened there.'

'Well, you'll have do that without my daughter.' A voice from nearby. He said, away from the phone, 'It's nobody. Keep at it, honey.'

That would be Trish. She'd be moving in with her father, Dance guessed. She was probably packing.

'Mr Martin, my specialty is interviewing people. I've spoken to hundreds of teenagers, often in traumatic situations. I promise you, I'll be very sensitive to Trish's frame of mind. I—'

He growled. 'And if you call us again, I'll get a restraining order against you.'

Dance said, 'Hmm, well, Mr Martin, there really isn't a mechanism for doing that. Why don't we just take a step back and—'

He hung up on her.

Dance wondered if one of the grounds for divorce had been mental cruelty against his ex, in addition to cheating on her.

She dropped the phone into the cradle. TJ was looking at her. 'Scratch her off the list. Probably didn't see anything anyway. Still—'

'You hate itches, boss.'

True, she did.

'Anything helpful on the canvassing?'

TJ had continued to talk to those who'd been at the club, sifting for insights, possible motives and suspects. 'Nothing more on revenge by disgruntled employees or patrons. I thought I'd check to see if there was a motive to hurt anyone in the band, or destroy careers.'

'Good.' She hadn't thought about that.

'But I don't think so. The music world's fragile nowadays – the margins aren't big enough to murder anyone to get ahead. Hey, boss, was wondering. Does "gruntled" mean you're happy?'

She rummaged in her drawer and found an old Timex, battery-powered. She strapped it on and glanced at the time. Then lowered her voice. 'How's the Serrano situation?'

He said, 'About an hour. It's set up. I just talked to Al Stemple.'

Stemple, big and quiet and rather scary, was the closest thing the CBI had to a cowboy. Well, to a John Wayne. An investigative agent, like any other, he specialized in tactical situations. Given the unstable nature of the Serrano situation, it was thought best to have a CBI strongman involved.

He rose and left. In his wake she was sure she detected a waft of patchouli aftershave or cologne.

Far out . . .

A few minutes later Dance happened to be looking into the doorway as Michael O'Neil appeared. He was in a dark plaid sports coat, navy blue shirt and jeans. Dance believed his clothes were better pressed now that he was divorced than when he'd been married to Anne, who was not known as the queen of domesticity. Though this might be her imagination, she allowed.

'Saw TJ. He was saying nothing turned up on the canvass?'

'No. We've talked to probably seven-eighths of the people who were at the club. No one spotted any potential perps.' She told him TJ had looked into jealous musicians too.

'Good call.'

'But nothing.' She asked him, 'Anything more on the theater?'

'Nope. Full canvass, security-video review. No vehicle. Nothing further. What was that about? Releasing the descrip of our boy? Overby?'

She puffed air from her lips. 'Came from Steve Foster. He's with us – CBI – in Sacramento. He's claiming it was an accident. Blaming, quote, "somebody" in his office. But *he* let it leak. Power play, I'm sure.'

'Brother.'

'It's not his case. He doesn't care.'

'You think our boy's rabbited?'

'*I'd* be gone,' she said. 'But then I didn't set up a stampede and kill three people. I don't know what makes him tick. He might be in Missouri or Washington State by now. He might be planning to attack the aquarium.'

Nodding, O'Neil extracted from his briefcase a thin manila folder with a metal fixture on top. Inside were a dozen sheets of paper. 'Crime Scene. Had them working non-stop. No surprise – our unsub's good. He wore cloth gloves.'

Latex gloves prevent a transfer of the perp's fingerprints to what he touches at a scene but nothing prevents a transfer of prints to the inside of those latex gloves. Careless perps often discard them, without considering that. Cloth gloves, however, neither transfer nor retain prints.

He continued, 'Prints on the Peterbilt truck key fob but none identifiable except the manager's and the driver's. The drop-box was negative too. No footprints. Nothing in the oil drum, with the fire, that's any use forensically.'

Dance said, 'I was thinking. It's got to be hard to drive a truck that big. Can we use that to narrow the field? Find anybody who's taken courses lately?'

'I thought the same thing. But checked it out online. Would take about a half-hour to learn to drive one, even if you had no experience. Probably couldn't back up or drive with a full load without practice but he basically just had to drive straight down the hill to the roadhouse.'

The Internet . . . Where you could learn everything from making a fertilizer bomb to baking a cherry pie to celebrate after you'd blown up your designated target.

O'Neil consulted his file. 'No video cameras in the area. Solitude Creek's too shallow for serious boating but in any case

I didn't get any hits in canvassing for fishermen. And no stolen kayaks or canoes.' He'd had the same idea as she.

Her phone dinged: a text from TJ. The Serrano case. She typed, '*KK.*' That was the new text message acknowledging 'understood and agreed'. A single K wasn't enough. She'd learned it from her son, Wes. She mentioned this to O'Neil. He nodded. 'My kids are saying "amen", a lot too. You notice?'

'I get "church". As in: "It's true." And also "It's a thing."'

'"Thing"?'

Dance was going to tell him that she'd first heard the expression when Maggie was talking to her friend Bethany on the phone and she'd said, 'Yeah, Mom and Jon, it's like a thing.' She instead told the detective: 'Means, I think, it's a phenomenon. More than what it seems. Significant.'

She wondered if he sensed the stumble and the over-explanation.

O'Neil said, '"Thing". Better than "phenomenon". I'd worry that crept into my kids' vocabulary.'

Dance laughed.

Michael O'Neil wasn't a chatterer. This was, for him, rambling.

Dance glanced down to the crime-scene file. She said, 'Oh, wanted to mention: Sorry we had to cancel the fishing.'

O'Neil lived for his boat, which he'd pilot out into Monterey Bay once a week at least. He often took his own children and Dance's. She herself had been a few times but her inner ear and waves were bad co-conspirators. If the Dramamine and patch didn't kick in, she'd end up hanging over the side, unpleasant for all involved. And the trip would be cut short. They'd talked about having a day on the water last weekend but before plans had been firmed up she and Boling had decided to take the children to San Francisco. Dance had not told O'Neil the reason they'd canceled. She suspected he'd guessed. But he didn't ask.

They talked for a few minutes about their children, plans for spring break. Dance mentioned Maggie's forthcoming talent show at school.

'She playing violin?'

Maggie's instrument. She was far more musical than her

mother, who was comfortable with a guitar but didn't have the ear for a fretless fingerboard. Dance told him, 'No, she's singing.'

O'Neil said, 'She's got a great voice. Remember, I took them to *The Lego Movie*. That song? "Everything Is Awesome"? She sang it all the way home. I know it by heart, by the way. I'll sing it for you some time.'

'She's doing that song from *Frozen*.'

'"Let It Go". I know that one too.' Being a single parent with custody could take the edge off the hardest major-crimes detective. Then O'Neil, studying her: 'What's wrong?'

Dance realized she'd been frowning. 'She's uneasy about the talent show. Usually you can't keep her offstage but, for this, she's reluctant.'

'She ever sung before in public?'

'Yep. A dozen times. And her voice's never been better. I was going to start her in lessons but all of a sudden she decided she didn't want to. It's funny. They whipsaw, you know, their moods. For a while Wes was depressed and Maggie was flitting around like Bella. Happy as could be. Now it's the other way round.' She explained that it might be a post-traumatic reaction to her husband's death.

He said softly, 'I know Bill died around this time of year.'

O'Neil had known Bill Swenson well; they'd worked together occasionally.

'I've thought of that. But when kids want to stonewall . . .'

O'Neil, whose children were close in age to Maggie, said, 'Don't I know. But – persistence.'

Dance nodded. 'So, Sunday, at seven? You and the kids want to come?' She dug through her purse. 'Hm. Have a hundred flyers in the car for her show. Thought I had one with me.' She snapped the Coach bag shut.

'Can I let you know? We might have plans. Bring a friend?'

'Of course.'

Had he been dating? she wondered. It *had* been a while since they'd talked socially. Well, *personally*. Why shouldn't he be going out with somebody? He'd been divorced for a while now. He was good-looking, in great shape, with a fine job. He was funny, kind . . . and had two adorable children whom his ex, in San Francisco, had little interest in.

Dance's mother called him 'the Catch', because he liked to fish . . . and because he was.

She glanced at the Timex. 'I've got to get into the field.'

'Our case?'

'No. The other thing.'

He sighed, glanced at her hip, where her weapon would otherwise have resided. 'I'll go with you.'

'Not for this. It's all right. I'll have backup. I have to handle it a particular way. This one's tricky.' She almost said, 'It's a thing,' but from O'Neil's concerned expression she knew he wouldn't have appreciated the levity.

CHAPTER 22

Charles Overby tapped a roll of fat above his belt. He wasn't alarmed but he knew he'd have to rein in the snacks that went down a little too easy at the Nineteenth Hole. Maybe go to red wine. He believed it had fewer calories than white.

No, a spritzer. After the martini, of course. And no artichoke dip. It was the devil.

On his desk were ordered stacks of documents – the sign of a sane mind and a productive body, he often said. The one that troubled him most was the pile that was topped with a sheet that read: 'Incident Report: Joaquin Serrano'. The other words that jumped out from the grayish boxes were 'Kathryn Dance'. He noted too: 'Disciplinary recommendations'.

His phone hummed with a text, which he read, and shaking his head for no one's benefit, he rose. He debated a jacket but decided no.

Down the hall, aware of the peculiar smell of a cleanser the staff had switched to recently. Why was he aware of that? he wondered. Because of the case. Small distractions dulled the concerns.

Serrano . . .

In the Guzman Connection task-force conference room, Carol Allerton sat alone, squeezing the life from a chamomile teabag. She leaned starboard, to make sure any spatter wouldn't hit the dozens of papers in front of her. She, too, was well ordered when it came to the stacks of documents in her cases.

'Charles.'

'Where is everybody?'

'The two Steves're in Salinas. FBI had somebody in town from one of their Oakland task forces. They're picking his brain.'

'Meetings, meetings, meetings,' Overby said, with the boredom of truth in his voice, though no contempt. 'Jimmy?'

'He said he had another case lead, something he was working on before we put Guzman together.'

'Well, we caught a lead in Serrano.' He held up his phone, on which he'd just gotten the text. She glanced at it, perhaps wondering why the show-and-tell. 'We have to move fast.'

'You've got Serrano's location?'

'Not that lucky. But TJ found this guy knows Serrano.'

'Who?'

'Wasn't more specific, except to say he wasn't a banger. Worked with Serrano or his brother or somebody. A painter, house painter. May know where Serrano's hiding out.'

'Really?' The woman's voice was throaty and sensual. Overby, married to the same woman for ever, noted her tone objectively. 'You should move on it. I'm going to call Sacramento and I'd love to be able to tell them that we're closer to nailing Serrano.'

She'd be thinking: Because CBI West Central was the outfit that let him slip away in the first place.

'Where is this guy?'

'Seaside. Works nights, TJ says. Name of Tomas Allende.'

'Not traditionally Mexican.' Allerton was speaking absently.

'I don't know. What would that be?'

'What? Oh, Spanish.'

'Well. Here's the address. Take Al Stemple with you. No reason to think it's hostile, but no reason to think it isn't. I'll call him.' Overby punched buttons.

Allerton rose and tugged down her close-fitting gray skirt. She, too, had a bit of fat over the belt. Other circumstances, he might've talked to her about how hard it was to lose those last twelve pounds. She pulled her jacket over her broad shoulders.

His phone clicked. 'Yeah?'

'Albert, 's Charles. Need you to go with Agent Allerton, follow up on a lead to Serrano . . . That's right . . . I don't know, parking lot?' He lifted an eyebrow to Allerton. She nodded. 'Good. Now.' He disconnected. 'Good luck,' Overby said and retreated to his office.

CHAPTER 23

Albert Stemple had been told he grunted a lot, though he didn't think that was the case. He never said much, didn't find it necessary most of the time, so he would respond to people with an *Ah* or *Oh*.

Maybe people *thought* words like that were grunts. I look like a guy who grunts, so people hear grunts.

The massive man, head free of hair and shaped like an egg, though shinier, stood with his arms crossed outside the rear door of CBI, looking over the parking lot. Since Stemple was the closest thing CBI had to a SWAT team, he'd been in more firefights and had more collars than any other agent in the division, which meant he had a price on that glossy head of his.

Stemple tended to check vistas and shadows regularly.

CBI's back door opened and Carol Allerton stepped outside, nodding to Stemple, taking in his jeans, black T-shirt and impressive Beretta .45, the only caliber a man should carry. He supposed the bump on her hip through her gray jacket was a teeny Glock. A 26, he guessed. Not bad. If you liked peashooters.

When she looked at his face with a bit of hesitation, Stemple knew she'd been considering the scars. You should see the other guys.

He nodded.

'Hi,' Allerton said.

'We're going to Seaside. A Serrano lead.'

'Right.'

'Hm.' Maybe grunt-like. 'I'll drive,' he told her.

'Hey,' came a woman's voice behind them.

Kathryn Dance walked up from the side of the building, where her car was parked, the gray Pathfinder. Nose art from her dogs decorated the back windows. Stemple liked her dogs; he knew them pretty well, being a regular visitor to the Deck. He was after Dance to let him borrow the flat-coated retriever, take her hunting and bring back a dressed duck or two for the family. He'd made the mistake of mentioning that in front of Dance's kids; the look in her eyes, the response, was a hard one to describe. It meant no in a lot of different ways.

Allerton was eyeing Dance neutrally as the CBI agent walked up. She looked around, then moved closer yet. 'Al.'

A nod.

'Carol, there's something I want to talk to you about. Both of you, really.'

'Sure, Kathryn.'

Stemple gave a second nod. Maybe a grunt.

'I heard you had a lead to Serrano.'

The DEA agent hesitated.

Dance said, 'Well, I know you do. TJ told me. He's my inside man. You're going to talk to this lead now?'

Allerton held her gaze. 'We are.'

Dance said, 'I want to interview him.'

'Well . . .'

'I know the turf, Carol. I don't know this particular subject but I know the crowd he'd hang with. That gives me a huge leg up.'

'But Charles,' Allerton said. 'He suspended you.'

Stemple watched Dance's lips tighten. 'All right. The other thing?' She glanced at Stemple, then decided, it seemed, to plunge ahead. 'You don't know Charles as well as I do. If I were a man and what happened with Serrano happened? He wouldn't've busted me. Hate to say it but . . .' Dance shook her head. 'You've been through this too, Carol. You know how it is.'

Her expression said: Women in law enforcement. Yes, I do.

Dance added, 'I'll give you full credit for everything I find out. And that'll go all the way to Washington. I'll disappear.'

'No, that's not necessary.'

'Actually, yeah, it is. Charles can't know anything, that I'm involved. All I want is to nail Serrano.'

'Sure,' Allerton said, nodding. 'I get it. Completely sub-rosa.'

Whatever that meant. Though Stemple hammered out a definition.

Now another glance his way.

Dance said, 'I may already be under the bus—'

'Charles'd do that to you?' Now Stemple couldn't control the grunt.

'—already under the bus, but we get Serrano back, Sacramento won't be clamoring for my head quite so loud. It's the only chance I've got to pull something out of the fire here.'

Allerton was scanning the parking lot, thoughtful, not looking for acquiring targets, though, as Stemple was doing. 'The fact is, Kathryn, I could use your help. I'm not the best interviewer in the world.'

'Deal, then?'

'Deal.'

Dance's eyes swiveled to Stemple.

'You asking me? I'm just backup. Do whatcha want.'

They walked to the car, Stemple easing into the driver's seat. The big Dodge bobbed under the weight. The women, too, got in. He fired up the growly engine and they squealed out of the lot toward the highway.

A half-hour later Stemple turned onto surface streets in Seaside and eased the cruiser along a crumbling asphalt road, bordered by grasses, dusty brush, rusting wire fences. A hundred yards along they came to a development, probably fifty years old, bungalows and Cape-style houses, tiny, all of them.

'That's it,' Allerton said, pointing to the scabbiest house there, a lopsided one-story structure that had last been painted a long, long time ago. White originally. Now, gray. The yard was half sand, half yellowing grass. Thirsty, Stemple thought. Everything was thirsty. This drought. Worst he could remember.

He shut the engine off. Everyone climbed out.

Stemple scanned the perimeter while the agents, looking around, headed toward the front door. Allerton knocked. No response. Dance pointed to the side, where there was a patio. They disappeared that way.

Stemple walked around the property, looked at the houses

nearby, wondered why somebody had taped a massive poster of a daisy in a window. Was it a sunscreen? Wouldn't a sunflower've made more sense?

Mostly, though, he was looking for threats.

This wasn't a cul-de-sac but it wasn't highly traveled. He counted four cars pass by, all seeming to contain families or individuals on their way to or from school, work or errands. That didn't mean there *weren't* gang-bangers inside, of course, with MAC-10s, Uzis or M4s. Gone were the days when crews conveniently piled into gang-mobiles, pimped-out low-rider Buicks with jacked-up suspensions. Now they tooled around in Acuras, Nissans and the occasional Beemer or Cayenne, depending on how the drug and arms trade had been lately.

But no one in any vehicle paid him any mind.

He walked back to the cracked sidewalk and was looking down at some vibrant purple plant, when there was from inside the bungalow a crash of something containing glass, a lot of glass.

Followed by a woman's scream.

CHAPTER 24

An hour later, back at CBI headquarters, Al Stemple was leaning back in a Guzman Connection task-force conference-room chair. It groaned under his weight.

The others were here too, the whole crew. The two Steves – Lu and Foster – along with Jimmy Gomez. Allerton, as well, was back from the Seaside bungalow mission.

'What happened to you?' Gomez asked her. She had a bandage on her arm.

'That lead to Serrano? He had a big-ass Doberman in the back bedroom. Sleeping dog, and all that. He woke up. Didn't like visitors.'

'You get bit?'

'Just scratched getting out of the way. Knocked over a table of crappy glass and china. Serves him right.'

'Al, you didn't shoot any dogs, did you?' Gomez feigned horror.

'Reasoned with it.'

Foster was on the phone, saying to a CHP trooper, 'Those're *your* procedures, not *my* procedures, and it's *my* procedures you're going to be following. Are we transparent on that? . . . I asked you a question . . . Are we transparent? . . . Good. No more of this shit.'

He hung up with nothing more.

What a dick, Stemple thought, and wondered if he'd have an excuse to dice the man verbally into little pieces. That'd be a challenge. Foster seemed like a good dicer too. It'd be fun.

Now that Foster had finished transparenting the Highway Patrol trooper, Allerton took the floor. 'The lead didn't quite pan out like we hoped. The Serrano Seaside connection.'

Gomez asked, 'Who was it?'

'A painter – a contractor, you know, a house painter. Not an artist. Tomas Allende. Serrano used to work with him. Uh-huh, he actually did day labor for a while before he got into turning people into skeletons.'

Foster grumbled, 'Whatta you mean didn't pan out?'

'I said didn't *quite* pan out. I'll tell you what we found.'

We.

Nobody noticed. Probably thinking she meant her and Stemple. Surprise, surprise, surprise.

The stocky woman rose and walked to the door, looked out, then closed it.

Gomez frowned. The two Steves simply watched her.

'I have to tell you, I didn't go alone. Kathryn came with me.'

'Kathryn Dance?' Gomez asked.

'How'd she do that?' Foster seemed both perplexed and put out by this information. Not an easy combo, Stemple thought. 'She's suspended. Or did something change that I haven't heard about?'

'Nothing's changed,' Allerton said.

'Then what do you mean she was there? I don't need her to fuck up another operation in this case.'

Stemple stuck his legs out and brought his boot heel down on the linoleum hard. Foster didn't notice the sound. Or didn't care if he did.

Gomez said, 'Steve, come on. We don't need that.'

'Need what? I'm saying it's because of her we're in this situation.'

Allerton: 'She asked and I said yes. She knows she made a mistake and she wants to make it right. Look, she was good, though, at the house in Seaside, Steve. She was. You should've seen her.'

'I did. With Serrano. I wasn't impressed. Who was?'

Stemple scratched a scar on his thigh, not new, but a .40 round leaves a thick streak and humidity could really kick off the itch.

'You can't bat a thousand every time,' Gomez said. Normally soft-spoken, he sounded brittle.

Thanks, Jimmy, Stemple thought.

Steve Lu, the chief of detectives from Salinas, said, 'Okay. She went. I don't see the harm. What happened?'

Allerton continued, 'The subject, our painter, used to work with Serrano? He was cooperating and telling us all kinds of things but swore he hadn't heard from Serrano for six months. He'd lost all contact. He was going legitimate. I mean, I believed him. Everything he was saying, completely credible. And Kathryn was all, "Sure, sure, I understand, interesting, thanks for your help." Then, bang, she pulled the rug out from underneath him. Just like that. Caught him in a dozen lies, went to work and in the end he talked.'

'What about the non-panning lead?' Foster grumbled.

'He didn't have Serrano's present location. Not surprising, considering Serrano's warranted and on the run. But the painter said the word is that he's still in the area. He didn't head out of state.' Allerton continued, 'But more important he gave up another name.'

'Who?'

'A woman was recently a girlfriend of Serrano's. Tia Alonzo. No warrants on her but she's keeping low. TJ Scanlon's on it, getting her whereabouts.'

'You really think Picasso's telling the truth?'

'Who?' Lu asked.

'The painter.' Foster sighed.

'Kathryn does. I do.'

'When'll we have a location to go with Señorita Alonzo?'

Allerton said, 'Soon, TJ said. He's convinced within a day or two.'

'Convinced.'

Allerton said, 'Now. With Kathryn. It was off the books.'

'Which means?' From Foster.

Sub-rosa . . .

'She didn't tell Overby.'

Foster: 'She snuck in to interview this dingo in Seaside?'

'Pretty much.'

'Jesus.'

Allerton said, 'I understand Charles is doing what he has to but she's too valuable to sit this out. What I want—'

Foster said, impatient, 'Yeah, yeah, she wants to go around Overby's back and stay on the team. On the sly.'

Sub-rosa . . .

Allerton snapped, 'Yes, Steve, that's exactly what she wants to do. And I say yes. She knows the area, knows these people. After all, she wasn't the only one who got taken in by Serrano. We watched the whole thing ourselves. Did anybody here suspect anything? I didn't.'

Finally the asshole fell quiet.

'I say yes,' said loyal Jimmy Gomez, nodding his crew-cut head.

'Can't hurt,' Lu agreed.

Foster looked Stemple up and down. The urge to dice returned. Foster said, 'What about you? How do you vote?'

Stemple replied, 'I'm just muscle. I don't get a vote.'

Foster turned and regarded the others. 'You've thought this through, all of you?'

'Thought it through?' From Gomez.

'Have you? Have you really? Well. Alternative A: Dance sits on the sidelines per orders and we handle it, the Guzman Connection, the hunt for Serrano, everything. She does that and, say Serrano nails a banger or, worse, an innocent. Even then she might just survive. She can claim she didn't have the chance to fix what got broke. Or Alternative B: she's back on the case, unofficial, and there's a screw-up, hers or anybody else's, that's it. Her career is over.'

Well, that was transparent enough.

Silence.

A second vote. The result was the same.

'You?' Allerton asked.

Foster muttered something.

Gomez: 'What?'

'Yeah, yeah. I'm on board. I got work to do.' He swung back to his keyboard and started typing.

CHAPTER **25**

After the Serrano mission, which had been somewhat successful, Kathryn Dance returned to the hunt for the Solitude Creek unsub.

She logged on to the National Crime Information Center to look for any similar incidents. The unsub was clearly a repetitive actor. Had he done this before?

NCIC revealed only one crime that echoed Solitude Creek, six months ago in Fort Worth, Texas. A man had wired shut the doors of the Prairie Valley Club, a small country-western venue, and set a fire just outside the back door. Two people were killed and dozens injured in the stampede. There was no connection to her case, though, since the perp, a paranoid schizophrenic homeless man, had died after accidentally setting himself alight too.

A search of the general media sent her to similar incidents, but nothing recent. She read about the Happy Land social-club fire in New York City in the eighties. Hundreds of people were packed into an illegal social club when a man who'd been ejected returned with a dollar's worth of gas and set the place on fire. Nearly ninety people died. In that case, there wasn't much of a stampede: people died so quickly in the smoke and flames that bodies were found still clutching their drinks or sitting upright on barstools.

The classic case of a deadly stampede, she found, was the Italian Hall disaster in Calumet, Michigan, in 1913. More than seventy striking mine workers and their families were killed in a crush at a Christmas party when someone yelled, 'Fire,' though there was none. It was believed that a thug connected with the mining company subject to the strike started the panic.

She found a number of accidental stampedes. Particularly dangerous were sporting events – the Hillsborough disaster in

Sheffield, England, which her father had witnessed, for instance. Soccer seemed to be the most dangerous of organized sports. Three hundred people had died in Chile, at Estadio Nacional, when an angered fan attacked a referee, resulting in police action that panicked the attendees. Before the 1985 European Cup final at Heysel Stadium in Belgium had begun, nearly forty people had died when Liverpool fans surged toward rival Juventus supporters. The tragedy led to a multi-year ban of English soccer teams playing on the Continent.

Even more deadly were stampedes during religious events.

During the Hajj, the Islamic religious pilgrimage, thousands had died over the years when crowds panicked and surged from one event to the next. Stoning the Devil, a station of the Hajj, had taken the most lives. Hundreds of similar occurrences.

Dance flipped through the documents cluttering her desk. Reports had come in of scores of tall, brown-haired men seen lurking suspiciously in the area. None of these sightings panned out. And the continued canvass of people who'd been at Solitude Creek Tuesday night had yielded nothing.

By six that evening she realized she was reading the same reports over and over.

She grabbed her purse and walked to the parking lot to head home. She was there in a half-hour. Jon Boling met her at the door, kissed her and handed her a glass of Chardonnay. 'You need it.'

'Oh, you bet I do.'

Dance went into the bedroom to de-cop herself. There was no gun to lockbox away tonight but she needed a shower and a change of clothes. She set the case files on her desk, stripped off the suit and stepped into steaming water. She'd been to no crime scenes other than the theater that day – at which there'd been no actual crime, no bodies, nothing graphic to witness; still, something about the Solitude Creek unsub made her feel unclean.

Then a fluffy towel to dry off. A fast collapse on the bed, eyes shut for three minutes. Then bounding up again. Dressing in jeans and a black T, a Kelly green sweater. Shoes? Hm. She needed something fun. Aldo's, in loud stripes. Silly. Good.

Downstairs, heading into the kitchen. 'Hey, hons,' Dance called.

Maggie, in jeans with Phineas and Ferb T-shirt, gave a nod. She seemed subdued again.

'All okay?'

'Yep.'

'What did you do today?'

'Stuff.' She disappeared into the den.

What was going on? Was it really nerves about the talent show? 'Let It Go' was a challenging tune, yes, but within Maggie's range. Lord knew she'd rehearsed plenty despite the deception the other night about not knowing the lyrics.

Was it something else? It was approaching that time in her life when hormones would soon be working their difficult changes in her body. Maybe they already were.

Adolescence. Wes was already going through it.

Heaven help us . . .

Or was it what she'd discussed with O'Neil? Her father's death.

But Maggie had seemed uninterested in talking about the subject. Dance had noted no unusual emotional affect patterns or kinesic messages when the subject of Bill came up. Still, kinesics is an imperfect science and, while Dance was talented when conversing with those she didn't know, witnesses and suspects, her skills sometimes failed her when it came to family and friends.

She now trailed her daughter into the den and sat down on the couch. 'Hey, babes. How's it going?'

'Yeah. Okay.' Maggie was instantly suspicious.

'You've been kind of moody lately. Anything you want to talk about?'

'I'm not moody.' She flipped through one of the Harry Potter books.

'How's "distracted"?' Dance smiled.

'Everything's fine.'

Thinking of the other children's movie song, 'Everything Is Awesome', which Michael O'Neil had threatened playfully to sing. Just like in that movie, where everything wasn't so awesome, Maggie wasn't fine.

She tried once or twice more to get her daughter to engage but she'd learned that it was impossible to do so if the children refused. The best solution was to wait for a different time.

Dance concluded with the standard, 'If there's anything you want to talk about, anything at all, let me know. Or I'll turn into a monster. You know what kind of monster I can be. Mom Monster. And how scary is *that*?'

Her smile was not reciprocated but Maggie tolerated the kiss on the head. Then Dance rose and stepped out onto the Deck, where Boling sat beneath the propane heater.

They spoke about the case – to the extent she felt comfortable – then about some of his projects, new code he was writing, the reasons why his college-level students hadn't finished their assignments.

'I wish I could give them a grade for the best excuse. I mean, there were A-pluses there.'

Dance glanced down at the end of the Deck, where Wes and two friends were intensely involved in a game. She recognized Donnie. She'd seen the other boy but couldn't come up with the name.

She whispered to Boling, 'And that's . . .'

'Nathan.'

'Right.'

He was taller than the others, stocky. The first time he'd been there he'd walked in with a stocking cap. Dance had started to say something, when Donnie noticed and, eyes wide, said, 'Dude? Seriously? Respect.'

'Oh, sorry.' The hat had vanished and he'd never worn it again.

The boys were now on the back deck playing the game they'd made up themselves. Its name was, she believed, Defend and Respond Expedition Service, or something similar. She supposed there was some shoot-'em side to it but that didn't bother her. Since it was played with paper and pen, a variation of a board game, she didn't mind a little military action. Dance kept her eye on video games and movies. TV shows now too. Cable opened the door to anything-goes. Wes had asked if he and Donnie could watch *Breaking Bad*. Dance had screened it first and loved the show but after the acid-dissolved body fell through a ceiling, she'd decided: No. Not for a few years.

But a game you played with paper and pen? How harmful could that be?

'You boys want to stay for dinner? Call your parents?'

Donnie said, 'Thanks, Mrs Dance, but I have to go home.'

'Yeah, me too,' Nathan said, looking embarrassed and guilty at the same time – the essential expressions of adolescence.

'Start packing up. We're going to eat soon.'

'Okay,' Donnie said.

She looked at her son and, when she spoke, she quashed 'honey', given that his peers were present. 'Wes, Jon and I were talking. You ever see Rashiv any more?'

Silence for a moment. 'Rashiv?'

'He was nice. I haven't seen him for a while.'

'I don't know. He's kind of . . . He's got a different bunch he hangs with.'

Dance thought this was too bad. The Indian American was, as Jon Boling had observed, funny and smart and polite. Which meant not only was he good company but he was a good influence too. Her son was getting to the point where, in the middle school he attended, there would be increasing temptations to steer toward the dark side. 'Well, if you see him, say hi for me.'

'Sure.'

After Wes's friends had left, Dance herded Maggie from the den and the two ladies prepared dinner. Whole Foods had been instrumental – sushi, a roast chicken, mashed potatoes, green beans and a complicated salad, which included cranberries, some kind of mystery seed, bits of cheese and impressive croûtons.

Boling set the table.

As she watched him her thoughts segued to the two of them, Dance and Boling.

The hours he spent with her and the children were pure comfort. The times she and he got away alone for a rare night at an inn were so very fine too. (He never stayed the night when the children were here.) All was good.

But Kathryn Dance wasn't long a widow. She monitored the

pulse of her figurative heart, on the lookout for subconscious blips that might sabotage the relationship – the first since Bill's death. She was not going to make fast decisions, for her own peace of mind, and the children: they were the north star by which she and Boling navigated their relationship. And it was Dance's job to be in control. To keep the speed brakes on.

Then her hand, holding a large spoon, paused as it scooped mashed potatoes from carton to bowl. And she asked herself: Or is there another reason I'm keeping things with Jon Boling slow?

He looked up from the table and caught her eye. He smiled. She sent one his way too.

'Dinner's ready!' she called.

Wes joined them, pulling a juice from the fridge.

'Put the phone away. No texting.'

'Mom, just—'

'Now. And how can you text and open a Tropicana?'

He mumbled but his eyes grew wide when he saw the potatoes. 'Awesome.'

As they sat down, Maggie said, 'Are we going to say grace?'

This was new. The Dance household was not particularly religious.

'We can if you'd like to. What do you want to say thanks for?'

'Thanks?'

'Grace is where you say thanks to God for something.'

'Oh,' Maggie said. 'I thought it was where you asked for something.'

'Not grace,' Boling explained. 'You can pray for things but grace is where you thank somebody else.'

'What did you want to ask for?' Dance looked at her daughter's face, which revealed no emotion.

'Nothing. I was just wondering. Can have I the butter, please?'

CHAPTER 26

Antioch March walked into a restaurant on Fisherman's Wharf and got a table near the window.

Tourism on steroids. Nothing like the days of Steinbeck's *Cannery Row*, he guessed.

He ordered a pineapple juice and looked at his prepaid once again. Nothing on the information he was expecting.

March ordered a calamari steak with steamed vegetables.

'Sorry, they're only sautéed. I don't think the chef—'

'That's okay. I'll take them that way.'

Another sip of juice. He opened his gym bag and began looking over maps and notes – what was planned for tomorrow. The theater had been denied him, set him back a day, but this would be just as good. Even better, he now reflected.

He glanced around the restaurant. He wasn't worried about being recognized. His appearance was very different from what had been reported. What a stroke of luck that the police had released his description to the public and not kept it to themselves. If the theater employee hadn't given that away, he might be in jail now.

Or dead.

He was studying a family nearby. Parents and two teenagers, all looking like they should be enjoying the pier more. In fact, it was a little anemic. Shopping mostly. No rides, except fifty cents bought little kids a turn on a space ship, up and down, in front of a shell shop.

Family . . .

Antioch March's father had been a salesman – yes, a real, honest-to-God *traveling* salesman. Industrial parts, American made (though maybe some components, tiny ones, had been teamed together in China. Dad, politically conservative, had been less than forthcoming about that).

The food came and he ate. He was hungry. It had been a long time since McBreakfast.

March's father was never home, his mother either, though she hadn't traveled much. She worked a lot, though young Andy could do the math. Shift over at five but not home till seven thirty or eight, for a shower, then downstairs to ask about her boy's day as she made him supper.

Not every day. But often enough. Andy didn't care. Mom could do what she wanted. He had what he needed. He had his video games.

'How's your calamari, sir?' the young waitress asked, as if she really, really cared.

'Good.'

She tipped him with a smile.

March used to think that was the reason he was drawn to, well, less healthy interests than his classmates: Dad never around, Mom tackling her own Get in her own special way. Plenty of free time as a boy. The solitary games.

Come on, Serena.

A little closer, Serena.

Look what I have for you, Serena . . .

Was he angry at their absence? March honestly couldn't say if he would have turned out different if he'd spent his evenings curled up in jammies as Mom or Dad read *Lord of the Rings* to him.

No, not much anger. Sure, Markiatikakis became March but that just made sense. He kept Antioch, didn't he?

Though I prefer Andy.

And he'd followed in his father's shoes. Life on the road. Life in business. And he *was* a salesman in a way.

In the employ of the website.

And working for his main boss.

The Get.

He could recall the exact moment of coining the term. In college. Hyde Park, U of C, the week of exams. He'd aced a few of them already and was prepared, completely prepared, for the rest. But he'd lain in bed, sweating and chewing on the inside of his cheek with compulsive molars. He'd tried video games, TV to calm down. No go. He'd finally given up and picked up a textbook for his Myths in the Classical World as Bases for Psychological Archetypes. He'd read the book several times and was prepared for the test but, as he flipped through the pages, he came across something he hadn't paid attention to. In the Oedipus story, where a son kills his father and sleeps with his mother, there was this line that referred to Oedipus as 'the get of Jocasta and Laius'.

The get . . .

What did that mean?

He'd looked it up. The word, as a noun, meant 'offspring'.

Despite his anxiety that night he'd laughed. Because in this context the word was perfect. Something within him, a creation in his own body, something he'd given birth to was turning on him. The way Oedipus would destroy father and mother both.

And – he couldn't help but think of the pun – whatever this feeling was, it forced young Antioch March to do whatever he could to 'get' peace of mind, comfort.

And so the hunger, the lack, the edge was named.

The Get.

He'd felt it all his life, sometimes quiescent, sometimes voracious. But he knew it would never go away. The Get could unspool within you anytime it wanted.

It wanted, not you. You didn't have a say.

And if you didn't satisfy the Get, well, there were consequences.

Somebody wasn't happy . . .

He'd talked to doctors about it, of course – well, shrinks. They understood; they called it something else but it was the same. They wanted him to talk about his issues, which meant he'd have to be open about Serena, the Intersection, about Todd. Which wasn't going to happen. Or they wanted to give him meds (and that made the Get mad, which was something you never, ever wanted to happen).

March tried to be temperate on his jobs. But the Asian family's death had been denied him, the theater disaster too.

What the hell?

'Miss? A Johnnie Walker Black. Neat.'

'Sure. Are you finished?'

'I am, yes.'

'A box?'

'What?'

'To take home with you?'

'No.' The Get made you rude sometimes. He smiled. 'It was very good. I'm just full. Thanks.'

The drink came. He sipped. He looked around him. A businesswoman eating dinner accompanied by an iPad and a glass of grapefruit-yellow wine glanced his way. She was around thirty-five, round but pretty. Sensuous enough, probably Calista-level sexy, to judge from her approach to eating the artichoke on her plate (food and sex, forever linked).

But his gaze angled away, avoiding her eyes.

No, not tonight.

Would he have a family some day with someone like her? He wondered what her name might be. Sandra. Joanne. Yes, she would be Joanne. Would he settle down with a Joanne after he got tired of the nights of Calistas and Tiffs?

March – yeah, yeah, so fucking handsome – could have asked Joanne, sitting over there with her artichoke and wine, a bit of butter on her cheek, to dinner tomorrow, and, in a month, a weekend getaway, and in a year to marry him. It would work. He could get it to work.

Except for one thing.

The Get wouldn't approve.

The Get didn't want him to have a social life, romantic life, family life.

He thought of the attack, at *Solitude* Creek.

How was that for a sign? Though Antioch March thought this in a droll way: he didn't believe in signs.

Solitude . . .

The family was preparing to leave, collecting phones, bags of chocolate sea otters, leftovers to be discarded in the morning. The father had the keys of his car out. Keys didn't jangle any more. They were quiet plastic fobs.

And, in this damn reflective mood, he couldn't help but think about the intersection. Well, upper case: the Intersection.

Serena had changed his life in one way but the Intersection had changed it most of all. Everything that came after was explained by what had happened where Route 36 met Mockingbird Road. Reeking of Midwest America.

After Uncle Jim's funeral, driving back.

'Nearer My God To Thee'.

'In Christ There Is No East Or West'.

The insipid, noncommittal Protestant hymns. They had no passion. Give me Bach or Mozart any day for gut-piercing Christian guilt. March had thought this even then, a boy.

It had been quiet in the Ford, the company car. His father, home for a change. His mother, being a wife for a change. Driving on the bleak November highway, winding, winding, pine turned gray by the mist, everything still.

Then around a bend, rocks and pines with stark black trunks.

Then: his mother gasping a brief inhaled scream.

The skid flinging him against the door, the brakes locking, then—

'Sir?'

March blinked.

'Here you go, sir.' The waitress set the bill in front of him. 'And at the bottom you can take a brief survey and maybe win a free dinner for the family.'

March laughed to himself.

For the family.

He doled out bills and didn't tell her that after his business was concluded here he wouldn't be coming back to the area again for quite a long time, if ever.

When March looked up, the couple and their children were gone.

It would be a busy day tomorrow. Time to get back to the inn.

His phone hummed with an email.

At last.

It was from a commercial service that ran DMV checks. The answer he'd been waiting for.

That morning as he'd enjoyed the Egg McMuffin and coffee,

parked near the multiplex that would have been his next target, March had noted an assortment of police cars and – this was curious – a gray Nissan Pathfinder.

He couldn't learn anything from the other vehicles or the uniformed or sport-coated men who climbed out of them. But the occupant of the Pathfinder, that was a different story. It wasn't an official car. Not a government plate. And no bumper stickers bragging about children, no Jesus fish. A private car.

But the driver *was* official. He could tell that from the way she strode up to the officers. The way they answered her questions, sometimes looking away. March was at a distance but he supposed she had a fierce gaze. Intense, at least.

Her posture, upright. March had sensed instinctively that this woman was one of the main investigators against him.

The search had revealed that the Pathfinder belonged to one Kathryn Dance.

A lovely name. Compelling.

He pictured her again and felt a stirring low in his belly. The Get was unspooling. It, too, was growing interested in Ms Dance. They both wanted to know more about her. They wanted to know *all* about her.

PRECAUTIONS

FRIDAY, APRIL 7

CHAPTER 27

'Never rains but it pours,' Michael O'Neil offered, walking into Dance's office.

TJ Scanlon glanced at the solid detective, who was sitting down across from her desk. 'I never quite got that. Does it mean, "We're in a desert area, so it doesn't rain but sometimes there's a downpour and we get flooded because, you know, there's no ground cover?"'

'I don't know. All I mean is, my plate's filling up.'

'With rain?' TJ asked.

'A homicide.'

'Oh. Sorry.' TJ often walked a fine line between jovial and flippant.

Dance asked, 'The missing farmer? Otto Grant?' She was thinking of the possible suicide, the man distraught about losing his land to the eminent domain action by the state. She couldn't imagine what he had gone through, losing the farm that had been in his family for so many years. She and the children had been at Safeway recently and she'd noticed yet more 8.5-by-11 sheets of paper, attention-getting yellow, with Grant's picture on them.

Have you seen this man? . . .

O'Neil shook his head. 'No, no, I mean another case altogether.' He handed Dance a half-dozen crime-scene photos. 'Jane Doe. Found this morning at the Cabrillo Beach Inn.'

A dive of a place, Dance knew. North of Monterey.

'Prints come back negative.'

The photo was of a young woman who'd been dead seven or eight hours, to guess from the lividity. She was pretty. She had been pretty.

'COD?'

'Asphyx. Plastic bag, rubber band.'

'Rape?'

'No. But maybe erotic asphyxia.'

Dance shook her head. Really? Risking death? How much better could an orgasm be?

'I'll get it on our internal wire,' TJ said. This would send the picture to every one of the CBI offices, where a facial-recognition scan would be run and compared with faces in the database.

'Thanks.'

TJ took the pictures off to scan them.

O'Neil continued, to Dance: 'The boyfriend's probably married. Panicked and took off with her purse. We're checking video nearby for tags and makes. Might find something.'

'Why wasn't she on the bed? I don't care how kinky I was, sex on the floor of *that* motel is just plain ick.'

O'Neil said, 'That's why I said *maybe* about the erotic asphyx. There were marks on her wrists. Somebody might've held her down while she died. Or it could have been part of their game. I'm keeping an open mind.'

'So,' she said slowly, 'you still with us on the Solitude Creek unsub?' She was afraid that the death – accidental or intentional – would derail him.

'No. Just complaining about the rain.'

'You still on the hate-crime case too?'

'Yeah.' A grimace. 'We had another.'

'No! What happened?'

'Another gay couple. Two men from Pacific Grove. Not far from you, down on Lighthouse. A rock through their window.'

'Any suspects?'

'Nope.' He shrugged. 'But, rain or not, I can work Solitude Creek.'

He was then looking down at the newspaper on Dance's chair. The front page contained a big picture of Brad Dannon. The fireman, in a suit and sporting a bright flag lapel pin, sat on the couch next to an Asian American reporter. *Hero Fireman Tells the Horror Story of Solitude Creek.*

'You interview him?' O'Neil asked.

She nodded and gave a sour laugh. 'Yep. And his ego.'

'Either of them helpful?'

'Uh-uh. In fairness, he was busy helping the injured. And we didn't know it was a crime scene at that point.'

'You ran the Serrano thing, in Seaside?'

'Yep.'

'How's that working out?' The question seemed brittle.

'It's moving along.' Then she didn't want to talk about it any more.

Her phone rang. 'Kathryn Dance.'

'Uhm, Mrs Dance. This's Trish Martin.'

The daughter of Michelle Cooper, the woman killed in Solitude Creek.

'Yes, Trish. Hi.' She glanced toward O'Neil. 'How're you doing?'

'Not so great. You know.'

'I'm sure it's difficult.' Thinking back to the days after Bill had died.

Not so great . . . Never so great.

'I heard, I mean, I was watching the news and they said he tried to do it again.'

'It's looking that way, yes.'

There was a long silence. 'You wanted to talk to me?'

'Just to ask what you saw that night.'

'Okay. I want to help. I want to help you get him. Fucker.'

'I'd appreciate that.'

'I can't talk here. My father'll be back soon. I'm at my mother's house. He'll be back and he doesn't want me to talk to you. Well, to anybody.'

'You're in Pebble Beach, right?'

'Yeah.'

'You drive?'

'Uh-huh.'

'Meet me at the Bagel Bakery on Forest. You know it?'

'Sure – I have to go he's coming back bye.' Spoken in one breath.

Click.

CHAPTER 28

She'd been crying.

Dance gave her credit for not trying to hide it. No makeup, no averted eyes. Tears and streaks present.

Trish Martin was sitting in the corner of the Bagel Bakery, toward the back, under a primitive but affecting acrylic painting of a dog carefully regarding a turtle. It was one of a dozen for sale on the walls, this batch by students, a card reported. Dance and the children came here regularly and she'd bought a few of the works from time to time. She really liked the dog and turtle.

'Hi.'

'Hey,' the girl said.

'How you doing?'

'Okay.'

'What do you want? I'll get it.' Dance was tempted to suggest cocoa but that smacked of youthening the girl, marginalizing her. She picked a compromise. 'I'm doing cappuccino.'

'Sure.'

'Cinnamon?'

'Sure.'

'Anything to eat?'

'No. Not hungry.' As if she'd never be again.

Dance placed the order and returned. Sat down. Automatically reaching for the plastic holster that held her Glock, which usually needed adjusting upon sitting. Her hand went to nothing and she remembered.

Then she was concentrating on the girl. Trish wore jeans and scuffed but expensive brown boots. Dance, a lover of footwear, spotted Italian. A black, scoop-neck sweater. A stocking cap, beige, pulled down over her hair. The sleeves of the sweater met her knuckles.

'Thanks for calling me. I appreciate it. I know what you're going through.'

'Totally.' Her keen eyes stabbed at Dance's. 'You have any idea who it is? Who killed my mother and those other people?'

And nearly you, Dance thought. 'Not much. It's not like any case I've ever seen.'

'He's a fucking sadist, whoever he is.'

Not technically but that would do.

Dance opened her notebook. 'Your father doesn't know you're here?'

'He's not so bad. This, like, freaked him out too. He's just being protective of me. You know.'

'I understand.'

'But I don't have much time. He's packing up stuff at his house now. He'll be back to Mom's soon.'

'Then let me get right to the questions.'

The drinks came, cardboard cups. They both sipped.

'Can you tell me what you remember?' Dance asked.

'The band had just started. I don't know, maybe the second or third song. And then . . .' After a deep breath, she gave much the same story as the other witnesses. The smell of smoke, though not seeing much. Then, almost as if somebody had flipped a switch, everyone in the audience had risen, knocking over tables, scattering drinks, pushing others aside and rushing for the exits.

Her expression mystified, she repeated, 'But there was no fire and still, you know, everybody went crazy. Five seconds, ten, from the first person who stood up. That was all it took.' She sighed. 'I think it was Mom. The first. She panicked. Then this bright light came on, pointed at the exit doors, you know, to show everybody where they were. I guess that was good but it made some of us panic more. They were so bright.'

She sipped a little from her cup, stared at the foam. Then: 'I got surrounded by this one bunch of people and my mother by another. She was screaming for me and I was screaming for her but we were going in different directions. There was no way to stop.' Her voice went low. 'I've never seen anything like that. It was like I was totally . . . I don't know, not even me. I was part of this thing. Nobody was listening to anybody else. We were just out of control.'

'And your mother?'

'She was going toward the fire doors. I could see her fight, trying to get back to me. I was going the opposite way – toward the kitchen, the group I was in. There wasn't an exit sign there but somebody said there was a door we could get out of.'

'And you escaped that way?'

'Eventually. But not at first. That's why it was so bad.' She teared, then wiped her eyes.

'What, Trish?'

'Somebody on the PA system said, "The fire's in the kitchen." Or something like that.'

Dance remembered Cohen had made the announcement.

'But somebody nearby saw that the kitchen was okay. No fire at all. We went in that direction. We tried to tell everybody else but nobody could hear us. You couldn't hear anything.'

Dance jotted down the girl's recollections. 'What's most important for us to find out is anything about him, this man. We have some description but it's not very much. We don't think he was in the club. He was outside. When did you and your mother get there?'

'I don't know, maybe seven fifteen.'

'I want you to think back. Now this guy—'

'The perp.'

Dance gave her a grin. 'We say "unsub". Unknown subject.'

'I say asshole.'

'Now, this asshole drove a truck from the warehouse to the club around eight. He had to've been there before. Did you see anybody hanging around, maybe near the warehouse? Checking out the club? Near the oil drum where he set the fire?'

Trish seemed to find more comfort in cupping the beverage between her fingers, her nails tipped with chipped black polish, than from drinking it.

A sigh. 'No. I can't remember anyone. You know, you go to a place, there's going to be a show, and you're just talking and thinking about what you're going to see and have for dinner, and you don't pay much attention.'

Much of Kathryn Dance's job had nothing to do with spotting deception on the part of unsubs: it was about helping witnesses unearth useful recollections.

Teenagers were among the worst when it came to remembering details. Their minds danced around so much, they were so distracted, that they observed little and recalled less – unless the topic interested them. Still, the images were often there. One task of an interviewer is to guide witnesses back to the time and place when they might have noted a tiny kernel that was nonetheless vital in nailing the suspect. As she considered how she might do this, she noted the girl's keyless fob sitting on the table beside her purse.

A Toyota logo from a local dealer.

'Prius?' Dance asked.

She nodded. 'My mom got it for me. How'd you know?'

'Guess.'

A sensible car. And an expensive one. Dance remembered, too, that the girl's father had driven a new Lexus.

'You like to drive?'

'Love it! When I'm upset I just drive up and down One. Big Sur and back.'

'Trish, I want you to think back to the parking lot that night.'

'I didn't see anybody in particular.'

'I understand. But what I'm wondering about is cars. We know this guy's pretty smart. There's no indication he's working with anyone so he'd have to drive to Solitude Creek but he wouldn't have parked too close to the club. He'd've been worried about video cameras or getting spotted climbing out of the truck, after he parked it, and getting into his own car.'

Trish frowned. 'A silver Honda.'

'What?'

'Or light-colored. We were pulling off the highway, off One, on the road that led to the club, and Mom said, "Wonder if it'll get stolen." It was parked by itself, on the other side of that line of trees that surrounded the parking lot. Of the club, you know.'

Dance recalled an area of weeds and dunes between the parking lot and Highway One.

'We'd just seen a news story about the gangs around here? They drive around in flatbeds and, you know, scoop up cars parked in deserted areas. That's what Mom was talking about.'

'You know the model?'

'No, not really. Just the style, you know. Accord or Civic. A lot of kids at school have them. Mom and I talked about calling the police to report it, so it wouldn't get stolen. But we didn't. I mean, if we'd done that, maybe . . .' She ran out of steam and cried quietly for a moment. Dance reached over and gripped her arm. Trish gave no response. She calmed eventually and took a sip from her cup. 'You think that's his car?' she asked.

Dance replied, 'Possibly. It's the sort of place somebody would park, out of the way. Did you notice the plate, what state it came from, the number?'

'No, just the color, silver. Or light-colored. Maybe gray.'

'And nobody nearby?'

'No. Sorry.'

'That's a big help, Trish.'

Dance hoped.

She sent a text to TJ to get a list of light-colored Honda owners in the area. She knew this was a weak lead. All law enforcers know that Honda Civics and Accords are close to the most plentiful sedans in America – and therefore the most difficult to trace. She wondered if their unsub had bought or stolen the car for that very reason.

She also asked TJ to hit the list of witnesses from Solitude Creek once more. And see if anyone had spotted the car and had any more information that could be helpful. He should put it out on the law-enforcement wire.

A moment later: *On the case, boss.* ☺

Trish glanced at her iPhone. 'It's late. I should go.' No teenager had a watch now. 'Dad'll be bringing his stuff back to the house soon. I should be there.' She finished her coffee quickly and pitched the cup into a rubbish bin.

Maybe destroying evidence of a furtive meeting.

'Thanks.' Trish inhaled and then, her voice breaking, said, 'Not okay.'

Dance lifted an eyebrow.

'You asked me how I was. And I said, "Okay." But I'm not okay.' She shivered and cried harder. Dance pulled a wad of napkins from the holder and handed them over.

Trish said, 'Not very fucking okay at all. Mom was, like, she wasn't the best mom in the world – she was more of a friend to me than a mom. Which drove me fucking crazy sometimes. Like she wanted to be my older sister or something. But despite all that crap, I miss her so much.'

'Your nose,' Dance said.. The girl wiped.

'And Dad's so different.'

'They had joint custody?'

'Mom had me most of the time. That's what she wanted and Dad didn't fight it. It was like he just wanted out.'

Fell for his secretary. Dance recalled her earlier scenario of the break-up.

'It's just going to be so weird, living in the house again, with him. They got divorced six years ago. Everybody tells me it goes away, all this stuff, what I'm feeling. Just time, it'll be all right.'

'Everybody's wrong,' Dance said.

'What?'

'I lost my husband a few years ago.'

'Hey, I'm sorry.'

A nod of acknowledgment. 'It doesn't go away. Ever. And it shouldn't. We should always miss certain people who've been in our lives. But there'll be islands, more and more of them.'

'Islands?'

'That's the way I thought of it. Islands – of times when you're content, you don't think about the loss. Now it's like your world's under water. All of it. But the water goes down and the islands come up. The water'll be there always but you'll find dry land again. That helped me get through it.'

'I should go. He'll be back soon.'

She rose and turned away. Dance did too. Then in an instant the girl turned and threw her arms around the agent, crying again. 'Islands,' she whispered. 'Thank you . . . Islands.'

CHAPTER 29

'Hello?'

Arthur K. Meddle turned from surveying the placement of chairs at the Bay View Center to see a man in the doorway.

'Help you? Hold on.' He turned away and shouted, 'Charlie, add another row. Come on. Four hundred. Got to be four hundred. Sorry. Help you?'

The man stepped closer. He seemed bored. 'Yessir. I'm a Monterey County fire inspector.'

Meddle gave a fast glance at the ID. 'Officer Dunn. Or inspector?'

'Officer.'

'Sure. What can I do for you?'

'You the manager?'

'That's right.'

The well-dressed polite fellow looked around the interior of the center, with furrowed brows. Then his eyes came back to Meddle. 'You may've heard, sir, about the incident at Solitude Creek? The club?'

'Oh, yeah. Terrible.'

'We're thinking it was done intentionally.'

'I heard that on the news.' Meddle didn't know this guy so he didn't add what he wanted to: 'What kind of crazy shit would do that?'

'The county board of supervisors and the Sheriff's Office – the Bureau of Investigation too – they're thinking he may try another attack.'

'No! Hell, is it really a terrorist? That's what Fox was saying. Was it O'Reilly? I don't remember.'

'Oh, I don't know. Between you and me, I'd think if it was terrorists, somebody would've taken credit for it. They do that.'

'True.'

'Anyway, sir, the county supervisors've issued a reg that requires any venues with events of over a hundred people have to postpone or pass a special inspection.'

'Postpone?'

'Or pass the inspection. We're making sure that what happened at Solitude Creek won't happen again. I mean they could catch the perp first. That's a possibility.'

'We can't very well cancel. Tonight? It's bringing in seven thousand dollars. It's a book signing. The author's publisher's paying for it. You know the economy out here. We can't afford to shut down.'

'Like I said, your choice.'

'What's this inspection? I've got a current occupancy cert.'

'No, this is different. We have to make sure the fire doors can't be blocked. You need to remove all the locks from the emergency-exit doors, or tape the latches down and chain off the area around them from the outside, so nobody can block them.'

'Like that guy did at the roadhouse, with the truck.'

'That's right,' Dunn said. 'Exactly. Everybody inside at this event tonight has to be able to get out, unobstructed.'

'Chain off an area outside the doors?'

'And I mean *chain* off. Literally. Ten feet away. So he can't block them. Frankly, it'd be easier to cancel the event.'

'You want me to cancel?'

'I'm just telling you the options.'

'But you're leaning toward our closing.'

'Easier for everybody,' Dunn said.

'Not for us.'

Seven thousand dollars . . .

'Look, I'm just saying,' Dunn said. 'Protect the exit area with chains and make sure the doors don't latch, so everybody can exit quickly in an emergency. Or you can cancel.'

Shit on a stick. As if he didn't have enough to do already. 'No, I'm not cancelling. But if people sneak in because we've left the doors unlatched, that'll be on you.'

'It's a book signing, right? You get a lot of gate-crashers at book signings?'

Meddle hesitated. 'It's not like a Stones concert.'

'So. There. Now, your smoke alarms? They've been tested recently?'

'We had an inspection ten, twelve days ago.'

'Good. Still, I'll double-check them.'

Meddle asked Dunn, 'For the chain, to block off the perimeter, any type in particular? Brand names?'

'I'd probably pick one that a truck couldn't break through.'

It sounded expensive. Meddle said, 'I'll go to Home Depot now.'

'Thank you, sir. I'm sure everything'll be fine . . . . What is this book thing anyway?'

Meddle explained, 'Hot new self-help thing. About living for tomorrow. I read it, like to keep informed about who appears here. The author says people live too much in the present. They need to live in the future more.'

'Like what? Time travel?' The inspector looked perplexed.

'No, no, just think about where you want to be in the future. Picture it, plan it, think it. So you'll reach your goals. The title is *Tomorrow Is the New Today*.'

Dunn frowned and nodded. 'I'll check those detectors now. You'd better measure for that chain.'

CHAPTER 30

Well, okay. Interesting.

Dance braked her SUV to a stop in one of the driveways that led to the Bureau of Investigation parking lot. She was between an unruly boxwood and a portion of a building occupied by a computer start-up.

Near the front door of CBI headquarters, Michael O'Neil stood in the lot talking to his ex-wife, Anne. Their two children – Amanda and Tyler, nine and ten – were in the back seat of her own SUV, visible through an open door. Anne's was a pearl-white Lexus, California tags.

The woman was dressed in clothes that were very, very different from what Dance recalled when Anne had lived on the Peninsula with Michael. Then, it was gossamer, close-fitting gypsy outfits. Lace and tulle, New Age jewelry. Boots with heels to propel her to a bit more height. Today, though: running shoes, jeans and a gray jacket of bulky wool. And, my God, a baseball cap. Exotic had become, well, cute and perky.

Who could have imagined?

It had been her decision to end the marriage and move to San Francisco. Rumors of a lover up there. Dance knew Anne was a talented photographer and the opportunities in the Bay City were far greater than here. She'd been a functional but unenthusiastic mother, a distant wife. The split hadn't been a surprise. Though it had certainly been inconveniently timed. Dance and O'Neil had always had an undeniable chemistry, which they let roam only professionally. He was married, and after Bill died, her interest in romance had vanished like fog in sunshine. Then, over time, Dance had decided for her sake and for the sake of the kids to wade into the dating pool. Slowly, feeling her way along, she'd met Jon Boling.

And, bang, O'Neil announced his divorce. Not long after, he'd asked her out. By then she and Boling were tight, however, and she'd declined.

It was a classic 'Send In The Clowns' moment, the Sondheim song about two potential lovers for whom the timing just wasn't cooperating.

O'Neil, gentleman that he was, accepted the situation. And they fell into 'another time, another place' mode. As for Boling – well, he'd said nothing about Dance's connection to the detective but his body language left no doubt that he sensed the dynamic. She did her best to reassure him, without offering too much (she knew very well that the intensity of denial is often in direct proportion to the truth being refuted).

She now noted: O'Neil had his hands comfortably at his sides, not in his pockets, or clutching crossed arms, either of which would have been a defensive gesture that meant: 'I just don't want you here, Anne.' Nor was he glancing involuntarily to his right or left, which was a manifestation of tension, discomfort and of a subconscious desire to flee from the person creating the stress.

No, they were, in fact, smiling. Something she said made him laugh.

Then Anne backed away, fishing keys from her purse, and O'Neil stepped closer and hugged her. No kiss, no fingers cupping her hair. Just a hug. Chaste as soccer players after scoring a goal.

Then he waved to the children and returned to the office. Anne fired up the SUV. She drove toward the exit.

And Dance suddenly recalled something else. The other night when she'd asked about O'Neil's new babysitter, his body language had changed.

New sitter?

Sort of.

So that's who it was. And the 'friend' at Maggie's recital? Anne, of course.

Dance watched Anne pull out of the lot.

Then a brief honk from behind the Pathfinder. Dance started. She glanced into the rear-view mirror and waved at the driver she'd been blocking, whispering a 'Sorry' that he couldn't hear. She headed to the CBI building, parked and climbed out.

Thinking of Anne and Michael, she found herself humming the song.

Let it go . . .

Inside Headquarters she found O'Neil in her office with TJ, poring over what turned out to be DMV records.

'Five thousand, give or take, Honda sedans in the three-county area. Gray, white, beige, anything light-colored.'

'Five thousand?' Ouch. As she sat down beside O'Neil, she smelled his aftershave, as last night . . . but it was slightly different.

Mixed with perfume?

O'Neil added, 'No reports of theft.'

TJ added, 'And none of the other people at the club, the ones I've talked to, remember it. The wheelbase and the track, they'll give us the model. Civic and Accord're different. Might help.'

Narrow the number down to 2500, she thought wryly. If – big if – it was even the unsub's vehicle.

'Want to take a look?' O'Neil asked. 'At where it was parked?'

Dance checked the time. It was three twenty. 'The kids are at Mom and Dad's.'

'Mine're covered too.'

I know.

She said, 'Let's take a drive.'

'For this, it's not Serrano. You going to take a weapon?'

He knew the rules. Wondered why he'd asked. 'I'm still Civ Div.'

A nod.

Dance told TJ to start canvassing the owners of light-colored Hondas.

In a half-hour she and O'Neil were at the roadhouse. The club was still closed and the trucking company, where she'd nearly received a concussion, was also dark. But there was some activity. A couple was laying flowers at the front entrance. Dance and O'Neil approached and she asked them if they'd been patrons the other night. They hadn't: the husband's cousin had died, and they were paying respects.

There also were some workers about two hundred feet from the club, in the direction of the path she'd taken the other day to the witness's house. It was a team of surveyors, with their tripod and instruments set up. They were engrossed in the obscure art of reckoning longitudes and latitudes, or whatever it was surveyors did.

'Maybe?' O'Neil asked. His voice sounded optimistic.

'Sure, let's give it a try.'

They approached and identified themselves.

The crew leader, a slim man, long hair under a cap, nodded. 'Oh. Hey. Terrible, what happened.'

Dance asked, 'Were you working here the day of the incident?'

'No, ma'am, we weren't. Had another job.'

O'Neil: 'Anytime before that?'

'No, sir. We just got the contract the other day.'

'Who're you working for?' Dance asked.

'Anderson Construction.'

A big commercial real-estate operation, based in Monterey.

'Know what the job is?'

'No, sir.'

They thanked the crew and wandered back toward the driveway. She said, 'We should talk to the company. They might've had other workers out on Tuesday. We'll see if they saw the Honda or anybody checking out the trucks or the club.' She called TJ Scanlon and put him on the assignment to find out who'd hired Anderson and see if either the developer or the construction company had had workers there the day of the incident or before.

'Will do, boss.'

She slipped the phone away.

O'Neil nodded. They continued past the roadhouse and headed down the driveway to the field where Michelle and Trish had seen the Honda.

Dance had wondered if she'd have to risk a call to Trish and find out exactly where the Honda had been parked but there was no need. It was clear from the trampled grass where it had turned off the driveway and bounded over the field of short grass and flowers to a stand of trees. Drought-stricken in most of the region, the ground was soggy from the creek, and the Honda's tires had left distinctive prints in the sandy mud. When the driver had reversed out, one had spun reaching for traction.

They stopped before they reached the tracks, however, and examined the ground carefully, then surveyed the surrounding area. Dance dug into her purse and pulled out elastic hair ties, four of them. She and O'Neil put them around their shoes – a trick she'd learned from her friends in New York, Lincoln Rhyme and Amelia Sachs. It would differentiate their shoeprints from those of the suspect when the forensics officers ran the scene.

'There,' O'Neil said, pointing into the trees. 'He got out of the car and walked back and forth to find a good route to circle around to the trucking company.'

Several cars drove past on the highway. One turned in at the next driveway. O'Neil was distracted and followed it until the lights vanished.

'What?'

'Just keeping an eye out.'

Guard dog. Because I don't have a weapon. Though the odds on their unsub charging out of the woods with blazing guns seemed rather narrow.

He turned back to the scene. They moved closer and Dance looked down, circling the area where the car had been, carefully so as not to disturb any evidence.

'Michael. Look. He wasn't alone.'

The solid detective crouched down and pulled out a small flashlight. He aimed it at what she'd seen. There were two sets of shoeprints, very different. One appeared to be running shoes, or boots, with complex treads. The other, longer, was smooth-soled.

O'Neil rose and, picking his steps carefully, walked around to the other side of where the car had been parked. Examined that area.

'No. Just one. Nobody got out on the passenger side.'

'Ah. Got it. He changed shoes. No, changed clothes altogether.'

'Had to be. Just in case somebody saw him.'

'We should get your CSU team here, search for trace, run the prints.'

The MCSO and the FBI had tread-mark databases for both tires and shoes. They might find the brand of shoe and narrow down the type of car, with some luck.

Though luck was not a commodity much in evidence in the Solitude Creek investigation.

CHAPTER 31

'*Tomorrow Is the New Today* . . . You have to think not about the present but about the future. You see, you blink and what was the future a moment ago is the present now. Are we good with that? Does that *speak* to you?'

The author looked like an author. No, not in a tweedy sport jacket with patches, a pipe, wrinkled pants. Which was, maybe, the way authors used to look, Ardel believed. This writer was in a black shirt, black pants and wore stylish glasses. Boots. Hm.

'So while you're focusing on the moment, you'll miss the most important part of your life: the rest of it.'

Fifty-nine-year-old Ardel Hopkins and her friend Sally Gelbert, sitting beside her, had come to the Bay View Center, off Cannery Row, right on the shoreline, because they were on diets.

The other option, as they'd debated what to do on this girls' night out, was to hit Carambas full-on, two hours. But that would mean six-hundred-calorie margaritas and those chips, then the enchiladas. Danger. So when Sally had seen that a famous author was appearing up the street, at the Bay View, they'd decided: perfect. One drink, a few chips, salsa, then culture.

Didn't preclude an ice-cream cone on the drive home.

Also, good news: like everyone else, Ardel had been worried about a crowded venue – after that terrible incident at Solitude Creek, intentionally caused by some madman. But she and Sally had checked out the Bay View hall and noted that the exit doors had been fixed so they couldn't be locked – the latches were taped down. And a thick chain prevented anyone from parking in front of the doors and blocking them.

All good. Mostly good – problem was, this guy Richard Stanton Keller, supposedly a self-help genius, was a bit boring.

Ardel whispered, 'Three names. That's a tip-off. Lot of words in his name. Lots of words in his book.'

Lots of words coming out of his mouth.

Sally nodded.

Keller was leaning forward to the microphone, before the audience of a good four hundred or so fans. He read and read and read.

Tomorrow Is the New Today.

Catchy. But it didn't make a lot of sense. Because when you hit tomorrow, it becomes today but then it's the old today and you have to look at tomorrow, which is the new today.

Like time-travel movies, which she also didn't enjoy.

She'd've preferred somebody who wrote fun and talked fun, like Janet Evanovich or John Gilstrap, but there were worse ways to spend an hour after digesting a very small – too small – portion of chips and one marg. Still, it was a pleasant venue for a book reading. The building was up on stilts and you could peer down and see, thirty or forty feet below, craggy rocks on which energetic waves were presently committing explosive suicide.

She tried to concentrate.

'I'll tell you a story. About my oldest son going away to college.'

Don't believe a word of it, Ardel thought.

'This is true, it really happened.'

Not a single word.

He started telling the story of his son doing something bad or the author doing something bad or the author's wife, the boy's mother, doing something bad because they'd been living for today and not tomorrow, which really was today. Hm. Did that mean—

Suddenly a loud bang, from somewhere outside the hall. Nearby.

Everyone looked toward the lobby. The author fell silent.

Now screams from outside too. Then another bang louder, closer.

That wasn't a backfire. Cars didn't backfire any more. Definitely a shot. Ardel knew it was a gunshot. She'd been to a range a couple of times when her husband was alive. She hadn't wanted to fire a gun, so she'd just sat back and watched the fanatics shiver with excitement over the weapons and talk shop.

Another shot – closer yet.

The manager hurried to a fire door, which he pushed open. A fast look out. He stepped back in fast.

'Listen! There's a guy with a gun. Outside. Coming this way!' He pulled the door shut but it swung open, thanks to the taped-down locks.

People were rising to their feet.

Another shot, two more. More screams from outside.

'Jesus Lord,' Ardel whispered.

'Ardie, what's going on?'

One man was on his feet, a big guy. Former military, it seemed. He, too, looked out. 'There he is! He's coming this way. He's got an automatic!'

Cries of 'No!', 'Jesus!', 'Call nine one one!'

Several people ran for the emergency exit. 'No, not that way!' someone called. 'He's out there. I think he's shooting people outside.'

'Get back!'

A brilliant security light came on. No! Ardel thought. All the easier to see his target.

The author didn't say, 'Stay calm,' or anything else. He leaped up and pushed some attendees out of the way, running for the lobby. A dozen people raced after him. They jammed the doorway. One woman screamed and fell back, clutching a horribly twisted arm.

Another shot from the direction of the lobby. Most of those who'd run that way returned to the main hall.

Ardel, crying, grabbed Sally's hand and they tried to move away from the exit doors. But it was impossible. They were trapped in a sweating knot of people, muscle to muscle.

'Calm down! Get back!' Ardel cried, her voice choking. Sally was sobbing too, as were dozens of others.

'Where're the police?'

'Get back, get off me . . .'

'Help me. My arm – I can't feel my arm!'

Deafening screams, screams so loud they threatened to break eardrums. As the mass pressed back from the exit doors, several people stumbled – one elderly man went down under a column of feet. He screamed as his leg bone snapped. Only through sheer strength, superhuman strength, it seemed, did two young men, maybe grandsons, manage to pry apart the crowd and get the man to his feet. He was pale and soon unconscious.

Two more shots, very close to the exit doors now.

The crowd surged away from the doors and toward the windows. Everyone was insane now, possessed with fury and panic. Slugging each other, trying to move back, thinking maybe, if anybody was thinking at all, that if they were not in the front line the bodies in front of them would take the bullets and the gunman would run out of ammunition or be shot by the police before he could kill more.

And moving relentlessly toward the only escape: windows.

Ardel heard a loud snap in her shoulder and her vision filled with yellow light, and pain, horrific pain, shot from her jaw to the base of her spine. A scream, lost amid the other screams. She couldn't even turn to look. Her head was sandwiched between one man's shoulder and another's chest.

'Ardie!' Sally called.

But Ardel had no idea where her friend was.

The voice on the PA – it wasn't the author's: he was long gone – cried, 'Get away from the door. He's almost here!'

A series of crashes, breaking glass, behind her and the mob surged in that direction, Ardel with them. Not that she had any choice: her feet were off the ground. Finally Ardel could turn her head and she saw attendees throwing chairs through the windows. Then silhouettes of desperate people climbing to the window frames, some cutting hands and arms on jutting shards of glass. They hesitated, then jumped.

She recalled looking out of the window earlier. It was three stories above the shoreline – you'd have to leap far out to hit the water, and even then it seemed there were rocks and concrete abutments just below the surface, some bristling with rebar steel rods.

People were looking down and screaming, perhaps seeing their friends and family hit the rocks.

'No! I'm not jumping!' Ardel shouted to no one in particular. And tried to use her good arm to scrabble in the other direction. She'd take her chance with the gunman.

But she had no say in the matter, no say at all. The writhing mass pressed closer and closer to the windows, where some people were hesitating and others pushing the reluctant ones down and climbing on their backs or chests or bellies to launch themselves into the questionable safety of the stony shoreline below.

'No, no, no!' Ardel gasped, as the cluster around her mounted the fallen bodies and made it to the sill. She couldn't look down, couldn't steady herself, couldn't even find a safe place to land, if there was such a place.

'Stop it!' she shouted to the crowd.

But then she was tumbling through space, curiously grateful, in those two or three seconds of free fall, to be out of the constrictor grasp of the surging crowd.

Then a jarring, breath-wrenching thud.

But she wasn't badly injured. She'd landed on top of the man who'd jumped just before her. He lay, unconscious, on the outcrop of rock, the right side of his face torn open, jaw and cheek and arm shattered. She'd even landed more or less on her feet, and slid back on her butt, avoiding what would have been a catastrophic, torturous collision of her shattered shoulder and the cracked rock.

A massive spray of pungent salt water flared over Ardel and those around her, sprawled and sitting and crawling on the stone, cold as ice.

Screams from the victims, roaring from the water.

She rose, unsteadily, looking around, clutching her shoulder.

By now the police would be swarming the hall, and the gunman shot or arrested. She'd just stay here and—

'Ah!' Ardel barked a scream as one of the falling patrons landed directly behind her, propelling her off the rock. She stumbled forward and fell into the raging water.

A wave was now receding, pulling her in the undertow, fast, away from the shore.

She inhaled at the pain and got only water. Retching, coughing, looking back for help, looking back to see how far she was from shore. Fifteen feet, then twenty, more. The chill stole her breath and her body began to shut down.

She glanced at her useless right arm, floating limp in the water.

Not that it mattered: even if it had worked perfectly fine, there was nothing she could do. Ardel Hopkins couldn't swim a stroke.

CHAPTER 32

Antioch March had returned from the Bay View Center and was sitting in his Honda parked about five blocks away from the venue, near the Sardine Factory, the wonderful restaurant featured in *Play Misty For Me*, the harrowing movie by Clint Eastwood. It was one of March's favorite flicks, about a beautiful woman obsessed with a radio disk jockey. Psychotically obsessed.

It was really about the Get, of course.

Anything to seize what she desired.

He stretched and reflected on the plan he'd just put into place. It'd gone quite well.

Forty minutes earlier he'd carted a Monterey Bay Aquarium shopping bag along Cannery Row, then slipped behind a restaurant near the Bay View Center. He'd changed into his 'uniform', militia chic, he joked to himself – camo, bandana, gloves, mask, boots. Then, ten minutes after the self-help author had started his reading, time for rampage.

He'd slipped out from the hiding spot and, firing his Glock, walked closer to the Bay View Center, aiming in the direction of people but not actually at them. Everyone scattered. Everyone screamed.

He made his way toward the center's fire-exit doors, shooting away. He figured he had about four minutes until police showed up.

Then, when people began leaping out of the windows, falling on the rocks and into the ocean, he'd turned and slipped back to his staging area. He stripped the camo off and was once again in T-shirt, windbreaker, shorts and flip-flops, pistol against his spine. The costume went into a mesh dive bag weighted with rocks and he'd tossed it into the bay, sinking thirty feet into the kelp.

Then, newly touristed, March made his way along the shore to where the Honda was parked. On a prepaid he called 911 and reported the gunman had moved off – toward Fisherman's Wharf, the opposite direction from where March now was. He then called a local TV station and said the same thing. Another call – to a Fisherman's Wharf restaurant, not the one he'd eaten at last night, to report that the crazed gunman was approaching. 'Run, run, get out!'

A lot of police – not everywhere, since this was a small community, but plenty of them. Not a single one paid any attention to him. Their focus was elsewhere. He'd wondered if they had any idea he'd masqueraded as the fire inspector, Dunn, to conveniently make sure that the exit doors were taped open. Probably not. The 'precautions' the venue used had assured the success of the attack.

He'd waited for a while but then decided he could return to, yes, the scene of the crime.

The streets were congested, of course, as he made his way toward the venue where the tragedy continued to unfold. In the water, he could see, a dozen police and Coast Guard boats cruised and floated, blue lights, searchlights. Some people bobbing, mostly divers. People on the rocks too, beneath the shattered windows of the venue. Some sat, seemingly numb. Some lay on their backs or sides. Rescue workers had carefully descended along a steep line of rock, slick with vegetation, like green hair, and salt water, to get to the injured. Several had lost their footing and gone into the ocean. A fireman was one of these, flailing in the water as it lifted and dropped him against the shore. Two fellow workers pulled him to safety.

He wasn't, March noted, the Hero Firefighter. But March was sure Brad Dannon would be there somewhere.

Through an alley and onto Cannery Row itself. Across the street and up the hill overlooking the Bay View Center.

What delicious chaos . . .

March eased close. He saw three body bags resting respectfully in the side driveway of the Bay View, near the emergency-exit doors, which were all wide open. Not a bad plan, this one, sending the self-helping book buyers out of the windows and onto the craggy rocks or into the breathlessly cold water.

March glanced down and noted another vehicle honking its way close to the Bay View.

Ah, what have we here?

My friend . . .

The gray Nissan Pathfinder featured an impromptu blue flasher on the dash. The vehicle parked near him – because of the congestion of the crowds and emergency vehicles it couldn't get close to the center itself.

Kathryn Dance climbed out, frowning. Looking around.

March had been to her house, of course, but hadn't been able to see much. There'd been dogs, people coming and going. He'd gotten some details about her life, her family, her friends, though he hadn't managed to get a good close look at her. Now he did. Quite attractive. A bit like that actress, Cate Blanchett. She wore a dark jacket and mid-calf skirt. Stylish boots. Her hair was back in a taut ponytail, secured by a bright red band.

Ah, interesting: in this outfit, with this hair, she looked a bit like Jessica, from the holy trinity of Antioch March's life, along with Serena and Todd.

She walked quickly up to several uniformed police and flashed her badge, though the officers seemed to know her. Others approached and gave her information, the way they'd greet a queen. His impression from the other day, at the theater, had been right: she's the one pursuing me. The lead detective, or whatever they called it. He supposed she was smart. She had a piercing, studious frown, an unyielding jaw.

In five minutes or so, she'd dealt with all the requests and had issued orders. She walked up to the bodies, looked down, grim-faced. Then into the hall itself.

When she was out of sight, Antioch March eased down the hill. Because of the congestion Dance had parked outside the police line perimeter and he was easily able to walk up to her car without being stopped.

Equally convenient, she'd been so focused on the Bay View Center disaster scene that she'd neglected to lock the SUV.

He looked around, saw nobody was paying him the least attention and popped open the driver's-side door.

CHAPTER 33

'About fifty people jumped. Most hit the rocks.' Dance was explaining this now to Charles Overby in her office at CBI head-quarters. O'Neil and TJ were present too. 'Half ended up in the water. The temperature was forty-five degrees. You can stay alive for a little while in water like that, some people can, but the ones who died couldn't swim or were stunned or injured by the fall. Then some were just picked up by the waves and slammed into the rocks. Knocked unconscious and drowned. Two got tangled in the kelp.'

'The count?'

O'Neil: 'Four dead, thirty-two injured. Twelve critical. Two are in comas from the fall and hypothermia. Three'll probably lose limbs from the fall to the rocks. No one missing. All accounted for.'

'No security?'

'No,' Dance said. 'The manager was in the front line, trying to help. The author? He hid in the bathroom. Women's room, actually. Then the shooter vanished – about three minutes before the police showed up. No sign whatsoever.'

'How did that happen?'

'We think he was wearing throwaways,' O'Neil said.

'The camo?'

Dance told her boss, 'There were plenty of places along the shore where he could have gotten out of sight, stripped, thrown everything into a shopping bag and strolled into the crowd, vanished.'

'There were reports he was headed toward Fisherman's Wharf.'

'We think he was behind that,' Dance explained. 'Called Dispatch, a TV station and another restaurant. Prepaid mobile. Bought in Chicago with cash about a month ago. And when I heard that I ran the call records the night of the Solitude Creek incident. Somebody called Sam Cohen from the parking lot and told him the fire was in the kitchen and backstage areas of the club. That sent more people into the crush.'

'The number the same?'

'No. But it was from Chicago too. Bought at the same time. I've sent a request to Chicago PD to see what they can find. I'm not holding my breath. Now, at the Bay View the manager said there was no security video. I saw cameras, in the hall and outside, but apparently they weren't hooked up.'

'And the unsub,' Overby said slowly, 'never went inside. Never actually hit anybody. Why?'

'The first question Michael and I asked about Solitude Creek. Why not just burn it down? Why not shoot his victims? He prefers them to kill themselves. He plays with perceptions, sensations, panic. It doesn't matter what people see. It's what they believe. That's his weapon, fear. And he knows what he's doing. I talked to one of the survivors. A woman named Ardel Hopkins. She was crushed in the mob and shattered her shoulder. She was about to drown but the Coast Guard fished her out. From what she said, it sounded just like Solitude Creek – people went insane. Nobody listened to reason. Security lights came on, bright ones. That added to the panic. Somebody must've broken a window and jumped. And the rest followed. Lemmings. Nobody looked to see if the shooter was actually inside. They just heard one person say, "Jump!" and they did. The manager said they'd just had a fire-department inspection – the venue could either cancel the event or submit to the inspection, which required them to make sure no vehicles could park in front of the exit doors and to tape the latches open.'

'At least the MCFD's being proactive. I didn't hear that. But it's ironic, hmm? The manager took all the right precautions – only *that* contributed to the frenzy.'

O'Neil said, 'Forensics is going over the site now. Oh, we did get the shoeprint analysis back from CSU – of the prints Kathryn and I found at Solitude Creek. And? Turns out the unsub's shoes're pretty rare.'

'What makes shoes rare?' Overby asked.

'Ones that cost about five thousand dollars a pair.'

'*What?*'

'The tool mark people're ninety percent sure. Louis Vuitton. I'm having somebody run sales throughout the country but, well, there's rare and then there's rare. They sell about four hundred pairs a year. And I'm betting our boy paid cash for those too. And the tire evidence for the Honda? Wheelbase, track and tires mean it's an Accord. Within the last four years.'

'Why's a man with five-thousand-dollar shoes driving a Honda?' Overby mused. Then obvious answer: 'Because it's the most common vehicle on the face of the earth.'

'Jesus. Five-thousand-dollar shoes.' Overby laughed. 'Who on earth is this guy?' He began to say something else but then glanced at his computer screen. 'Well. Oh.'

'What, Charles?'

He read for a moment. 'This's from the Pipeline wire – Oakland task force. Two bangers burned down one of the G-eight-two's warehouses. The one on Everly Street.'

'Burned it down?' Dance grimaced. She explained to O'Neil, 'We found the place was a front, about a month ago. We could've raided it but decided to let it keep operating and put surveillance on it. So we could get the IDs of trucks headed south.' She sighed. 'Now the G-eight-twos'll find someplace else and we'll have no idea where. This'll set us back.'

Overby continued to read: 'Was loaded with about ten thousand rounds of ammo. Quite the fireworks display.'

Dance said, 'I don't get it. The 'house was neutral territory. All the crews knew that. Doesn't make sense to take the place out.'

'Well, somebody didn't go along with the neutrality part,' O'Neil said. 'Maybe a renegade outfit from the south. Or here.'

Overby continued to read. Then looked up. 'Except it's odd. The guys who torched the place were white. At least, that's what the video showed. All the crews involved in Pipeline're black or Lat. But maybe they stepped on the wrong toes.'

'And the owner wouldn't do it for the insurance. Not with ammo inside,' Dance said. 'He'd wait till it was empty.'

Overby added, 'Oakland PD and DEA have a partial on the arsonists' license tag. Checking now. And video in the area, witnesses.' Shaking his head, he turned from the screen.

Just then TJ Scanlon appeared in the office. He nodded to everyone. 'Just want to keep you in the loop. I got some info on Anderson Construction.'

Ah. Dance explained to Overby that they'd found a crew of surveyors near the roadhouse. She'd hoped a construction worker might have seen the unsub near Solitude Creek.

'Anderson's been approached by a company in Nevada to do some development in the area. Nobody from Anderson has been at the site in two weeks. But they think the Nevada company's had some people over there recently. I've left messages.'

'Thanks, TJ. Get on home now.'

'See you in the a.m. Night, all.'

Overby left as well, then Michael O'Neil after him.

Dance noted the time: it was nearly eleven p.m. As she ordered files on her desk, she glanced at her computer, on which was streaming a local TV news account of the Bay View incident, the sound down. Who was on but Brad Dannon, the Hero Firefighter. He hadn't been the first on the scene this time but a close second or third. She watched the stark images. The blood on the doorway, the shards of glass from the shattered windows and the rocks, the huddled survivors who'd been fished from the water and wrapped in thin, efficient hypothermia blankets. People stumbling through the parking lot and among the crowd of onlookers, calling out, pathetic, for their missing relatives or friends.

A new, related story appeared. Dance turned the volume up. Henderson Jobbing had been sued by eighteen people for negligence in not securing their vehicles and keys. The commentators said bankruptcy was likely, not because of liability – it probably wasn't responsible legally – but because defending the suit would be so expensive that it would have to close down.

'The company has been a Monterey employer for years, providing warehouse services and running trucks throughout the state . . . and internationally as well. A local success story, but now, it seems, it will be shuttering its doors for good.'

Dance turned away from the screen. And thought, too, about poor Sam Cohen. The roadhouse would surely close, as well.

This is something you never recover from. Ever.

She pulled out her phone and made a call.

'Kathryn,' the man's voice said.

'You still here, Rey?'

'Sure am.'

Rey Carreneo was an agent she described as older in heart than in years. The man had been a patrol officer in Reno, Nevada, where he'd got quite the lesson in policing. He'd had a rich past, some good, some dark, and he bore a tiny scar in the Y between his thumb and forefinger; it was where a gang tat had resided not too many years ago before he'd had it removed.

'Need some help.'

'Sure, Kathryn. The Serrano case?'

'No, this is our Solitude Creek unsub. I need you to look into a couple of things. Can I come to your office in five?'

'I'll be here.'

CHAPTER 34

Antioch March sat parked in the Honda, observing a house fifty feet away and waiting for the right moment to change Kathryn Dance's life for ever.

He shifted. A big man, March didn't much care for the Accord. At home he drove a full-size Mercedes, and AMG, over 500 horsepower. A present from his boss. Here, though, of course, he needed to keep a low profile.

Squinting as he looked over the house.

He was there because he'd found some quite helpful information in Dance's Pathfinder not long ago, and an obvious plan had presented itself. On the seat beside him were his ski mask, the cotton gloves and a tire iron. He pictured dear Kathryn's face when she learned of the tragedy here. Would she cry? Scream? Both March and the Get wondered.

He was intermittently listening to the account of the Bay View disaster and to an audiobook, Keith Hopkins's brilliant *Death and Renewal*. March had failed as an academic because of the Get, not because of his intelligence: he had always read a great deal. He preferred non-fiction – biographies and histories primarily. *Renewal* was a scholarly work about death and social structure in ancient Rome, an era that fascinated him. The battles, the spreading of the empire, the culture. Gladiatorial contests were one of the topics covered in the book and they were of particular interest to March. He'd read whatever he could find on them, but there was little scholarship on gladiators and their world. It was astonishing to March that the bulk of the books on the topic were romance novels, featuring muscular men sweating through the strappy leather garb that encased them.

Romance novels!

My God.

He shut off the audiobook and stared at the house. He wondered how long he'd have to wait.

March relaxed, sat back.

What interested him about gladiators, of course, wasn't the erotic side – hetero or homo – which was a product of Hollywood and, apparently, popular publishing. No, it was the institutionalization of death that was so captivating to him.

History taught, history explained. A man can't be judged by one day: you have to examine his whole life to see trends, to see who he really is. The great leveling of time.

Mankind in general, the same.

And the world of gladiatorial contests had informed Antioch March's being. Now, the combat itself was interesting and complicated. It had begun in a very modest form as a tribute to a deceased relative, called the *munus*, a fight between two or three professionals, sometimes to the death, sometimes not. Eventually Roman officials combined the *munera* and non-combative entertainments, like sporting events, popular with the citizenry, into gladiatorial (the word referred to 'swordsmen') shows.

A fan of video games forever – he still played them regularly to relax – March had decided to create one himself. It would be about gladiatorial contests, a first-person game, where you see the action as if you were participating in it. The enemy comes at you and you must fight for your survival (or, as in some of the games, you sneak up behind your foe and slit his or her throat). Thanks to books like the one he was listening to and other research, he'd learned all he needed to about the contests themselves. The next step would be learning how to craft video games. He'd played them, many to the end, for nearly twenty years and had a good idea of how they worked but he would have to learn the mechanics of putting one together and find a computer person to help.

He spent hours fantasizing about the game and imagining what it would be like to play. He even had a title: *The Blood of All*. It was from a poem, perhaps by Catullus, a paean to a particular gladiator, Verus, in first-century Rome. He knew the last stanza by heart.

> *O Verus, you have fought forty contests and have*
> *Been offered the wooden Rudis of freedom*
> *Three times and yet declined the chance to retire.*
> *Soon we will gather to see the sword*
> *In your hand pierce the heart of your foes.*
> *Praise to you, who has chosen not to walk through*
> *The Gates of Life but to give us*
> *What we desire most, what we live for:*
> *The blood of all.*

He'd worked on the game off and on for years. If it became a hit, of course, he'd have to be careful to remain anonymous. A game designer would get some publicity and he supposed it wasn't good for someone who spent his days doing, well, what he did, to be too much in the public eye. But then he figured that the project wouldn't draw attention to him – not like a famous author. He'd never have four hundred people at a book signing, like I'm-a-Coward Richard Stanton Keller had had tonight.

Tomorrow Is the New Today. He smiled, thinking: Well, it sure wasn't for some of the people in attendance at the Bay View.

Another glance at the house. A light was on. But—

Just then his phone hummed with a text.

He squinted and picked up the unit.

What the hell's this? he thought. No. Oh, no . . .

The plans for the evening had changed.

CHAPTER 35

'How bad?' Jon Boling asked.

'I don't want to talk about my day. Let's talk about yours.'

Boling smiled. 'I'm not sure how captivating an article on flaws in Boolean search logic will be. How about we play roast beef sandwich?'

She smiled, too, and kissed him. 'I'm starved. Thanks.'

He whipped up plates and brought them onto the Deck, set out a glowing candle. Dance couldn't help but think: lighting it for the dead at Bay View Center.

He opened a bottle of Jack London Cabernet. The wine wasn't bad but she really liked the wolf on the label.

'What've the munchkins been up to?' she asked, as they sipped wine and ate the sandwiches and potato salad.

'Mags was still moody.'

Dance shook her head. 'I'll sit down with her again. See if I can pry it out of her.'

'But she seems to like her club. She was Skyping with them for an hour or so.'

'Oh, what's it called? The Secrets Club.'

'That's it. Bethany and Cara. Lucie too, I think. Pretty exclusive, it sounds like.'

'You kept an eye on it?'

'I did.'

Dance's rule was that the children could Skype or go online only if an adult was nearby and checking in occasionally.

'An official club?' she asked.

'I'm not sure Pacific Heights Grade School requires much in the way of charter for a club to be official.'

'Good point . . . Secrets Club,' she mused. 'And what do they do? Gossip about their American Girl dolls?'

'I asked her and she said it was a secret.'

They both laughed.

Boling waved off another pour of wine. Since the children were here, he was present only until bedtime, then would drive back home. Just like he never drank when he was chauffeuring them anywhere.

'And Wes?'

'Donnie came over for a while. I like him. Really smart. I was teaching them how to code. He picked it up fast.'

'What do you think about that game they're playing now – Defend and Respond Expedition? What is it again?'

'Service.'

'Right.'

'I have no idea what it's about but what I'm fascinated with is that they're rejecting the computer model. Writing out their battle plans, or whatever they do, sort of like football plays. Or like the old Battleships game. Remember?'

'Sure.'

'It's a return to traditional game practices. I think there's even an aspect where they do a scavenger hunt or something outside, find clues in the park or down by the shore. They're out in the real world, ride their bikes, get some exercise.'

'Like I used to play when I was a girl.'

'Have to say I was pretty box-oriented, even that age.'

Boxes. Computers.

She said, 'I heard people're going back to paper books, away from e-books.'

'True,' he said. 'I prefer the paper ones. And, besides, given my typical reading material, you're probably not going to find *Vector Modeling and Cosine Similarity as Applied to Search Engine Algorithms* on Kindle.'

Dance nodded. 'They're making a movie of that, aren't they?'

'Pixar.'

Patsy and Dylan wandered out onto the Deck. Molecules of roast beef aroma carry far on nights like that. They plopped down and Boling furtively, but not too, slipped them bits. He asked Dance, 'Okay, how bad was it?'

She lowered her head, sipped wine again.

He said, 'You didn't want to talk about it. But maybe you do.'

'It's bad, Jon. This guy, we don't have a clue what he's up to. Tonight— Did you hear the news?'

'Gunman, but he wasn't actually shooting people. Just making them panic. They jumped into the water. Four or five dead.'

Dance fell silent, looked out over the tiny amber lights in the backyard. As she leaned back, a bone somewhere in her shoulder popped. Didn't used to happen. She stared up through the pines at the stars. This was the Peninsula of Fog but there were moments where the temperature and moisture partnered to turn the air into glass and, with little ambient illumination here, you sometimes could peer up through a tunnel between the pines and see the start of the universe.

'Stay,' she said.

Boling looked down at the dogs. They were asleep.

He glanced at her.

A smile. 'You. Not them.'

'Stay?'

'The night.'

He didn't need to say, 'But the children.' Kathryn Dance was not somebody you needed to remind when it came to the obvious.

And he didn't need to hesitate. He leaned over and kissed her hard. Her hand went around his neck and she pulled him to her.

Neither asked about finishing dinner. They picked up their half-empty plates and carried them inside to the sink. Then Dance ushered the dogs in, and locked the doors.

Boling took her hand and led her up the stairs.

FLASH MOB

SATURDAY, APRIL 8

CHAPTER 36

The alarm went off at seven thirty.

A classical tune – Dance, a musician, never did well with dissonance. It was the 'Toccata and Fugue', *Phantom of the Opera* – no, not *that* one. An earlier version.

She opened her eyes and fumbled for the stop button.

Yes, it was Saturday. But the unsub was still out there. Time to get up.

She turned to see Jon Boling brush back his thinning hair. He wasn't self-conscious: it was only that strands were sticking out sideways. He wore only a T-shirt, gray, which she vaguely remembered him pulling on somewhere north of midnight. She was in a Victoria's Secret thing, silk and pink and just a little outrageous. Because, how often?

He kissed her forehead.

She kissed his mouth.

No regrets about his staying. None at all.

She'd wondered what her reaction would be. Even now, hearing the creak of a door downstairs, a latch, muted voices, the tink-tink of cereal bowls, she knew it was the right decision. Time to step forward. They'd been dating a year, a little more. She now marshaled arguments and prepared a public-relations campaign for the children, thought about what they would and wouldn't think, say, do when they saw a man come down the stairs. They'd have a clue about what had been going on: Dance had had The Talk with them, several years ago. (The reactions: Maggie had nodded matter-of-factly, as if confirming what she'd known for years; Wes had blushed furiously and finally, encouraged to ask a question, any question, about the process, wondered, 'Aren't there, like, any other ways?' Dance, struggling to keep a straight face.)

So. They were about to confront the fact that Mom had had a man stay over, albeit a man they knew well, liked and who was more relative to them than her own sister was an aunt (flighty, charming and occasionally exasperating, New Age Betsey lived in the hills of Santa Barbara).

Let's see what the next half-hour holds.

Dance considered just throwing on a robe but opted for a shower. She slipped into the bathroom and, when out, dressed in jeans and a pink work shirt while Boling, looking a bit uneasy, brushed his teeth. He, too, dressed.

'Okay,' he said slowly.

'No.'

'No?' he asked.

'You were looking at the window. You can't jump out of it. You're going to come downstairs with me and we'll have my famous French toast. I only make it on special occasions.'

'Is this special?'

She didn't answer. She kissed him fast.

He said, 'All right. Let's go see the kids.'

As it turned out, however, it wasn't just the kids that Dance and Boling saw.

As they stepped to the bottom of the stairs and into the kitchen, Dance nearly ran into Michael O'Neil, who was holding a glass of orange juice and walking to the table.

'Oh,' she whispered.

'Morning. Hi, Jon.'

'Michael.'

O'Neil, his face completely neutral, said, 'Wes let me in. I tried to call but your phone was off.'

She'd shut it off intentionally before easing into bed, not wanting to risk a call – that is, risk hearing O'Neil's ringtone, an Irish ballad, courtesy of the kids – at a moment like that. She'd fallen asleep before turning it back on. Careless. Unprofessional.

'I . . .' she began, but could think of not a single syllable to utter past that. She glanced toward the busy bees hard at work on breakfast.

'Hi, Mom!' Maggie said. 'There was this show on TV about badgers and there's this one kind, a honey badger, and this bird called a honeyguide leads it to a beehive and a badger rips it open and eats honey and its coat is so thick it doesn't get stung. Hi, Jon.'

As if he'd lived there for years.

Wes, on his phone, nodded a cheerful greeting with a smile to both mother and boyfriend.

Mother and daughter went to work, wrangling breakfast – including honey for the French toast, of course. Dance glanced toward Wes. 'Who?' she whispered, nodding at his phone.

'Donnie.'

'Say hi for me and then hang up.'

Wes said hi, kept talking and, under her gaze, clicked off.

O'Neil, who might very well have spent the night with Ms Ex-O'Neil, kept his eyes on the juice. From his solid frame, a dozen kinesic messages were firing, like cylinders in a sports car. Or a white SUV, made by the Lexus division of Toyota Motors.

Enough, she told herself.

Let it go . . .

Boling made coffee. 'Michael?' Lifting a cup.

'Sure.' Then O'Neil added to Dance, 'Something's come up. That's what I was trying to get in touch with you about.'

'Solitude Creek?'

'Right.'

Dance didn't need to glance at the children, from whom she kept most aspects of her job. It was O'Neil who nodded toward the front hall. She told Maggie to set the table. Boling grilled the toast and made bacon. Wes had taken to texting again but Dance said nothing about it.

As she followed O'Neil, she realized that her top button was undone; she'd been distracted earlier. She fixed it with a gesture she tried to make casual but that she was sure drew attention to the V of flesh, dotted with faint freckles. And silently gave a word of thanks to whatever impulse had told her not to go with the robe and lacy Victoria's Secret gown before heading downstairs.

'There's a lead we ought to follow up on. Out of town.'

'The unsub's Honda?'

'No. The alert we've got for online activity.'

She and O'Neil had spoken to Amy Grabe, San Francisco, and she'd had the FBI's powerful online monitoring network search for any references to either of the two attacks. It was not unheard of for witnesses to unintentionally post helpful information about crimes; there had even been instances when the perp had bragged about his cleverness. 'Last night somebody posted a clip on Vidster.'

Dance knew it. A YouTube competitor.

'What was it?'

'Some of the press footage – shot of a TV screen – of the roadhouse. And stills of other incidents.'

'Others?'

'Not related to what happened here. It was a rant by somebody named Ahmed. He said this is what Islam will do to the West, that sort of thing. Didn't take credit for it exactly but we should check it out.'

'What other incidents?'

'Some foreign. A beheading of Christians in Iraq, a car bomb outside of Paris. A train wreck in New York, derailment. And then another stampede – a few years ago in Fort Worth. A nightclub.'

'I read about that. But the perp died in the incident. A homeless guy.'

'Well, Ahmed claims he was jihadist.'

O'Neil scrolled through his phone. He displayed some clips. Bodies close up, lying in their desperate still poses, asleep for ever.

'And that was supposedly the work of some terror cell?'

'More or less.'

'Have we got his address?'

'Not yet. Soon, the tech people said.'

'Mom!' Maggie called.

'Be right there.'

He slipped the phone away and they walked into the kitchen. O'Neil said, 'I should go.'

'Aw, no, stay!' Wes said.

Dance said nothing.

'Yeah, Michael. Pleeeease.' Maggie was in her persuasive mode.

Boling said, 'Come on, have something. It's Kathryn's secret recipe.'

She said, 'Eggs, milk. But don't tell anybody.'

'Sure, I guess.'

They all sat at the table and Dance dished up.

Wes said, 'Wow, I saw on the news that guy did another one.'

Dance said, 'It looks that way.'

'Did another what?' Maggie asked.

'Hurt some people at the Bay View Center.'

Her daughter asked quietly, 'Did anybody die?'

Dance never over-explained but she always answered their questions truthfully and directly. 'Yes.'

'Oh.'

They ate in silence for a while. Dance had little appetite. Boling and O'Neil did. So did Wes.

She sipped coffee and noted that Maggie was troubled again and was now picking at her French toast. 'Honey?' she whispered, lowering her head. 'What's wrong?'

'Nothing. I'm just not hungry any more.'

'Drink your juice.'

She had a minuscule sip. Her face was now very clouded. After a moment she said, 'Mom? I was thinking.'

'What?'

'Nothing.'

Dance glanced at the others, then said to her daughter, 'Let's go on the Deck.'

Maggie rose and, with a glance toward Boling, then O'Neil, Dance followed her outside. She knew that the serious conversation, postponed the other night, was now going to happen.

'Come on, hon. Tell me. You've been sad for a long time now.'

Maggie looked at a hummingbird, hovering over the feeder.

'I don't think I want to sing that song tomorrow.'

'Why?'

'I don't know. Clara's not performing.'

'Clara just had her appendix out. Your whole class is doing something.'

The name of the show was *Mrs Bendix's Sixth Grade Class's Got Talent!*, which told it all. There were to be skits, dance performances, piano recitals, violin solos. Her teacher had persuaded Maggie to sing after she'd performed a perfect solo of 'America The Beautiful' at an assembly.

'I keep forgetting the words.'

'Really?' Dance's tone called her on the lie.

'Well, like, sometimes I forget them.'

'We'll work on it together. I'll get the Martin out. Okay? It'll be fun.'

For a moment Maggie's face was so dismayed that Dance felt alarm. What was this all about?

'Honey?'

A dark look.

'If you don't want to sing, you don't have to.'

'I . . . Really?' Her face blossomed.

'Really. I'll call Mrs Bendix.'

'Tell her I have a sore throat.'

'Mags. We don't lie.'

'It gets sore sometimes.'

'I'll tell her you're not comfortable singing. You can do the Bach invention on your violin. That's beautiful.'

'Really? It's okay?'

'Of course.'

'Even if . . .' Her voice faded and her eyes fled to the tiny band-throated hummer, sipping sugar water.

'Even if what?'

'Nothing.' Maggie beamed. 'Thanks, Mommy! Love you, love you!' She ran off, back to breakfast, happier than Dance had seen her in weeks.

Whatever was motivating her not to sing, Dance knew she'd made the right decision. As a mother, you had to prioritize. And forcing her daughter to sing in a sixth-grade talent show was not an important issue. She called the teacher and left a message, relaying the news. If there was any problem, Mrs Bendix could call her back. Otherwise, they'd be at the school at six thirty tomorrow, violin in hand.

Dance returned to the kitchen table, and as she ate a mouthful of toast O'Neil's phone beeped. He took a look at the screen. 'Got it.'

'The address of the guy who posted?'

'His service area.' He scooted back in the chair. 'They're still working on his name and exact address.'

'Jon . . .' Dance began.

'I'll get the gang to practices,' he said, smiling. 'No worries.'

Wes for tennis. Maggie'd taken up gymnastics – something she hadn't been interested in until her friend Bethany, the cheerleader, had suggested she try it.

'And Quinzos after,' Boling told the kids. 'Only be sure you don't tell your mother. Oh, oops!'

Maggie laughed. Wes gave a thumbs-up.

'Thanks.' Dance kissed him.

O'Neil was on the phone now. 'Really, okay. Good. Can you get a state plane?'

Plane?

He disconnected. 'Got it.'

'Where're we headed?' Dance wiped some honey from her finger.

'LA. Well, south. Orange County.'

'I'll go pack.'

CHAPTER 37

Antioch March opened his eyes and tried to recall where he was.

Oh. Right.

A motel off the 101.

After getting the Google alert on his phone, he'd tried to make it all the way to his destination last night. But there'd been delays. He'd needed to steal a car – an old black Chevy, it turned out – from the long-term lot at Monterey Regional Airport. He'd thought there was a possibility he'd have to abandon his wheels when he arrived at the destination and he wasn't prepared to lose the Honda just yet.

There were better ways to get an untraceable car than theft, much better, but this matter was urgent and he'd had no choice but to steal the vehicle. Hotwiring, it turned out, was really quite simple: pull the ignition harness bundle out, gang together everything but the – in this case – blue wire. Rig a toggle, then touch the blue wire to the bound leads (let go right away or you'll ruin the starter). Then pop the cover off the lock assembly and knock out the steering-wheel pin. Easy.

Still, he hadn't hit the road until about two a.m.

Several hours later, fatigue had caught up with him there, near Oxnard, and he'd had to stop for some rest. He imagined what would have happened if he'd dipped to snoozing and run off the road. The Highway Patrol, suspecting drinking, would have possibly found the Glock 9mm and a car registration that had someone else's name on it. And the evening would not have gone well.

So he'd made a stop there, at a dive of a motel, along with truck drivers, Disney-bound tourists and college students, whose energy for copulation was quite astonishing, as well as noisy.

Now, close to eight a.m., March rose slowly to waking, thinking about the dream he'd just had.

Often Serena. Sometimes Jessica.

This one had been about Todd.

Todd at Harrison Gorge. It was in upstate New York, on a busy river, one that led ultimately to the Hudson.

The park and nearby town, Colonial era, was a romantic getaway, four hours from Manhattan. The day he was thinking of, the Day of Todd, was nestled in the midst of leaf season. Officially out of school then, working in sales, he'd been in Ithaca, New York, a call. He'd kept some sentimental ties to academia by working for a company that sold audio-visual equipment to colleges. After a lackluster pitch at Cornell, he'd recognized the symptoms: edgy, depressed. The Get was prodding. He'd cancelled a second meeting and left, driving back to his motel.

He'd seen the park on the way and decided, on a whim, to check it out. March spent an hour hiking along the trails, surrounded by leaves spectacular even in light mellowed by low-hanging clouds. March had his camera and shot some pictures as he walked. The rocks, brown and gray like ancient bone, and stark tree trunks impressed him more than the colors.

Click, click, click . . .

March had spotted a sign, Harrison Gorge, and followed the arrow.

Although the weather had thinned the visitors, he came upon a cluster of people – mostly young, rugged outdoor people, rock-climbing people. Helmets and ropes and well-used backpacks. One young man had stood off to the side, looking down at the water. Someone had called his name.

Todd . . .

Blonde, cut and muscled, about March's age. Lean, handsome face. Eyes that would probably be confident at any other time. But not today. Then his companions were gone. Todd was now alone.

And March had approached.

Listen, Todd, I know it's a big leap. I know you're scared. But come on, don't worry. Everything'll be fine. If you never try something, you never know, do you?

I see you have a Get of your own to scratch.

Come on . . . A little closer, closer.

Go for it, Todd. Go for it.

Yes, yes, yes . . .

Antioch March smiled at the memory. It seemed both from another life and as real as yesterday.

He stretched. Okay. Time to get to work. He showered and dressed. He looked in the mirror and his face grew wry. The blond hair was just plain odd.

He made coffee in the cheap unit on the desk and used the powdered creamer. Breakfast was included but he certainly wouldn't go to the common room, where others might see him. The description of the man who had 'allegedly' caused the Solitude Creek tragedy did not include his face. But he thought it best to be cautious. He sipped the pungent brew and turned on the TV.

March finished packing. He dumped the coffee out, wiped away fingerprints throughout the place using a sanitizer wipe (plain cloth doesn't work). He stepped outside into the clear, cool air. Gazing around, at the oak and brush, the brown hills, the parking lot for anyone watching him, any threats.

None.

Then he slipped into the car, which was parked in the back. Toggle the power. Blue wire to the bundle.

The car started.

Then he was on the road again, piloting the cigarette-smoke-scented Chevy Malibu, heading south.

Two hours later he was in Orange County, closing in on the apartment of the man who'd posted the bizarre Vidster rant by someone named or nicknamed Ahmed, linking the Solitude Creek incident and several other mass tragedies to fundamentalist Islamist terror.

And putting Antioch March in a spotlight he could not afford to be in.

CHAPTER 38

After the autobot had alerted March last night to the video, he'd called in some favors to find the address of the poster. It was in Tustin, a pleasant, nondescript suburb in the heart of Orange County. He now passed a lot of stores, restaurants, strip malls, modest homes.

March found Ahmed's apartment in a quiet residential area, and parked the Chevy Malibu four blocks away, in front of an empty storefront. No security cameras to record the tag number, or him, though he was at the moment largely unrecognizable. The workman's beige jacket was a thick one for this hot Southern California weather and he was sweating under it and the baseball cap. But nothing to do about that. He was used to being physically uncomfortable on the job. The Get always put you through your paces.

Especially irritating were the flesh-colored cotton gloves.

He supposed, too, he was upset that he'd had to make the trip in the first place. He longed to be back in Monterey. He didn't want Kathryn Dance's reprieve to last much longer.

But when your profession is death you need to be willing to do what's necessary to protect yourself. Be patient, he told the Get. We'll return to our lovely Kathryn in due time.

March clicked the toggle off, climbed out and pulled on black-framed glasses with fake lenses. Looked at his reflection in the window.

Porn star meets *Mad Men* . . .

Then he snagged his gym bag from the back seat. No key, so he had to leave the car unlocked. This didn't, however, seem like a place where car theft was a big risk. Again, no choice.

Then, head down, he walked an indirect route to the one-story, ranch-style apartment complex.

In the courtyard, he paused. Another glance around. No security videos. No one visible. He stepped up to ground-floor apartment 236, listened. Faint music came from inside. Pop music.

He reached into his pocket with his right hand, gripping the gun, and with his left rapped on the door. 'Excuse me?'

The music went down. 'Who's there?'

'Your neighbor.' He stood directly in front of the peephole to prove he was white. And therefore no threat. It seemed like that sort of neighborhood.

The chain, then the latch.

The man inside could be big. Dangerous. And armed.

The door opened. Hm. Ahmed was indeed big, yes, but mostly fat. Pear-shaped. He was also probably not an Ahmed since he was as Anglo as they came. About forty, curly hair. A goatee, shaved head. And a dozen tats, the biggest of which were the American flag and an eagle.

No gun, though one would have looked right at home in his belt.

'Which unit you from?' he asked.

March shoved his Glock into the man's thick chest. Pushed him back into the room.

'Fuck. No. What is this?'

'Sssh.' March frisked him. Then collected the gym bag, closed and latched the door.

Five minutes later the heavyset man, crying, was lying on his back, hands and feet bound with duct tape.

'Please, don't hurt me. I don't— What do you want? Please, no!'

March got down to the fun and soon had his answers. Stan Prescott was not, of course, a terrorist. He was a Christian. A well-thumbed Bible sat beside a well-sat-in armchair. By profession, a bartender. But his avocation was – he might have said – patriot.

After being caressed by the muzzle of March's Glock, he'd admitted he'd posted the images and claimed credit in the name of Allah, or whatever the fine print read, to arouse anti-Islam sentiment in the country. Was he crazy? March reflected. Everyone with half a brain would see through the plan. And those who believed the claims? Well, that was one group that nobody needed to convert.

Stupid on all fronts. Not the least because he'd picked the wrong person to draw attention to.

But, of course, Prescott had his own Get: the need to keep his country safe and free . . . from anyone who wasn't American. That is, Christian American. That is, white Christian American. What he hadn't learned was that you need to treat the Get like an animal that's only partly domesticated. You can't be stupid: it'll kill its owner as fast as anyone else.

'Give me your passcode. Your computer.'

The man did, instantly.

March was surveying Prescott's files. Looking at all the man's pseudonymous diatribes against America. He looked over the dozens of grim photos of beheadings, bombs and other supposedly terrorist attacks that no self-respecting jihadist would have been behind. He had quite the collection of gruesome pictures.

He got the passcodes to Prescott's Vidster account and blog, and took everything down.

'What's this about, man? Come on! Are you working for them? You seem like one of us!'

Them . . .

It occurred to March that there might be a benefit here: if the authorities had seen the post, the terror angle would lodge in their minds as a motive for what had happened. That would obscure just a bit more the real reason for the attacks in Monterey, which had, of course, to be kept completely secret.

'I'm sorry. I'll do whatever you want. Jesus, man. Come on. We're both . . . alike, you know.'

White.

March shut down the laptop. He looked around the room, then dragged a pole lamp over, positioned it above the man's sweating face.

'What're you doing?'

March walked to the front door and fetched his gym bag.

'What're you doing?' Prescott repeated, more desperate.

March crouched down and examined the man's face closely. He patted him on the shoulder, said, 'Don't you worry.'

And unzipped the bag.

CHAPTER 39

'This's it,' Michael O'Neil said, pulling the rental car into the parking lot of Stan Prescott's apartment complex in Tustin, California.

They parked several units down from Prescott's to wait for an Orange County deputy to join them.

In the time it had taken the state jet to whisk Dance and O'Neil from Monterey Regional Airport to John Wayne, Orange County, O'Neil's computer people had the identity of the man who'd posted that clip of the Solitude Creek deaths.

Stanley Prescott, aka Ahmed, was a forty-one-year-old bartender. Single. The information gathered also revealed that he had been working in his club's Long Beach location at the time of the Solitude Creek and Bay View disasters, so he wasn't the unsub.

His Facebook and blog profile revealed he was essentially a rabid bigot. It was obvious that he was claiming Solitude Creek and the other incidents were the work of Muslims to incite anti-Islamic sentiment.

People could be such idiots.

This news was discouraging, since he'd probably had no connection whatsoever to either of the attacks and had simply pulled violent pictures and videos randomly from the web to repost. Still, as they were there, they would talk to him. Maybe the unsub had emailed or posted something on this man's blog.

As they waited for the Orange County deputy to arrive, O'Neil took a call. He nodded and Dance noted he lifted an eyebrow. He had a brief conversation, then hung up.

'Otto Grant. Remember?'

Of course she did. The farmer whose land had been confiscated under eminent domain. The possible suicide.

'Santa Cruz police found a body in the water by the pier. Male. Same age and build. They'll run the scene and get me the report.'

How sad, she reflected. 'Did he have family?'

'He was a widower. Grown children. Farming must've been his whole life, maybe all he had left.'

'A hard way to go. Drowning.'

'I don't know,' O'Neil mused. 'In that water? You'd be numb after three, four minutes. Then . . . nothing. Worse ways to die than going to sleep in the Bay.'

Dance and O'Neil had to wait only a few minutes for the Orange County deputy to arrive. They waved him over. The stocky uniformed man's name was Rick Martinez.

'We've been following the wire about your perp. The Solitude Creek thing. The other one too. The author signing. Last night. Man, that's terrible. I've never heard anything like this. This terror thing?' A nod toward the apartment. 'Is Prescott your doer?'

Dance said, 'We know he's not. But we're hoping there's a chance of some connection between him and our unsub.'

'Sure. How do you want to handle it?' He was speaking to O'Neil.

'Agent Dance'll wait here. I'll go to the front door, you go around back, if you would. If everything's clear, Agent Dance'll do the interrogation.'

Wait here. Her lips tightened.

'No warrants. He had a drunk and disorderly a few years ago, assault too, and he owns weapons, so we'll handle it cautiously.'

The two men headed up the sidewalk, past a row of dying bushes and healthy succulents, another testament to the water problems suffered by the Golden State.

O'Neil waited near Prescott's door, out of sight of the peephole and side window, which was curtained. Martinez, bulky and imposing, continued around the side of the complex to the rear.

O'Neil gave it three or four minutes, then knocked. 'Stanley Prescott? Sheriff's deputy. Please open the door.'

Once more.

He tried the door. It was unlocked. He glanced back at Dance. Held her eye for a moment. Then pushed inside.

No more than a minute later she heard two stunning gunshots, followed by one more.

CHAPTER 40

Antioch March was running.

Full out, a sprint. He realized he was still holding his Glock and slipped it into his pocket. He pulled his gym bag higher on his shoulder and kept going.

Ski mask? he wondered. No, that would definitely draw attention. Glancing back, he noticed that no one was in pursuit. Wouldn't last long. People would be calling in the incident all over the neighborhood. Tustin wasn't the sort of place where gunshots would be ignored.

And he knew one person who definitely was calling for backup at this moment: the woman he'd spotted outside the apartment, Kathryn Dance. She was here! She hadn't seen him, as she sprinted fast to the front door of Prescott's apartment, cell phone in hand. He might've gotten closer to her, tried for a shot. But she was, of course, armed and, he imagined, good with a gun.

Huntress . . .

And there were probably other deputies nearby. Maybe dozens. And, now, more on the way.

Running faster. Gasping.

For a moment he'd been mystified as to how they'd learned about pathetic Stanley Prescott. Then, of course: just like him, they had an autobot scanning the Internet for any references to the Solitude Creek or Bay View incidents, blog posts or clips on YouTube or Vidster or the other services. She'd received the same sort of alert he had and had sped there too. He wondered if she'd driven. Maybe they'd driven in tandem down from Monterey.

Sucking air into his lungs. March was in good shape, yes, but he'd never run this fast in his life.

The Chevy was a block away.

Go, go. Move!

He was upset that he hadn't had time to grab Prescott's computer. But his only thoughts were escape. It had been chaos in the apartment.

Two shots to forestall any pursuit. As the large man went down, clutching the wound, March began his sprint.

Now he saw the car. The Chevy.

Another look back. No one yet.

His feet slapping, the heavy gym bag bouncing on his back. There'd be bruises tomorrow.

If he lived till tomorrow.

His heart labored and the pain crept into his chest and jaw. I'm too young for a fucking heart attack. His mouth filled with saliva and he spat.

Finally he slowed and, chest heaving, walked casually to the stolen car. He gripped the door handle and pulled it open, looking around again. He fell into the driver's seat and pressed back against the headrest, catching his breath. A few people were nearby but no one apparently had seen the sprint. They didn't look his way. The strollers and dog walkers and joggers continued what they were doing.

Then he was tricking the ignition wires to start the vehicle. It chugged to life.

March signaled and looked over his shoulder. He pulled carefully into the street, no hurry, and started west, then turned south along surface streets.

He'd be back in Monterey in five hours. On the whole—

A flash caught his eye. He glanced up into the rearview mirror and saw two police cars, blue lights flaring, beginning to speed his way.

Maybe a coincidence.

No . . . They were after him. One of the goddamn stroller pushers or dog walkers *had* reported him.

March made a skidding turn, pressed the accelerator to the floor and pulled his Glock from his jacket pocket.

CHAPTER **41**

Dance ran into the shaded area behind Stan Prescott's apartment and dropped to her knees beside the two men.

Michael O'Neil knelt over Deputy Martinez, who lay on his back, conscious but bewildered, fearful.

Martinez gasped, 'I didn't see him. Where'd he come from?'

O'Neil said, 'Climbed out through the bathroom window.'

'It doesn't hurt. Why doesn't it hurt? Am I dying? I heard that if you don't hurt you might be dying. Am I?'

'You'll be fine,' O'Neil said, though he clearly wasn't sure.

One round had slammed into Martinez's chest, stopped by his body armor. The second had caught him high in the arm. The wound was a bleeder, brachial artery. O'Neil was applying direct pressure. Dance pulled a locking-blade knife from a holster on the deputy's belt, flicked it open and cut Martinez's sleeve off. This she tied around his shoulder. Using a small branch she'd found in the yard nearby, she tightened the cloth ring until the bleeding slowed.

The wounded deputy gasped, 'Got off one round. I missed. Shit.'

'I called it in,' O'Neil said, nodding toward Martinez's Motorola.

Backup would arrive soon enough. Dance supposed everybody on the block had told 911 about the gunfire, too. She could hear sirens, coming from several directions.

'Where is he?' O'Neil said.

'Didn't see him,' Dance replied. 'Prescott?'

'Dead. Hang in there, Martinez. You're doing fine. You a lefty?'

'No.'

'Good. You'll be pitching a softball with the kids in a few weeks.'

'I can lose the arm.'

Dance blinked.

'All we play is soccer.' He smiled.

'You'll be fine,' O'Neil repeated.

Sirens now in front of the apartment complex. Dance rose – O'Neil manned the tourniquet – and jogged to the front. She returned a moment later, with two officers and two medical techs with a gurney.

The latter two took over the treatment, and Dance and O'Neil stepped aside to let them work. They explained to the Orange County deputies what had happened.

One took a call on his mobile. He said a few words and disconnected. 'We have a lead. Man lives about three blocks from here saw a white male, tall, blond. He was running fast down the street. Got into a car and took off. The guy said it was suspicious. Got the tag. Black Chevy. Monterey, registered to a man his wife tells us is out of town for a week. Left it at Monterey Airport two days ago.'

'That's our unsub.'

'Cars in pursuit now. Headed north on Cumberland.'

'We'll want to go,' Dance said, glancing at O'Neil who had already called up a map on his phone.

Whatever the protocols of lending vehicles to out-of-county law, the deputy didn't hesitate. 'Take Martinez's cruiser. You'll need the sound and lights.'

CHAPTER 42

Antioch March was sure he couldn't beat the officers at the freeway game.

He knew this not from any research but from *COPS*, the TV show, and other programs about high-speed pursuits in the LA area. Nail strips, the PIT maneuver and a thousand troopers with nothing better to do than catch you. Escaping by car was the fantasy of bad movies and contrived thrillers.

The Chevy was fast, the suspension okay. And this time of mid-morning, the traffic was light. But he wasn't going to get much farther. And bailing out and running wasn't an option either.

Stay calm. Think.

What were his options?

The part of suburban Orange County he sped through now was residential. He could 'jack another car, he supposed, but that would buy time only.

He needed population. People, and a lot of them.

And then he saw it.

Ahead of him, less than a mile, March estimated. Perfect!

A glance in the mirror. The cars were in pursuit, sirens and lights. But they were holding back. As long as they could see him, there was no need to try anything dramatic and endanger lives.

March sped up and covered the distance in less than a minute. Then he executed a fast turn to the right, through a wooden gate and began easing through a crowd of people.

Glorious . . . Lots and lots of people.

He began to honk and flash his lights. The crowd moved out of the way, most of them frowning, though some probably suspecting a medical emergency or another legitimate reason for the car's frantic approach.

Then, the way clear, he aimed the Chevy toward a gate in a six-foot-high metal fence. He floored the accelerator.

With smoking tires the vehicle slammed into the mesh, airbag deploying and then shrinking fast. The impact swung the gate wide open. It also sent two people sprawling to the pavement. One was a man on stilts, dressed like a cowboy, and the other, gender indeterminate, wore a purple cat costume and held a matching parasol that read, 'Welcome, Guests!'

CHAPTER 43

Dance had brought the children there a few years ago.

Global Adventure World was a theme park in Orange County, a smaller-size version of nearby Universal and Disney. Filled with typical rides, animatronics, holographic wonders, theaters featuring live and filmed shows, costumed characters from the parent company's films and TV programs. Also concession stands galore, ready to help you gain back in one day those three pounds you struggled to lose before your vacation.

As they sped to the front gate, where a dozen police cars were parked, Dance said, 'Odd choice for a getaway.'

O'Neil nodded. Security in these parks was the best in the nation. Tall fences. High-quality CCTV cameras were disguised as rocks or branches or hidden in light poles and rides, and undercover guards, unarmed but equipped with high-tech com equipment, roamed the grounds, resembling typical tourists. And it wasn't as if the unsub had tried to slip inside subtly to get lost in the crowd. No, he'd made as explosive an entrance as possible, crashing into a front gate, injuring two costumed employees then leaping through the breach and sprinting inside.

A hundred park visitors were standing in a loose crowd, some distance from the car. Looking over the crumpled vehicle, faint smoke wafting above. Easily half were taking pictures and videos.

Dance and O'Neil met with the incident supervisor from the Orange County Sheriff's Office, Sergeant George Ralston, a tall, round African American.

O'Neil asked, 'Any sightings?'

Ralston replied, 'None. Hey, Herb. Whatta you know?'

Another man joined them. He was tall and solid and, Dance thought, a former cop. Introductions were made. He was the head of security for the park, Herbert Southern.

'No sign yet.'

Dance asked, 'Are you following him on security cameras?'

Southern said, 'We were – sent our people after him. But he disappeared. Got lost in a crowd waiting for the Tornado Alley ride. Named after the cartoon? One of the most popular here. Hundred people were queued up. Security went through the crowd but they couldn't find him.'

Dance supposed they weren't particularly aggressive. Didn't want to spook the patrons. She imagined the key word had been *subtle*. Make sure the customers feel safe.

'Description?' Dance asked.

Ralston offered, 'White male, over six feet. Longish blond hair, green baseball cap, unknown logo. Sunglasses. Dark pants, light shirt, beige jacket. Wool or cotton. Gym bag. White.'

Blond hair. Of course he'd dyed it after Foster's leak to the press.

'Your security get a close-up of his face?' O'Neil asked.

'No. Kept his head down.'

Dance said, 'Well, he's not wearing any of those clothes any more. If he didn't have a change of clothes with him in the bag, and I'll bet he did, he's bought a souvenir jacket and shorts and running shoes. And the gym bag is in a Global shopping bag right now. He can't change his hair color so he'll have a different sort of hat. Cowboy maybe.'

One of the big hits from the studio last year, a Wild West animation had won Oscars for something.

'And some people thought he was wearing gloves. Light-colored ones.'

'He was,' O'Neil said. 'For the fingerprints.'

'What's this about?' Southern asked.

'He's wanted in connection with a homicide in Monterey,' Dance explained.

'The roadhouse thing?' Ralston asked. 'And the other one, right? On the wire. Last night.'

'That's right,' O'Neil confirmed.

Dance added, 'We came down here to look for a possible witness. The unsub beat us to it. He was at the apartment in Tustin – he killed the wit just before we got there.'

O'Neil's face grew still. 'Your deputy was wounded. Martinez. He'll be okay, I heard, but he took a round in the arm.'

'Ricky.' Ralston nodded. 'Sure. I know him.'

The security man took a call, listened. 'Thanks.' He disconnected and said, 'Nothing. Well, we've got all the exits covered. This is the only park exit but there are service entrances with gates.'

Ralston said, 'I've got officers headed there now. He's armed. I don't want your boys and girls approaching,' he said to the security head.

'No. We'll work with your folks. Call 'em if they see anything. I've told 'em.'

Ralston added to Dance and O'Neil: 'I've got teams circling the outer perimeter. There's no way he'll get out unseen.'

Southern shook his head, looking over the growing crowd of park-goers. These were *his* people, those he was in charge of protecting. Dismayed, he said, 'Hostages?'

But, to Dance, a taking seemed unlikely. The strategy was that you negotiated only to buy time to talk reason into the hostage-taker or to get a sniper into position for a kill shot. You never gave him his freedom. This unsub was smart – no, brilliant. He'd guess that grabbing a hostage was a futile proposition.

She explained this, glancing at O'Neil, who agreed.

Then she said, 'Here's a thought. We don't have a solid facial ID but he doesn't know that. Can we—' Dance looked around and saw a business office nearby. 'Can we get a hundred printouts?'

'Of what?'

O'Neil was nodding. He got it. 'Of anything with a man's face. Distribute them to officers and security people. Walk through the park, just looking at them from time to time and scanning the crowd.'

'And keeping an eye out for anybody tall and blond, whatever he's wearing. Anybody who turns away or avoids eye contact, that'll be him.'

Southern walked to the office and a few minutes later came back with a stack of paper. He held one up. 'Message from our new manager. Just saying hi to all the employees, happy to be working with you, that sort of thing.'

'Excellent,' Dance said. It had a face shot of the man, which from more than three feet away could very well be a security camera image of their unsub.

Southern and Ralston divided the sheets to distribute to the officers and guards and sent them on their way.

Dance took one and handed another to O'Neil.

The sergeant said, 'You want radios?'

'Phone's fine for me.'

O'Neil nodded too and they both typed Ralston's number into theirs.

Then: 'And Agent Dance needs a weapon.'

'What?' she asked. 'No.'

'Kathryn,' O'Neil said firmly.

The Orange County sergeant looked at her curiously.

'I'm assigned to the Civil Division of the CBI, not authorized to carry,' she explained.

'Oh,' Ralston said. That settled it. It would be illegal to hand over a weapon.

O'Neil sighed and said, 'Then why don't you stay near the entrance and—'

Wait here . . .

But Dance was already walking through an open turnstile, right under the nose of a large and disturbingly realistic grizzly bear in a Viking helmet, glaring down at her angrily.

CHAPTER 44

Antioch March was, more or less, in the center of the theme park, near one of the rides – a roundy-round thing for younger kids, where they sat strapped into fiberglass leaves, like lettuce wraps from a Chinese restaurant. The ride would have made him puke.

Nearby was a jungle tour – where the guests were startled by the fierce appearances of oversized carnivores. They were the characters from a huge hit film, a blockbuster. March had seen it. The movie was gruesome and simple. But effective at shocking the audience. As gruesome and simple usually were.

The fake canyon he was now walking through reminded him of the Harrison Gorge. It was strikingly similar. He could smell the moist stone, the leaves, the loam, the dirt, the water. He could see, vividly, Todd. More than the colored leaves. Far more clearly than the leaves.

Focus here, he told himself. You need to get out, and soon. In an hour there'd be a thousand officers poking under every poly-vinyl triceratops and singing bush in the place.

And then he saw them.

Two young men, dressed like tourists but clearly security guards, were glancing at printouts and scanning the crowd.

Hell. Had they gotten an image of him as he sprinted through the gate? He'd seen the dozens of security cameras hidden in trees and in the fake rocks of the exhibits.

March was different in appearance now – he'd done the quick change right in the middle of a crowd waiting for some insane roller-coaster, Tornado Alley, not in a restroom, whose front doors he was sure would be monitored by cameras. But had they gotten a picture after he changed?

Out. You need to get out—

Then he turned and, to his shock, another officer was walking in March's direction, glancing at his sheet and then at people nearby – men, tall men. He was more than thirty feet away.

The pathway here was fairly narrow and his only option was to keep on walking, nonchalantly, with the crowd he found himself in. Or to turn and walk away, which would seem suspicious.

His pistol was in the shopping bag he carried. He didn't want to use it but he might have to. He maintained his stroll in the direction he'd started, glancing at a map he'd picked up of the park. He paused and asked a couple for directions. The husband glanced at the map, then pointed to a pathway nearby.

The officer continued in their direction, casually, too casually, looking around.

March chatted to the couple – a pleasant duo with southern accents – and felt the cop's eyes scan them, then look elsewhere. March glanced over his shoulder and saw the officer walking away, not reaching for radio or phone.

Ah, yes, trying to trick him. They didn't have a clue what he looked like. The sheet of paper was either blank or an advertising flier. They expected he'd see it, then turn and flee, give himself away.

Nice try.

He wondered if the ploy had been Kathryn Dance's. Betcha, he told the Get.

March turned to the husband, who had been so helpful, and said, 'That's odd.'

'What's that?'

'Over there. Uniformed policeman in the park. With the printout?'

The couple both squinted. The husband said, 'Oh, yeah. And there're some men over there too with fliers. See them?'

'Undercover security,' March said.

'What's that about?' the wife asked.

'Probably nothing. I just . . . I hope it's not terrorists or anything.'

'Terrorists,' the wife whispered.

'Yeah, did you hear that story on Fox? Or CNN? There were reports of a possible terrorist attack in LA.'

'No!'

'Rumors, that's all. You know how the police always say that and then nothing happens. Most of the time.' March shrugged. 'Anyway, have fun.'

A quarter-mile down the winding paths, Antioch March found another couple who looked promising. He walked up to them, brandishing the map and nodded.

'Hi, sorry to bother you.'

'Sure,' said the husband. He and his wife were with their three children, about eight through twelve.

March asked this man, too, for directions. Where a particular restaurant was. He was supposed to meet his family there. The couple consulted the map.

The husband said, 'There you be. Bit of a hike but you're going the right way.'

March knew where the restaurant was and that proceeding toward it would give him an excuse to stroll along with the couple.

'Thanks.' They all started to move in that direction.

'Come here every year,' the husband said, as they walked along. 'You?'

March said, 'No, first time. Josh was too young. He's five now.' They meandered past two uniformed officers consulting their advertising fliers. The men didn't even glance toward him.

'I hear you. Beth and Richard,' the wife said, nodding toward her brood, 'took them to Disney when they were three and four. Scared to death of Goofy. They weren't too sure about Tinker Bell either.'

March laughed.

The husband: 'Wait till they can appreciate it. Even the kids' tickets're ridiculous. Break the bank.'

As March walked with them, chatting about the rides, he looked around him. Into the trees, the rocks – well, fake rocks – the lampposts, the grounds. Studying carefully. He was learning some things about theme parks. In truth, he'd never been to one. That had been as far removed from his parents' idea of entertainment as one could imagine. Go downstairs, play video games, Andy. Go play.

Interesting, what he was noticing.

Then March said to the couple, 'There's another one.' A frown. 'What's that?'

'Another cop. Or whoever it is. With that sheet of paper. I've seen about ten of them.'

The wife: 'Yeah, I saw some too. What's that about?'

March: 'It's like they're looking for somebody.'

'Maybe somebody broke in without paying.'

'I don't think,' March said slowly, 'they'd go to that much trouble for somebody like that.'

'Probably not,' the wife said. 'Hm. Look, two more.'

'Odd,' the husband said.

'I hope it's nothing too serious,' March said. 'Maybe . . . Excuse me . . . A text.' He frowned as he looked at his phone, holding the screen so they couldn't see it. He pretended to read. 'Oh. Well.' He'd nearly said, 'Jesus.' But he'd noted the wife wore a cross and he needed his new friends to be with him. Completely with him.

'What?'

'That was from my wife. She's up at the restaurant. *She* just got a text from her mother. It was on the news. They're talking about some kind of a terrorist thing in the park.'

'Terrorists?' the wife blurted. 'Here?' Six or seven people turned toward them.

March didn't answer. He looked around, frowning. He began texting. The message was not, however, to the imaginary wife. It was going out to various blog sites, as well as legitimate news organizations, Twitter.

Rumors that terrorist rams front gate at Global Adventure Park. Suicide bomber loose in park.

March looked up. 'I've got to get to my wife and son.' But he looked at his phone again. 'No, no!'

'What is it, Mister?'

'My brother. In Seattle. He's watching CNN and, it looks like somebody rammed the front gate. Some guy with a backpack. He's here in the park!'

'Oh, Bill. Kids! Come here! Kids, stop, come over here.'

'What ride are Sandy and Dwight on?' the husband asked. Voice breathless.

'One of the roller-coasters, I don't know. Call them and let them know.'

A voice behind him. Another couple. 'Did you mention a terrorist or something? I saw all the police. With those handouts.'

March said, 'I just heard, somebody crashed into the front gate and got into the park with a bomb and a machine-gun.'

'Gun too?' the husband of the first couple asked.

March brandished his phone. 'My brother. That's the story. Suicide bomber, they're saying. He's armed. And there may be others.'

'Fuck no.'

The good Christian wife didn't correct her husband's language.

'Well, that's what he heard. CNN and Fox.'

Now all the adults were making calls or texting. Some seeking confirmation. But others would be spreading the lie.

One woman said desperately into her iPhone: 'Honey, where are you and the kids? Well, get out. Just leave now. There're terrorists in the park! . . . Yeah, we saw them too! If there are that many police something bad is happening. Get out! . . . I will. I'll be there as soon as I can.'

March turned.

Ah, fantastic! A tour guide was passing, holding aloft a folded umbrella so his group could see him. Sixty or so kids, from a private high school in Ohio, according to their matching T-shirts.

March began to speak to the leader but he didn't have to say anything. The wife of the first couple said, 'Did you hear anything about terrorists in the park? Do you know where it's safe?'

The guide blinked, lowered the umbrella. 'No, what do you mean?'

The word spread among the students like flames through dry California brush. 'Terrorists.' Some of the girls in the group started to cry. A few boys too. Phones emerged. Texts and voice calls.

Breathlessly March added, 'In the park. He rammed the gate. Suicide bomber. But he's got guns too. There may be more than one.' He held up his phone for proof.

Wonderful adolescent cries and screams.

The Get was pleased.

Now there was a good-size crowd in this area of the park. People uncertain about where to go. All talking, checking phones, making calls or texting. Gathering children.

And looking for someone with a backpack bomb, a suicide vest, a machine-gun, an RPG.

One man stormed up to a deputy holding one of the ID sheets and confronted him. Others joined in.

'The hell are you doing about it?'

'Why aren't there any announcements?'

'Do you even *know*?'

The officer was flustered. Looking around. Another patron, then two more accosted the cop, demanding why they were covering up an attack and not evacuating. Was it so the amusement park wouldn't lose face – or tax money the park would pay the county? The officer denied terrorists. But nobody was listening.

March stepped aside, watching the growing agitation of the crowd. Now about two hundred people were milling about, shouting at concession-stand employees, groundskeepers, costumed characters.

Time to ratchet things up, March decided. He called 911.

'Police and fire, what's your emergency?'

'My family's in Global Adventure. Somebody crashed into the gate and he's loose. It's a terrorist. They've seen him. He's got a bomb!'

The dispatcher: 'We have a report of an accident but there's no report of any terror—'

'Jesus, there he is! He's got a bomb! And a gun too.'

'Sir, what's your name and location? Please—'

He disconnected and walked farther around the perimeter of the park, making a circle back toward the entrance. Looking in the trees, looking behind the buildings.

He made another voice call, to a local news affiliate. 'Please, you have to help! We're in Global Adventure World, the park, you know. Orange County. We're hiding. My family's hiding but he's nearby. It's a terrorist. A man with a machine-gun. And another one with a bomb! Please . . . There's a terror attack going on! A suicide bomber. He crashed through the gate and he's in the park. I'm looking at him now.'

'Sir, please, what's your name?'

'Jesus, he's coming this way.'

He disconnected and continued to walk through the park, noting the increasing number of people on their phones, standing in protective clusters. Some were walking off the paths and into the bushes, peering out – as if in a scene from one of the amusement-park parent company's movies: the innocent about to be devoured by aliens.

March hurried along the pathway. He was about to play the scenario all over again, walking up to another family and stabbing them with panic, when the husband gripped March's arm.

'Hey!'

Wide-eyed, the man said, 'Mister, you have family here?'

'Yeah, they're over at Tornado Alley. Why?'

'There're terrorists in the park. A half-dozen. They're going to blow up some of the rides.'

The wife was sobbing.

'No!' March said. He looked at his phone. 'Hell, you're right. It's my wife. Texting. CNN has the story. Terror alert. Suicide bomber in the park.'

'That's why the police. They're all over the place.'

'And they're not saying anything!' March snapped.

He'd thought he'd have to spread the rumor a half-dozen more times but, nope, it wasn't necessary. The stories buzzed like locusts. One bomber, a dozen. Machine-guns. Al Qaeda. ISIS. Pakistan. Syria.

'What're we going to do? How do we get out?'

March shouted, 'There's only one way I know about. The front entrance. They don't have emergency exits, I heard.'

'No exits? Didn't they think something like this could happen?'

'We're going to be trapped here!'

March waved his arm. 'No, we're not. Let's go!'

The crowd was now moving in the general direction of the park entrance. What had started as a cluster of a hundred was swelling to three, four, five times that number. March walked with them for a ways, then stepped off the path into the bushes and let skittish cattle continue their quickening drive to what they hoped was safety.

CHAPTER 45

What's going on? Dance wondered.

She and O'Neil were back at the Global Adventure entrance, having heard reports that for some reason hundreds – no, thousands of park guests were moving in this direction. The agent and detective were outside the entrance turnstiles and fence.

The patrons clustering on the other side, waiting to exit, were edgy, anxious. Some exchanged harsh words. A shoving match or two broke out when people cut into the line ahead of the others to leave. The crush could have been relieved if the wide gate was functioning but the unsub's steamy Chevy still blocked it.

Dance thought of the Liverpool fans clustering outside Hillsborough Stadium, the disaster her father had told her about.

Twenty-five years ago. I still have nightmares . . .

O'Neil and Dance walked up to the head of park security and Sergeant Ralston.

Dance asked, 'What is all this?'

Both Herb Southern and Ralston were on their phones. Ralston said, 'Jesus.' Whatever he'd learned was very troubling.

Southern disconnected.

'There's panicking inside. A couple guests beat up one of my security guards. I don't know why.'

Ralston hung up too. 'Okay, this is a problem. We're getting calls from everybody – the Sheriff's Office, media, FBI, Homeland. Reports terrorists're in the park. Machine-guns. Suicide vests. Fucking rumors but nine one one's flooded, circuits're almost overloaded.'

Dance muttered, 'He's doing it.'

'Your perp?'

She nodded.

O'Neil said, 'All it took was him telling a few people the rumor, one news report, a few blog posts, and it's spread like fire.'

'It's what he does. He starts panics. And he's real good at it.'

O'Neil said, 'He's going to try to get out this way, thinking we can't check everybody.'

'That's pretty damn close to true,' Sergeant Ralston muttered.

Herb Southern walked to the turnstiles, on the other side of which a crowd thirty or forty deep jostled to get out. 'There's no emergency!' he shouted to the crowd. 'You're safe. You can stay in the park. Don't push. Don't push!'

Everyone ignored him.

Dance asked, 'What's the procedure if it *were* a terror attack?'

'Lockdown. Get everybody off the rides and have them wait where security tells them. We have designated places of cover from gunmen and bad weather, fire.'

'Evacuation?'

'Not a mass evacuation,' Southern said, staring at the growing sea of patrons. 'Ma'am, today's a slow day but we've still got thirteen thousand souls in the park at this moment. If they all head out together – well, you can imagine.'

The crowd was swelling as people from inside the park joined the other exiting patrons in bottlenecks between two gift shops, which jutted into the entrance walkway. Every face seemed terrified.

At the turnstiles serious fights were starting to break out and there were more and more instances of people shoving others aside and jumping the barriers, which led to more panic. The crowd was now fifty or sixty deep. And growing. One woman screamed as she was jammed against a fence. Her wrist had broken. Two guards got to her and managed to calm that cluster of patrons. But as soon as they did another fight broke out, more pushing, more screams. Dance watched two other patrons fall. They were trampled before guards got them to their feet. The workers' faces were as alarmed as their guests'.

Dance said, 'It's on the borderline of manageable. We'll be okay as long as nothing more sets them—'

From the distance came a half-dozen gunshots.

'Hell,' she muttered.

Then, over the loudspeaker: '*Emergency evacuation. All guests. There are terrorists in the park. Suicide bomber in the park. This is not a drill. Everyone evacuate immediately!*'

'That's not procedure!' Southern snapped, his face in shock.

'*All guests, this is an emergency. Evacuate at once. There is a suicide bomber in the park.*'

'It's him. He got into the security command post somehow.'

O'Neil snapped: 'Get a team there now!'

Ralston lifted his radio, made a call.

The security man was on his phone. 'Derek, what's going on? . . . Is he in the CP? . . . Okay, find out. Cut the power to the PA system.'

'*Evacuate! Evacuate immediately. We have shooting victims! If you've been wounded, seek cover immediately. Medical teams are on the way!*'

Southern explained to Dance and O'Neil, 'We've got a network of underground tunnels – where our security office is. We take sick guests out that way, pickpockets, people're drunk. It's the command post too. He's in there. He's going to try to get out through the tunnels. There's an exit to a parking lot on the far edge of the property . . . Oh, Jesus . . . Look!'

A wave of a thousand, two thousand people was now charging the exit.

'Get back, it's all right!' the security head yelled to them. Pointless, as before.

Parents had abandoned strollers and were carrying their screaming children. The people waiting at the turnstiles turned back and saw the tide approaching.

The screams rose and those behind the patrons in front began scrabbling over the others to get to the turnstiles. Some began running through the broken gate, climbing over the unsub's Chevy. One man fell on his back and lay still.

Dance, O'Neil and Southern ran forward, holding their palms up to stanch the flow of human bodies, shouting that there was no attack.

But the crowd had no rational mind. Safety, escape – those were the only things that mattered.

A creature . . . not human . . .

'They're going to be crushed,' Dance said.

O'Neil: 'The gate. We have to get it open. Now!'

He, Ralston and a half-dozen park workers ran to the unsub's car and, by using pure muscle, pulled it back – five feet, ten, twenty. They then grabbed the gate and swung it open. It screeched on the concrete.

O'Neil leaped aside as the tide, twenty bodies wide, swarmed through the open space. Others continued to push through or leap over the turnstiles.

A mother, holding a young child of about four, staggered through the gate, then turned toward an empty part of the parking lot and stumbled in that direction. Dance noticed that her arm was badly broken. She got about ten steps toward a bench, then eased her daughter to the asphalt and collapsed. Dance ran to help.

She had just gotten to the woman when there was a shattering of glass and dozens of people leaped onto the sidewalk. They'd broken a large window of one of the gift shops and were fleeing out of the park through the gap. This herd soon swelled to several hundred.

They were bearing down on Dance, the woman and her child. Even though they were out of the park, panic had seized them and they were sprinting madly.

'Get up!' Dance cried to the groggy mother, scooping up the child by the waist. The crowd was forty feet away, thirty.

The woman suddenly gripped Dance's collar. Unbalanced by her awkward crouch, the agent fell backward. She landed hard, still clasping the child. Stunned, she looked up to see a wall of a hundred patrons stampeding directly for them. To judge from their feral eyes, not a single one even saw them, let alone had any intention of turning aside.

CHAPTER 46

As a matter of pride, Antioch March would have preferred to start the panic without firing any shots.

What a lovely idea. Words alone causing so much destruction and chaos. In fact, he would have preferred to start the madness by merely asking questions, not using fake texts from a fake wife.

'Who do you think those guards are looking for?'

'Have you heard anything in the news about any terrorist threats here?'

Subtlety, finesse. Let the victims use their own imagination.

Stampedes, he'd learned, can begin with nothing more than a hint, as insubstantial as a moth's wing, that you won't get what you desire. Or that what you fear will destroy you. Thanks, Dad . . . Desire and fear were the keys to success in sales, his father had told him.

March was presently hiding in the trunk of a Nissan Altima, which was still parked in one of the garages at Global Adventure World. He was quite hot in the ski mask and cloth gloves.

Getting out of the park itself had been relatively easy, thanks to the massive herd of gazelle fleeing the terrorist lion. He'd even caught a fast glimpse of his beloved Kathryn, staring with wide eyes at the surging crowd, not seeing him. But the rest of his getaway – escaping from the area – was more of a problem. As the crowd surged out, March had diverted into the garage, where he began looking for a certain type of car. Finally he found what he sought: a rental (with a big trunk) that had a hotel valet ticket, good for three more days, on the dash. That meant the family had already checked in and wasn't leaving Orange County for a while; therefore, no luggage in the trunk in the immediate future. Sure, maybe Billy or Suzy had bought some souvenirs but, if so, they'd probably lost them in the crush.

He'd jimmied the door, popped the trunk – found it empty, good. Then climbed in, along with the shopping bag containing his gym bag and gun, and closed it. True, he might have to shoot his way out of this, if the driver and family did decide to toss something back here. But he didn't have a lot of options.

Would there be roadblocks, would they open the trunk?

Again, no choice.

He assessed the situation. He'd lost one of the burner phones on the sprint to the Chevy in Tustin, which'd have some information on it he would rather they didn't have but nothing critical. No prints. He'd worn gloves whenever he used the unit. He wished he'd gotten Prescott's computer. But a fast look had revealed nothing obviously incriminating on the laptop. No, no direct leads to him. Even brilliant Kathryn Dance would be hard pressed to connect those dots.

Now, an hour after the panic, he heard the grit of footsteps approach and the click of the locks. He gripped the gun. But the trunk didn't pop. Then doors opening and closing. Somber voices. Adults. A third door closed. A teenage boy, he deduced from the kid's tone.

The engine started and they were driving, but very stop-and-go; the lines to exit would be long, of course. The car radio was on but he couldn't hear much. Man, it was hot. He hoped he didn't faint before the family got to their destination.

More conversation. He could discern the woman's, though not the man's, voice. A matter of pitch, maybe.

'Police there. A roadblock.'

The man muttered something angrily. Probably about the delay, the congestion.

March wiped sweat from his eyes and gripped his pistol.

The car squealed to a stop.

He could hear an indistinct voice from outside, asking questions. A female voice. Was it Kathryn Dance's?

No, these were line officers. Not the Great Strategist, the woman so intent on capturing him . . . and the Get.

Wiping sweat.

Silence.

Trunk inspection? Shoot the cop, commandeer the car and drive like hell.

No option.

Footsteps.

But then the car started forward again. The radio grew louder. The boy said he was hungry. The man – father, surely – muttered something unintelligible. The mother said, 'At the hotel.'

After forty minutes they made several turns and stopped. The radio went silent and the car was put in park. Doors opened and closed.

The valet took charge of the car and drove for five minutes, up a series of ramps. Then he parked. Closed the door, locked it and left.

March gave it five minutes and, when he heard nothing outside, pulled the emergency release cord, climbed out as quickly as he could and looked around the garage.

Empty. And no CCTV.

He walked back and forth, stumbling like a drunk, to revive the circulation in his legs. Once, he had to sit down and lower his head to his shaking knees.

Then on his feet again and into the hotel itself. A Hyatt. He went into the restroom in the lobby and examined himself in the mirror. He didn't look too bad. The glistening head, which he'd shaved the minute he'd heard his description on the radio several days ago, showed a bit of stubble. Like Walter White on *Breaking Bad*. He opened the Global Adventure shopping bag and pulled out his gym satchel. From this he retrieved the blond wig, which he'd been wearing since the shaving, at least when he was out in public.

Porn star meets Mad Men . . .

March pitched into the trash the wig, baseball cap and the worker's jacket he'd worn at Stan Prescott's apartment and when he'd first broken into the theme park. (He'd stripped them off as he'd stood in the interminable queue near the Tornado Alley roller-coaster, and donned a souvenir jacket that he'd bought. Nobody noticed the quick change: everyone was watching the flamboyant ride, racing overhead.)

He now dumped the Global jacket and shopping bag, too.

Then outside into the lobby. He got a look at the TV in the bar, reporting on the event at the theme park. No pictures of him, no artist's rendering, no reference to Solitude Creek.

In the gift shop he bought a windbreaker, sunglasses and a tote – into which went his gym bag.

He took a cab to a downtown Hertz office to rent a car. There he told the clerk he'd be dropping off the rental in San Diego in three days – the police could be looking for rentals to the Monterey area. He'd call later to extend the rental and ultimately switch the drop-off to somewhere in Central California. A flight might be safer but he had only the one pistol: he couldn't afford to leave it here – there was no way of getting a new weapon in California.

And he knew he'd need it before the week was out.

With his mind racing – Kathryn Dance figured prominently – March took surface streets and local roads on a mazelike route for miles, meandering north, until he figured it was safe to hop on the Ventura Freeway, the 101.

North. He'd be back on the Peninsula in five hours.

CHAPTER 47

Simple.

But effective.

Dance and O'Neil were at the front entrance to Global Adventure World, near the shattered gate. The unsub's stolen Chevy sat nearby; under it, oil and coolant pooled. The panic had stopped and several thousand people meandered about in the front area of the park, not sure what to do.

Three dozen had been injured, none critically. Opening the two gates – the main and the disabled entrances – had largely relieved the pressure of the masses.

Dance had nearly been trampled but the security chief, Herb Southern, had saved her, the woman who'd fallen and her daughter. He'd driven a golf cart directly between them and the surging mass.

'Go on,' Dance now said to Southern and Sergeant Ralston. They continued explaining to the Monterey law enforcers what had happened.

Simple, effective.

No, the unsub hadn't escaped through the security tunnels lacing the theme park. He hadn't even given the fake terrorist announcement. Apparently he'd noticed entrances to the tunnels, as well as an extensive PA system, speakers hidden in trees and landscaping. He'd pulled on a ski mask and waylaid one of the security guards – easily spotted because he was carrying one of the fake ID fliers.

The guard – his name was Bob – was present there too. He continued, 'Then he asked about the tunnels. I didn't want to tell him but he had the gun. He was right beside me. It was . . . terrible.'

Dance said, 'I'm sure it was. Of course.'

Bob, miserable, continued in a choked voice: 'He took my wallet and called somebody. Gave my address. Told his friend to go there and keep an eye on my family. I had to do exactly what he told me.'

Ralston added to Dance and O'Neil, 'We've got somebody on the house already.'

O'Neil said, 'There's no evidence anybody's working with him. I think that was a sham.'

'I didn't want to help,' the shaken employee said.

'It's all right, Bob,' Southern said, 'There was a panic and some injuries 'cause of it but nobody badly hurt. You did what you had to. I would've done the same thing.'

'I was supposed to go down in the tunnel and give it five minutes, then he'd fire the gun. He promised me he wasn't going to shoot anybody. He was just doing it to escape. If I thought he was going to shoot anybody, really was, I wouldn't've done it. I—'

'It's okay, Bob.'

The man swallowed. 'And I did what he wanted. I grabbed the microphone and said what I was supposed to.'

Dance shook her head, looking over the milling crowd, now easily three thousand people. As at Solitude Creek, in the snap of a finger they'd calmed, once they were out of the park and police on loudspeakers had reassured them there were no terrorists.

Their unsub had walked right out in the midst of escaping attendees. He didn't even need a disguise. He could've had a black hood on and been carrying a machine-gun and nobody would've spotted him.

O'Neil took a call. 'That's right . . . Yes . . . They're set up?' He thanked the caller and disconnected. He looked at the others. 'Highway Patrol. All the roadblocks're up. They worked fast. Not every exit route, but the main ones. And random stops, traffic headed away from the park.'

Officers were checking out the bus lines too. And taxis.

No sign of a six-foot-plus man, solid build, blond hair, holding a white gym bag (or Global Adventure World shopping bag *holding* a gym bag).

Finally the staff who'd been manning the security video reported that there was nothing on any of the many minutes of tape that might help them. The crowds had been too thick.

Dance looked over the masses and didn't even bother canvassing.

O'Neil said, 'Back to Prescott's?'

'Sure.'

In a half-hour they were there – the traffic was, of course, thick as honey; even the lights and siren in Deputy Martinez's cruiser couldn't speed them along very much. They arrived just as the crime-scene crew was finishing up.

A tech said, 'Your man knew what he was doing. Cloth gloves.'

'I know.'

'Didn't find much.'

Looking down at Prescott, on his back, suffocated with duct tape. The image was stark and clear: he was under a bright floor lamp.

O'Neil asked, 'Why was he killed?'

Dance speculated, 'Something in that picture of Solitude Creek he included in the post? Clues?'

The rant had been taken down but O'Neil had made a copy earlier. They looked it over again, carefully. The Vidster post was a video but the image from Solitude Creek was a still. It was a news photo, taken of the aftermath of the tragedy, when the bodies had been removed from the floor, which was covered with litter, purses, scraps of clothing, overturned furniture.

Neither of the officers could see anything revealing.

O'Neil offered, 'Maybe our unsub just didn't want any attention drawn to Solitude Creek.'

Dance nodded. 'It got him noted by the feds.'

Both the CBI and MCSO had received calls from Homeland Security, since the incident was linked to potential terrorism, though agents reviewed the matter and decided it wasn't terrorist-related – wasn't even a federal crime.

'That could be.' She examined the body again, seeing the face, clear under the bright lamp. The look of horror, eyes wide. She supposed it would have taken him four or five minutes to die. The unsub'd used this means of death for the quiet, she guessed.

An officer appeared in the doorway. He nodded to those inside and said, 'Detective O'Neil?'

'Yes?'

'We did a canvass of the neighborhood, following the route your unsub escaped down. And found this.' He held up a plastic evidence bag containing a Nokia phone. 'Guy walking a dog said he saw it fall out of the perp's pocket when he was running to the Chevy, the getaway vehicle.'

Dance and O'Neil shared a look. Guardedly optimistic. The phone was clearly a prepaid burner – they were invariably cheap, like this model. So it was unlikely they could trace it back to the man. But it might have helpful information inside.

'Can we get the prints from the man who found it?'

The uniform smiled. 'He never touched it. He used a plastic bag. He watches all the crime-scene shows, he said.'

Dance took the phone and, through the plastic, tried the keys. 'Passcode protected. Well, one way or the other, we'll get inside.' She said to the Orange County detective, 'I'll want to take his computer and the unsub's phone into custody. You all right with that?'

'Sure.'

O'Neil couldn't have done this, not without Orange County's okay, since the crime had occurred there and Monterey had no jurisdiction. The CBI, however, trumped county public-safety departments and she could take the evidence. Her intention, however, was not to deliver the phone and victim's computer to the CBI's small forensic department – they actually farmed out physical-evidence work to the Monterey lab most of the time – but to have Jon Boling analyze them. The former wonder boy in Silicon Valley, occasionally consulted for the CBI, FBI and other law-enforcement groups that needed IT or computer assistance. Computer forensic science is an art and he was good at it.

A woman officer with Crime Scene handed the computer over to Dance, who signed a chain-of-custody card for it and the phone. She stepped outside and slipped the plastic bags into her suitcase.

They arranged with the lead detective for the reports from

there and the theme park to be sent to Monterey. In silence they walked to the rental car and headed for the airport. After a day like that, the idea of flying commercial, with the many hassles, had no appeal whatsoever; Dance reminded herself to do something nice for Charles Overby, thanking him for the pricey state jet.

Maybe she'd bake him a cake.

CHAPTER 48

Dance and O'Neil's flight from John Wayne Airport in Orange County to Monterey landed at six. A young uniformed officer with the Monterey County Sheriff's Office greeted them.

Dance knew him well. Gabriel Rivera was a young deputy who worked frequently with O'Neil. The round, cheerful man, with a well-tended mustache that rivaled Steve Foster's, wanted to be a detective, like his mentor, and was known for putting in long hours.

'Detective, Agent Dance.'

She shook his hand.

'I've got the preliminary from the scene in Santa Cruz. Otto Grant.'

Dance recalled O'Neil had received the phone call about the discovery of a body in the Bay.

Worse ways to die than going to sleep in the Bay . . .

He handed O'Neil a manila envelope and the detective extracted the contents, copies of handwritten notes and some photos.

Dance glanced at the crime-scene photos. Hard to make an ID from them alone: he'd been in the water for some time and, though the chill would otherwise preserve flesh, critters had been dining. Much of the remains had been reduced to bone.

'I haven't contacted the family yet,' Rivera said. 'We've got a DNA sample from them and the lab's running it now. Should be about twenty-four hours.' A nod at a close-up of the corpse's hands. 'No fingerprints, of course.'

O'Neil squinted at one image. 'Not Grant.'

'It's—'

'Not him. Grant had had a knee replacement. Two of 'em. That man's got both knees intact. Maybe homeless, maybe a drifter, fell asleep on the beach and got washed out to sea. Anyway, it's not him.'

'Okay, Detective. I'll let everybody know.'

'Oh, Gabriel?'

'Yessir?'

'Saves time to learn everything you can about whoever you're searching for.'

'I'll remember that, sir.' The deputy took the envelope back and returned to his squad car.

Dance and O'Neil walked to short-term parking and collected his vehicle. The fog was back, and the evening promised chill.

'Solitude Creek . . . Bay View . . . What on earth is he up to?' Dance mused.

O'Neil remained silent. A mood seemed to be on him. Understandable, of course: a deputy had been shot, a witness killed and their suspect had escaped. Yet she sensed there was something else on O'Neil's mind.

His window was down and cold air streamed into the car. She thought about asking him to roll it up but chose not to, for some reason. She turned the heater up higher.

Well, if he wanted to talk, fine; it wasn't her role to pry anything out of him, unlike with her daughter. She pulled out her phone to call Boling but somehow the idea of having a cheerful conversation with him didn't appeal; it also seemed a bit passive-aggressive – payback for O'Neil's mood. She texted, instead, saying she'd be home soon.

Almost immediately her phone dinged with a reply. *Miss you. WDYWFD?*

She answered back that leftovers were good, and asked about the kids.

He sent another, saying Maggie was Skyping with Bethany and Carrie (*Secrets Club teleconference*), Wes was out with Donnie, biking (*back @ 7, promised*).

She typed: *C U soon. XO*

Dance did make a voice call – to Charles Overby. 'You're on speaker with me and Michael,' she told him.

Her boss called, 'Michael, hello.'

'Charles.'

She had, of course, called in from time to time to let him know how the incident in Orange County was proceeding. She now said, 'No indication that Prescott was anything more than an oddball – a redneck, if they have rednecks in Orange County – stirring up anti-Islamic sentiment. Our office down there'll canvass his friends and family, coworkers but I'm sure that the profile'll be just that. We've got custody of his computer and a phone the unsub dropped. I'd like to have Jon Boling crack the passcodes and take a peek.'

'That's good. Sure. And, if I recall, he's not very expensive.'

Dance let that go.

Overby added, 'Any thoughts about why our boy would travel all that way to kill him?'

O'Neil explained the theory that Prescott had brought unwanted federal scrutiny to the incident with the 'terrorist' comments. 'That's all we can think of.'

They arranged a meeting tomorrow in Overby's office, to review the crime-scene reports from the sheriff's office in Orange County.

Dance clicked the phone off. Then made another call.

'Hey, boss. You back from La-La Land?'

'Just landed,' she told TJ Scanlon. 'Eleven tomorrow in Overby's office. On Solitude Creek and Bay View.'

'Be there with bells on.'

She asked, 'And Serrano? The second lead? What's the name again?'

'Ah, Señorita Alonzo. Serrano's former squeeze. Moss Landing tomorrow at nine? Good for you?'

'Yep. I'll coordinate with Al.'

'Foster'll be out. Steve Two and Jimmy'll be there.'

'Thanks. See you tomorrow.'

They disconnected.

Silence for some moments.

'Look out,' she said sharply, pointing ahead.

Two flashes of yellow, close-set eyes.

'I got it,' he said, braking.

They cruised past the deer as it debated who would win the collision.

O'Neil hadn't, however, seen the creature at first. He'd been distracted. Mind elsewhere.

More silence. His body language revealed tension.

Another five minutes. Finally she'd had enough. She was going to pry a confession out of him, but just at that moment his phone rang. He unholstered it and hit accept. He listened, grim. 'Where?'

Her heart sank. Had the unsub returned so quickly and committed yet another mass attack?

'I'm headed in that direction now. I can be there in fifteen.'

He disconnected.

'Another one?'

'Not our unsub. A hate crime again.' He sighed, shaking his head.

'Anybody in custody?'

'No, a homeowner found his wall graffitied. I'm going to swing by and poke around the neighborhood. It's in Pacific Grove, not far from you. I'll take you home first.'

'No, I'll go with you.'

'You sure?'

'Yes.'

He hit the flasher lights and sped up, though minding the slippery road.

She asked, 'You think there's a chance you'll find the perp there?'

'He can't be too far away. The graffiti? The paint's still wet.'

CHAPTER 49

'Well, there you have it. Welcome to Berlin, nineteen thirty-eight.'

Dance and O'Neil were standing next to David Goldschmidt, who ran one of the nicer furniture stores downtown. The slim, balding man was bundled into a navy watch coat and wore jeans. His sockless feet were in Topsiders. They were in his side yard.

Goldschmidt was a bit of a celebrity in the area: the *Monterey Herald* had run an article on him last week. When Hamas had begun firing missiles from Gaza into Israel not long ago he'd volunteered to help. At forty, he was too old to serve in the Israeli army – the age limit was twenty-three – but he had spent several months helping with medical and provisions support. However, she recalled that, according to the article, while on a kibbutz outside Tel Aviv years before, Goldschmidt had served in combat.

The publicity was probably why he'd been targeted.

And what a cruel attack it was.

On the side of his beautiful Victorian house there was a swastika in bright red paint and below it: 'Die Jew.'

The paint dripped from the symbol and words like blood from deep wounds.

The three stood in his side yard surrounded by a foggy dusk, the air fragrant with mulch from the Goldschmidts' beautiful garden.

'In all my years,' he muttered.

'Did you catch a glimpse of anyone?'

'No, I didn't know about it until I heard the shout from across the street – ah, here.'

A woman, mid-fifties, in jeans and a leather jacket, approached. 'Dave, I'm so sorry. Hello.'

O'Neil and Dance introduced themselves.

'I'm Sara Peabody. I saw them. I'm the one who called the

police. I shouted. I guess I shouldn't have. I should've just called you first. Maybe they'd be in jail now. But I just, you know, lost it.'

'Them?' O'Neil asked.

'Two, that's right. I was looking through the trees there, see? I didn't have a good view. So, young, old? Male, female? I couldn't say. I'd guess men, wouldn't you think?'

O'Neil said, 'Generally that's the case in hate crimes. But not always.'

'One stood guard, it looked like, and the other jumped over the fence and sprayed those terrible things. The other one, the guard, he took pictures or a video of the first. Like a souvenir. Disgusting.'

Goldschmidt sighed.

Dance asked, 'Have you been threatened recently by anyone?'

'No, no. I don't think it's personal. This's got to be part of what's going on, don't you think? The black churches, that gay center?'

O'Neil: 'I'd say so, yes. The handwriting looks similar to the other attacks, spray paint in red. Looks like the same color.'

'Well, I want it gone. Can you take pictures and samples of the paint or whatever you want to do? I'm painting over it tonight. My wife's back from Seattle tomorrow morning. I will not let her see this.'

'Sure,' O'Neil told him. 'We'll get our crime-scene people here in the next hour. They'll be fast.' He looked around. 'I'll canvass the neighbors now.'

'Brother. After all these years,' Goldschmidt muttered angrily. 'Sometimes I think we're not making any progress at all.' Dance looked him over, his body language of defiance, determination, his still eyes as he took in the obscene symbol and words.

O'Neil asked Dance if she'd take his and the neighbor's statements.

'Sure.'

He wandered up the street to interview other neighbors who might have seen the vandalism.

Dance looked over the yard. No footsteps in the grass, of course. Maybe the CS team could pull a print from the fence the perp had vaulted but that would be a long shot. Ah, but a moment of hope. Nestled under the eaves was a video security camera.

But Goldschmidt shook his head. 'It's on but it doesn't record. The monitor's in the bedroom and I was in the den when they were here. We only use it after we're in bed. In case there's a noise.'

Dance texted Boling that she'd be a bit later than she'd planned. He replied that Maggie was still Skyping and Wes had not returned yet – but he had ten minutes until the promised deadline. Leftovers were heating.

Michael O'Neil was up the street and Dance had nothing more to do there. She started her own canvass, going the other way. The houses had no view of Goldschmidt's but the vandals might have parked in front of one. Those who were home, however, had seen nothing and Dance spotted no deception. As horrific as vandalism is, there's not much risk of physical assault and witnesses are more eager to come forward than if they've seen a murder, rape or assault.

Two more houses, dark and unoccupied.

She was about to return to the crime scene when she noticed one more house – it was on the other side of a city park, which was a known migration stop for monarch butterflies. The tree-filled park was about two acres in size.

The house bordered Asilomar, the conference area, and beyond that was the coastal park at Spanish Bay. It also overlooked a sandy shoulder, a perfect place for the perps to leave their car and hike through the park to get to Goldschmidt's. Maybe these homeowners had seen them.

She waded into the park now, moving slowly: the place hadn't been trimmed recently – budget issues, she supposed – and underbrush might trip her.

Any risk? she wondered, pausing. No. The perps would have headed off as soon as they'd finished. If not, surely they'd done so when they'd seen the blue-and-white flashing lights on O'Neil's car.

She started through the dark preserve once more.

CHAPTER 50

'Dude, somebody's coming. I'm like sure.'

Wolverine was saying this.

'Sssh.' Darth waved him quiet.

'Let's just go. Yo.'

Darth ignored him and scanned the dusk-lit scene. The two boys remained motionless, still as snipers, in the large backyard of the house that the owners, weird, had named Junipero Manor or something, nestled in mossy trees like something out of *The Hobbit*, all bent and gnarly. A house with a name. Weird.

The ocean was not far away and Darth could hear the water smashing on the rocks, the seals, gulls. Good. It covered up the noise of their movement.

'I'm saying, we should book.' Wolverine was in a navy jacket. Baseball cap, black, backward. Darth was wearing jeans, a black shirt and hoodie. Darth liked to think of him and his friend by their code names when they were out fucking up somebody's house or a church. Felt like soldiers, felt like superheroes.

They were both slim, young. Darth was bigger, older by a year and change, though they were in the same grade. The two hid behind a bush that smelled of pee, and his knees felt moisture from the fog-damp sand.

'Dude?' Wolverine whispered more desperately. 'Now! Let's history, man. We gotta get out of here.'

Darth shifted. And: *clink, clink.*

'Jesus, quiet!'

Darth set the backpack down carefully and rearranged the cans of red spray paint, put a T-shirt between them. Hoisted the canvas satchel once more.

'Really, man.' Wolverine wasn't exactly living up to his nickname. But Darth was patient with his friend. The bitch got freaked a lot. And, church, Darth was a little tweaked at the moment too, with some asshole prowling around, getting closer.

But he was leader of the crew and he now commanded, 'Chill.'

Wolverine nodded.

Okay, he was a pussy but he also was the one who'd spotted somebody coming through the park. Sure, they ought to leave. Darth didn't have any hassle with that idea. But they fucking couldn't because the fucking Jew had found the bikes and rolled them into his garage. Just after they'd tagged the wall, and got over the fence out of the yard, some bitch from across the street had come out and started screaming, stop, what're you doing, how hateful and who did they think they were . . .

Blah, blah . . .

They didn't want to get seen so they'd run in this direction and hidden in some bushes, watching Goldshit come out, spot the bikes, cart them away and – fucker – throw them into the garage.

Then the flashing lights.

And now the footsteps.

Who? Goldshit? The woman who'd snitched?

But why would they be here? No, it probably was a cop. And if so they'd be armed with a Taser and a Glock and one of those big fucking flashlights that could cave your head in. When Darth had been in juvie, he'd celled with a kid whose head'd been caved in by one of those.

Footsteps getting closer but still half a basketball court away.

'Why're we waiting?'

The why was something Darth didn't have the time – or the inclination – to explain: that if Darth's dad found out his bike was gone, out would come the branch and Darth'd get bloody.

Closer. The probably cop was moving slow but headed in their exact direction.

Darth nodded toward a garden shack at the back of Junipero Manor.

They slipped closer to the lopsided structure and crouched between it and a tangled bush. The cop didn't have a flashlight out. Just was walking slowly, stopping, listening. Playing it cautious, as if the dudes he was after were stone cold. Anybody who'd sneak up to a house and write, *Die Jew* with a fat-ass swastika on it, probably was.

And, yeah, Darth thought, guess what? We are.

Totally stone cold . . .

Darth whispered, 'Got an idea. I'm going to lead 'em off.'

'But you'll . . . What're you gonna do?'

'I'll head that way into the park, make some noise or something and then you can run.'

'Yeah? What'll happen to you?'

'Nobody can touch me,' Darth whispered, mouth close to ear. 'Track and field, remember? I'll be fine.' Darth's father had made sure he'd gotten trophies in every event he could in T and F (it'd be the branch if he didn't).

'You cool?'

'Yeah.' His friend's green eyes looked uncertain.

'Okay, just stay here and . . . give me sixty seconds to get into position. When you count sixty, run – that way. Asilomar. And just keep going. They'll start after you but I'll make a shitload of noise and lead 'em off.'

'Okay. Sixty.'

Then Darth gave a smile. 'Yo. We did good tonight.'

A nod. A fist bump.

'Start counting.' Darth moved as quietly as he could into the woods away from the shed. As he did so he looked around. Ah, there, excellent. He found a perfect weapon. A rock about ten inches long, sharp at one end. He picked it up and hefted it. Good, good.

Darth had no intention of running. He was pissed off that they'd been pushed into a corner and pissed that the Jew had taken his bike. What he was going to do as soon as Wolverine took off was come up behind the cop, distracted by the noise of his friend's footsteps.

Then Darth'd slam the rock into the cop's head, knock him out.

And get the asshole's gun, which would be a slick and smooth Glock or Beretta or something.

He felt a chill of pleasure and enjoyed a brief fantasy of his father coming into his bedroom, pushing him down on the bed, facedown, lifting the branch . . . and Darth twisting away, grabbing the automatic from under the pillow and watching his father's terrified face stare into the muzzle of a fucking nine-mil.

Would he pull the trigger?

No. Yes. Maybe.

He silently made his way around the cop, looking carefully where he put his feet.

Okay, Wolverine. Up to you now.

About fifteen seconds left in the count. He gripped the rock and moved a bit closer to him.

Only, wait, weird. It wasn't a him. It was a woman. Was it the bitch across from Goldshit's? No, no, that didn't make sense. It'd have to be a cop, just a woman cop.

Could Darth drop a girl?

Then decided: What the fuck difference does it make? Of course he could.

Then he had a weird thought: Wolverine – his real name was Wes – his mother, Mrs Dance, was a cop. What if this was her? It was too dark to see anything but long hair. But then Darth, well, Donnie Verso, remembered that Wes had said his mother was out of town. Some big case she was working on.

So, whoever she was, it wasn't Mrs Dance.

Okay. He moved a bit closer, then paused, kneading the rock. He crouched and got ready to sprint up behind her and take the bitch out. In less than a minute he'd have his gun.

CHAPTER 51

Kathryn Dance continued toward the large Victorian house on the far edge of the park.

She was disappointed to see that while the porch lights were on the rest of the house seemed dark. Too bad. Despite O'Neil's assessment she was still inclined to lay the crime at the feet of a biker gang. The family here might have heard the throaty clatter of a 'cycle engine, maybe peeked out of the front window and gotten a good view. Make and model of the bike possibly, descriptions.

Still, someone might be home. That a lead was unlikely was no reason to ignore it.

Unleashed . . .

As she approached the large, rustic yard surrounding the house, she paused once more. Now she heard footsteps. Two sets, in fact. One in front of her some distance away; others, closer, to her right, moving behind. She squinted into the darkness but could see nothing. Deer, most likely. The population of the critters around here was huge.

Of course, she wondered, too, if she'd been too hasty in dismissing the possibility that the perps were still here. True, an ordinary perp would be long gone. Hey, let's get the hell out of here. We've done the deed. Enough. But this wasn't a burglary or mugging or 'Let's torch the Porta Potti for the hell of it' kind of vandalism. This was different. And it wasn't unreasonable to think that the perps in this case would remain to watch the reaction, the dismay of the victims.

Deer?

She heard a branch snap not far away, but couldn't tell exactly where it had come from.

Okay. Time to leave, she told herself. Now.

A crackle of underbrush.

And then—

A mobile phone started to ring – from about thirty feet in front of her.

'Shit!' a voice called from behind – close. Jesus, somebody'd been flanking her. One of the perps.

'Run, run!' A male voice, from the direction of the ringtone.

And she heard two sets of sprinting footsteps, heading away from her. She saw no one. She thought about ordering them to stop but, unarmed, she didn't want to give her position away.

Dance lifted her phone and hit a speed-dial button.

'Kathryn.'

'Michael. They're here, east at the end of the road. Junipero Drive.'

'The perps? From Goldschmidt's?'

'Right. What I'm saying.'

'What were you doing?'

What the hell was he asking this for? She snapped, 'Call it in. They split up. One headed toward town. The other to Asilomar.'

'Where are you?'

Why was he asking? 'Where I just said. East, end of the road. A three-story Victorian.'

'I'll make the call.' Then he grumbled, 'Now get back here.'

A half-hour later Dance and O'Neil were with the crime-scene unit at Goldschmidt's house.

A Pacific Grove Police Department car pulled up and two officers got out.

O'Neil nodded. 'Anything?'

'Nope. We locked down Sunset, Asilomar, Ocean View and Lighthouse. But they must've gotten to their car before we set up the roadblocks.'

'Footprints?'

The wry smile on the face of one of the officers attested to the fact that they all knew: the ground here was mostly sand, and if you expected footprints for the electrostatic impression machine, you were going to be disappointed.

David Goldschmidt approached, carrying a roller and a can of paint. He set them down. He was interested to learn that Dance had had an encounter with the perps near the house up the street, Junipero Manor.

He said, 'You were close to them, sounds like.'

'Fairly. They'd split up. One was probably twenty feet away, the other fifty.'

'What did they look like?' His gray eyes narrowed. He focused intently, as if he wanted to learn all he could about those who had defiled his home.

She explained, 'Too dark to see much.' Pacific Grove was not known for abundant street lighting.

'Twenty feet, you said? And you saw nothing?'

A nod toward the park. 'Dark, I was saying.'

'Ah.' His eyes returned to the defiled side of his house.

'I'm sorry for this, Mr Goldschmidt.'

'Well, thank you for your prompt response.' His mind was elsewhere.

Dance nodded and handed him one of her cards. 'If you can think of anything else, please let me know.'

'Oh, I will.' He looked over the streets, eyes keen.

She watched him put the card into his back pocket, then walked to O'Neil's car. The detective started the engine.

Dance started to get in. Then paused, said, 'Give me a minute.' And returned to the house. 'Mr Goldschmidt?'

'Agent Dance. Yes?'

'A word?'

'Sure.'

'The law on self-defense in California is very clear.'

'Is that right?'

'Yes. And there are very few circumstances that will justify killing someone.'

'I watch *Nancy Grace*. I know that. Why do you bring it up?'

'You seemed interested in getting a clear description of the perps who committed this crime. Clearer than what you might've seen on a security video.' She glanced at the camera under his eaves.

'Like I told you, I didn't see them on the monitor. No, no, I was just thinking: what if I see them in town, or in the neighborhood? I could call the police. If I had a good description.'

'I'm simply telling you that it is a crime to harm an individual unless you truly believe yourself or another to be in danger. And damage to property is not a justifiable reason to use force.'

'I imagine these people are willing to do a lot more than paint messages. But why are we even having this conversation? There's no reason for them to come back, now, is there? They've already done the damage.'

'Do you own a gun?'

'I do, yes. Here's where you ask me if it's registered. Surely you know, in California you don't have to register guns you owned before January first. You may have to jump through hoops to get a conceal/carry permit. Which I don't have. But the shotgun that I own does not have to be registered.'

'I'm just telling you that the self-defense right is much more limited than most people think.'

'Most people maybe. But I'm quite versed in the law of the land. *Nancy Grace*, as I was saying.' His smile was assured, his light eyes narrow. 'Goodnight, Agent Dance. And thank you again.'

CHAPTER 52

Michael O'Neil pulled up to Dance's house and braked to a stop.

She read texts. 'From our office in LA. Orange County'll upload the crime-scene and canvassing reports to you early tomorrow.'

He grunted. 'Good.'

She flipped the lever and pushed open the door, then stepped outside, as O'Neil popped the trunk. He didn't get out. Dance walked back to get her suitcase and her laptop bag.

A wedge of light filled the front yard and Jon Boling was stepping out.

As if O'Neil suddenly felt he was being rude, or inconsiderate, he glanced at Boling, then Dance. He climbed out of the car.

To Boling, O'Neil said, 'Jon. Sorry it's late. I kidnapped her for an operation on the way home.'

'Nothing serious, I hope.'

'Another hate crime. Not too far from here.'

'Oh, no. Anyone hurt?'

'No. The perps got away, though.'

'Sorry.'

Dance carried her wheelie to the porch and Boling took it from her.

'Just to let you know,' he said, 'Wes came in about forty minutes late.'

She sighed. 'I'll talk to him.'

'I think a girl said no to his invite to the graduation dance or something. He was in a mood. I tried to get him to help me hack some code. But he wasn't interested – how 'bout that? So has to be love sickness.'

'Well, we have something official I'm hoping you can help us with,' she said.

'Sure. What can I do?'

She reminded him of the clip that had been posted last night – of the Solitude Creek tragedy.

'Right.' To Michael: 'What you were telling us this morning, breakfast.'

O'Neil nodded. Dance explained what Stan Prescott had done and that he'd been killed in Orange County – by the Solitude Creek unsub – without going into the part when she and O'Neil had both been in the line of fire.

'Killed? Why?'

'We aren't sure yet. Now, there may be a connection between the unsub and this Prescott. Not likely, but possible. I've got his computer and the unsub's phone. Can you crack the passcodes and run a forensic analysis?'

'What kind of box is it?'

'Asus laptop. Nothing fancy. Windows password protected. And a Nokia.'

'Be happy to. I like playing deputy. I want a badge some day. Or, like on Castle, one of those windbreakers. Mine could say, *Geek*.'

O'Neil laughed.

She handed the items over. Without prompting from her, Boling signed the chain-of-custody card.

'It's been dusted for prints but—'

'I'll wear my Playtex Living gloves. I'll take a peek now but I'll probably need the big guns to crack it. I'll start first thing in the morning.'

'Thanks,' she said.

O'Neil added, 'Oh, and it's been swept for explosives.'

'Always a plus.'

'Thanks, Jon.'

'The kids've eaten. We've got plenty of leftover leftovers. Why don't you stay for dinner?'

'No, thanks,' O'Neil said. 'We've got plans at home.'

'Sure.'

Boling gave a friendly nod. 'See you later, Michael.'

'Night.'

O'Neil said to Dance, 'Overby's at eleven. See you then.' He walked back to the car.

Dance put her hand on the door knob. Released it. Turned and strode to the car before he'd gotten in. She looked up into his dark eyes; she was not a short woman but O'Neil was six inches taller.

'Anything else?' O'Neil asked.

Which was exactly the wrong thing to say.

'Actually, Michael, there is.'

They rarely used each other's first names. This was a shot across the bow. 'I want to know what's on your mind. And if you say, "Nothing," I'm probably going to scream.'

'Been a long day.'

'That's as much of a screamer as a man saying, "Nothing."'

'Didn't know that's a gender issue.'

'You're right. But *you*'re the one acting out here.'

'Acting out.'

'Yes.'

'Well, if I'm pissed off, it's because this hasn't been the most successful operation on record. Losing the perp is one thing. But we also got an officer wounded down there.'

'And that was unfortunate. But *we* didn't get him shot. He got himself shot by not being aware of his surroundings. Basic street procedures, and I'm not even a street cop. But come on. No bullshit. Tell me.'

The jaw and tongue form an obvious configuration to make the nasal occlusive sound – that is, a word beginning with the consonant *n*. O'Neil's face was clearly forming it, a preface to the word *nothing*. Instead he said, 'You're making a mistake.'

'Mistake?'

'Okay. The truth?'

As opposed to what? she thought, and lifted an ironic eyebrow.

'The Guzman Connection, Serrano.'

This surprised her. She was sure he'd been upset to find Jon Boling had spent the night.

'How do you mean? What about Serrano?'

'I don't like you involved, not the way you're handling it.'

This was news to her. O'Neil wasn't involved in either Operation Pipeline or the subset, the Guzman Connection and the Serrano matter.

'Why?'

'I just don't.'

As if that told her anything. She sighed.

'Let somebody else run it.'

'Who? I'm the only one.'

This wasn't completely accurate, and his silence called her on the matter. She was angry that she felt defensive. 'I want to run it.'

'I heard you with TJ. The Serrano thing tomorrow. You're going along.'

'That's the whole point, Michael.'

'Al's going to be there.'

'Why not a whole team?'

'Because that'll set off alarms.'

'And what if some banger finds out you're in Motel Six with one of his boys and he sends in a team of shooters?'

'I've thought about that. It's an acceptable risk.'

'Oh, define that.'

'Michael.'

'Just take a weapon. That's all I'm saying.'

Oh, so that's what this was about. 'I'm Civ Div, and I—'

'You are not. You're full investigative. That's the way you're acting, at least.'

'Well, I can't have a gun. Procedures. There's no alternative.'

'Take one anyway. A Bodyguard, a Nano. I'll give you one of mine.'

'It's a breach of—'

'It's only a breach if you get caught.'

'And getting caught could ruin everything.'

'Okay, Serrano's your priority. You want to play that out, fine.'

Like he was giving her permission.

'Then give up Solitude Creek. I'll run it with my people. Coordinate with TJ and Rey. Even bring Connie Ramirez in.' His voice was raw, like a purple line of storm cloud moving in. He added, 'CBI'll get full credit.'

She scoffed, 'You think I care about that?'

His eyes looked away, answering: No, of course not. His comment had been a reflexive jab.

'Michael, I can't give the case up. Simple as that.'

'Why not?'

Because she couldn't.

He persisted, 'Tonight, at the Goldschmidt house, you weren't even supposed to be canvassing. You were supposed to stay at the scene.'

'"*Supposed* to"?' Her voice was raw.

'And I find out you're down near Junipero Manor, with the perps? You should've called me first. If they'd stayed around, they might have had something else in mind – nailing the law that's after them, for instance. Some neo-Nazi assholes, who cart around Glock forties?'

O'Neil continued, 'Or in Tustin today, if the unsub had turned right coming out of Prescott's apartment, after shooting the deputy, not left, he would've run right up on you.'

'We didn't know he was there. We were going to talk to a witness.'

'We *never* know what direction a case'll take.'

'You want me to sit in a room and talk my suspects into confessing on Skype? It doesn't work that way, Michael.'

'Remember your kids.'

'Don't bring my children into this,' she snapped.

'Somebody has to,' he muttered, in his infuriatingly calm, though ominous, tone. 'Nailing the Solitude Creek unsub, Kathryn? It doesn't have to be you.' He dropped into the front seat of the car, fired it up.

O'Neil didn't skid angrily out of the driveway – he wasn't that way. On the other hand, neither did he stop, reverse and return to apologize.

She watched the taillights until they disappeared in the fog.

It doesn't have to be you . . .

Except, Michael, yes, it does.

CHAPTER 53

Wes was in bed, texting, when she went in to say good night.

'Hey.'

'Hi,' he replied.

'Got home late, I heard.'

'Yeah. Flat tire. Had to leave my bike at Donnie's.'

'You didn't call for a ride? Jon could've picked you up.'

'Yeah, well. I was bummed about Karen. The dance. She's going with Randy.'

True, not true? It seemed deceptive. But after this impossible day, her kinesic skills weren't firing on all cylinders. Besides, it would exhaust and alarm you to analyze everything children said.

She didn't push. 'When you say you'll be home in fifteen, you'll be home in fifteen. There'll be consequences if this happens again.'

'Yeah. Okay.'

'Helmets?'

'Yeah, Mom. Helmets.'

'Night.' She kissed him.

Into the next bedroom.

'Mags?'

Maggie was asleep. Dance tucked the blankets around her and latched her window. Kissed her head.

At close to midnight she and Boling walked upstairs to her bedroom. He had here a set of clothes in a gym bag, which represented a tentative escalation in their relationship. This was fine with her: some clothes, not wardrobes' worth.

No rush . . .

She showered and dressed in PJs and crawled into bed next to him. They lay thigh to thigh, and she sensed he was ready to talk about her day if she wished but wasn't going to push it.

Thank you, she thought silently, and squeezed his hand as a gesture of the thought, which she knew he understood. She wondered if he'd heard the argument between her and Michael O'Neil.

She asked, 'How's Mags doing?'

'I kept an eye on the Skype session with the Secrets Club gang. Bethany's quite the young lady. I expect to see her as the head of the State Department in a few years. The White House is an option too. I think they were using codes. I couldn't figure them out. Like they've created their own language.'

Dance laughed. 'If they put half that energy into schoolwork.'

'When I was a kid and supposed to take a shower, I spent more time running the water, getting a towel wet and rubbing dirt from the floor on the washcloth than if I'd just jumped in. Something about getting away with it.'

'Did it work?'

'Not once. But I kept trying. Oh, not to worry, I'm over shower-cheating now.'

Her mind returned to the argument she'd had with O'Neil. Her gut clenched and she felt a flash of anger. She realized that Boling was saying something else.

'Hmm?'

'Just goodnight.' He kissed her cheek.

'Night.'

Boling rolled over on his side and in a few minutes he was in enviable sleep.

Dance realized she was staring intently at the ceiling. Then she told herself to relax. But how ridiculous an order was that?

She continued to wrestle with the greater implication of O'Neil's words, which he had not spoken to her. That if she had taken a weapon, yes, maybe they would have stopped the Solitude Creek killer today. Maybe she would have been closer to the door and seen him trying to escape.

And if anyone else died in another attack, that would be on her shoulders.

But if she had, and word had gotten back to CBI headquarters that she'd broken protocol with a pistol, it would have been the end of her involvement in the case and, more important, her secret role in the Serrano matter. She wasn't willing to do that. Michael had to understand.

Except, obviously, he didn't.

She, too, rolled over, back to the man beside her, hoping for prompt sleep.

It was nearly dawn before her addled mind stumbled into nonsensical thought and, finally, dreamless dark.

THE SECRETS CLUB

SUNDAY, APRIL 9

CHAPTER 54

'Did you hear from TJ? The lead came through, got a location and we'd better move on it.'

Those words, uttered by Al Stemple, were virtually one sentence, one breath. And not a single grunt. He knew he wasn't known for speedy anything and the fact that he was taking a let's-go attitude with the Guzman Connection task force was meant to convey: Time's a-wasting, boys and girls.

Carol Allerton, Jimmy Gomez and Stephen Lu were in the war room. Lu asked, 'Lead?'

Stemple grumbled, looking at his watch, 'Yeah, yeah. Lead to Tia Alonzo, Serrano's skirt.'

Drawing a glance from Allerton.

Oh, please . . .

Lu said, 'Where?'

Stemple wondered where Lu got his clothes. He had to have a size-thirteen neck. Tiny. His white shirt and black slacks bagged. 'Houseboat off Moss Landing.'

'Houseboat?'

What I said, Stemple thought.

'She with anybody?' Gomez asked.

'No, just her. Was with some guy but he left, TJ said.' He lowered his voice. 'Kathryn's outside. She'll go with us. So, draw straws. Jimmy?'

'Sure, I'll go.'

Lu said, 'Why don't we all go?'

Allerton: 'I need somebody here. I've got to finish these transcripts from Oakland. The prosecutor needs them in a couple of hours and I don't think I'm going to make it. '

Lu said, 'Sure. I can do that. Happy to help out.' That defined Steve Two. Somebody else might've said, 'Oh, I just *looooove* paperwork. Can't get enough.' But sincerity was baked into his core. He returned to the tasks on his desk.

Gomez pulled on his tan sports jacket, checked his Glock. As if the bullets had fallen out between the last time he'd checked and now. 'After you, Al.'

Together the men walked out into the parking lot.

Kathryn Dance was waiting.

'Hey,' Gomez said.

'Jimmy.' She nodded. And they walked toward Stemple's cruiser.

Looking around, Dance asked, 'Charles doesn't know I'm here, does he? You're sure?'

'Not from us,' Gomez confirmed. 'We Fab Four took a vow of silence. Even Steve Foster's agreed. He can be a . . . you know.'

'I do.'

It was transparent, Stemple thought.

They climbed into the car. Stemple started the engine and sped west on 68, heading for Highway One, which would get them to Moss Landing in twenty minutes.

'Who's this Tia we're going to see?' Gomez asked. Then: 'Whoa.'

Stemple never paid much attention to speed limits.

Dance said, 'Tia Alonzo. Use to be an exotic dancer.'

'Love that. "Exotic".'

'And model. Wannabe, of course. Serrano met her at a party and they, well, kept up partying for a month or two. It ended but they hook up occasionally. TJ found Tia's gotten a couple of texts from Serrano lately. He's checking her sheet now, seeing if there's any paper we can use to leverage her into helping us. Or maybe she'll just cooperate. Out of the goodness of her heart.'

Now, yeah, Stemple grunted.

A real houseboat.

Rundown but Al Stemple liked it.

About forty feet long, fifteen wide, a squat whitewashed structure on top of pontoons.

Wouldn't mind something like that.

Moss Landing was a stretch of marinas, shops and restaurants scattered along a sandy road that paralleled Highway One. The houseboat was anchored in a secluded area of docks. In its heyday, the years of plentiful fish, the Steinbeck years, this spot had been home to hundreds of fifty- and sixty-foot fishing boats. No longer. Some pleasure craft, a few small fishing operations – party boats and commercial – and then, like here, a houseboat or two.

Stemple parked about a hundred feet from the place. The three CBI agents climbed from the car and slowly made their way toward the boat. A beat-up Toyota was parked in the weed-filled lot in front of the vessel. Or house. Or whatever.

'One car only. But doesn't mean she's alone.' Stemple made a fast security sweep. And returned. 'Looks good to me.'

Dance regarded her phone. She said to Gomez, 'TJ. He's telling me no paper on Alonzo. Yellow sheet – lewd and lascivious, prostitution, public drunkenness. Years ago. She's been a good girl since.'

'Nothing violent, then.'

'Nup. But we have to assume she's armed.'

Gomez said, 'And you're not, right?'

'Nope. Stay close, Jimmy.'

'Oh, I will.'

'And, Al, don't watch the perimeter.'

'Gotcha.'

They approached the boat, which was called the *Lazy Mary*. Stemple didn't like the name. Wasn't elegant. If he had a houseboat, he'd call it something like *Diamond Stud*. No, too tacky. *Home of the Brave*. Good. He liked it.

Near shore was a breakwater, so the occasionally ornery Monterey Bay waters didn't intrude here. Today the *Lazy Mary* rose and fell, Stemple decided, lazily.

Gomez glanced at Dance, who nodded and said, 'Let's do it.'

They walked over a short gangplank and onto the deck, painted gray, scabby. Gomez knocked on the door.

It opened and they stepped inside.

Stemple looked out over the marina, adjusted his Beretta on his wide hip and crossed his arms.

CHAPTER 55

Fifteen minutes later Gomez, Stemple and Dance were driving back to headquarters.

She called the task force and got Carol Allerton.

'It's Kathryn. You're on speaker here with Jimmy and Al.'

'You're speakered as well. Steve Foster's back. And Steve Two, too.' Uncharacteristic humor from a DEA agent.

'Steve and Steve,' Dance said.

'Hi, Kathryn.' Lu, of course, since the greeting sounded warm.

'Yeah?' A gruff voice. Did Foster ever utter a cheerful syllable?

'We just left Moss Landing,' Dance said.

'And?' Foster grumbled.

'Tia Alonzo hasn't seen Serrano for a month. I believed her.'

Silence from Foster now. He didn't say what he wanted to.

Dance continued, 'But she gave up another name. Pete or Pedro Escalanza. TJ's going to track it down. Ninety percent the guy's got Serrano's present whereabouts.'

'Lead to a lead to a lead,' Foster said, with buoyant cynicism.

Allerton asked, 'So, at the houseboat. It was productive.'

'That's right.'

'And you're okay. Jimmy's okay?'

'I'm good,' Gomez said.

'Tia was saying this Escalanza, he's got access to some of Serrano's accounts. If we play it right, we might be able to pick up his credit-card numbers, track him in real time.'

'Or maybe we'll find another lead,' Foster chimed in. 'Let's be transparent here. I'm not overly reassured.'

Stemple coughed.

Dance said, 'The best we could do, Steve.'

Allerton said, 'I'll tell Charles.'

'Thanks.'

'We're coming back in.' Dance disconnected.

Stemple said, 'Life's a fucking checkers game. No, chess. You play chess, Jimmy?'

'No. You?'

'Yeah, I play chess.'

'Really?' Gomez asked.

'Why really? Because I bench-press three hundred and group my rounds touching at fifty feet – if I'm using the long barrel?'

'I don't know. You just don't seem like a chess player.'

'Mostly people think I tap dance for a hobby.'

In a half-hour, eleven a.m., she was back in CBI headquarters, making for Overby's office, in the company of TJ Scanlon.

As they walked along, she checked her phone again. Texts from her mother, Boling. Maggie, silly and happy – because, of course, she'd been pardoned from the cruel and unusual punishment of singing in her class's talent show.

Nothing from O'Neil.

Did she expect an apology? The hard words had been motivated by his concern for her but she'd found them patronizing. That was difficult for her to get past.

She supposed the frisson between them would dissipate, like smoke from a brief fire. This happened from time to time, head butting. Still, they had had such a complicated history, personal and professional, that she never knew if the flare would spread like a wind-fueled brushfire racing over the dry, bristly coat of the landscape in this state. Destructive, even fatal. She'd never prepared for a final rift with Michael O'Neil because, well, it was unimaginable.

A glance at her phone once more. Nothing.

Let it go . . .

They arrived at Overby's office and the CBI head waved them inside. 'Just found something interesting. Got a call from Oakland PD. The arson?'

Dance nodded and explained to TJ about the Operation Pipeline warehouse that some crew had burned down.

'But – it wasn't a gang that did it.'

Dance cocked her head.

Her boss continued, 'Mercenaries.'

TJ said, 'Working *for* a crew, then. Didn't want to get their dainty little fingers dirty.'

'No. Not working for a crew. They got out of the country but left some tracks behind. Guess where they were based? Baja.'

'But not working for one of the Mexican cartels?'

'No. Working for someone else.'

Dance understood. 'Well, well: Santos hired them. *He* was behind it.'

'Bingo,' Overby said.

Chihuahua Police Commissioner Ramón Santos, who'd called the other day to excoriate the US contingent of Operation Pipeline for not doing enough to stanch the flow of guns into his country.

'He took matters into his own hands.'

'Oakland DEA contacted some of their people in Mexico and confirmed it.'

Dance grimaced. 'Thought he was taking down a source for the guns? Well, he shot himself in the foot. That warehouse was a great source for intel. Does he know he's set us back a month with his little fireworks display?'

'He will,' Overby said, 'after I call him this afternoon.'

Whatever else about his personal style, Overby combined right-eousness and indignation very, very well.

'So Santos,' TJ said, 'has got an interesting approach to enforcing the law. He *breaks* the law.'

Then a sound behind her, paper shuffling, footsteps. Michael O'Neil came into the office.

'Ah, Michael.'

'Charles.'

She looked his way. He nodded to everyone. 'Morning.'

Overby said, 'Okay, the Solitude Creek unsub. Where are we?'

O'Neil glanced toward Dance. She said, 'Well, all we have are dead ends with the unsub's Honda. But Jon Boling's hacking into the unsub's phone now. It might be the burner he used to call Sam Cohen or the one at the Bay View Center, where he called nine one one, the media and the restaurant on Fisherman's Wharf after the Bay View incident. Or maybe another one. Jon's also cracking Stan Prescott's computer – the man killed in Orange County. We hope it gives us some clue why the unsub went to all that trouble to murder him. And TJ? Update on Anderson Construction?'

The young agent reminded Overby that he was trying to track down officials from the Nevada corporation hiring Anderson to do some construction work in the Solitude Creek area. In hopes of finding some witnesses. 'They're taking their sweet time getting back to me. Weekend-itis maybe. I'll definitely squeeze them tomorrow. And I'm keeping up canvassing people who were at the roadhouse that day. But same old. No leads.'

Overby nodded and looked at O'Neil, who was opening his briefcase and extracting a folder. 'Crime-scene report from Orange County?' Overby asked.

'That's it. Not much. Some trace elements. Footprints that probably are the Louis Vuitton. They have good security video at the Global Adventure theme park but all it shows is the crash, then our man jumping over the car through the gate. The teams down there canvassed a hundred people but nobody saw anybody who could've been him.'

He added, 'And some OC detectives looked over Prescott, fine-tooth comb. Talked to most of his friends, bosses, co-workers. All his redneck buddies. No connection to our unsub. He just randomly pulled the picture of Solitude Creek off the web and posted it in his rant.'

Dance said, 'So, he just had the bad luck to pick our boy's attack to use in his post.'

O'Neil continued, 'There were nearly four thousand texts and voice calls out of the park, once the rumors started to spread. Some of those would be his prepaid mobiles. But Orange County can't devote manpower to go through every one and try to narrow it down.'

Overby said, 'He caused all that chaos by a few phone calls?'

'Pretty much that's it. But he was smart. He spread the rumors verbally in the park too. And the patrons helped him out, of course, when they texted and tweeted. Online media and TV picked up the story in seconds, and then those who weren't at the park would text their family members and friends who were inside.'

Overby nodded. 'Chain reaction.'

'Flash mob,' Dance said. 'No prints on anything, not even shell casings – at either scene, Prescott's apartment or the theme park. And the car he stole from the airport here?' O'Neil explained it had been a sloppy theft, suggesting he wasn't a pro at the art.

But, she reflected, it had worked.

Overby's cheek twitched up. 'So, nothing other than the phone.'

O'Neil said, 'I've found something else, though. Not really a lead. But it's something to throw into the mix about our unsub.'

'What's that?' TJ asked.

'Remember that Jane Doe?' He spread out the photos that Dance had seen. 'The asphyx?' O'Neil explained about the homicide he was working, the attractive young woman found in a seedy motel, the bag rubber-banded over her head.

Never rains but it pours . . .

'Could have been consensual sex gone wrong, could have been intentional. We don't know for sure. Except for this.' He opened the folder and extracted a photograph. It was a still from a security video. The picture was black-and-white but it clearly showed a light-colored Honda Accord.

'No tag number,' Dance noted, shaking her head.

Sometimes it was that easy. Not often. Not now.

'Where was it?'

'A block from the motel where our Jane Doe died. I had some MCSO officers canvassing all the businesses around the area and one came back with this.' Tapping the picture.

'The connection, though?' Overby asked.

O'Neil pulled another crime-scene picture out of the back of the folder and set it beside the Jane Doe. It was of Stan Prescott's body.

Looking from one to the other, Dance said, 'It's the same pose as Prescott, same cause of death. Asphyxiation. Both lying on their backs. Both images are stark: the victims are lying in pools of bright light from nearby lamps.'

'Why would he kill *her*?' Overby wondered aloud.

Dance offered, 'The TOD on the Jane Doe was just after Foster leaked the info about what the unsub was wearing. Maybe she'd seen his outfit – the worker's jacket with the logo he'd worn to Solitude Creek. And he realized she could ID him.'

O'Neil: 'Could be why she didn't have a phone or computer or notebook. That could lead to him. The scenario: she wasn't from here. They met in a bar, had a one- or two-night thing. They were going their separate ways but he had to take her out.'

Dance asked, 'But why the parallel means of death?'

'Sadism,' Overby suggested.

Maybe. That wasn't, however, a question that interested Dance at this point. She had only one query in mind: was their unsub back in town, with another venue in his sights?

CHAPTER 56

Antioch March was thinking of Calista Sommers.

The police still didn't have her name. In the media, she was referred to as Jane Doe. A picture had been released. Her death was either murder or some kind of weird sado-sexual thing.

He just happened to be driving near the bar where he'd picked her up earlier in the week.

A martini for her, a pineapple juice for him.

She'd still be alive if she hadn't been brash enough to fling open his closet in search of a robe. Modesty. That was what'd killed her. She'd have seen the outfit that he'd worn at Solitude Creek, when he'd moved the truck to block the exit doors. At that point, the announcement had not been made that a witness had seen him – so he hadn't thought anything of it. Shortly thereafter, at the movie theater, he'd learned that the public had gotten the word. Why on earth they'd released his description he still couldn't fathom.

The police's disclosure not only saved him at the theater incident it had got Calista dead. As soon as he'd left the McDonald's near the theater, after learning of Ms Agent Dance, he'd taken a drive to Calista's motel in Carmel. Hoping she hadn't heard the description broadcast. But no. She'd been pleasantly surprised to see him. He asked if she wanted to take a drive. And once they were under way, how 'bout an adventure? Some little no-tell motel?

'You naughty boy . . .'

You're so fucking handsome . . .

And then . . .

Sorry, Calista.

'No, no . . . .'

He pictured her on the floor of the cheap place, shivering as she died. The plastic bag over her head. Five, six minutes was all it had taken.

He now tucked away the happy memory and continued to one of the places he'd found a few days ago, perfect for another attack: a church reception hall.

It was astonishing to him, the number of people killed in stampedes related to religion.

Mecca. Never do Mecca.

How anybody could manage to hang on to faith after hearing about those deaths was beyond him. Thousands had died.

India was pretty bad too, crowds of hundreds of thousands. Oh, what he could do with a herd like that . . .

Ahead he could see the venue he'd checked out earlier. There was a church supper planned there tonight. The site was particularly good. Two exit doors that could be bound shut with flower-arranging wire. Perfect.

This also happened to be an African-American church. And someone in the area, conveniently, had been targeting ethnic facilities just like this. That meant the people would be particularly paranoid, fast to escape if there was any sign of threat.

Fast to crush their fellow congregants to save themselves.

He'd start a small fire outside, just like he'd done in Solitude Creek. That would be enough, smoke wafting in. They'd be thinking the neo-Nazis had returned and, tired of simple-minded graffiti, were now intent on doing the real thing. Burn them to the ground. March thought it would be—

But, no, what was this?

As he approached he noted a sign on the billboard out front. *Dine with Jesus Supper Postponed. Join us for Services next week. Pray for the victims of Solitude Creek and the Bay View Center.*

March sighed. He guessed he should have anticipated that. The bigger venues were probably robo-calling ticket holders and cancelling shows.

He wondered if Kathryn Dance was behind this.

Maybe not behind. But involved.

Well, he certainly couldn't leave the area just yet. So, what to do? Out-think them, out-think dear Kathryn. Well, performance venues were out, reception halls too. Maybe weddings were going on but they would probably have been moved outside – the weather was temperate enough for that.

What venue wouldn't be closed down?

Movie theaters, but they wouldn't work. After the abortive attempt the other day, sure, cineplexes with substantial crowds would have guards, if not police.

What else would remain open?

Ah, wait. Here's a thought: management of hotels would resist closing, certainly on a nice Sunday afternoon, everybody in for brunch or an early supper.

Hotel or inn . . . Yes.

Some ideas began to form. Good, a solid plan.

But he'd pursue it only after he had completed his immediate task – the errand that had been interrupted by his trip to Orange County after the Bay View incident.

The task of slowing down, if not stopping completely, his pursuers.

Well, one pursuer. Singular.

He smiled. Yes, truly singular.

What better word to describe Kathryn Dance, of whom he'd dreamed at glorious length last night?

CHAPTER 57

The Kathryn Dance Situation.

That's how Jon Boling had come to think of it. The phrase could have a negative connotation but he didn't mean it like that. Boling, a product of academia who made his living in the world of computers, was analytical by nature.

This drab, gray Sunday he was bicycling down Ocean Avenue in Carmel, the main shopping drag, while his partner at the college, Lily, chipped away at Stanley Prescott's and his killer's passcode. There was nothing more for him to do until she finished, so he'd taken a ride. Besides, he had an errand that needed attending to.

He was not paying much attention to the pretty scenery but was, instead, reflecting on the nature of the KD Situation.

Yes, he loved her. No question about that. The tug in his gut whenever he saw her. He could, always, call up the smell of her hair as they lay together. He could see the sparkle in her green eyes, hear her breezy laugh. They gave to each other, didn't hesitate to speak about their vulnerabilities. He remembered feeling her pain when the worst – to her – happened: she'd fail to catch a perp. He'd wrap his arms around her at moments like that and she'd yield to the comfort. Not completely. But to a degree. This was love.

He continued downhill. Don't fail me here, he thought to the brakes. It was a long, fast stretch straight down to the rocks and traffic at the beach. He eased to a stop at an intersection, then continued.

And the children, he loved them too. Wes and Maggie . . . He'd always wanted to be a father, but that hadn't worked out. No dark angst there but it was a gap he was determined to fill and fill soon. Boling admitted he wasn't a natural parent but he worked hard. And he could see that the effort had paid off. When he'd first met Kathryn, the children were moody, depressed from time to time, Wes more but Maggie too. After all, they hadn't been without their father for all that long. They still grew morose or attitudinal at times.

But wasn't that just life? Adolescents and adults.

So, a lyrical comfort with Kathryn, a rapport with the children . . . and even the formidable Edie Dance liked him – enough. Stuart, of course, and Boling had become solid friends.

But something wasn't quite right. Hence, the 'situation'.

Suggesting issues requiring consideration. Formulation. Adjustment. Solution.

Jon Boling hardly knew kinesics but he'd learned enough from Kathryn to be aware of tension. And when was it most in evidence? Not when she was entangled in a case. Not when one of the kids was sick. But when she and Boling and Michael O'Neil were in the same room together.

Computer code, the language Jon Boling spoke most fluently, is written according to the laws of logic. The parameters are clear and allow for not a single mis-spaced character. He wished he could write out a program on the Kathryn Dance Situation, compile it and have his answer pulsing on a monitor in front of him.

```
<!DOCTYPE html>
<html>
<body>

<h1>The Kathryn Dance Situation</h1>

<p> Love her.</p>

<p>Love the children.</p>

<p>It works, many, many ways.</p>
```

Jon Boling liked Michael O'Neil a great deal. He was a solid, decent man. A good father, who'd kept his path during a divorce from a faithless and frivolous wife. And to hear Kathryn tell it, he was one hell of a law enforcer. But there was another factor in the code Boling was now writing.

Michael O'Neil loves Kathryn.

A stretch of flat surface, and Boling pulled off to the sidewalk. He texted the college's computer-science department, where Lily was hard at work on cracking Stan Prescott's computer and the unsub's phone.

Lily, quite a beauty she was. Smart as could be.

There was no progress. But Boling had confidence she'd find the passwords.

Back to the Situation. And the big question: did Kathryn love Michael?

He'd lain awake a number of nights wondering, tagging her words and looks and gestures with meaning, wondering, wondering . . . and replaying certain images and words over the past year. The radiance of her eyes, the lift of her lips when she smiled, characterized by faint, charming wrinkles.

What are Kathryn's true feelings?

Boling recalled overhearing the fight she and O'Neil had had last night. Raw. Sharp words, back and forth. Then he pictured her returning to the house and her face changing, melting, relaxing, growing comfortable once more. Boling and Dance had laughed, had some turkey reinvented into something innovative, salad, wine. And the hard day in Orange County, the hard words fired by Michael O'Neil fell away.

Do Kathryn and Jon have a future?

He now eased to a stop outside the store he'd bicycled ten miles to come to. It was, like most stores and houses in Carmel, on the borderline between quaint and precious. The décor was Bavarian ski resort, not uncommon here, though Boling suspected the downtown saw snow once a decade at most.

He unstrapped his almond-shaped helmet and slung it over the handlebars. He leaned the bike up against a nearby fence. Didn't bother with the lock. Nobody was going to steal a bike in daylight in downtown Carmel. That would be like trying to run a gun show in Berkeley.

Jon Boling had done some research on By the Sea Jewelry, the store he was walking toward now. It was just what he needed. Glancing at the beautiful antique engagement and wedding rings in the window, he pushed inside. The door opened with a jingle from a cowbell, both incongruous and perfectly apt.

Five minutes later he was outside once again.

Do Kathryn and Jon have a future?

Boling opened the By the Sea Jewelry bag and peered into the box inside. Good. He slipped it into his jacket pocket. He found himself smiling.

Helmet on. Time to head back to her house.

There were several ways to get there. The shorter was to go back up Ocean Avenue. But that was a steep hill, made for the thighs of a twenty-year-old. The other option, longer, was to bike downhill toward the beach, then meander along Seventeen Mile Drive back to Pacific Grove.

Pretty and, yes, far easier.

A glance at his watch. He'd be back to Dance's in thirty minutes this way. He turned the bike down the steep hill and caught a glimpse of the ocean, beach, rocks, shrouded in mist.

What a view.

He pushed off, keeping tension on the rear brake mostly – the incline was so severe that hitting the front one alone would catapult him head over heels if he had to stop fast. It seemed to him that the rear responded slowly, wobbling with some vibration. It felt different from when he'd biked there, just minutes ago. But the sensation was simply a rough patch of asphalt, he guessed. Or maybe even his imagination. Now, no traffic in front, he let up on the brake handles. The speed increased and Boling enjoyed the wind streaming against his face, enjoyed the hum it made in his helmet. Thinking of the bag inside his pocket.

<p>The Kathryn Dance Situation has been resolved. </p>

</body>
</html>

CHAPTER 58

Dance and her father were on the Deck that warm Sunday afternoon, pleasant, though under gray skies – overcast for a change, no fog. Natives knew the difference. As often on the Peninsula, the sky promised rain but deceived. The drought grew worse every year. Solitude Creek, for instance, had at one point been eight, nine feet deep, she'd learned. Now it was a quarter that. Less in some places.

She thought again about the reeds and grass, the decaying buildings behind the parking lot on the shores of the creek.

Annette, the sobbing witness.

Trish, the motherless child.

The bodies in the roadhouse, the blood. The stain in the shape of a heart.

She was talented . . .

Picturing Solitude Creek itself, the gray expanse of water, bordered by reeds and grasses.

It was then that she had a thought. 'Excuse me a sec,' she said to Stuart.

'Sure, honey.'

She pulled out her phone and texted Rey Carreneo with yet another assignment.

He responded as crisply as his shirts were starched.

K, Kathryn. On it right now.

She put her phone away.

'When's brunch?' Maggie asked, poking her head out of the door.

'Jon'll be home anytime.' She looked at her Timex. He was ten minutes late. It wasn't like him not to call.

'K.' The girl vanished.

Her phone hummed.

Maybe that's him. But no.

'TJ.'

He and several MCSO deputies had been systematically contacting venues with public performances or large social events and asking them to cancel.

'I think we've got most of the big ones. Concerts, church services, plays, sports events – praise the Lord it's not March Madness or we'd have riots on our hands. By the way, boss, I am not the most popular man on the Peninsula – in the eyes of the Chamber of Commerce and assorted wedding parties, *persona non grata*. The Robertsons are *not* inviting me to the rescheduled reception.'

Dance thanked him and they disconnected.

Stuart asked, 'How's it going?'

She shrugged. 'Ruining people's Sunday.'

'So, Maggie's not singing in the talent show?'

'No, she didn't want to. I was going to push it but . . .' A shrug.

Stuart smiled. 'Sometimes you let it go.' He knew he'd made a pun on the song his granddaughter was going to have sung. Dance laughed, reflecting that the song title had become a theme of hers over the past few days.

'When's brunch?' Wes called from the doorway, echoing his sister.

Dance glanced at her phone. Still no word from Boling. 'We'll get things started.'

She and Stuart walked into the kitchen. She Keuriged some coffee for them both and prowled through the fridge.

She glanced toward her son.

'No texting at the table.'

'We're not eating yet.'

A look from Mom. The mobile disappeared into his back pocket.

'So, what's on the wish list for brunch?'

Maggie: 'Waf—'

'—cakes,' her brother chimed in.

'Wafcakes. Good.'

Maggie poured an orange juice and sipped. 'When are you going to get married?' she asked, like a father to a pregnant daughter.

Stuart chuckled.

Dance froze. Then: 'I'm too busy to be thinking about getting married.'

'Excuses, excuses, excuses . . . Are you marrying Jon or Michael?'

'What? Maggie!'

Then the phone was ringing. Wes was closest and he answered. 'Hello?'

They weren't supposed to answer with their name or 'Dance residence'. Security starts early in a law-enforcement household.

'Sure.' He looked at his sister. 'For you. Bethany.'

Maggie took the cordless phone and wandered off. Dance checked her own cell for updates. Nothing from Jon. She called him and the line went right to voice mail.

'Hey, it's me. You on your way? Just checking.'

Dance disconnected and happened to glance toward her daughter on the phone. Bethany Meyer, the future secretary of state, was a precocious eleven-year-old, polite enough, though Dance thought of her as over-assembled. She believed kids that age should wear jeans or shorts and T-shirts most of the time, not dress up as if they were going for movie auditions every day. Her parents were well off, true, but they sank way too much money into the girl's clothes. And such fastidious makeup? On a girl her age? In a word, no.

Suddenly she noticed Maggie's body language change abruptly. Her shoulders rose and her head drooped. One knee went forward – a sign of a subconscious, if not physical, desire to flee or fight. She was getting troubling news. Her daughter continued to talk a bit more, then disconnected. She returned to the kitchen.

'Mags, everything all right?'

'Yeah, it's fine. Why not?' Jittery.

Dance looked at her sternly.

'Everything's, like, fine.'

'Watch the "like". What did Bethany have to say?'

'Nothing. Just stuff.'

'Nothing?'

'Uh-uh.'

Dance gave her a probing look, which was conspicuously ignored, and began to assemble the ingredients for the meal. 'Blueberries?'

Maggie didn't answer.

Dance repeated the question.

'Yeah, sure.'

Dance tried the proven tactic of diversion. 'Hey, you all looking forward to the concert? Neil Hartman?'

The new Dylan . . .

'I guess,' Maggie said, less than enthusiastic.

A glance at Wes, who was, in turn, sneaking a look at his phone. He put it away fast. 'Yeah, yeah . . . can't wait.' More enthusiastic but more distracted, as well. Dance at least was looking forward to seeing Hartman. She reminded herself to check the tickets to see where the seats were. She'd left Kayleigh's envelope in the glove compartment of the Pathfinder.

A moment later, Wes: 'Hey, Mom,' Wes said. 'Can I go meet Donnie?'

'What about brunch?'

'Can I do Starbucks instead? Please, please?' He was cheerful, almost silly. She debated, extracted a five from her purse and handed it over.

'Thanks.'

'Can I go too?' Maggie asked.

'No,' Wes said.

'Mom!'

'Come on, honey,' Stuart said. 'I want to have brunch with you.'

Maggie glanced at her brother darkly, then said, 'Okay, Grandpa.'

'Bye, Mom,' Wes said.

'Wait!'

He stopped and looked at her with small alarm in his face.

'Helmet.' She pointed.

'Oh.' He stared at it. 'Well, we're walking. I've still got that flat.'

'All the way downtown?'

'Yeah.'

'All right.'

'Yeah. Bye, Grandpa.'

Stuart said, 'Don't get a double shot of espresso. Remember what happened last time.'

Dance hadn't heard about that incident. And didn't want to know.

The door closed. Dance started to call Boling again when she noted that Maggie's face was still troubled. 'You wouldn't've had any fun with them.'

'I know.'

Dance began to say something to her, make a joke, when her cell rang again. She answered. 'Michael.'

'Listen. May have our Solitude Creek unsub. A PG patrolman spotted a silver Honda Accord at the Del Monte View Inn.'

Dance knew it, a big luxury non-chain hotel not far from where she lived.

'It's parked right behind the building. The driver was tall. Sunglasses. Hat but maybe he has a shaved head. Worker's jacket. He's inside now.'

'Tag?'

'Delaware. But how's this? It's registered to layers of shell corporations, including an offshore.'

'Really? Interesting.'

'I've got teams on the way there. Rolling up silent.'

'You know the place? There're two lots. Have the teams stage in the bottom one.'

'Already ordered it,' he said.

'I'm ten minutes, Michael. I'm moving.'

She turned to her father and daughter, to see Stuart already on his feet, reading the recipe on the back of the Bisquick box.

She laughed. He looked as serious as an engineer about to power up a nuclear reactor. 'Thanks, Dad. Love you both.'

CHAPTER 59

As he walked to Starbucks to meet Wes, Donnie Verso was thinking about their friendship.

The kid wasn't like Nathan or Lann or Vince or Peter. Not *that* stand-up. And wasn't quite thinking right, the way he ought to if he wanted to hang with the Defend and Respond crew. Not muting his phone and alerting the bitch cop just as Donnie was about to crack her skull open and get her gun. Your phone, dude? Seriously? (Though, afterward, he thought maybe that *had* worked out for the best.)

Yeah, yeah, he was good backup, a good lookout – he'd saved Donnie's ass a couple of times, warning him that somebody was about to see him tagging a church or stealing a watch from Rite Aid.

But Donnie just couldn't get Wes to go the extra step.

Oh, he wanted to. That was obvious. Because Wes was mad. Oh, yeah. Totally mad. Wes was as pissed off at his father for being dead as Donnie was at his for being alive. That kind of anger usually pushed you dark really fast. But the dude was hanging back.

He was sure the kid could do it, if he wanted to, even though they'd known each other only a month. Donnie had seen the twelve-year-old Wes around middle school from time to time, and hadn't thought anything of him. A church humper? Probably. Science club? Probably. Another time, Donnie might've wailed on him. (Or Donnie and Nathan together, since Wes wasn't small.) But there were other, easier, targets at school.

He was thinking of the first time they'd really spoken. One day after school Donnie and Nathan had gotten this pussy grade-schooler down by Asilomar and fucked him up a little, nothing bad. While they were doing it Donnie had looked up and seen Wes standing there. Like he was curious was all.

Wes had watched then pedalled off, not fast, not scared, like no worries.

The next day at school, Donnie'd cornered him and said, 'The fuck you were looking at yesterday?'

And Wes said, 'Nobody special.'

'Fuck you,' Donnie'd said. Not being able to think of anything better. 'You tell anybody what you saw and you're fucked.'

Wes said, 'I coulda told somebody but I didn't. 'Cause, duh, you're here and not behind bars.'

'Fuck off.'

Wes just walked away slow, like he'd biked away the day before. *No cares . . .*

Then a couple days later Wes came up to Donnie in the hall and gave him a copy of *Hitman*, the video game where you could go around fucking people up, killing them for assignments and even strangling girls. He said, 'My mom won't let me play. But it's a good game. You want it?'

Then a week later Wes was sitting outside and Donnie came by and said, 'I couldn't play it, I don't have Xbox, but I got *Call of Duty*. I traded it at Games Plus. You want to play sometime?'

'My mom won't let me play that either. At your house, yeah.'

It took a couple weeks of games and pizza and just hanging out before Wes said, 'My father's dead.'

Donnie, who'd heard, said, 'Yeah, I heard. Sucks.'

Nothing more for another week. Then Donnie sat down at the lunch table and they talked about shit for a while and asked, 'I heard your dad was FBI. Somebody killed him?'

'Accident.'

'Like a car?'

'A truck.'

Wes sounded as calm as Donnie's mother after she took her little white pills.

'You want to fuck up the driver?'

'Yeah, but he's gone. Didn't even live here.'

'Wish somebody'd run into my father. Don't you want to fuck things up sometimes?'

'Explode, yeah,' Wes had said. 'And my mom's going out with this guy. A computer guy. He's okay. He hacks code real good. But it's like my dad never even existed, you know. And I can't say anything.'

''Cause you'll get the crap beat out of you.'

Wes had just repeated, 'Explode.'

They hung out some more and finally Donnie let him into the Defend and Respond Expedition Service game. He needed a partner because Lann, fuck him, had moved.

Donnie, who spent hours a day at video games, had made up the game himself. Defend and Respond Expedition Service. But they thought of it as what it really was: DARES. Well, *dares*.

Donnie and now Wes were on one side, Vincent and Nathan on the second. One team *dared* the other to do something totally fucked up: steal something, shoot pictures up a girl's skirt, piss on a teacher's lesson plan. You got a point if you met the challenge – and came back with proof. At the end of the month, whoever had the most points won. They wrote it up like a board game with fake countries and codes and names – Darth and Wolverine – so that any parents looking the game over would just think it was like *Lord of the Rings* or *Harry Potter* or whatever.

Wes hadn't been sure about joining at first. Donnie's crew wasn't Wes's flavor. But Donnie could see he was interested and, after the first couple dares, even though he only watched Donnie's back, it was way clear that he got a high out of it. Like he'd almost smiled in Asilomar that time, watching Donnie and Nathan beat the crap out of the whiny little Lat.

But would he really come around? Donnie Verso wondered again.

He walked into Starbucks, got a coffee and sat down next to Wes, who was texting. He glanced up, nodded and put his phone away.

'Hey.'

They bumped fists.

For the next ten minutes they talked, in whispers, about how best to get into Goldshit's garage and steal their bikes back. Wes thought it was smart not to do it just the two of them but get Nathan and Vincent too.

Donnie thought that wasn't a bad idea.

After a few minutes, Wes said, 'I heard Kerry and Gayle'll be at Foster's. Want to go up there?'

'Is Tiff with them?'

'I don't know. I just heard Kerry and Gayle.'

'K. Let's go.'

They headed out and turned north, making for the old department store, now a restaurant – at least on the first floor.

They got about one block and Donnie laughed and slapped Wes's arm. 'Look who it is.'

It was that prick Rashiv. Mrs Dance had mentioned him the other night. Donnie and his DARES crew had wailed on him about six weeks or so ago. Donnie didn't quite know why, maybe because Rashiv wasn't even a democratic US citizen and he should go back to where he came from, Syria or India or wherever. But mostly they'd pounded on him and pulled his pants down and launched his book bag into the water off Lovers' Point because it was something to do.

And here he was now.

Rashiv glanced up and, terror in his eyes, saw Donnie and Wes walking right toward him. They were on Lighthouse, the main commercial street in Pacific Grove, and plenty of people were around so the kid didn't think he was going to get lashed but he still looked plenty scared.

'Yo, bitch,' Donnie said.

Rashiv nodded. He was a way skinny little guy.

'Whatchu up to, bitch?'

A shrug. 'Nothing.' Looking for a place to run, just in case Donnie decided to lash on him even with people around.

Wes just looking at him with this blank expression.

'Hey, Wes.'

No response from Wolverine.

Rashiv said, 'Haven't seen you for a while. I called.'

'Busy.'

Donnie said, '*You* been busy too, Rashit?' It was funny how a question could be both friendly and threatening.

'Sorta. Yeah. You know, school.'

Wes said, 'What's that?' Squinting at a book the boy was carrying.

'Just some manga.'

'Let me see.'

'I don't—'

Wes lifted it away. He laughed in shock. 'Japanese edition of *Death Note* – it's signed by Ohba.'

Shit, Donnie thought. Holy shit. One of the best, kick-ass manga comics of all time. And signed by the author? Donnie said, 'I figured you'd beat off to *Sailor Moon*.'

Death Note was about a high-school student who has a secret notebook that gives him the power to kill anyone just by knowing their name and face. Fuck, this was pure solid, the most righteous of any manga or anime in the world.

Wes flipped through it. 'I'm going to borrow it.'

'Wait!' Rashiv said, eyes wide.

'I'm just going to read it.'

'No, you're not! You're never going to give it back. My parents brought it to me from Japan!' Rashiv reached forward and gripped Wes's arm. 'No! Please!'

Wes turned to him with a look that sent some ice even down Donnie's back. 'Get your hand off me. Or you know what?' He nodded toward Donnie. 'We'll totally fuck you up.'

The boy dropped his hand and stared in pure misery as Donnie and Wes walked leisurely away, sipping their coffee.

And with that – *totally fuck you up* – Donnie knew that, at last, Wes was one of them.

CHAPTER 60

Dance's Pathfinder careened along the hilly stretch of Highway 68.

Not a good vehicle to be executing these maneuvers.

And not a good driver to be attempting them. Kathryn Dance had her talents but motoring wasn't one of them.

'Where are you, Michael?'

'Twenty minutes. There's a cruiser there now. CHP happened to be nearby.'

'I'll be there in three.'

Whoa, a faint skid and a blare of horn. You're allowed to honk angrily at a large Nissan SUV straying over the centerline toward you, even if there *is* a flashing blue light on the dashboard.

She tossed the phone onto the seat next to her. Get serious here.

Bounding into the lower lot at the inn, the Pathfinder sped up to the Highway Patrol trooper, dressed crisp, as they always looked, standing next to the Pacific Grove cop, whom she knew.

'Charlie.'

'Kathryn.'

'Agent Dance,' the CHP trooper said. 'I got the call. This is the Solitude Creek suspect?'

'We think so. Where is he?'

Charlie offered, 'Headed inside just after he parked. He didn't spot me, I'm sure.'

'Where's the car?'

'Follow me.'

They eased along the path, through gardens of pine and succulents. They paused behind a large bush.

The silver Honda was parked near the loading dock of the large hotel, a stone-and-glass structure that featured about two hundred rooms. The dining room was top notch and on Sunday it did a huge brunch business. Dance and her late husband, Bill, had come here several times for romantic busman-holiday weekends, while Stuart and Edie kept the kids.

Two more patrol cars pulled up quietly, filled with three MCSO deputies. Dance waved them over. Another car arrived. O'Neil. He climbed out and hurried along the path, joining his fellow officers.

'There's the car.' Dance pointed.

O'Neil glanced at her, then said to the others: 'What he's going to rig, incendiaries, flash bangs, whatever it is, probably isn't life-threatening in itself. That's not what turns him on. He wants to kill with the panic, people trampling each other – because they can't get out. You have to tell people that there's no real danger. They might not listen. They won't want to. But you have to try.

'But, remember, at Bay View he was armed. Nine mil. Plenty of ammo.'

They started to leave and go inside.

Which was when, with a *whump*, rather quiet actually, the Honda began to burn. In seconds the fire was raging. The device, whatever it might be, was in the trunk. Just above the gas tank. Dance imagined the unsub had drilled or punched a hole into it, to accelerate the blaze.

She then noticed smoke being drawn into the HVAC system, just like at Solitude Creek.

'The exit doors – he's probably wired them shut. Get 'em open, now! All of them.'

CHAPTER 61

Always happened, the orderly reflected.

The two elevators in this part of Monterey Bay Hospital were pretty dependable. But what happens, a woman comes in, contractions counting down, and car number one is out of commission.

'You'll be fine,' the thirty-five-year-old career medical worker told her. He turned his kindly face, under a fringe of curly hair, toward her.

'Ah, ah, ah. Thanks. My husband's on his way.' *Gasp.* 'Oh, my.'

The orderly had been on duty since five a.m. He was beat. Sundays were the days of rest for almost everybody – but not hospital workers. He eased the wheelchair a bit closer to the door, through the group of eight or nine visitors and medicos waiting for the car. He didn't think there'd be any problem with getting on the next ride. *They* weren't about to deliver.

The blonde, in her late twenties, was sweating fiercely. The orderly was happy to see a wedding ring on her finger. He was old-fashioned.

She grimaced in pain.

Come on, he thought to the car. A glance at the indicator. Second floor.

Come on.

'Where is he? Your husband?' Making conversation, putting her at ease.

'Fishing.'

'What's he fish for?'

'Ah, ah, ah . . . Salmon.'

So he was on a party boat. Four hours minimum. Was he out of his mind? She looked like she was ready to pop at any minute.

She glanced up. 'I'm two weeks early.'

The orderly smiled. 'My son was two weeks late. Still's never on time.'

'Daughter.' A nod toward the impressive belly. She gave another assortment of gasps.

Then, the car. The doors opened and people streamed out.

'Like one of those funny cars at a circus, all the clowns.'

The woman in labor didn't laugh. Okay. But he got a smile from a nurse and an elderly couple, carrying a balloon reading, 'IT'S A BOY!!!'

After the car had emptied one person pushed on first – a doctor, natch. Then the orderly wheeled his passenger – well, technically, *two* passengers – on and turned her, facing out. The others walked in as well, jockeying for space. As in all hospitals, the elevators were large – to accommodate gurneys – but with the other car out, this one filled up fast. Several said they'd wait. A dozen, fourteen people climbed on. The orderly looked at the maximum weight. How the hell helpful was that? He supposed the buzzer would sound if it was too heavy; it had a safety system like that, of course.

He hoped.

It was really packed, stifling. Hot too.

'Ah, ah, ah . . .'

'You'll be fine. We're three minutes away and the staff's all ready for you.'

'Thank y-aaaah.'

The door closed. She was in the far right-hand corner of the car, the orderly behind her, his back to the wall. He was extremely claustrophobic but, for some reason, being in this position, having no one behind him, kept the discomfort at bay.

A businessman looked around. Frowned. 'Shit, it's hot in here. Oh, sorry.'

Maybe directed to the pregnant woman, as if the fetus might be shocked. But, the orderly thought, shit, it *is* hot. Prodding the claustrophobia to squirm.

The elderly couple was discussing their granddaughter's choice of a name for the boy who'd just been born. The orderly heard the beep of phone keys. The doctor, natch again, had pulled out his mobile.

'I'm confirming a reservation . . .'

Blah, blah, blah.

The restaurant apparently didn't have a particular table he'd requested earlier. And he wasn't happy.

The car stopped at the second floor.

Three people got off. Five got on. Net gain. Ugh. And one was a biker. The Harley-Davidson variety. Black leather jacket, boots, stocking cap. And chains. Why did anybody need to wear chains? There was protest in the form of sighs and a glare or two (he could've waited) and the doors closed and the car rose slowly, bobbing under the weight. Not because he looked dangerous, which he did, but at his size. They were completely packed in now, belly to back. Man could've waited for the next trip.

This is hell.

Shit.

'Ah, ah, ah . . .' the woman gasped.

'Almost there,' the orderly said, reassuring himself as much as the pregnant woman.

Not that it worked.

As the car climbed toward floor three, conversation slowed, except for the complaining doctor, who was abrasively asking to talk to somebody in charge. 'Well, I don't know. Maybe the restaurant manager? Is that so very hard to figure out?'

Almost there . . .

Seconds unreeled like hours.

Jesus Christ. Get to the floor. Open the fucking door!

But the door didn't open. In fact, the elevator didn't even make it to the third floor. It bounced to a stop somewhere between two and three.

No, no, please. He believed he thought this. But the prayer or plea might have been uttered aloud. Several people looked his way. That might, however, have been from the look of encroaching panic on his sweaty face.

'It's all right. I'm sure it'll get moving soon.' It was the doctor, slipping his phone away, who'd offered this reassurance to the orderly.

And the pregnant woman in the wheelchair wiped abundant sweat from her forehead, tucked stringy hair behind her ears and tried to steady her breathing.

'Ah, ah, ah. I think it's coming. I think the baby's coming . . .'

CHAPTER 62

In surgical scrubs, cap and booties, Antioch March left the engineering room on the top floor of Monterey Bay Hospital, where he'd just cut the power to east wing elevator car number two. Twenty minutes earlier he'd done the same to car one, when it was empty. That drove the passengers to the second car, which guaranteed it would be packed when disaster struck.

Which it was. He was watching the video image of the interior from the camera inside. Of particular interest was the pregnant woman, whose head was tilted back and who was gasping. Her face wincing in pain. Even better was the expression of the orderly accompanying her. Panic starting to form. Exquisite.

March imagined what it was like in there. A dozen – no, more – belly to back, side to side, the air becoming denser and more useless. Hotter too. The power loss had taken out the air-conditioning unit as well.

He closed up his computer, tossed his tools into the tote bag. He left the top floor, the fifth, then headed to the basement. He didn't have much time, he knew. The repair crews had already been summoned to fix car one and, given their location in Salinas, could be there in twenty minutes. Car two, the occupied one, would be their priority once they arrived. The hospital maintenance staff, too, would head up to the infrastructure room on the top floor and look over the system. They'd see the vandalism immediately and might rig a solution, though given the dangerous nature of a two-thousand-pound piece of machinery, they'd probably wait for the pros.

Not much time, no, but he'd choreographed this attack as skillfully as the others. After deciding, at the aborted-church-supper hall, that a hotel would make a good target he'd come up with a plan that he believed even the brilliant Kathryn Dance could not anticipate.

He had *appeared* to attack the nearby inn, setting fire to the Honda – he needed to dump it anyway. The police would concentrate on that, and assume the hotel was the target, while he hurried on foot to the hospital a half-mile away.

They wouldn't consider the hospital a likely venue for an attack and wouldn't have added extra guards, he speculated, because there wasn't any one particular area of concentration: patients, visitors and doctors were spread out over several large buildings, which had numerous exits.

No, the charming and not unattractive Ms Kathryn Dance was clever but she'd surely miss that those oversize elevator cars in a hospital would be a perfect site for the panic game.

He now doubled-stepped down to the basement and peered out. He was in scrubs, yes, but had no ID pinned to the breast so he had to be careful. The corridor was empty. He stopped in the storeroom and collected a gallon container of a substance he'd found there earlier, on recon.

Diethyl ether.

Ether was a clear liquid, nowadays used as a solvent and cleanser mostly but years ago it was the anesthetic of choice. Famed dentist William T. G. Morton, of Boston, was the first to use inhaled ether to put patients under for medical procedures. The substance was soon praised as better than chloroform because there was a large gap between the recommended dosage and how much ether it would take to kill you; with chloroform that window of safety was much smaller.

However, ether did have one disadvantage: patients who were administered the drug occasionally caught fire. Sometimes they even exploded (he'd seen the remarkable pictures). Ether and oxygen or, even better, ether and nitrous oxide – laughing gas – could be as dangerous as dynamite.

Hence the chemical had been relegated to other uses, like here – a solvent. But March had been delighted to find some during his reconnaissance.

March now made his way to the elevator-room door. He opened it and dumped some of the liquid on the floor of the elevator shaft pit, holding his breath (ether may occasionally have blown up patients but it was a very efficient anesthetic).

He tossed a match into the puddle and it ignited explosively. The liquid was perfect since it burned hot but without any smoke; this would delay the fire department's arrival, since no automatic alarm would be activated. Meanwhile, though, the passengers would feel the heat rising from beneath them and smell the smoke from the Honda burning at the inn. They would be convinced the hospital was on fire and that they were about to be roasted alive.

Now Dr March walked casually along the corridor, head down, and took the exit to the hospital's parking garage.

He pictured the people in the elevator car and reflected that they were in absolutely no physical danger from what he'd done. The smoke was faint, the fire would burn itself out in ten minutes, the car's emergency brakes would not give out and send it plummeting to the ground.

They would be completely fine.

As long as they didn't panic.

CHAPTER 63

Got to get out, got to get out . . .

Please, please, please, please, please.

The orderly was paralyzed with terror. Emergency lights had come on – the car was brightly lit – and it didn't seem to be in danger of falling. But the sense of confinement had its slimy tentacles around him, choking, choking . . .

'Help us!' an older woman was crying.

Three or four people were pounding on the doors. Like ritual drums, sacrificial drums.

'You smell that?' somebody called. 'Smoke.'

'Christ. There's a fire.'

The orderly gasped. We're going to burn to death. But he considered *this* possibility in a curiously detached way. A searing, painful death was horrific but not as bad as the clutching, the confinement.

Tears filled his eyes. He hadn't known you could cry from fear.

'Is anybody there?' a woman nurse, in limp green scrubs, was shouting into the intercom. There'd been no message from security through the speaker.

'It's hot, it's hot!' A woman's voice. 'The flames're right under us. Help!'

'I can't breathe.'

'I've got to get out.'

The pregnant woman was crying. 'My baby, my baby.'

The orderly ripped his shirt open, lifted his head and tried to find some better air. But he could only fill his lungs with stinking, moist, used breath.

In the corner, a woman vomited.

'Oh, Jesus, lady, all over me.' The man beside her, forties, in shorts and a T-shirt, tried to leap back, getting away from the mess. But there was no place to go and the man behind him shoved back.

'Fuck you.'

The smell overwhelmed the orderly and it was all he could do to control his own gut.

Not so lucky with the woman beside him. She, too, was sick.

Phone calls:

'Yes, nine one one, we're trapped in an elevator and nobody's doing anything.'

'We're in a car, an elevator in the hospital. East Wing. We can't breathe.'

Somebody shouted: 'Don't both call at once! Are you fucking crazy? You'll block the circuits!'

'What – were you born in the fifties? They can handle more than—'

Then an otherworldly scream filled the car: the biker had lost control, lost it completely. Screaming, he grabbed the shoulders of the elderly woman in front of him and boosted himself up onto the crowd.

The orderly heard a snap as the woman's clavicle broke and she screamed and fainted. The biker didn't even notice; he scrabbled forward atop the shoulders and necks and heads of the others and slammed into the elevator door, breaking nails as he tried to pull the panels open. He was screaming and sobbing. Tears and sweat flowed like water from a cracked pipe.

A slim African-American woman, an aide, in what used to be called candy stripers, colorful scrubs with teddy bears on them, muscled her way forward and gripped him by the collar. 'We'll be okay. It'll be all right.'

Another scream from the huge man, the sound piercing.

She was unfazed. 'Are you listening? We'll be all right. Breathe slowly.'

The biker's red, bearded face leaned toward hers. Close. He gripped her neck. He was looking past her and for a moment it seemed as if he'd snap bones.

'Breathe,' she said. 'Slow.'

And he started to.

'You're all right. Everybody's all right. Nothing's happened to us. We're fine. There're sprinklers. The fire department's on its way.'

This calmed the biker and four or five of the passengers, but among the others panic was growing.

'Where the fuck are they?'

'Jesus, Jesus. We're going to die!'

'No no no!'

'I feel the heat, the flames. You feel that?'

'It's underneath us. It's getting hotter!'

'No, please! Somebody.'

'Hey!' the biker shouted, in a booming voice. 'Just, everybody chill!'

Some people did. But others were still in the grip of panic. They began pounding on the walls, screaming, ripping the hair and clothes of their fellows to get to the door. One woman, in her forties, knocked the biker aside, jammed her nails into the seam between the sliding doors and tried to force them open, just as he had attempted. 'Relax, relax,' the big man said. And pulled her away.

A man screamed into the intercom, 'Why aren't you answering? Why aren't they answering? Nobody's answering.'

Sobbing, cries.

Someone defecated.

The orderly realized he'd bitten his tongue. He tasted blood.

'The walls! They're hot. And the smoke.'

'We're going burn to death!'

The orderly looked at the doctor. He was unconscious. A heart attack? Had he fainted?

'Can't you hear us? We're stuck.'

'No, no!'

More screams.

'It's not that hot!' the biker called. 'I don't think the fire's that close. We're going to be okay.'

The nurse said, 'Listen to him! We'll be all right.'

And, slowly, the panicked passengers began to calm.

Which had no effect on the orderly. He couldn't take the

confinement for a moment longer. Suddenly he was consumed by a wholly new level of panic. He turned his back to the people in the car and whispered, 'I'm sorry.' To his wife and son.

His last words before panic became something else. A snake winding through his mouth and into his gut.

Frenzy . . .

Sobbing, he tore the pocket from his scrubs, wadded it into a ball and stuffed it down his own throat. Inhaling the cloth into his windpipe.

Die, please let me die . . . Please let this horror be over.

The suffocation was terrible, but nothing compared to the claustrophobia.

Please let me . . . let me . . .

His vision went black.

CHAPTER 64

'Listen to me!' Kathryn Dance shouted. 'Listen!'

'I've got my orders.'

She was on the east wing third floor of the hospital, speaking to one of the maintenance men.

'We need that door open now.'

'Lady, Officer, sorry. We gotta wait for the elevator repair people. These things are dangerous. It's not gonna fall. There's no fire. I mean, there was a little one but it's out now and—'

'You don't understand. The people inside, they're going to hurt themselves. They don't know there's no fire.'

She was in front of the doors to elevator number two. From inside she could hear screams and thuds.

'Well, I'm not authorized.'

'Oh, Jesus Christ.' Dance stepped past him and grabbed a screwdriver from his tool kit, a long one.'

'Hey, you can't—'

'Let her, Harry,' another worker said. 'It don't sound too good in there.'

The screams were louder now.

'Fuck,' Harry muttered. 'I'll do it.'

He took the screwdriver and set it down, then extracted a separate tool from the bag, an elevator door key. He slipped it into the hole and a moment later was muscling aside the doors.

Dance dropped to her belly, hit by the disgusting smell wafting out of the car, vomit, sweat, feces, urine. She squinted. Security lights, mounted on the CCTV camera inside the elevator, were glaring into her face. The ceiling of the car was about eighteen inches above the hospital's linoleum floor. To Dance's surprise, the passengers were fairly calm, their attention on two of their fellows: a pregnant woman, the source of the screaming. And a man passed out, though standing; his face an eerie blue. He was dressed in the uniform of a hospital orderly.

'The fire's out! You're safe!' This was the best way to convince them to calm, she'd decided. Telling them it was a prank, much less an intentional attack, didn't seem advisable.

Somebody was trying to give the orderly the Heimlich maneuver but could get no leverage.

'He's dying!' somebody called, nodding at the orderly. One of the male passengers suddenly snapped and lunged forward, stepped on a fellow occupant, a petite woman, and boosted himself up. 'I need out, I need out! Now!' He grabbed Dance's collar, trying to pull himself out. Still, he tugged fiercely. Dance screamed as her head was jammed into the gap, the metal ceiling of the car cutting into her cheek.

'No, listen!'

But he wasn't listening.

'Stop!'

She felt the growing strains of panic grip her. She began pounding the man's hand. Useless. Her head, sideways, was partly inside now, wedged completely still. She was feeling dizzy from the fumes and the dismal air. And that unbearable feeling of being unable to move. She tasted blood, dripping from the gash into her mouth.

Jesus . . .

No choice.

Sorry.

Dance reared her head back, clamped her teeth around the man's thumb and, tasting blood and tobacco, bit down hard with her molars.

He screamed and released her.

'That man!' she shouted, pointing to the orderly. 'Get him over here.'

Several of the passengers grabbed the man's collar and waist and pulled him off the floor. Then, together, they all handed him overhead, mosh-pit style. Dance gestured for two medics from Emergency to help and together they boosted the man up to the gap and got him out.

One ER worker said, 'We'll get him downstairs.' They placed him on a gurney and sprinted away.

Michael O'Neil came running up. 'Fire's out in the basement. You all right?' He frowned, looking at her face.

'Fine.'

Dance peered back into the car. Brother. She shouted over her shoulder, 'How long till we can raise the car?'

'Fifteen, twenty minutes, I'd guess,' the maintenance man said.

'Okay, then we need an ob-gyn here. Now.'

'I'll get one,' a male nurse behind her called.

Dance added, 'And make it the skinniest one you've got on staff.'

CHAPTER **65**

Dance said, 'I should've thought more clearly. This unsub . . . he's too fucking smart.'

A word that rarely escaped her lips.

They were in the lobby of the hospital, waiting for the Monterey County Crime Scene Unit officers to report what they'd found in the elevator motor room, the car itself and the pit in the basement.

After the Honda had started to burn in earnest and the officers had raced into the inn, Dance had checked two exit doors, found them unencumbered – and paused. She looked over the establishment.

'No,' she'd muttered. The inn was one story and, though built into a hill, the incline was minimal. To escape, all you had to do was pitch a chair through a window and step outside, safe as long as you minded the broken glass.

Then she'd noted the smoke wafting into the woods and had seen, behind them, the hospital.

She'd said to O'Neil, 'I don't think it's the inn that's his target.'

'What then?'

'Hospital.'

He'd considered this. 'A lot of exits.'

She'd suggested that he might hit a closed-off interior area. 'Surgical suite?'

'There wouldn't be enough people for a stampede. Good security. And—'

'Cafeteria? Waiting room.' Then: 'Elevator.'

O'Neil'd said, 'That's it.'

And they'd started jogging along the quarter-mile path that led to the hospital.

Now, in the third-floor lobby by the elevator, a nurse wandered up the hall. 'You're Special Agent Dance?'

'That's right.'

'You wanted to know. You asked earlier? The baby's fine. A girl. Mother has a broken arm – somebody stepped on it – but she'll be okay. She asked for your name. I think she wants to thank you. Can I give it to her?'

Dance handed her a card, wondering if the newborn was about to get a different given name than Mom and Dad had originally planned.

'And the orderly?'

'Heimlich didn't work – not with cloth stuck in the windpipe. But we did a tracheotomy. Looks like he swallowed it himself. Attempted suicide. He'll be okay. He's pretty shaken up. Claustrophobia's his big fear.'

A doctor, a tall African American, approached. He examined her cheek. 'Not too bad.' He offered her an antiseptic pad. She thanked him, tore it open and pressed the cloth against the cut, wincing at the brief pain. 'I'll bandage it up, you want.'

'I'll see. Maybe I'll come by the ER later. Thanks.'

O'Neil's phone rang. He took the call. After disconnecting, he said, 'Downstairs. Crime Scene's released the basement. There isn't much. But I'm going to take a look. You want to come?'

Just then her phone hummed. She glanced at it. 'You go on. I'll be a minute.' She answered. 'Mags.'

'Mom.'

'Everything all right?'

'Yeah, yeah. Fine. I finished the book report. It's five pages.'

'Good. We'll go over it when I'm home.'

'Mom.'

Of course she'd known there was another agenda. No child calls about book reports. No hurry. Give her time.

'What, hons?'

'Mom, I was thinking?'

'Yes, wonderful child?'

'I think I'll sing at the show, the talent show. I think I want to.'

Dance gave it a moment. 'Do you really want to?'

'Uh-huh.'

'Why'd you change your mind?'

'I don't know. I just did.'

'And this's something you really want to do?'

'Cross my heart.'

Those words tend to be an indicator of deception. But the fact that she was going to sing even if she didn't want to wasn't necessarily bad. It's a positive developmental step toward adulthood to take on a challenge even if you'd rather not.

'That's great, honey. Everybody'll love to hear you. All right, good. I'm proud of you.'

'I'm going to go practice now.'

'Don't overdo your voice. You probably know the song backwards by now. Hey, honey, is Jon there?'

'No, just Grandpa and me.'

'Okay. I'll see you soon.'

'Bye.'

'Love you.'

Where was Boling? Lost in the world of supercomputers, she guessed, still trying to crack the code of Stan Prescott's computer and the mobile that the unsub had dropped in Orange County. But his not calling? That was odd.

Dance turned to see her mother walking quickly toward her.

'Katie! You're all right?' she called, when she was still some distance away. Heads turned at the urgent words, as the stocky woman with short salt-and-pepper hair strode forward.

'Sure. Fine.' They hugged.

Edie Dance was a cardiac nurse here. She surveyed the elevator car. The blood, vomit, metal battered by fists. Edie shook her head, then hugged her daughter. 'How horrible,' she whispered. 'Somebody did this on purpose?'

'Yes.'

'Are— Oh, your face.'

'Nothing. Got scratched a little, getting into the car.'

'I can't imagine what it would be like to be trapped in there. How many people?'

'About fifteen. Pregnant woman. She'll be okay. Baby's fine. One close call.'

'No!'

'He tried to kill himself. He couldn't take the panic.'

Edie Dance looked around. 'Is Michael here?'

'He's meeting with his crime-scene people. They're running scenes in the basement and next door, at the inn.'

'Ah.' Edie's eyes remained down the hall. 'How's he doing? Haven't seen him for a while.'

'Michael? Fine.'

Body-language skill is such a blessing . . . and a curse. Her mother had something to say, and Dance wondered if she was supposed to pry it out of her. That was often the case with Edie Dance.

But she didn't have to.

Her mother said, 'I saw Anne O'Neil the other day.'

'You did?'

'She was with the kids. At Whole Foods. Or does she go by her maiden name now?'

Dance touched her sore face. 'No, she kept O'Neil.'

'Thought she was living in San Francisco.'

'Last I heard she was.'

'So Michael hasn't mentioned anything about it?'

'No. But we haven't had much of chance for personal conversation.' She nodded at the elevator. 'The case and all.'

'I suppose not.'

Dance sometimes wondered where her mother's loyalties lay. Recently Edie had been fast to tell her that Boling appeared to be moving away – without having mentioned anything to Dance. As it turned out, he only had a business trip and was planning to take Dance and the children with him for part of it – a mini-vacation in Southern California. True, Edie had her daughter's and grandchildren's interests at heart but Dance thought she'd been a bit too fast to relay what turned out to be a misunderstanding.

Now she was telling Dance that the man who'd once been a potential partner might not be as divorced as he seemed to be.

But Edie was not a gossip or a sniper. So, Dance speculated, this would have to do with protecting her daughter's heart, as any good parent would do. Though the information was irrelevant, of course. She was Jon Boling's partner now.

Edie expected her to say something more on the topic, she sensed. But Dance chose to deflect: 'Maggie's going to sing in the show after all.'

'Really? Wonderful. What changed her mind?'

'I don't know.'

Children were mysteries and you could go nuts trying to figure out patterns.

'Your dad and I'll be there. What time is it again?'

'Seven.'

'Dinner after?'

'I think that should work.'

Her mother was looking at her critically. 'And, Katie, I'd really get that face taken care of.'

'A lift?' Dance asked.

Mother and daughter smiled.

Her phone buzzed. Ah, at last.

'Jon, where've you been? We—'

'Is this Kathryn?' A man's voice. Not Boling's.

Her heart went cold. 'Yes. Who's this?'

'I'm Officer Taylor, Carmel Police. I found you on Mr Boling's speed-dial list. You're a friend, a co-worker?'

'Yes. Friend. I'm Kathryn Dance. Special agent with the CBI.'

A pause. Then: 'Oh. Agent Dance.'

'What's happened?' Dance whispered. She was deluged with an ice-cold memory – of the trooper calling her after her husband had been killed.

'I'm afraid I have to tell you that Mr Boling's been in an accident.'

CHAPTER 66

Antioch March was back in his suite at the Cedar Hills Inn.

He'd finished the workout at the inn's luxurious health club and was enjoying a pineapple juice in his room, watching the news reports of the event at the hospital.

Not a single fatality.

Antioch March was mildly disappointed but the Get was satisfied. For the time being. Always for the time being.

Somebody's not happy . . .

His phone rang. Both caller and callee were on new burner phones. But he knew who it was: his boss. Christopher Jenkins ran the Hand to Heart website. He gave March his assignments to travel to non-profit humanitarian groups, who would then sign up for the site. Jenkins also arranged for March's other jobs, which were the real moneymakers for the company.

'Hi,' he said.

No names, of course.

'Just wanted to tell you, the client's extremely satisfied.'

'Good.' What else was there to say? March had done what he'd been contracted to do in the Monterey area. He'd also eliminated evidence and witnesses and cut all ties that could potentially link the incident to the client, who was paying Jenkins a great deal of money for March's services. The client wasn't the nicest guy in the world – in fact, he could be quite a prick – but one thing about him: he paid well and on time.

'He's sent eighty percent. It's gone through proper channels.'

Bitcoin and the other weird new payment systems were clever in theory as a mechanism to pay anonymously for the sort of work that March performed but they were coming under increasing scrutiny. So Jenkins – the businessman in the operation – had decided to resort to good old-fashioned cash. 'Channels' meant he'd received a FedEx box containing 'documents', which in a way it did, though each document would have a picture of Benjamin Franklin on it.

Antioch March had eight safe-deposit boxes around the country, each with about a million inside it.

Jenkins continued, 'Wanted to tell you. Found a restaurant we have to try. *Foie gras* is the best. I mean, the best. And they serve the Château d'Yquem in Waterford. Oh, and the red wine? Pétrus.' A chuckle. 'We had two bottles.'

March didn't know the wines but he assumed they were expensive. Maybe Jenkins had even poured some for him in the past. The two men had worked together for about six years, and from day one, Jenkins had treated March to fancy dinners, like the one he was describing now. They were okay. But the elaborate meals didn't really move March, in the same way the Vuitton and the Coach and the Italian suits didn't. He accepted the gifts but was forever surprised that Jenkins didn't notice his indifference. Or maybe he did but didn't care. Just like March's lethargy at certain other times, in his connection with Jenkins.

His boss now added, 'Just had a proposal. I'll tell you about it when I'm out.'

They were always vague when they were on the phone. Yes, these were prepaid mobiles but listenable to if one were inclined to listen, and traceable if one were inclined to trace.

And people like Kathryn Dance would be more than happy to do both.

'I'll be in tomorrow night,' Jenkins said.

'Good.' March tried to be enthusiastic. There was another reason Jenkins was coming to the inn, of course. Which March could have done without. But he could live with it: anything for the Get.

'Thanks again for all your work. This is a good one. This's a winner. And it'll open up a lot of doors for us. Well, think we've been talking long enough. Night.'

They hung up.

March checked the news, but there was nothing yet about Jon Boling's death due to a bicycle malfunction. He supposed that with both brakes out the bike would have been doing fifty or sixty when Dance's boyfriend had slammed into the traffic or rocks at Carmel Beach. March wasn't sure exactly how close Dance was to Boling but he knew he was more than a casual date; in her Pathfinder, at the Bay View Center, he'd found a card he'd sent her. A silly thing, funny. Signed, *Love, J.* March had noted the return address and driven there straight from the scene of the attack.

Motivated by both a need to distract the huntress and a bit of jealousy (he found he desired Kathryn even more than Calista), he'd waited outside Boling's house, planning to beat him to death, a robbery gone wrong. Or coma him, at the least. But the man still hadn't returned when March got the text about foolish Stan Prescott down in Orange County and he'd had to leave.

He'd followed Boling later and decided he liked the idea of a bike accident better than an obvious attack.

March looked at his shaved scalp in the mirror. He didn't like it. He looked a bit like Chris Jenkins, now he thought about it. And reflected that it was ironic that Jenkins – former military, crack shot, familiar with all sorts of weapons, with friends among the security and mercenary crowd – was the businessman who never got out into the field to run the assignments.

And Antioch March, who was essentially a misplaced academic, was the one fulfilling them.

But it worked to everybody's advantage. Jenkins lacked the finesse to set up the deaths the way March did, the intellect to foresee what the police and witnesses would do.

March, on the other hand, had no talent for dealing with clients. Negotiating, vetting to make sure they were not law, structuring payment terms, maintaining the Hand to Heart website.

March finished his juice.

The client is extremely satisfied . . .

Which, March thought, was the ultimate goal of his father, the salesman, as well.

He flopped down in the sumptuous bed. He had many plans to make. But at the moment he preferred his thoughts to dwell upon . . . who else? The captivating Kathryn Dance.

CHAPTER 67

At CBI headquarters once more.

Dance had hit the restroom to scrub the face wound but she assessed it as minor. A little sting. There'd be a bruise. Nothing more.

She turned the corner to the Gals' Wing. It being the weekend, the office wasn't staffed with assistants. She walked past Maryellen Kresbach's station and into her own office.

'Hey.' Jon Boling, sitting in the chair across the desk, smiled.

'Jon!' She strode to him fast and started to throw her arms around his shoulders, then saw him wince in anticipation. She stopped. 'How are you?'

'Fine. Relatively speaking. But sore. Really sore.' His face was bruised and he had two bandages, on his cheek and neck. His wrist was wrapped in beige elastic.

'What happened?'

'Lost the brakes on Ocean.'

The main street leading down to the beach in Carmel. Very steep.

'No!'

'They felt funny, when I started off, so I got about a half-block from the store . . . the store I was at and I pulled over. That's when they popped. Both of the brake shoes.'

'Jon!'

'I steered into bushes, and that slowed me down. Went through them and hit the curb and a car at the stop sign.'

'The brakes?' she asked. 'You think they were tampered with?'

'Tampered with? Why would . . . Oh. Your unsub, you're thinking?'

'Maybe. To slow me down, distract me.'

'But how did he put us together?'

'Nothing about this guy would surprise me. You notice anybody near your bike?'

'No. I had an errand. Left the bike outside. Only five minutes. I wasn't paying any attention.' Then Boling was looking her over. 'But . . . what happened to you?'

'Nothing critical. I got banged up getting into an elevator.'

'Well, that must have been quite an entrance.'

She told him of the latest attack. 'Nobody hurt badly.'

Then her eyes strayed to what was on her desk in front of him: Stan Prescott's Asus computer. Beside it was a portable hard drive. 'You cracked it?'

'Well, my partner did.'

'Partner?'

'Lily.'

Dance glanced at him with a playful frown. 'Lily. Is this where I start to be jealous?'

'Ah, Lily . . . My main squeeze. She's a second-generation Blue Gene/P four-way symmetric multiprocessor supercomputer with node-to-node logic communication. But as sexy as that is, you've got a better body.'

At that moment O'Neil walked through the door. He blinked. That wasn't – it seemed – a reaction to Boling's comment about Dance. He was staring at the bandages and bruises. 'Jon, Jesus. What happened?'

'The dangers of going green. Bike accident. Banged up a little. I was lucky.'

Dance said, 'Maybe intentional.'

'So he knows who's out to stop him,' O'Neil said to Dance. 'I'll order a protective detail to keep an eye on your place.'

Not a bad idea. She'd also make sure the children didn't go anywhere alone. Certainly Wes couldn't take any more bike rides with Donnie. Not until the unsub was caught.

O'Neil had his mobile out. He said to Boling, 'I'll order one for you too, if you want.'

There was a pause. Dance said, 'Just one. For my house is fine.'

'Sure.' And O'Neil phoned the request in. After a brief conversation he hung up. 'There'll be an undercover out front in the evenings. Random drive-bys too. During the day.' He had ordered protection for her parents too.

She thanked him. Then glanced toward Boling. 'Jon got into Stan Prescott's computer. And phone.'

'Great.'

Boling handed her the small USB-powered hard drive. The computer forensic protocol was that you backed up the suspect's drive onto an external because there were often software booby traps in the computer itself.

She plugged it in and nodded at her keyboard. He took over.

'I've got access to Prescott's emails and the websites he visited. You should review it yourself but I didn't see any connection to the Solitude Creek incident or Bay View. No personal connection, I mean. He didn't correspond with anybody about them – and he didn't delete anything about them either. I reconstructed the deleted files. All of them. Looks like he downloaded the pictures of Solitude Creek from a pay site.'

'Pay site? What's that? I thought they were from a TV newscast.'

'They were originally. But somebody uploaded them to a commercial site where members can see graphic violence – stills and movies. Do you know about them?'

Neither Dance nor O'Neil did.

'Oh, well, here, take a look.' He hesitated a moment. 'You'd better brace yourself.'

'Brace?'

He typed and a page loaded.

Dance's eyes widened. 'Oh, my. What's this?'

O'Neil walked around and stood on Dance's other side. The three of them stared at the website. It was called Cyber-Necro. com and the opening graphic revealed a computer-generated image of a man plunging a knife into the belly of a buxom woman strapped down to a medieval table.

Boling said, 'It's a pay site devoted to graphic images of murder and rape victims, disasters, crimes scenes, accidents, medical procedures. The Solitude Creek pictures were in the section on "Theater and Sporting Events Deaths".'

'That's actually a category?'

'Yep. People pay a lot of money to see those pictures and videos. I couldn't tell you why. Maybe a shrink could. Voyeurism, sexual, sadistic. Who knows? I've gotten quite an education in the past few hours. There're hundreds of sites like this. I might write a paper on it. Some sites are like this one.' He nodded at the screen. 'Real deaths and injuries. But you can also get custom-made videos. Actresses – usually actresses – being shot or stabbed or hit by arrows. Strangulation and asphyxia're popular too. Sexual assaults. Some hard-core. And the weapons? The special effects're good. Shockingly good. You'd almost think the women were actually being killed but they keep appearing in other clips. It seems some men have favorite actresses they want to see killed. Over and over.'

O'Neil whispered, 'I've never heard of this.'

'A whole underground, I found.' Boling typed. 'Here're the pictures of Solitude Creek.'

The page on Cyber-Necro.com showing pictures of the disaster had about fifteen pictures. Most were from the media, shot afterward, depicting blood. Some were bad phone videos, low resolution, taken inside during the crush.

Dance and O'Neil glanced at each other. They'd both be thinking the same thing: was there anything in the videos or pictures that might help the case?

'How can we watch the videos?' Dance asked.

'You join. A hundred a month and you can download whatever you want.'

Dance went to the home page and signed up.

Boling added, 'If you want, you can get a discount if you join Cyber-Necro's sister site at the same time.'

'What's that?' she asked.

Boling smiled. 'I think it's called Sluts-On-Demand.'

Dance nodded. 'Probably just the one. It's going to be hard enough to get Charles to sign off on my expense account as it is.'

In a half-hour they'd downloaded all of the clips and images of Solitude Creek. She wondered who'd taken the videos. During the canvassing she'd asked if anyone had done so; no one admitted it, perhaps not wishing to seem heartless.

But they found nothing helpful. The images, video and still, were low resolution and murky. No clues.

One picture Dance stared at for a long moment. It was a still image similar to the one Prescott had used for his phony jihad rant on Vidster. It showed the interior of the club, taken several days after the event, according to the time stamp.

'What?' O'Neil asked, seeing her face.

'Oh, I couldn't place that face.' She pointed. Although the focus of the pictures was the bloodstains, in the mirror behind the bar you could see several faces. They were indistinct but the one she indicated was fairly visible.

'It's the US Congressman.'

'Congressman?'

'Nashima. Daniel Nashima. He must've come back to examine the club after the police released the scene.'

Boling said, 'If it's an election year, he'll be talking about reforms in fire codes and all that. Not to be cynical.'

Dance said, 'Really appreciate all this. Thanks, Jon.'

'Wish I'd been more helpful.'

'That's the thing about policing,' O'Neil said. 'Even when it doesn't pan out, you've got to do the work anyway.'

So Prescott's computer was a bust. But then Dance asked, 'What about the unsub's phone?'

The burner he'd dropped during the pursuit in Orange County.

'It's a prepaid from a Chicago exchange.'

'Like the one he used at the site of the Bay View Center disaster to lead police into thinking the killer was headed toward Fisherman's Wharf.'

Boling added, 'My guess is he goes through a phone every few days. This one has only a few texts on it. To and from a prepaid with a California exchange.' He consulted his notes. 'Incoming: "Very pleased so far. Second installment en route." Outgoing: "Good. Thanks." Incoming: "What's next?" Outgoing: "Cleaning up. All will be good. Will be in touch."'

'Well,' Dance whispered.

O'Neil was nodding. 'There's our answer.'

She said, 'Sure is.'

Boling said, 'Sorry? What do you mean?'

She explained, 'Our unsub is a pro. He's working for somebody.'

Dance then placed a call to TJ Scanlon, gave him the number of the California phone and asked him to contact the service provider and see if it was still active.

'On it, boss.'

Then a thought occurred to her. She considered it. Interesting idea. She said to O'Neil. 'Do you have the pictures of your Jane Doe, the one we think our unsub killed?'

'Sure.'

He went onto the MCSO secure server and called them up.

On her computer she accessed the images of Stan Prescott.

O'Neil said, 'Right. Like we were saying: Same sort of MO. Strangled or asphyxia. On their backs.'

'And,' she said, 'look. They're both under lights.'

'Maybe they just fell there.'

'No. I don't think so. I think he moved the lamps so he could get pictures on his cell phone. It occurred to me when I was looking at the crime-scene pictures on that website – those bodies were all well-lit too.'

O'Neil nodded, now understanding. 'Proof of death.'

'Exactly.'

'What do you mean?' Boling asked.

'He needed clear pictures to prove that the witnesses'd been eliminated. That line in the text about "cleaning up". He's making a lot of money on this job and he wants to be sure the man who's hired him is confident he's not leaving any traces.'

Five-thousand-dollar shoes . . .

O'Neil said, 'Brilliant. He's targeted a couple of venues to make it look like this's the work of a psycho. But, no, he's got a specific venue in mind. He was hired to destroy it.'

'Or a person,' Dance said, after a moment. 'He *could've* been hired to destroy a location, sure. But also to kill somebody specific.'

O'Neil nodded. 'Sure. Makes sense. But if it's an individual, then who?'

Dance offered, 'At the hospital, no one in the elevator could have been the intended victim.'

'Because how could he know who'd be in that car at that time? And at the Bay View Center – that venue wouldn't've worked either.'

'No,' O'Neil said. 'The people who died all drowned. He couldn't be sure he'd get a specific target there. How'd he know who'd jump into the bay? No, it was Solitude Creek. His target was there, in the audience.'

O'Neil: 'The panic starts. The unsub's changed out of his workman's clothes. He's in the audience. He gets close to the victim and kills him or her. Trips them maybe, crushes their throat, breaks a rib that pierces their lung.'

'He'd be in the mob too. But no—'

'Right.' O'Neil carried through on her thought: 'He's a big guy. He can survive a bit of jostling.'

'Besides, remember, there was no fire. It wasn't like he was going to burn to death. He knew most people would get out okay.'

O'Neil was scrolling through his mobile. 'There were three deaths at Solitude Creek. Guess we'll have to look at all the victims.'

It was then that she had one of those moments.

A to B to Z . . .

'Let's go for a drive,' said Kathryn Dance.

'Me?' Boling asked.

She smiled.

'No. Better if it's just Michael and me.'

CHAPTER 68

'Oh. Hi, Mrs Dance. I mean, Agent Dance.'

'Hello, Trish. This is Detective O'Neil with the Monterey County Sheriff's Office.'

Nervous. Naturally.

'Hi.'

The detective nodded down to her. 'Hello, Trish. I'm sorry about your mother.'

'Yeah. Thanks. It's, you know, tough.'

'I'm sure it is.'

The three stood on the front porch of one of the nicest houses Dance had ever seen. Easily seven thousand square feet. Stone and glass and chrome. A Beverly Hills house, a Malibu house. A rich producer's or film star's house.

A moving company truck was parked by the garage. The workers were carrying boxes and furniture into the house, not out.

She'd known Frederick was moving back in but she appreciated this physical evidence regarding who had hired the Solitude Creek unsub.

Dance asked, 'Is your father home?'

'No. He's taking my aunt and uncle to the airport. But he could be back soon.'

A conspiratorial smile. 'We won't be long. I know he's not a big fan of mine. Do you mind if we ask you a few more questions?'

'You want to come in?'

'Thank you.'

They walked into the entryway – bigger than Dance's living room and kitchen combined – then entered a study. Sumptuous leather and metal furniture. The couch alone could have been traded in for a new Pathfinder. They all sat.

'Uhm, the thing is, I didn't tell my father we talked, you and me,' the girl said.

'We'll play along.' Dance gave a smile. 'If he comes back.'

Relief flooded Trish's eyes. 'Thanks. Like, really.'

'Sure.'

'I heard he did the same thing at the Bay View Center.'

O'Neil said, 'And the hospital, the fire in the elevator.'

'Why's he doing it?'

They, of course, demurred on the suspected motive. Dance said, 'We don't know. There doesn't seem to be any clear reason. Now, Trish, I'm sorry to ask but I need to know a little more about your mother's death. Some of the facts. Are you up for that?'

She was still. She took a deep breath, then nodded. 'If it'll help you catch this asshole.'

'I hope it will.'

'Okay, sure. I guess.'

Dance said, 'Go back to that night. At the Solitude Creek Club. After you and your mother got separated.'

A nod.

O'Neil, who'd read the account, said, 'If I understand, you were being swept toward the kitchen and she was in the crowd going for the exit doors.'

'That's right.'

Dance asked, 'But before you got into the kitchen, you could see your mother, right?'

Eyes hollow, she nodded. 'Yeah. With the emergency lights. I could see good.'

'Trish, this is a hard question but I have to know. Did it look to you like somebody hurt your mother intentionally? Pushed her out of the way? On to the floor? To save themselves?' She was hardly going to suggest to the girl that her father had hired someone to kill Michelle Cooper, his ex-wife.

The girl said, 'Oh, are you thinking of arresting some of the people in the crowd?'

'Whenever somebody dies, it's important to get the exact details.'

'For the reports,' O'Neil added.

Trish was shaking her head. 'I don't know. The last time I saw her—' She choked, then continued, 'The last time I saw her, she was waving at me and then she disappeared behind the pillar, near the last exit door.'

'Did you see anybody beside her, holding her, pushing her?'

'No. But the next thing I knew I was in the kitchen and then we were falling out onto the gravel and grass, and everybody was screaming and crying.'

Tears streaked her cheeks. Dance dug into her purse and found a pack of Kleenex. 'Here you go.'

Trish opened the pack and pulled a few out, wiped and blew.

Dance was disappointed she hadn't provided anything concrete. But Dance and O'Neil had other facts to uncover – slowly and with finesse.

'Thanks, Trish, this's been helpful.'

'Sure.' She sniffed.

O'Neil delivered his line, according to their script: 'I don't think we have anything else.'

Dance looked around the room. 'Your father's moving back. Where does he live now?'

'Yeah. He lives in a place in Carmel Valley now.'

'Nice.'

'Not really. Not his place. It's a total dive. And with me in school – Carmel High's a mile away – it made sense for him to move here. Like . . .' She glanced around her. 'Not really too shabby, huh?'

O'Neil asked, 'Was this your house when your folks were married?'

Finesse . . .

'That's right.'

Dance offered another glance to O'Neil. The cheating husband had lost it in the property settlement. Now he was back in. He couldn't take title – it would be part of the bequest to Trish from her mother. But when she came of age he would work on her to get it transferred back to him. Motive one for Frederick Martin to be the killer. She suspected there was another too.

'Was it a tough divorce?' O'Neil asked. Good delivery, Dance thought. They'd rehearsed the line on the drive here.

'Oh, yeah, really mean. It was awful. They said really bad things about each other.'

'I'm sorry,' Dance offered.

'It totally sucked, yeah.'

Dance added, 'Hard about the money too, I imagine. The alimony payments?'

'Oh, yeah. I think they called it something else.'

'Maintenance,' O'Neil chimed in. Of the two of them, Dance and O'Neil, he was the only one with first-hand experience of the dissolution of a marriage.

'Oh, yeah, that's it. They don't know that I know. But I heard them talk. Really big checks. Like fifteen thousand a month.'

Dance assumed that, while child support would go on as long as Trish was under eighteen, maintenance payments would terminate upon the death or remarriage of the ex-spouse. So Martin would save nearly two hundred K a year. For a man living in a small house in the valley, presumably with limited income, that could be a huge windfall.

Motive number two.

And Martin would have known Michelle would be at the club. He would have given instructions to the unsub to make sure the girl was safe.

Or would he?

Dance felt her gut flip. If the girl had died too, was her father the beneficiary of *her* will? Would he have gotten the entire house and estate back?

Then Trish was saying, 'It's, like, too bad Dad'll lose all that.'

'Too bad . . . what?' Dance asked.

'I mean, he does okay at his job but he could really use that money. Trying to go back to school and everything.'

Silence for a moment. The girl's words spun like a top through Dance's thoughts.

'Your mother was paying your *father* alimony?' she asked.

'Yeah.'

O'Neil asked, 'Why did your parents get divorced?'

Trish looked down. 'My mom kind of cheated on him. And he's such a nice guy. Really cool. But Mom, she just sort of . . . you know, she ran around a lot. And not just with one guy but a bunch of them. Dad worked part time to raise me and put Mom through school. He didn't finish his degree. So when he found out she'd been cheating on him and went for the divorce, the judge made her pay alimony. I mean, maintenance. Man, I don't know what he's going to do now for money.'

Frederick Martin's motive for killing his wife vanished.

Dance would have TJ check out the facts but she'd be very surprised to find any variation. It was obvious the girl was telling the truth.

'Well, thanks for your help, Trish. I'll let you know if we find anything else.'

'You really think somebody hurt Mom on purpose, to get out of the club?'

'It doesn't seem likely, what we're learning,' O'Neil said.

'If they did,' the girl said, 'I don't really blame them. What happened that night, the panic and everything, it wasn't human beings doing that. Like you can't blame a tornado or an earthquake. They don't think, they don't plan on doing anything bad. They just happen.'

CHAPTER 69

At her desk, O'Neil beside her, Dance answered the phone. ''Lo?'

'Boss.'

'TJ. On speaker with Michael,' Dance told him.

'Hey, Michael. I love it when people say they're on speaker. Think of all the juicy things they were about to say but can't.'

'TJ?'

'I pulled strings and got into the courthouse. Yes, on Sunday. The girl's story checks out. Trish. It's confirmed. I read the settlement agreement and court documents, talked to the lawyers. Frederick Martin had zero to gain if his ex was gone. He had *negative* to gain – except it's not like you gain anything negative. You know. Anyway, it's going to cost him a lot now that she's dead. Michelle didn't leave much to her daughter either. The house, in trust, is hers but it's mortgaged to the throat. Trish gets a small stipend. Somebody named Juan got the rest but it's only fifty K. Not worth killing for. Yep, I said Juan. I'm betting the pool boy.'

Dance sighed.

'Good theory, though, boss. You've got two more fatalities at Solitude Creek. Maybe they were the intended victims.'

O'Neil said, 'We thought of that and I looked at them, TJ. One was a college student, one was a woman in her twenties – there with a bachelorette party. No motive that we could find.'

'Back to Square A. You need me in the office, boss?'

'No. Just track down that company in Nevada, the one doing the surveying at Solitude Creek. Give me an update in the morning.'

'Will do, boss.' He disconnected.

O'Neil seemed preoccupied.

Dance looked at the time. She said, 'Oh, wanted to ask. You

do any more thinking about Maggie's talent show? Tonight at seven?'

We might have plans. I'll let you know. Bring a friend?

'Oh, I should've mentioned. Can't make it. Tell her I'm sorry.'

'Sure. No worries.'

Together they walked out of the office and made their way to the exit. Dance noticed the Guzman Connection task-force conference room was dark, Foster, Steve Two, Allerton and Gomez gone for the night.

In the parking lot O'Neil and Dance walked to their cars, parked beside each other.

'What a case, hmm?'

'Yep,' he replied. They stood together for a moment. Then he said, 'Night.'

That was all. She nodded. They got into the cruiser and the Pathfinder respectively, and without another look they drove to the highway and turned in different directions.

A half-hour later she was home.

'Mom!' Maggie was waiting on the front porch.

Dance had called and told her daughter she was on the way. But Maggie looked agitated. Had she been concerned that Dance was going to be late? Or was she troubled that her mother had shown up on time and there was no excuse to miss the show? Even though Maggie'd changed her mind about singing Dance knew she wasn't looking forward to it.

'Give me a few minutes and then we'll be on our way. Go get dressed.'

Her daughter had a special costume for the event.

Together they walked inside and Maggie disappeared into her room. Dance kissed Boling.

He whispered, 'How're you feeling?' Touching her face gently.

'Fine. You?'

'My bandage's bigger than your bandage.'

She laughed and kissed him again. 'We'll compare bruises later.' She saw Wes and Donnie on the back porch. They weren't playing their game but intently looking over a Japanese comic. 'Hi, boys!'

'Hi, Mrs Dance.'

'Hey, Mom.'

'We leave in fifteen. Donnie, you want to come to Maggie's class's show? At the grade school. It's at seven. We can have you home by nine.'

'No, that's okay. I've gotta get home.'

Wes slipped the comic into his book bag.

Dance had a sip of the wine Boling had ready for her, then headed upstairs for a shower and a change of clothes.

She stripped off her outfit, which she now detected smelled of smoke – oil and rubber smoke. Might be destined for the trash. She ran the shower and stepped under the stream of hot water, feeling a one-two stab of pain: the right side of her torso from the pulled muscle and her cut cheek. She let the water pound her for five full minutes, then stepped out and toweled off.

Examining the facial injury, she noted that the cut would leave a scar and that the bruise was striving to conquer more of her face. Probably should have had it looked at in the ER, after all.

She thought wryly of the curious dynamics of her life. Caught in a stampeding herd of theme-park patrons, squeezing into an elevator car to rescue a pregnant woman and a choking victim . . . and now off to a ten-year-old's talent show.

Then she was dressed – black blouse, fancy jeans and navy jacket. Gold Aldos with exotic heels. A look in the mirror. She let her hair hang loose, better to conceal the banged-up jaw and cheek.

Downstairs she called, 'Donnie. Did you bike over? I didn't see it.'

The boy stared at her for a moment.

Wes said, 'No, we left them at his house.'

'You want a ride home? It's on the way to Maggie's school.'

Donnie glanced at Wes, then turned back. 'No, thanks, Mrs Dance. I'll walk. I feel like it.'

'Okay. Come on, Wes, we have to go.'

He and Donnie bumped fists and her son joined her in the front entryway.

'Maggie!' Dance called.

Her daughter appeared.

Boling said, 'Well, look at you.'

She gave a shy smile.

Dance said, 'Beautiful, Mags.'

'Thank you.' In a stilted tone. Formality is a form of deflection.

'Really.'

Maggie *was* looking pretty. Her outfit was a white sequined dress that Dance had snagged at Macy's. It was the perfect outfit for singing a song by an ice queen or princess or whatever Elsa was. Light blue leggings too and white shoes.

They walked to the car, Boling slightly limpier than Dance, climbed in and belted up. Dance was behind the wheel. Into the street. She honked and Donnie Verso turned and waved. Then Dance hit the CD player and they listened to the infectious 'Happy' by Pharrell Williams. Boling tried to sing along. 'Hopeless,' he said.

It was.

'I'll work on it.'

'I wouldn't really worry about it,' Wes said. Everyone laughed. Dance changed the song to a Broken Bells tune.

In ten minutes they were at Maggie's grade school. The lot was full. Dance parked near the gym and they got out. She locked the vehicle. 'Let's go to the green room.'

'What's that?' Maggie asked.

'It's the place backstage where they have the snacks.'

'Let's go!' Wes said.

Dance put her arm around Maggie. 'Come on, Elsa. Time to wow the audience.'

Her daughter said nothing.

CHAPTER 70

'Working late, sir? And on Sunday.'

O'Neil looked up at Gabriel Rivera. The junior deputy, in uniform as always, stood in the doorway of O'Neil's small work-space in the Sheriff's Office building in Salinas. He discouraged the 'sir' but the young man was unshakeable in his respect. 'Looks like you are too.'

'Well, we get triple time, right?'

O'Neil smiled. 'What's up?'

'They got an ID on the body in Santa Cruz. You were right. Homeless guy living off and on in a shelter. Blood work-up, he was way drunk.' The big man shook his head. 'As for Grant? Nothing, sir. Just no sign at all. Any other ideas? I'm at a loss.'

With the Solitude Creek unsub on the loose, O'Neil had had to delegate much of the Otto Grant disappearance to others. There'd been no sightings of the farmer who'd lost his property.

'You've expanded to surrounding counties?'

'All through the Central Valley. Zip.'

'And nothing online since his last post?'

'Nothing after five days ago.'

That was when the farmer had written another diatribe against the state.

You STOLE my property thru the travasty called eminent domain!

'You run his posts by Dr Shepherd?'

'I did,' Rivera said. 'He agrees that the comments could support a suicide but there weren't any other indications I could find. He didn't put his affairs in order. Didn't take out any life insurance. No goodbye calls to neighbors or army buddies or relatives.'

'And any place he'd run to?'

'Checked the lakes he likes to fish at, where he's rented cabins. A casino in Nevada he went to some. Nothing.'

O'Neil didn't bother to ask about credit-card or mobile-phone tracing. Rivera had checked all that first.

'Probably not much else to do until some campers find the body. Or fishermen.'

Worse ways to die than going to sleep in the Bay . . .

'And on our Jane Doe?'

O'Neil looked at the picture of the woman who'd died of asphyxiation, possibly another victim of the unsub. Lying on her back, face up, under the light in the cheap motel room.

'I've heard back from Nevada, Oregon, Arizona, Colorado. No matches in driver's-license-photo databases. But facial recognition equipment . . .' He shrugged. 'You know. Can be hit or miss. The pix're on the missing-persons wires, state and fed. She's young, has to have family're worried about her.'

'Not much more we can do.'

'You staying?' Rivera asked.

'A while.'

'Night, then.'

'You too, Gabe.'

O'Neil stretched. He glanced down at a pink phone-message slip, a call he'd returned earlier that day.

Anne called.

He thought about his ex. Then about Maggie's recital, soon to get under way. He was sorry to be absent. He hoped she wouldn't be disappointed.

Jon will be there . . .

Though her boyfriend's presence wasn't the reason he couldn't go. Not at all. He *did* have plans this evening. Just curious that Dance would mention Boling. O'Neil had assumed that he'd be in attendance.

Jon will be there . . .

Enough. Let it go.

Back to work.

The preliminary crime-scene report from the hospital was open on his desk and Michael O'Neil was reading through it. Eighty percent of a cop's job is paper or bytes.

He took notes from the new report, then opened some of the

earlier ones to compare data: from the Solitude Creek incident, the Bay View Center and Orange County.

. . . footprint seventeen inches from driver's door of suspect's vehicle revealed one partial three-quarter-inch front tread mark, not identifiable . . .

Reading, reading, reading.

And thinking: There probably was a time when it might've worked between us, Kathryn and me. But that's over. Circumstances have changed.

Wait. No. That wasn't right.

There'd been a time when it *would* have worked out. Not 'might'.

But he was accurate when he'd said circumstances had changed. So what would have been — and what would have been good, really good — wasn't going to happen now.

Circumstances. Changed.

That was life. Look at Anne, his ex. She'd definitely changed. He'd been surprised, nearly shocked, to get that phone call from her last week. She'd sounded like the person he remembered from when they'd met, years ago. She'd been reasonable and funny and generous.

He then reminded himself sternly he was not thinking about Kathryn Dance any more.

Get. Back. To. It.

. . . accelerant was diethyl ether, approximately 600 ml, ignited by a Diamond Strike Anywhere match, recovered from the site of the burn. Not traceable. Generic . . .

Kathryn was with Jon Boling.

So O'Neil would go in a different direction too.

Best for everybody. For his children, for Dance, for Boling. He was convinced this was the right thing to do.

. . . Statement by witness 43 at Bay View Center crime scene, James Kellogg: 'I was, what it was I was standing near the street, the one that goes through Cannery Row. I'm not from here, so I don't remember what it was. And I'm like what's all this, all the police stuff going on? Was it terrorists? I'd heard shots or firecrackers earlier, like five minutes earlier but I didn't know. I

didn't see anything – I looked around – but I didn't see anything weird, you know. I mean, I did. But I thought it was a normal crime, not like the attack at the club.

'*This guy, he was tall, over six feet, wearing shorts, sunglasses and a hat – I think he was blond though, you could see that. He was looking around and he went to a car, this SUV, and looked in and opened the door. And I could see he was looking through a woman's purse. I thought he was going to steal something. But he just put it back. So he wasn't a thief.*'

'*What kind of SUV was it?*'

'*Oh, it was a Nissan Pathfinder. Gray. And the reason he didn't steal anything was that it had to be a police car. It had flashing blue lights on the dashboard.*'

O'Neil froze. He scooted back in his chair. No! Oh, hell. The unsub had been through Dance's car. He'd gotten her ID, knew where she lived. Had followed her. And had seen her and Jon Boling together. That was how he'd known to target Boling, tamper with his bike. And—

Another thought hit him. Dance had told him she'd had flyers about the event in her vehicle. The unsub could easily have seen them.

A school auditorium. A perfect venue for an attack.

He grabbed his phone and called Central Dispatch.

'Hello?'

'Sharon. Michael O'Neil. There's a possible two-four-five in progress at Pacific Hills Grade School. PG. Have units roll up silent. I'm going to get more info and I'll advise through you.'

'Roger. I'll get 'em rolling. And await further.'

They disconnected.

How to handle it? If he ordered an evacuation and the unsub had locked the doors already, that might result in the very stampede and crush that O'Neil had to avoid.

Or was it even too late to do anything?

He'd call Dance and warn her. She could see if there was a way to get the parents and children out quietly before the unsub made a move.

O'Neil grabbed his mobile and hit speed-dial button one.

CHAPTER 71

Wes and Jon Boling were chowing down on green-room goodies.

Not like at Madison Square Garden or MGM Grand where, Dance suspected, Dom Pérignon and caviar were the fare backstage. This was Ritz crackers, Doritos, juice boxes and milk (the school, like Dance's house, was a soda-free zone).

Then the audience grew silent: the show was about to get under way. Boling whispered they were going to find their seats and he and Wes left.

Dance remained, looking over her daughter as they stood together, near the entrance to the stage. Maggie gazed out at the audience, probably two hundred people.

Her poor face was taut, unhappy.

Dance's phone grew busy: it was on mute but she felt the vibration. She'd get it in a minute. She was now concentrating on her daughter. 'Maggie?'

The child looked up. She seemed about to cry.

What on earth was going on? Weeks of angst about the performance. A roller-coaster of emotion.

And then Dance made a sudden shift. She moved from mom to law enforcer. That had been her mistake, looking at her daughter's plight. Dance had been viewing the discomfort as a question of nerves, of typical pre-adolescent distress. In fact, she should have been looking at the whole matter as a crime. She should have been thinking of plots, motives, *modi operandi*.

A to B to Z . . .

She knew instantly what was going on. So clear. All the pieces were there. She just hadn't thought to put them together. Now she understood the truth: her daughter was being extorted.

By Bethany and the Secrets Club . . .

Dance guessed that Bethany, so polite on the surface, was an expert at subtle bullying, using secrets as weapons. To join the club, you had to share a secret, something embarrassing: a wet bed, stolen money, a broken vase at home, a lie to a parent or teacher, something sexual. Then Bethany and her crew would have leverage to get the members of the club to do what they wanted.

Maggie's reluctance to perform was obvious now. She wasn't going to sing 'Let It Go' at all. The girls in the club had probably forced her to learn a very different song, maybe something off-color, embarrassing – maybe ridiculing Mrs Bendix, their teacher, a wonderful woman but heavyset, a careless dresser. An easy target for juvenile cruelty.

Dance recalled that when she'd agreed that Maggie didn't have to appear at the show, her daughter had been so relieved: Mom would back her up against the club. But comfort hadn't lasted long. The recent call from Bethany had been an ominous reminder that, whatever her mother had agreed to, Maggie was going to sing.

Or her secret would be revealed.

She was furious. Dance found her palms sweating. Those little bitches . . .

Her phone buzzed again. She ignored it once more.

She put her arm around Maggie's shoulders. 'Honey, let's talk for a minute.'

'I—'

'Let's talk.' A smile.

They walked to the back of the green-room area. From there they could see one of Maggie's classmates, Amy Grantham, performing a dance scene from *The Nutcracker*. She was good. Dance looked out at the audience. She saw her parents, sitting in the center, with Wes and Boling now near them, a jacket draped over the chair reserved for her.

She turned back to her daughter.

Dance had decided. Maggie was *not* going perform. No question. Whatever the secret was, she'd have her tell her now. Revealing it would defuse their power over her.

Anyway, how terrible could a ten-year-old's indiscretion possibly be?

Another tremble of her phone.

Three times. She'd ignored it long it enough. She tugged her phone from its holster. Not a call: it was a text. From Michael O'Neil.

She read it, noting that it was in all caps.

Well. Hmm.

'What's wrong, Mom?'

'Just a second, honey.'

She hit speed-dial button number one.

Click.

'Kathryn! You saw my text?'

'I—'

'The unsub went through your Pathfinder. At the Bay View Center. We've got to assume he knows about Maggie's concert. I have a team on the way. We don't know what he has planned but you have to evacuate the school. Only keep it quiet. Check all the exits – they're probably wired shut or something.' This was more than Michael O'Neil usually said in half an hour. 'So, you've got to see if Maintenance has wire cutters. But it's got to be subtle. If you can start getting people out—'

'Michael.'

'It's seven twenty, so following his profile, he could attack at any time. He waits for the show to start and—'

'It's outside.'

'I . . . What?'

'The show? Maggie's concert? We're on the soccer field behind the school. We're not in the gym or the assembly hall.'

'Oh. Outside.'

'No risk of confinement. Stampede.'

'No.'

'Even the green room – it's just a curtained-off area outside.'

'You're outside,' he repeated.

'Right. But thanks.'

'Well . . . Good.' After a pause he said, 'And tell Maggie good luck. I wish I could be there.'

'Night, Michael.'

They disconnected.

Outside . . .

The relief in his voice had been so dramatic, it was nearly comical.

Then she turned her attention back to her daughter.

'Honey, Mags . . . Listen. I need you to tell me something. Whatever it is, it's fine.'

'Huh?'

'I know why you're upset.'

'I'm not upset.' Maggie looked down at her crisp, shiny dress and smoothed it. One of her better kinesic tells.

'I think you are. You're not happy about performing.'

'Yes, I am.'

'There's something else. Tell me.'

'I don't want to talk about it.'

'Listen to me. We love each other and sometimes it's not good enough for people who love each other to say that. They have to talk. Tell me the truth. Why don't you want to sing?'

Maybe, Dance wondered, the Secrets Club and queen bitch Bethany were forcing her daughter to throw a pie at the teacher or a water balloon. Even worse? She thought of Stephen King's *Carrie*, drenching the girl in blood onstage.

'Honey?' Dance said softly.

Maggie looked at her, then away and gasped, 'It's terrible.'

She burst into racking tears.

CHAPTER 72

Kathryn Dance sat next to Jon Boling and her son in the third row, her parents nearby, watching the procession of performers in *Mrs Bendix's Sixth Grade Class's Got Talent!*.

'How you doing there?' Dance whispered to Boling. It was astonishing how many forgotten lines, missed dance steps and off-tone notes could be crammed into one hour.

'Better than any reality show on TV,' Boling responded.

True, Dance conceded. He'd managed, yet again, to bring a new perspective.

There'd been several scenes from plays, featuring three or four students together (the class numbered thirty-six), which cut the show's running time down considerably. And solo performances were hardly full-length Rachmaninoff piano concerti. They tended to be Suzuki pieces or abbreviated Katy Perry hits.

'The Cup Song' had been performed six times.

It was close to eight thirty before Maggie's turn came. Mrs Bendix announced her and, in her shimmering dress, she walked confidently from the wings.

Dance took a deep breath. She found her hand gripping Boling's, the bandaged one. Hard. He adjusted it.

'Sorry,' she whispered.

He kissed her hair.

At the microphone, she looked over the audience. 'I'm Maggie and I'm going to sing "Let It Go" from *Frozen*, which is a super movie, in my opinion better than *The Lego Movie* and most of the Barbie ones. And if anybody here hasn't seen it I think you should. Like, right away. I mean, right away.'

A glance at Mom, acknowledging the slip of lazy preposition. Dance smiled and nodded.

Then Maggie grew quiet and lowered her head. She remembered: 'Oh, and I want to thank Mrs Gallard for accompanying me.'

She nodded to her music teacher.

The piano began, the haunting minor-key intro to the beautiful song. Then the piano went quiet, a pause . . . and right on the beat, Maggie filled the silence with the first words of the lyrics. She sang slow and soft at first, just as in the movie, then growing in volume, her timbre firm, singing from her chest. Dance snuck a peek. Most of the audience was captivated, heads bobbing in time to the tune. And nearly every child was mouthing, if not singing, along.

When it came to the bridge, bordering on operatic recitative, Maggie nailed it perfectly. Then back to the final verse and the brilliant offhand dismissal about the cold never bothering her anyway.

The applause began, loud and genuine. Dance knew the audience was considering a standing ovation, but since there'd been none earlier, there could be none now. Not that it mattered, Dance could see that Maggie was ecstatic. She beamed and curtseyed, a maneuver she'd practiced almost as much as the song.

Dance blew her daughter a kiss. She set her head against Boling as he hugged her.

Wes said, 'Wow. Jackie Evancho.'

Not quite. But Dance decided definitely to add voice to the violin lessons this year. She exhaled a laugh.

'What?' Edie Dance asked her daughter.

'Just she did a good job.'

'She did.'

Dance didn't tell her mother that the laugh wasn't prompted by Maggie's performance but from the discussion in the green room a half-hour earlier.

'Honey?'

'It's terrible.'

When the tears had stopped, Dance had told Maggie, 'I know what's going on, Mags. About the club.'

'Club?'

Dance had explained she knew about the Secrets Club and their extortion.

Maggie had looked at her as if her mother had just said that Monterey Bay was filled with chocolate milk. 'Mom, like, no. Bethany's neat, no, she wouldn't do anything like that. I mean, sometimes she's all, I'm the leader, blah, blah, and everything. But that's okay. We voted her president.'

'What did she say when she called this morning? You were upset.'

She'd hesitated.

'Tell me, Mags.'

'I'd told her you said I didn't have to sing but she said she'd talked to everybody in the club and they really, really wanted me to. I mean, everybody.'

'Sing "Let It Go"?'

'Yeah.'

'Why?'

'Because, I mean, they were saying I was sort of the star of the club. They thought I was so good. They don't have a lot of things they can do, most of the girls. I mean, Leigh does batons. But Bethany and Carrie? You saw them try to do that scene from *Kung Fu Panda*?'

'It was pretty bad.'

'Uh-huh. I'm the only musical one. And they said nobody wants to hear a stupid violin thing. And they were like the club would look really bad if one of us didn't do something awesome at the show.'

'So they weren't going to expose your secret or anything?'

'They wouldn't do that.'

'Can you tell me yours?'

'I can't.'

'Please. I won't tell a soul.'

There'd been a moment's pause. Maggie'd looked around. 'I guess. You won't tell anybody?'

'Promise.'

Whispering: 'I don't like Justin Bieber. He's not cute and I don't like what he does onstage.'

Dance had waited. Then: 'That's it? That's your secret?'

'Yeah.'

'Then why don't you want to sing, honey?'

Her eyes had clouded with tears again. 'Because I'm afraid this terrible thing's going to happen. It'll be, you know, the worst. I'll be up there in front of everybody.'

'What?'

'You know you were telling me about our bodies and when you get older things happen?'

My God, she was worried she'd get her period onstage. Dance was about to bring up the subject when Maggie said, 'Billy Truesdale.'

'Billy. He's in your class, right?'

A nod. 'He's my age.'

Dance recalled their birthdays were about the same time of year. She took out a tissue and dried her daughter's eyes.

'What about him?'

'Okay,' Maggie had said, sniffling. 'He was singing last month, in assembly. He was really good and he was singing the national anthem. But then . . . but then when he sang a high note, something happened, and his voice got all weird and it like cracked. And he couldn't sing any more. Everybody laughed at him. He ran out of the auditorium, crying. And afterward I heard somebody say it was because of his age. His voice was changing.' She choked. 'I'm like the *same* age. It's going to happen to me. I know it. I'll go out onstage – and you know that note in the song, the high note? I know it'll happen!'

Dance had clamped her teeth together and inhaled hard through her nose to keep the smile from blossoming on her face. And she'd reflected on one of the basic aspects of parenting: you think you've figured out every possible permutation and plan accordingly and you still get slammed from out of the blue.

Dance had wiped Maggie's tears once again, then hugged her daughter. 'Mags, there's something I've got to tell you.'

THE BLOOD OF ALL

MONDAY, APRIL 10

CHAPTER 73

Dance awoke early and surveyed the aftermath of the Secrets Club pajama party, which she'd hosted after the show.

The living room was not bad for a gaggle of ten- and eleven-year-old girls. Pizza crusts on most of the tables, popcorn on the floor, glitter from who knew what makeup experiment, some nail polish where it shouldn't be, clothes scattered everywhere from an impromptu fashion show.

Could've been a lot worse.

Arriving at the house last night, Maggie had been pure celeb, red-carpet celeb. Whatever other clubs were part of the social structure of Pacific Hills, the Secrets Sisters ruled.

And, Dance had been pleased to learn (one of the reasons for the pizza and pajama party at her place), the girls were all quite nice. Yes, Bethany would probably someday be an inside-the-Beltway force whom no one would want to argue with from across the aisle. Heaven help Leigh's husband. And Carrie could write code that impressed even Jon Boling. But the girls were uniformly polite, generous, funny.

Edie Dance had stayed the night too and would cater the breakfast – making her daughter's signature hybrids: panfles or wafcakes – then get the girls ready for pickup by their parents. Because of the show last night, the school had a delayed opening today.

Now, dressed for work, Dance said, 'Thanks, Mom.' She hugged her. 'Don't you dare clean up. I'll do that when I'm home.'

'Bye, dear.'

As Dance was heading for the door, Bethany appeared, wearing Hello Kitty PJs. There was definitely an insidious aspect to the cartoon feline, Dance had decided long ago.

'Yes, Bethany?'

'Mrs Dance, I have something to talk to you about.' Dead serious.

Dance turned to her and nodded, concentrating. 'What is it?'

'We all talked about it last night and we decided that you can be in the Secrets Club.'

'Really?'

'Yes, we like you. You're actually pretty cool. But you have to tell us a secret to get in. That's what, you know –'

'– makes it the Secrets Club.'

'Uh-huh.'

Dance played along. 'An important secret?'

'Any secret.'

Dance happened to be looking at a picture of her and Jon Boling, taken by the waiter at a wine tasting on a weekend away in Napa not long ago.

No.

A glance into the kitchen. 'Okay, I've got one.'

'What is it?' The freckled girl's eyes went wide.

'When I was your age, at dinner, I'd put butter on the broccoli and feed it to our dog when my mother wasn't looking.'

'Her?' Bethany glanced at Edie Dance, in the other room.

'Her. Now, I'm trusting you. You won't tell.'

'No. I won't tell. I don't like broccoli either.'

Dance said, 'Pretty much sucks, doesn't it?'

Bethany nodded as if considering a litigant's petition. Then passed judgment. 'That's a good secret. We'll vote you in.' She turned and trotted back to the den, where the other girls were waking.

The official, and presumably only, adult member of the Pacific Hills Secrets Club now left the house. She nodded at the MCSO deputy keeping guard and smiled. He waved back. Then Dance jumped into her SUV and drove to headquarters. She'd no sooner walked into the lobby than Rey Carreneo spotted her and said, 'Looked into it, the situation you asked me about.' He handed her a folder. 'All in there.'

'Thanks.'

'Anything else, Kathryn?'

'Not yet. But stay close.'

'Sure.'

Dance flipped through the folder, skimmed. She closed it and walked through the corridors to Overby's office. Her boss gestured her inside, dropping his landline phone into its cradle. 'Sacramento.' He said this with a grimace. An explanation would logically follow that but none was forthcoming and she didn't press it. She supposed he'd been dinged because of the latest incident on the Peninsula – the hospital attack – and the corollary: the tardiness of finding the Solitude Creek killer. Or the Oakland warehouse fire, which had damaged Operation Pipeline. Or the Serrano operation.

Or just because bureaucracy was bureaucracy.

As she sat down in one of the office chairs, Michael O'Neil stepped into the office too.

'Michael, greetings,' Overby said.

'Charles.' Then to Dance a nod. She thought he looked tired, as he sat heavily beside her.

'What do you have?'

The deputy answered, 'The preliminary report from the hospital. Not much, sorry to say. But not surprising. Given how smart this guy is.'

'How did he do it, the elevator?'

'There's not a lot of security video but it seems he dressed in scrubs – cap and booties too – and stole a key from the maintenance room. He got into the elevator motor room on the top floor, cut the wires feeding both cars. Primary and backup. CSU took tool marks but you know how helpful those are.'

'There was some power,' Dance said, recalling the blinding glare from the lights attached to the security camera. She explained this.

O'Neil said, 'Probably battery backup for that in the car itself. But it must not've been connected to the intercom.' He glanced at his notes. 'There was a fire in the elevator shaft but it was from ether. Hot burn but no smoke. What people smelled was from the burning Honda. We think he did that to make sure the fire alarms didn't go off. That would send an automatic notice to the fire department. They'd be there in five, ten minutes. He wanted to keep the carnage going for as long as he could.'

'Well,' Overby said.

Dance added, 'And we have no idea what he's driving now. There's no security video in the garage at the hospital. If that's, in fact, where he parked. Or, for all we know, he hiked a mile to where he left his new wheels.'

She explained that while she believed the unsub was a pro, hired by somebody else, their one suspect – Frederick Martin – had not panned out. The other victims at Solitude Creek seemed unlikely targets for a pro. 'We're back to thinking somebody may have been targeting the venues themselves. The roadhouse, the Bay View Center or the hospital. But why? We just don't know.'

She noted that Overby wasn't fully attentive. He was staring at his computer screen, which showed a streaming newscast from a local TV station. The Hero Fireman was giving another interview – this time about his efforts at the hospital incident.

Overby muted the set. 'I read an article one time. It was pretty interesting. About a fireman in Buffalo, New York. You ever hear about it?'

There were presumably a lot of firemen in Buffalo, Dance reflected. But you usually let Charles Overby run with whatever it was he was running with. 'No, Charles.'

'Nup.'

'He was pretty good at his job. Brave. There'd be a fire in an apartment. He'd race in, make his way around the flames, save a family or the pet dog. Happened three or four times. He knew just where the fire'd started, how best to fight it. Amazing how he saved people. His truck was usually first on the scene and he could read a fire like nobody else. That's what they say: reading a fire. Firemen say that, I mean.

'Well, guess what, boys and girls? The fireman set the fires himself. Not because he was a pyromaniac, if that's what they call those people. No, he didn't care about the fires. He cared about the prestige. The glory. He basked in it. Went away for attempted murder, in addition to the arson, burglary and assault charges. I think they dropped the vandalism. Didn't need it, really.'

He stabbed a finger at the TV. 'Have you noticed that Brad Dannon has been on the scene of the disasters pretty damn fast? And that he was real eager to talk to the media about what he did? "Hero". That's what they're calling him. So. You think *he* might be the perp, your unsub?' A faint smile of triumph.

'I—' Dance began.

'Wonder why we didn't think of that before?'

Dance wished he hadn't added that last sentence. Throughout his monologue she'd been trying to figure out some way to side-line him before he tossed out a line like that.

Well, nothing to do.

She set the folder she'd just received on his desk. 'Actually, Charles, I did wonder if Brad might be a suspect. So I had Rey Carreneo check him out.' She tapped the file. 'He correlated his whereabouts and checked phone records. After Bay View, we've got the unsub's prepaid number. There was no connection. He's innocent. His boss at MCFD says he's usually on the scene in the first ten minutes of a call. He cruises around the county with a scanner, even when he's off duty. Oh, and he's known for being a real pain in the ass.'

A pause.

'Oh. Good. Great minds think alike.' And the look on his face wasn't sheepishness for having been out-thought, Dance believed: it was pure relief that he hadn't offered up the theory at a press conference only to recant a few hours later based on the findings of his suspended underling.

Dance's mobile hummed. It was TJ Scanlon.

'Hey.'

'Boss, I've been plundering various and sundry records. Real estate, deeds, construction permits. Per your request.'

She knew he had. 'Yes?'

'Dusty. You'd think everything would be online but, un-uh. I've been prowling through shelves, back rooms. Caverns. Where are you?'

'Charles's office.'

'I'll be there in one. You're going to want to see this.'

He arrived in less time than that. And his flecked Jefferson Airplane T-shirt and, yes, dusty jeans attested to his old-fashioned detective work.

Caverns . . .

He held a folder similar to the one she'd just passed to Overby.

'Michael, Charles. Hey, boss. Okay. Check this out. Nobody got back to me from that Nevada company, the one planning the construction near Solitude Creek? So I thought I'd do some digging. Try to find shareholders, whatever. Well, the company's owned by an *anonymous* trust. I tried to get a look at the trust but it's not public. I could, though, find out who represents it. Barrett Stone, a lawyer in San Francisco. How's that for a lawyer's name? I'd want him representing me, I'll tell you. Okay, I'll get to the point. The phone company coughed up his call log for me, and I looked them over. Guess who the lawyer's been calling? Three calls in the past two days.'

Overby lifted his palms.

'Sam Cohen. So I called *him*. And found out that Stone, on behalf of the trust, made a cash offer to buy the roadhouse and the property it sits on.'

'So, there's a motive,' Dance said. 'Ruin the business, then buy up the land cheap. Build a new development on it. Maybe buy Henderson Jobbing too, now that they're going out of business.'

O'Neil asked, 'How do we find out who's behind the trust? . . . I don't know if we've got enough for a warrant.'

'I did the next best thing. I pulled together some of Stone's more prominent clients. Recognize anyone?' He set a sheet of paper in front of them.

One name was highlighted in yellow. He'd also drawn an exclamation point next to it.

Neither was necessary.

Dance blinked. 'Hm.'

'Well,' Overby said. 'This's going to be . . . I don't know what this is going to be.'

'Awkward' came first to Dance's mind. Then: 'explosive'.

Overby looked from her to O'Neil. 'You'd better get on it right now. Good luck.'

Meaning he was already thinking about how to extricate himself from the train wreck about to occur.

CHAPTER 74

En route to Salinas.

Kathryn Dance was piecing together a portrait of the man now suspected of hiring the Solitude Creek Unsub. She was online. Michael O'Neil, driving.

Forty-one-year-old Congressman Daniel Nashima had represented what was now the Twentieth Congressional District of California for eight terms. He was a Democrat but a moderate one, advocating socially liberal positions, like gay marriage and a woman's right to choose, but pushing for lower taxes on the wealthy ('Most of the one percent got that way by working hard, not by inheriting their money').

Nashima himself was a living example of that philosophy. He'd made a lot of money through Internet start-ups and real-estate deals. His goal of financial success, however, didn't vitiate his do-good attitude, of course. If anything, the altruism deflected attention from his capitalistic side. You tend not to think of a man's net worth when he's hauling forty-pound blocks of concrete off victims trapped in earthquake rubble.

Nashima's performance in Congress was stellar. He showed up for the majority of votes, he reached across the aisle, he served on the hardworking committees, Ethics and Homeland Security, without complaint. His term in office had never been tainted with the least scandal: he'd gotten divorced before commencing a romantic liaison with a lobbyist (who had no connection with him professionally), and in his closest brush with crime, it had been discovered that his housekeeper had herself forged visas – he had been duped like everyone else. Dance and O'Neil were accompanied by Albert Stemple and a Monterey County Sheriff's Office deputy. Dance had learned that Nashima was a hunter and had a conceal-carry permit.

They now arrived at his office in Santa Cruz. In a strip mall, next to a surfboard rental and sales shop, whose posters suggested you could walk to Maverick, site of the most righteous surfing on the west coast (it was fifty miles north).

With Stemple remaining outside, lookout, the other three stepped inside. The Congressman's assistant, a pretty, diminutive Japanese-American woman, looked them over, hostile, then walked to the back of the suite. She returned a moment later and ushered them inside.

After introductions, Nashima calmly surveyed them all. 'And what can I do for you?'

Shields were displayed, identifications offered.

Nashima was still examining hers when Dance took the lead. 'Congressman, we'd like to ask about your connection with Solitude Creek.'

'I don't understand.' The man sat back, relaxed though stony-faced. His movement and gestures were precise.

'Please. It'll be easier for everybody if you cooperate.'

'*Cooperate?* About what? You walk in here, accusation all over your face. Obviously you think I did something wrong. I don't have any idea what. Give me a clue.'

His indignation was credible. But that was common among the High Machiavellians – expert deceivers – when they were called on lies they'd just told.

Calmly she persisted, 'Are you trying to purchase property on Solitude Creek north off Highway One, the building and the land the roadhouse is located on?'

He blinked. Was this the point where he would demand a lawyer?

'As a matter of fact, I'm not, no.'

The first phrase was often a deception flag. Like: 'I swear'. Or 'I'm not going to lie to you'.

'Well, your attorney made an offer for the property.'

A pause. It could mean a lie was coming and he was trying to figure out what they knew. Or that he was furious.

'Is that right? I wasn't aware of it.'

'You're denying that Barrett Stone, your lawyer, talked to Sam Cohen and made an offer to buy the property?'

The Congressman sighed. And lowered his head. 'You are, of course, investigating the terrible incident at the roadhouse.' He nodded. 'I remember you, Agent Dance. You were there the next day.'

O'Neil said, 'And you came back a few days later to look over the property you wanted to buy.'

He nodded. 'You're thinking I orchestrated the attack to drive the property value down. Ah, and presumably the second attack at Cannery Row was to cover up the motive for the first attack. Make it look like some kind of psycho was involved. Oh, and the hospital too, sure.'

He was sounding oddly confident. Still, what else was he going to say?

'I have alibis for one or all of the incidents . . . Oh, but that's not what you're thinking, I'm sure. No. You're thinking I *hired* this psycho.'

Dance remained silent. In the art of interrogation and interviewing, all too often the officer responds to comments or questions posed by the subject. Keep mum and let them talk. (Dance had once gotten a full confession by asking a suspected murderer, 'So, you come to Monterey often?')

Daniel Nashima now rose. He looked both law enforcers over carefully. Then set his hands, palms down, on the desk. His face revealed no emotion whatsoever as he said, 'All right. I'll confess. I'll confess to everything. But on one condition.'

CHAPTER 75

Donnie and Wes were hanging on Mrs Dance's back porch, huddling in the back, along with Nathan (Neo, from the Matrix) and Vince (Vulcan – no, not the race of the dudes from *Star Trek* but the X-Man).

Fritos and orange juice and a little smuggled Red Bull were the hors d'oeuvres and cocktails of the hour.

'So, what're you? Like grounded?' slim, pimply Vince asked.

Wes sighed. 'My mother's running that case, that thing at Solitude Creek, where the people got killed. And the Bay View Center?'

Nathan: 'No shit. Where people jumped into the water and drowned. She's doing that?'

'And she's like all paranoid he's going to come around and mess with us.'

'Get a piece, dude. Really. Waste him, the fucker shows up.'

'I don't think so,' Wes said.

Vince asked, 'How're you gonna play the game, man? Jesus.'

Wes shrugged. 'I gotta have rides to school and home. But I can still get away. Just have to be careful about it. Not when my mom's here. But Jon? I can tell him I've got a headache or need to take a nap. Get out through my window. I don't know. I'll figure it out.'

Donnie waved to Mrs Dance's boyfriend, Jon, who, Donnie thought, was spying on them, though maybe not. The guy actually seemed friendly enough and sure as shit knew machines: he hacked epic code and showed Donnie how to write script for games. Donnie had this fantasy about taking the Defend and Respond Expedition Service game onto the net, making millions. Where you'd fuck with people in the virtual world.

Yeah, it could be a good game. Mucho more interesting than wasting zombies with machine-guns.

Donnie shifted on the bench and he must've winced. Wes noticed. 'Yo, what's wrong?'

'Nothing, bitch. I'm fine.'

Except he wasn't fine. His father'd noticed the missing bike and, even though he seemed to believe the lie that Donnie had lent it to a friend, he'd whacked him a half-dozen times with the branch for not asking permission to lend out a present. ('And you know how much it cost?') He was under orders to produce the bike tomorrow, or face even worse punishment.

And, with Donnie's father, worse always meant worse.

Big Nathan, who didn't take as many showers as he ought to, moved his hair out of his eyes. 'So here.' He flashed a picture on his Galaxy of a stop sign, uprooted and sitting in Vince's garage. His mother never used the place. His father might have killed himself in there – that was the rumor – so nobody in the family ever went inside or did anything with it. So it had sort of become their clubhouse.

'Can I get an amen?' Nathan asked. 'Team Two scores.'

Fist bumps.

'Cool,' said Wes. 'How much did it weigh?'

'Tons,' Vince said. 'We both had to carry it.'

'I could have,' Nathan said fast. 'Just, it was long, you know. Hard to get a handle on.'

If anybody could muscle it, Neo could. He was a big fucker.

'Nobody saw you?' Donnie asked.

'Naw. Maybe one kid but we looked at him, like, you say anything and you're frigging dead.'

Nathan said 'frig' instead of 'fuck'. He'd come around, Donnie thought. Wes had.

We'll totally fuck you up . . .

Donnie pulled out the official Defend and Respond game score sheet, illustrated by him personally. Titans, X-Men, Fantastic Four, zombies everywhere. A couple of the hot girls from *True Blood*.

He wrote on the Nathan/Vince side: *Challenge 5, completed.*

Donnie had come up with the idea of challenging the team to steal a stop sign, not just any sign. No 'Yield', no 'School

X-ing', no 'No Parking'. But a real fucking stop sign at a four-way intersection. Copping that would mean they'd have to be at an intersection, where it'd be riskier to get caught. And then, too, a missing stop sign would mean that a car might fuck up another in a crash.

Vince grimaced. 'Only, like a half-hour later, not even, there was another one up.'

'That's fucked up,' Donnie said, disappointed.

Wes gave a sour laugh. 'Who drives around with signs to put up?'

'Dunno. Just was like all that work was wasted,' Vince said.

Nathan slapped his arm. 'Shit, dude. We got the point.' A stab at the score sheet. 'Am I right, ladies?'

Donnie would've liked a big fucking car crash but the challenge hadn't been to keep stealing stop signs until there was a big fucking car crash; it was steal a fucking stop sign. Period.

'Dude,' Wes was talking to him. 'Show 'em.'

Donnie pulled his iPhone out and displayed the *Die Jew* picture.

Nathan didn't seem happy. He and Vince were down two points.

Vince said, 'That thing, that's Indian.'

Impatiently, Donnie said, 'What thing? And what Indian? Like Raj?'

'What's Raj?' Wes said.

His mother didn't let Wes and his sister, Maggie, watch much TV.

Donnie scoffed. 'Raj, man, the brainiac on *Big Bang Theory*. Jesus.'

'Oh. Sure.' Nathan seemed to have no clue.

Vince said, 'No, what I'm saying, Indian like bows and arrows and tepees.'

'It's called a swastika,' Wes said. 'The Nazis used it.'

Donnie added, 'The Indians did too. I saw a special. I don't know.'

Nathan asked, 'Is a swasti-whatever, is it like a blade you throw? I mean, are those knives on the end?'

Wes said, 'It's just a symbol. On their flag.'

'The Indians?'

Wes cocked his head. 'No, dude. The Nazis.'

'Who were they again?' Nathan asked.

Donnie muttered, 'They and the Jews had a big war.'

'Yeah?'

'*Game of Thrones*. Like that.'

Donnie's shoulders rose and fell. 'I guess. I don't know. Couple hundred years ago, I think.' Then he was tired of history. He added their point to the score sheet.

Nathan said, 'Okay. Our turn. We're challenging Darth and Wolverine to the following dare. You know Sally Caruthers, the cheerleader? We challenge you to get some Visine in her drink at school. It gives you the runs.'

'That's way gross,' Wes said.

Donnie liked the idea of the challenge and knew it wasn't a bad idea to stop dissing Jews and blacks for a while. But he said, 'Yeah, yeah, but the game's on hold for a couple days.'

'Yeah?' asked Nathan, frowning.

Wes sighed. 'The asshole, the house we tagged, perped our bikes.'

'Put 'em in his garage. Me and Wes were talking about it, what to do.'

Wes said, 'To get 'em back.'

Donnie nodded for Wes to continue.

'And we need some help. Backup, you know. You up for that?'

Vince considered it. 'We'll help you but we get a point.' Tapping the score sheet.

Nathan said, 'Dude, that's mad brilliant.'

Donnie furrowed his brow. He was, though, only pretending to debate. He didn't care about the point. The fact was that for the plan *he* had in mind, which he hadn't told Wes about, he definitely needed the others.

Finally he said, 'All right, you ladies get a point.' And popped the Red Bulls and passed the cans around.

CHAPTER 76

They were driving along Highway One, O'Neil behind the wheel of his patrol car, Dance in the front passenger seat. In the back were Al Stemple and their confessing suspect, Congressman Daniel Nashima.

This was the condition to his confession: a drive to the scene of the crime, where he'd tell her everything she wanted to know.

He wasn't under arrest, so no cuffs, but he had been searched for weapons. Which had amused him.

The compact man was silent, staring out of the window at the passing sights – agricultural fields of Brussels sprouts and artichokes on the right; to the west, the water side, were small businesses (souvenir shacks and restaurants) and marinas, increasingly downscale as they moved north.

Finally they turned off the highway and took the driveway to the parking lot; the roadhouse was boarded up. The trucking business was operating but Dance wondered for how long: she remembered the story on the news about the company's probable bankruptcy.

O'Neil was about to stop but Nashima directed him to the end of the lot, not far from where Dance had discovered the path that led to where she'd found the witness in the trailer, Annette, addicted to cigarettes and music.

'Let's take a walk,' Nashima said.

Dance and O'Neil exchanged glances as together they climbed from the car and followed Nashima as he started along the path. Stemple plodded behind, boot falls noisy on the gritty asphalt. Both he and O'Neil kept their hands near their weapons. The unsub, armed with at least one nine-millimeter pistol, was still at large, of course.

Was he headed for the cluster of residential houses? And why did he seem to have no interest in the roadhouse itself?

I'll confess . . .

He didn't get far along the path, however, before he turned left and walked toward Solitude Creek, through the grass and around the ruins she'd seen earlier, the remnants of concrete floors, fences, walls and posts. As they got closer to the water, she found a barrier of rusting chain-link separating them from the glistening creek.

He turned to them. 'When I said I didn't know if the lawyer made an offer, that's because of a blind trust.'

'We know about it,' Dance said.

'I put all my assets in it when I took office. Barrett controls everything as trustee. But he knows my general investment and planning strategies. And when he heard about the roadhouse, I imagine he made the offer because he knew I was interested in all the property here.

'But the trust sets out the guidelines he has to follow in purchasing property and he'll stick to those. He'll buy it if the conditions are right; he won't if they're not. I can't tell him to do anything about it.'

Dance was beginning to feel her A-to-B-to-Z thinking might end up short of the twenty-sixth letter.

The Congressman said, 'If you know about the trust then you know about the company it owns. The LLC in Nevada.'

'Yes, planning to do some construction here.'

'That company also owns all of this.' He waved his hand. He seemed to indicate everything from the parking lot, along the shore of Solitude Creek almost to the development where Dance had discovered Annette.

Nashima continued, 'The company I'm referring to is Kodoku Ogawa Limited. The Japanese words mean "Solitude Creek".' He fell silent momentarily. 'Curious about the word for "solitude", though. In Japanese, it also means isolation, desolation, detachment. "Solitude" in English suggests something healthy, regenerative.' He turned to them with a searing gaze. 'Have you figured out the purpose of Kodoku Ogawa Limited yet?'

No one responded. Stemple was gazing out over the grassy expanse, arms crossed.

Nashima walked to an ancient fencepost topped with rusted barbed wire. He touched it gingerly. 'In nineteen forty-two, President Franklin Roosevelt signed Executive Order Ninety Sixty-six, which gave military officers the right to exclude any person they saw fit from quote "designated military areas". You know what those military areas were? All of the state of California and much of Oregon, Washington and Arizona. And who got excluded? People of Japanese ancestry.'

'The internment,' Dance said.

Nashima muttered, 'A nice word for pogrom.' He continued, 'Nearly one hundred and twenty thousand people were forced out of their homes and into camps. Over sixty percent were US citizens. Children, the elderly, the mentally handicapped among them.' He laughed harshly. 'Spies? Saboteurs? They were as loyal as German Americans or Italian Americans. Or any Americans, for that matter. If there was such a risk, then why in Hawaii, where only a small minority of Japanese were rounded up, was there *no* espionage or sabotage among the tens of thousands who remained free?'

'And this was one of those camps?'

'The Solitude Creek Relocation Center. It extended from that crest there all the way to the highway. It was a charming place,' he said bitterly. 'People lived in large barracks, divided into twenty-foot apartments, with walls that didn't go up all the way to the ceiling. There were only communal latrines, not separated by gender. There was virtually no privacy at all. The camp was surrounded by barbed wire, five strand, and there were machine-gun towers every few hundred feet.

'There was never enough food – diet was rice and vegetables, and if the prisoners wanted anything more than that, they had to grow it themselves. But, of course, they couldn't just stroll down the road and buy a couple of chickens, could they? And they couldn't fish in the creek because they might swim away and slit the throats of Americans nearby or radio the longitude and latitude of Fort Ord to the hundreds of Japanese submarines in Monterey Bay just waiting for that information,' he scoffed.

He strode to a reedy plot of sand. 'I've reconstructed about where my relatives were incarcerated.' He looked the spot over.

'It was here that my grandfather died. He had a heart attack. The doctor wasn't in the camp that day. They had to call one from Fort Ord. But it took a while because, of course, the yellow menace would feign a heart attack to escape, so they had to find some armed soldiers to guard the medical workers. He was dead before help arrived.'

'I'm sorry,' O'Neil muttered.

'He, like my grandmother, was a *nisei* – second generation, born here. My father was a *sansei*, third generation. They were citizens of the United States.' He looked at them with still, cool eyes. 'We need to keep the memory of what happened here alive. I've always planned to build a museum to do that. On this very site, where my relatives were so badly treated.

'The sign at the entrance will read "*Solitude Creek Kyōseishū yōsho Museum and Memorial*". That means "concentration camp". Not "relocation center". That's not what it was.'

Almost as an afterthought he said, 'Before you go to a judge to get warrants to arrest me, look up the corporate documents for Kodoku. It's a non-profit. I won't make a penny on it. Oh, and about murdering people to buy some property cheap? You'll see from the plans we'll be filing for permits, I don't need the road-house. If Sam Cohen sells we'd just doze the club down for an extension of the parking lot. If not, we'll buy some of the property closer to Highway One. Or, if Sam would like to keep the land, he could tear down the building and put up a restaurant.' The Congressman cocked his head. 'I can guarantee him a good supply of clientele if he puts sushi and sashimi on the menu.' His eyes strayed to the waving grasses, the ripples on gray Solitude Creek.

'I know what you're thinking: I could have told you this in my office, yes. But I don't think we can ever miss an opportunity to remind ourselves that hate persists. What happened here happened only seventy years ago.' A nod at the concrete borders along Solitude Creek. 'That's a drop in the bucket of time. And look now, on the Peninsula. Those terrible hate crimes over the past month. Synagogues, black churches.'

He shook his head and turned back toward the parking lot. 'We haven't learned a thing. I sometimes doubt we ever will.'

CHAPTER 77

'That didn't go well,' Dance muttered.

She and O'Neil were in her office.

'Better than it could have gone. I don't think there'll be any lawsuits for . . . Well, I don't know what Nashima would sue for.'

'Wrongful accusation?' she suggested, only half joking. She looked over the case material spread out on her desk and pinned to the whiteboard nearby. Evidence, reference to statements, details of the crimes. And photos, those terrible photos.

Dance's phone rang. But it wasn't Barrett Stone, Esq., asking where he could serve the papers. TJ sounded sheepish as he said, 'Well, okay, boss, I guess I will admit that I didn't exactly look over all those facts and figures. I mean, longitude and latitude of the deeds and the plots or plats, whatever they are, and—'

'Is Nashima innocent, TJ? That's all I want to know.'

'As the driven snow. Which is an expression I don't get any more than "When it rains, it pours." The Nevada company's construction plans have nothing to do with the roadhouse; it's all the site of the old relocation camp and an area toward Highway One. And he was telling the truth: all the companies involved are non-profits. Any earnings have to be spent on education and support of the museum and other human-rights organizations.'

Nail in the coffin, Dance thought. Reflecting that *that* was one expression leaving little doubt as to meaning.

Another: back to the drawing board.

O'Neil's phone buzzed. He glanced at caller ID. 'My boss.' The Monterey County sheriff. 'Brother. Wonder what's up.' He answered. 'Ted. Did Nashima call to complain? The Congressman? . . . No. Well, he might. I thought that's what you were calling about.'

Then she noticed O'Neil stiffen. Shoulders up, head down. 'Really? . . . Are they sure? I'm here with Kathryn now. We can be there in twenty minutes. What's the internet address?'

He jotted something down.

'We'll check it out on the way.' He disconnected. He looked at her with an expression she rarely saw on his face.

Dance lifted her eyebrows. 'We?'

'The case I was working on, about the man who went missing, Otto Grant.'

She recalled: the farmer who had gone bankrupt after his property was taken by the state. 'You thought he might be a suicide?'

'That's what happened, right. Hanged himself. A shack out in Salinas Valley.' He rose. 'Let's go.'

She asked, 'Me? It's your case. You want me along?'

'Actually, turns out, it's *our* case now.'

CHAPTER 78

Michael O'Neil piloted his unmarked Dodge into the countryside, east of Salinas, a huge swathe of farm country, flat and, thanks to the precious water, green with young plants. Dance skimmed the blog entry Otto Grant had posted just before he'd taken his life, several hours ago. 'Explains a lot,' she said. 'Explains everything.'

The reason the Otto Grant case was now both of theirs was simple: Grant was the man who'd hired the Solitude Creek unsub to wreak havoc on Monterey County. In revenge for the eminent-domain action that had led to his bankruptcy.

'As much of an oddball as we thought?'

She scanned more. Didn't answer.

'Read it to me.'

'*Over the past few months readers of this BLOG have followed the chronicle of the Destruction of my life by the state of California. For those of you just "tuning in" I owned a farm off San Juan Grade Road, 239 acres of very fine land which I inherited from my Father, who inherited it from his Father.*

'*Last year the state decided to steal two thirds of that property – the most valuable – under the totalitarian "law" known as eminent domain. And WHY did they want to take it from me? Because a nearby landfill, filled with garbage and trash, was nearly full to capacity and so they turned their sights on my land to turn it into a dump.*

'*The Founding Fathers approved laws that let the government take citizens' land provided they give "JUST COMPENSATION" for it. I'm an American and a patriot and this is the best country on earth but do you think Thomas Jefferson would allow taking all this property and then arguing about the value? Of course he wouldn't. Because HE was a gentleman and a scholar.*

'*I was given compensation equal to land used for grazing not farming. Even though it was a working vegetable farm and there are no livestock for miles around. I had to sell the remaining land because there wasn't enough to cover expenses.*

'*After paying off the mortgages I was left with $150,000. Which may seem like a princely sum except I then got a tax bill for $70,000!! It was only a matter of time until I ended up homeless.*

'*Well, by now you know what I did. I did NOT pay the taxes. I took every last penny and gave it to a man I had met a few years ago. A soldier of fortune, you could say. If you wonder who's at fault for what happened at Solitude Creek and Bay View Center and the hospital, look into a mirror. YOU! Maybe next time you'll think twice about stealing a man's soul, his heart, his livelihood, his immortality and discover within you a conscience.*'

Dance said, 'That's it.'

'Phew. That's enough.'

'One hundred fifty thousand for the job. No wonder our unsub can afford Vuitton shoes.'

They drove in silence for a few moments.

'You can't sympathize but you almost want to,' O'Neil said.

This was true, Dance reflected. Bizarre though it was, the letter revealed how the man had been so sadly derailed.

In fifteen minutes, O'Neil pulled onto a dirt road, where an MCSO cruiser was parked. The officer gestured them on. About a hundred yards farther on they came to an abandoned house. Two more cruisers were there, along with the medical examiner's bus. The officers waved to O'Neil and Dance as they climbed out of the car and made their way to the front door of the shack.

'Door was unlocked when we got here, Detective, but he had quite a fortress inside. He was ready for battle if we came for him before his hired gun finished with the revenge.'

Dance noted the thick wooden boards bolted over the windows of the one-story structure. The back door, the officer explained, was sealed too, similarly, and the front was reinforced with metal panels and multiple locks. It would have taken a battering ram to get inside.

She spotted a rifle, some scatterguns. Plenty of ammo.

Crime Scene had arrived too, dolled up in their Tyvek jump-suits, booties and hoods.

'You can look around,' one officer said, 'just mind the routine. Nothing's bagged or logged yet.'

Meaning: keep your hands to yourselves and wear booties.

They donned the light blue footwear and stepped inside. It was largely what she'd expected: the filthy cabin, latticed with beams overhead, was dingy and sad. Minimal furniture, second-hand. Jugs of water, cans of Chef Boyardee entrees and vegetables and peaches. Thousands of legal papers and several books of California statutes, well thumbed, with portions highlighted in yellow marker. The air was fetid. He'd used a bucket for his toilet. The mattress was covered with a gray sheet. The blanket was an incongruous pink.

'Where's the body?' O'Neil asked one of the officers.

'In there, sir.'

They walked into the back bedroom, which was barren of furniture. Otto Grant, disheveled and dusty, lay on his back in front of an open window. He'd hanged himself from a ceiling beam. The medical team had untied the nylon rope and lowered him to the floor, presumably to try to save him, though the lividity of the face and the extended neck told her that Grant had died well before they had arrived.

The window, wide open. She supposed he'd chosen this as the site of his death so he could look out over the pleasant hills in the distance, some magnolia and oak nearby, a field of budding vegetables. Better to gaze at as your vision went to black and your heart shut down than a wall of scuffed, stained sheetrock.

'Michael? Kathryn?'

With a last look at the man who'd caused so much pain to so many, O'Neil and Dance stepped back into the living room to meet the head of the CSU examination team, dressed in overalls and a hood.

'Hey, Carlos,' Dance said.

The lean Latino CSU officer, Carlos Batillo, nodded a greeting. He walked to the card table that Grant had been using for his desk. The man's computer and a portable router sat on it. It was open to his blog, the entry that Dance had read to O'Neil on the drive there.

'Find anything else on it?' O'Neil asked.

'Bare bones. News stories about the stampedes. Some articles on eminent domain.'

Dance nodded at a Nokia mobile. 'We know he hired somebody to handle the attacks. He's the one we want now – the "soldier of fortune" he referred to. Our unsub. Any text or call-log data that could be helpful? Or is it pass coded?'

'No code.' Batillo picked it up with a gloved hand. 'It's a California exchange, prepaid.'

When he told her the number Dance nodded. 'The unsub called it from his burner, the one he dropped in Orange County. Can I see the log?'

She and O'Neil moved closer together and looked down, as the CSU officer scrolled.

'Hold it,' Dance said. 'Okay, that's the number of the phone the unsub dropped. And the others are the ones he bought at the same time, in Chicago.'

Batillo gave a brief laugh. Perhaps that she'd memorized the numbers. He continued, 'No voice mail. Fair number of texts back and forth.' He scrolled through them. 'Here's one. Grant says he has, quote, "the last of your" money. "I know you wanted more and I wish I could have paid you more."' The officer read on. '"I know the risks you took. I'm For Ever in your debt." "For Ever" capitalized. He does that a lot. Then, going back . . . Grant tells him the targets were perfect: the roadhouse, the Bay View Center, the Monterey Bay Hospital, "probably better the church didn't work out".'

'He was going to attack a church?' Dance asked, shaking her head.

Batillo read one more. '"Thanks for the ammo."'

Soldier of fortune . . .

The officer slipped the phone into a bag with a chain-of-custody card attached. He signed it and put the sealed bag into a large plastic container resembling a laundry basket.

She glanced down at a treatise on the law of eminent domain.

'How'd he meet the doer?' Dance wondered aloud. 'He said a few years ago.'

Batillo said, 'I saw some texts about "the gun show". "Enjoyed talking weapons with you."'

'And I found the ammo I think he was talking about. Brick of twelve gauge and two twenty-three. "Arlington Heights Guns and Sporting Goods" on the label.'

'Chicago,' Dance said.

O'Neil said wryly, 'Tough manhunt. Six million people.'

'We've got the gun-show reference. The ammo. The phones.' She shrugged and offered a smile. 'Needle in a haystack, I know. Right up there with "When it rains it pours." But that doesn't mean the needle isn't there.'

Forty minutes later she was back in her office, scrolling through the crime-scene pictures of the Otto Grant suicide – the rest of the report wouldn't be ready for a day or two – and considering how to narrow down the task of finding their unsub in the Windy City, or wherever he might be. Page after page . . . Dance found herself staring at the pictures of Prescott and the woman he'd killed, positioned under the lights to get pictures for proof of death. If only she could let her eyes be theirs for a brief moment before they had glazed over, and darkness embraced them.

To catch a fleeting glimpse of the man who'd done this.

Who are you? Are you headed back to your home in Chicago, or somewhere else?

And are you working for someone else now, a new job? Nearby? Or in a different part of the world?

Questions she would answer, whether it took a week, a month, a year.

CHAPTER 79

Maggie's eyes were wide and even Dance's adolescent, seen-it-all son was impressed.

They were backstage at the Monterey Performing Arts Center with Neil Hartman himself. The lanky man in his early thirties, dark curly hair and a lean face, looked every inch the country-western star, though that genre was only part of his repertoire. His songs and performance style were very similar to Kayleigh Towne's – she was Dance's performer friend, based in Fresno.

When Dance and the kids had been ushered into the green room, the musician had smiled and introduced everyone to the band members present. 'Kayleigh sends her best,' he told her.

'Where's her show tonight?'

'Denver. Big house, five thousand plus.'

Dance said, 'She's doing well.'

'I'll head out there after tomorrow's show. Maybe we'll get to Aspen.' He was grinning shyly.

That answered one of Dance's questions. The beautiful singer-songwriter hadn't been dating anyone seriously for a time. There were worse romantic options than a Portland troubadour with dreamy eyes and a lifestyle that seemed more mom-and-pop than Rolling Stones.

'Uhm . . .' Maggie began.

'Yes, young lady?' Hartman asked, smiling.

'Ask him, Mags.'

'Can I have your autograph?'

He laughed. 'Do you one better.' He walked to a box, found a T-shirt in Maggie's size. It featured a photo from one of his recent CDs – Hartman and his golden retriever sitting on a front porch. He signed it to her with a glittery marker.

'Oh, wow.'

'Mags?'

'Thank you!'

For Wes, the gift was age-appropriate: a black T-shirt with 'NHB'.

'Cool. Thanks.'

'Hey, you guys want to noodle around on a git-fiddle or keyboard?'

'Yeah? Can we?' Wes asked.

'Sure.'

'Wooee!' Maggie sat down at the keyboard – Dance cranked the volume down – and Hartman handed Wes an old Martin. You couldn't live in the Dance household without knowing something about musical instruments, and though Maggie was the real talent, Wes could chord and play a few flat-pick licks.

When he started 'Stairway To Heaven', Hartman and Dance glanced at each other and laughed. The song that will never die.

They talked about the show tonight. Hartman was growing in popularity but not at the Kayleigh Towne level yet, though his Grammy win had guaranteed a sold-out house at the performing arts center – nearly a thousand people were coming to see him.

With the children occupied in the corner, the adults spoke in low voices.

'I heard you got him. The guy behind the attacks.'

'Well, the one who hired him.'

'Grant, right? He lost his farm.'

'That's him. But we still don't have the hit man he hired. But we will. We'll get him.'

'Kayleigh said something about you being . . . persistent.'

Dance laughed. 'That's what she said, hm?' Her kinesic skills told her that Hartman was translating. Maybe 'obstinate' or 'pig-headed' had been the young woman's choice. She and Kayleigh were a lot alike in that regard.

'I thought we were going to have to cancel the show.'

Dance had been fully prepared to do just that – if they hadn't closed the case before the concert.

'You hear about Sam Cohen?'

'No, what?'

'He's going to rebuild the roadhouse. A dozen or so of us are doing some benefit concerts, donating the money to him. He's going to tear down the old building and put up a new one. He didn't want to at first but we were . . .' he laughed '. . . persistent.'

'Great news. I'm really happy.'

Maybe you *can* recover from some things, Sam. Maybe you can.

Hartman's drummer appeared in the doorway, smiled at the kids, then said, 'Let's play.'

Hartman gave the children a thumbs-up. 'You got your chops down, both of you. Next time I'm in town, we'll work up some tunes, I'll get you out on stage with me.'

'No way!' Wes said.

'Sure.'

'Excellent!'

Maggie frowned, considering something. 'Can I cover a Patsy Cline song?'

Dance said, 'Mags, why don't you sing a Neil Hartman?'

Hartman laughed. 'I think Ms Cline would be honored. We'll make it happen.'

'Hey, gang, let's head to our seats.'

'Bye, Mr Hartman. Thanks.'

Wes handed over the guitar and, looking at his phone, headed toward the door.

'Young man.'

'Thanks.'

'Say hi to Kayleigh for us.' Dance gave him a smile.

They left the green room and walked into the theater, which was filling up. There were about eight hundred people, Dance estimated.

Year ago, she had dreamed of being a musician, appearing in halls like this. She had tried and tried, but however hard she worked, there came the point when her skill just didn't make the final bump into the professional world. There came advanced degrees, a stint as a jury consultant, offering her kinesic skills commercially, then law enforcement. A wonderful job, a challenging job . . . And yet, what she wouldn't have given to have the talent to make places like this her home.

But then the nostalgia faded as the cop within her resurfaced. Dance was, of course, aware that she was in a crowded venue that would be a perfect target for their unsub at-large. He was surely a hundred miles away by now. But just because Otto Grant had said he'd gotten sufficient revenge didn't mean he hadn't had his man set up a whopper of a finale. On the way back from Grant's shack, she'd arranged for a full sweep of the concert hall and for police to be stationed at each exit door.

Even now she remained vigilant. She noted the location of the exits, fire hoses and extinguishers. She could see no potential sniper nests. And checked that the red lights on the security cameras glowed healthily and, because those models didn't sport lights, unlike the one in the hospital elevator, she checked for emergency lighting: there were a dozen halogens that would turn the place to bright noon in the event of trouble.

Finally, confident of their security, Kathryn Dance sat back, crossed her legs and enjoyed the exhilaration that always accompanies dimming lights in a concert hall.

CHAPTER 80

Antioch March was enjoying another pineapple juice and studying the TV screen in the Cedar Hills Inn.

The hotel was so posh that it featured a very special television – one with 4K resolution. This was known as ultra-high-definition video. It was nearly double the current standard: 1920 wide by 1080 high.

It was ethereal, the depth of the imagery.

He was presently watching an underwater video, shot in 4K, flowing from his computer, via HDMI cable, onto the fifty-four-inch screen.

Astonishing. The kelp was real. The sunfish. The eels. The coral. All real. The sharks especially, with their supple gray skin, their singular eyes, their choreography of motion, like elegant fencers.

So beautiful. So rich. You were there, you were part of the ocean. Part of the chain of nature.

There was not, as yet, much content in 4K – you needed special cameras to shoot it – but it was coming. If only the family on the rocks at Asilomar had lingered but a minute longer he might have given the Get their ultra-high-definition deaths: his Samsung Galaxy featured such a camera.

Somebody's not happy . . .

The landline phone rang and he snagged it, eyes still on the waving kelp, so real it might have been floating in the room around him.

The receptionist announced that a Fred Johnson had arrived.

'Thank you. Send him over.' Wondering why that pseudonym.

A few minutes later Christopher Jenkins was at the door.

March let his boss into the entryway. A handshake and then into the luxurious suite. Once the door was closed, a hug too.

Mildly reciprocated.

Jenkins, who, yes, resembled March somewhat, was in his fifties, broad-shouldered, compact – a good foot shorter than his employee – and tanned. His hair was blond, close-cropped and flat against his skull. A military bearing because he had been military. He glanced up at March's shaved head.

'Hmm.'

'Had to.'

'Looks good.'

Jenkins didn't really think so, March could see, but he'd never say a word against his favorite employee's appearance. To March, Jenkins seemed no older than when the two men had met six years ago. He was a bit heavier, more solid. Jenkins had his own Get, but it wasn't March's. Amassing money was what numbed Jenkins's demon. Whether buying a Ferrari for himself or taking a boy out for a thousand-dollar dinner or finding a Cartier bauble . . . that was what kept Jenkins's Get at bay.

Odd, how their respective compulsions worked. Symbiotic.

'Carole says hello.'

'And to her too.'

One of the girls Jenkins had dated on and off. March wasn't sure why he kept the façade. Who cared nowadays? Besides, you can't cheat the Get, which knows what you want and when you want it, so why complicate things? Life's too short.

'Your drive good?'

'Fine.' Jenkins had a faint Bostonian drawl. He'd lived in a suburb of Bean Town before the army.

March had ordered the best – well, the most expensive – wine on the list, a Château Who Knew from France. A 1995. Had to be good: it was six hundred dollars. It was already open. He'd had a taste. It was okay. Not as good as Dole.

'Well. Excellent!' Jenkins said, looking over the label – all Greek to him, a private joke, considering March's heritage.

He allowed Jenkins to pour him some of the sludgy wine and they tapped glasses, toasting their success. Over the past few days they'd made several hundred thousand dollars.

'Always loved it here, the Cedar Hills.'

Chris Jenkins reminded March of the people in those infomercials:

371

the handsome man, next to the beautiful woman, on a Florida or Hawaiian porch, boats in the background, palms nearby, talking about how they'd made millions with hardly any effort in the real-estate market or by inventing things. In Jenkins's case, selling something very, very rare and valuable.

The men sat on the couch. They regarded the crystal TV screen, on which fish swam and kelp waved, hypnotic.

'Good picture. Four K. Man, that's beautiful. We'll keep that in mind.' Jenkins set the glass down. 'Now where are we?'

'All good.'

'What about Otto Grant? I heard the news. They seemed to buy it.'

'They did.'

March paused the shark video and called up another video file on his computer. The video, a high-definition (only 2K), showed Otto Grant, kicking in the last moments of his life, trying to get leverage to pull himself up and somehow unhook the rope from where March had tied it to stage the suicide. He struggled for a time, then shivered and went limp.

'Did he come?'

There was a rumor that upon being hanged, men sometimes ejaculated. Neither had been able to confirm this.

'Just peed.'

'Ah.'

'I left evidence in the shack that the man he hired is from Chicago and has already left to go back there, left right after the incident in the hospital. Solid leads. Phone calls, proxies, emails. They'll sniff up that tree for a while.'

'Good.'

'Now, you were mentioning a new job.' March knew Jenkins had come to Carmel for another reason, but he wouldn't've made up the part about a new job entirely.

'Client's in Lausanne, so he wants it to happen anywhere but Europe. He mentioned Latin America.'

'Any preferences as to how?'

'He was thinking a fall, maybe a cable car.'

March laughed. He could hotwire an ignition, he could disable an elevator. That was the extent of his mechanical engineering skills. 'I don't think so. A bus?'

'A bus would work, I'd think.'

'Send me the details.'

Glasses clinked again. March had sipped the wine once. He'd also eyed the pineapple juice.

Jenkins laughed and handed the juice glass to March, making sure their fingers brushed once more. 'Just don't mix it with Saint Estèphe.'

March let his boss's hand linger on his for a moment.

'Dinner?' Jenkins asked.

'Not hungry.'

March never was, not at times like this. All the work, hoping it would pay off. The way he planned out the jobs, well, it was fragile. There was a lot that could go wrong. Wasting all that time and money, the risk. Anyway, what it came down to: when the Get was hungry, March was not.

'Oh, here. I brought you something.' Jenkins dug in his Vuitton backpack. He handed over a small box. March opened it. 'Well.'

'Victoria Beckham.'

They were sunglasses, blue lenses.

Jenkins said, 'Italian. And the lenses change color in the sun. Or get darker. I don't know. I think there are instructions. You'll love them.'

'Thanks. They're really something.'

Though March's first thought was: wearing bright blue sunglasses on a job, where you would want to be as inconspicuous as possible?

Maybe I'll go to the beach sometime. On vacation.

Would you let me do that, Get? Just relax?

He tried them on.

'They're you,' Jenkins whispered, squeezing March's biceps.

March put the glasses away and picked up the remote.

Click. The hypnotic ballet of sea creatures resumed on the TV. 'Extraordinary. Four K,' he said reverently. 'Who shot this?'

'Teenager, believe it or not.'

'Four K. Hmm. Wave of the future.'

Jenkins asked, 'What's the plan?'

'We need to stop her.'

'That investigator? Dance?'

'That's right.' He explained that the attempt to injure her boyfriend, somebody named Boling, hadn't worked out. Now they needed to do something more efficient.

'We're leaving tomorrow. Why do anything? We'll be a thousand miles away by noon.'

'No. We have to stop her. She won't rest until she gets us.'

'You're sure?'

'Yes,' March said, staring at the sharks.

'What do you have in mind?'

Dance, he'd seen when he'd slipped into her Pathfinder at the Bay View crime scene, was presently attending a concert at the Performing Arts Center in Monterey. He'd thought momentarily about staging a final attack there, with the chance that she'd be severely injured or killed. But coming after Grant's suicide that would be suspicious.

Besides, there was another reason he didn't want her dead.

He looked over the notes he'd jotted after getting the information on the man's license plate. 'There's a close associate. Named TJ Scanlon. Lives in Carmel Valley. We'll kill him, make it look gang-related. It'll deflect her. She'll drop everything and go after them.'

'Why not just kill her?'

March could think of no answer. Just: 'It's better this way.'

Another reason . . .

He jabbed a finger at the TV screen. 'Ah, watch. This is it.'

On the screen a hammerhead shark, awkward yet elegant, swam toward the camera, then veered upward and, as casually as a human swatting a mosquito, opened its mouth and neatly removed the leg of a surfer treading water overhead. The shark and limb vanished as the massive cloud of red streamed like smoke into the scene, eventually obscuring the mutilated young man, writhing as he died.

'Well,' Jenkins said. 'Four K. Excellent.' He lifted a glass of wine.

March nodded. He stared at the imagery for a moment longer and shut the set off. He picked up the Louis Vuitton bag, checked that the hunting knife and gun were still inside, and gestured his boss toward the door. 'After you.'

CHAPTER **81**

This was an era he knew nothing about, didn't care for, didn't appreciate.

The sixties in the US. At least *this* part of the sixties.

Antioch March believed it was called the counterculture and, for some reason, CBI agent TJ Scanlon loved it.

As they stood in the living room of the three-bedroom ranch-style house in Carmel Valley, March and Jenkins surveyed the place. Orange and brown dominated. Carpet, furniture, table-cloths. On the wall were posters – nice ones, framed – of Jimi Hendrix at Woodstock, the Mamas and the Papas, Jefferson Airplane. The doors were strings of colorful beads that clicked when you pushed them, gun in hand, to make sure you were alone. And, yes, a lava lamp.

'Sets you on edge, doesn't it?' Jenkins asked.

It did.

In his gloved hand March clicked on a black light. The ultra-violet rays spectacularly lit up what had been a dull poster of a ship improbably sailing through the sky.

He shut the light off again.

A glance at a large peace symbol, reminiscent of the Mercedes Benz emblem on his car back home. The sixties' icon was made out of shells.

On edge . . .

He told the Get to relax; it was, he suspected, still angry that the Asian family on the rocks had missed the opportunity to die spectacular deaths in the icy bay.

Somebody's not happy . . .

You will be soon.

They had parked two blocks away and made their way to Scanlon's house through woods, out of sight of any of the neighbors. March, the technician of the two, had examined the man's place carefully from the distance. Then, convinced it was unoccupied, he'd slipped up and peered through the windows. No alarms, no security cameras. The lock had been easily jimmied. Then, prepared to flee in case they'd missed an alarm, they'd waited before preparing the room for the events tonight.

March now turned from the bizarre décor and looked over the cot they'd set up. TJ Scanlon's final resting place. The young man would be tied down and tortured. You didn't need much. March had his knife and he'd found a pair of pliers. Pain was simple. You didn't need to get elaborate.

He'd staged the scene rather well also, he thought. They'd bought a bottle of rubbing alcohol, to enhance the agent's agony, from a convenience store in the barrio of Salinas, a place known for gangs, and they'd picked up some trash and discarded rags in the area too. A little research had revealed the colors and signs of the K-101s, which was a crew that the CBI had had some run-ins with, arresting a few lieutenant-level bangers. March had tagged the signs on Scanlon's wall, right above the spot where he would die. Presumably after giving up all sorts of helpful information about ongoing investigations into the gang.

March wondered what 'TJ' stood for. He didn't bother to prowl through paperwork to find out.

Thomas Jefferson?

Jenkins was asking, 'What if he's not coming home tonight. Maybe—'

And just then there came the sound of a car on the long gravel drive, approaching.

'That's him?'

March eased up to the window to look out.

Which gave Jenkins a chance to put his hand on March's spine. *It's all right.*

'Yep.'

Scanlon was alone in the car. And there were no other vehicles with him.

Suddenly the Get slipped a regret into March's head that it wasn't Kathryn Dance whom he was about to work on after all.

March vetoed the idea. No. This was the way to handle it.

Which irritated the Get, and for a moment March felt inflamed and edgy.

Fuck you, he thought. I've got *some* say in this.

Silently the two men stepped behind the front door. March looked out of the peephole, gripping the hammer he'd break Scanlon's arm with as soon as he walked inside, grab his gun.

He saw the young man walking, head down, to the gate in the picket fence in front of his house. He opened it and started up the winding walk, minding where he put his feet. If Scanlon had front lights he hadn't turned them on.

Scanlon walked onto the low porch, then stepped to the side. They heard the mailbox open. A brief laugh, faint, at something he'd received – or hadn't received. Then gritty footsteps on the redwood planks, moving toward the front door.

The sound of a key in the lock.

Then . . . nothing.

Jenkins turned, frowning. March took a firmer grip on the hammer. He peeked outside through a curtained window. He was staring at the empty porch.

'Leave!' March whispered harshly. 'Now!'

Jenkins frowned but he followed March instinctively. They got only three feet back into the living room when a half-dozen Monterey County Sheriff's deputies, in tactical gear, flooded into the room from behind the beads covering the doorway to the kitchen. 'Hands where we can see them! On the ground, on the ground! Now!'

And the front door exploded inward. Two other tactical officers charged in too. Scanlon, his own weapon drawn, followed.

'Christ!' Jenkins cried. 'No, no, no . . .'

March backed up, hands raised, and eased to his knees. Jenkins started to, as well, but his hand dropped to his side, as if to steady himself as he sank down.

March looked at his eyes. He'd seen the expression before. The gaze wasn't defiance. It was resignation. And he knew what was coming next.

Calmly he said to Jenkins, 'No, Chris.'

But what was about to happen was inevitable.

The small pistol was in the man's tanned hand, drawn leisurely from his hip pocket. He swung it forward but it got no farther than four o'clock before two officers fired simultaneously. Head and chest. Huge explosions that deafened March. Jenkins crumpled, eyes nearly closed, and landed in a pile on the floor.

'Shots fired. Suspect down. Medic, medic, medic!' One officer who'd fired dropped his radio and hurried forward, pistol still pointed toward Jenkins, though from the spatter it was clear he was no threat. Another two cuffed March.

The policeman removed the small gun from Jenkins's hand, unloaded it and locked the slide back.

The others hurried through the place, opening doors. Shouts of 'Clear!' echoed.

March continued to gaze down at his boss.

Maybe Jenkins had actually believed he could shoot his way out of the situation. But that was unlikely. He'd chosen to take his own life. It wasn't uncommon; suicide by cop, it was called. For those who lacked the courage to put a gun to their head and pull the trigger.

He stared at Jenkins's body on the floor, the blood spreading in the shag carpet, a twitch of a finger.

Other officers streamed inside, accompanying two emergency medical technicians. They bent to the fallen man. But a fast check of vitals confirmed what was obvious.

'He's gone. I'll tell the ME.'

Another man, in a body-armor vest, walked inside and looked down at his captives. He recognized him from outside the movie theater the other morning and from the Bay View Center. Kathryn Dance's colleague.

'Detective O'Neil,' one of the deputies called. 'We're clear of threat.' The officer handed O'Neil March's wallet. Jenkins's too. O'Neil flipped through them.

He walked to the door and said, 'It's clear, Kathryn.'

She walked inside, glancing at the corpse matter-of-factly. Then her green eyes fixed on March's. He felt an odd sensation, looking at her. Was it a comfort? He believed so. Outrageous, under the circumstances. But there it was. He nearly smiled. She was even more beautiful than he'd believed. And how much she resembled Jessica!

O'Neil handed her the men's IDs. 'The deceased's Chris Jenkins.' Then a nod. 'And you got it right, Kathryn. He's Antioch March.'

Got it right?

He wasn't the least surprised his beautiful Kathryn had out-thought him.

'Read him his rights and let's get him to CBI.'

CHAPTER 82

'It was the lights, Antioch.'

'Andy, please. Lights?'

'The lights in the security cameras of the venues where you staged the attacks.'

Dance scooted her chair closer, here in the larger of the interview rooms, the one, in fact, where the Serrano incident had begun. She was already wearing her dark-framed predator specs. Examining March carefully. A trim-fitting light blue dress shirt, dark slacks. Both seemed expensive. She couldn't see his shoes from where she sat: were they the five-grand pair?

He still seemed a bit mystified at the officers' sudden appearance at TJ's, though the explanation was rather simple.

Just after the Neil Hartman concert had started Dance had found herself thinking once more of her observation a few moments earlier: about the security lights at the hospital, and at the venues the unsub had attacked. They'd all been been equipped with lights, while most security cameras – like the ones she'd just noted at the Performing Arts Center – were not. She recalled the witnesses telling her that bright lights had come on around the time of the panic at the roadhouse and the author's signing; she herself had seen them blazing from the camera in the elevator.

She'd ducked into the lobby of the concert hall and, from her phone, checked the photos of the three crime scenes. The cameras were all the same.

She told March this and added, 'All the venues had just been inspected by an insurance or fire inspector, I remembered. Except it wasn't an official. It was you, mounting the cameras when the manager wasn't looking. Fire Inspector Dunn.'

Dance continued, 'You moved lamps over two of your other victims: Calista Sommers and Stan Prescott. Oh, I see your expression. Yes, we know about Calista. She's not Jane Doe any more. We finally got her ID. Missing-person memo from Washington State.

'Calista . . . Stan Prescott. And Otto Grant. He was hanged in front of an open window. Lots of light there, as well. Every time somebody died because of you, you wanted lights. Why? For Calista and Prescott, we thought it was to take pictures of the bodies. Were you filming at the venues too?'

Just after she'd had this thought, at the concert hall earlier, she'd called O'Neil and had a crime-scene team seize and dismantle the security camera in the elevator. They found a cellular module in it.

She had remembered that at Solitude Creek she'd wondered why the security video that Sam Cohen had shown them seemed to come from a different angle than that of the camera she'd seen in the club. That was, she realized, because there were two cameras – with March's pointed, as Trish Martin had said, at the blocked exit doors. To see the tragedy most clearly.

'The cameras were streaming the stampedes, full high-def, brightly lit. But why? So Grant could gloat over his revenge? Maybe. But if he planned to kill himself he wouldn't be around very long to enjoy the show.' Through the lenses of the steely glances Dance probed his face. 'And then I remembered the bucket.'

'Bucket?'

'Why did Grant have a bucket for a toilet? If he'd vanished on his own, well, wouldn't he just go outside for the bathroom? *Kidnappers* have buckets for the victims to use because they're handcuffed or taped.'

He squinted slightly. A kinesic tell that meant she'd struck a nerve. He'd made a mistake there.

'And the venues that were attacked, Solitude Creek and the Bay View Center? Grant's complaint was with the *government*. He would've hired somebody to attack state buildings, not private ones, if he'd really wanted revenge.

'Which meant maybe Otto Grant had been set up as a fall

guy. You went online and found somebody who'd been posting anti-government statements. A perfect choice. You made contact, pretended you were sympathetic, then kidnapped him and stuck him in that cabin until it was time to finish up here. Made his death look like a suicide. All the texts and the call-log records we found? About payments and what a good job his supposed hitman had done? They were both your phones; you just called and texted yourself, then planted one on Grant.'

She now placed her hands flat on the table. 'So. Grant was a set-up. But then who was the real client who'd hired you?'

She'd eliminated Michelle Cooper's husband – Frederick Martin. Brad, the fireman. And Daniel Nashima.

Another suspect had arisen briefly. Upon learning that it was Mexican Commissioner Ramón Santos's mercenaries who'd orchestrated the arson of the warehouse in Oakland, Dance had wondered if he'd been behind the entire plot, suspecting Henderson Jobbing and Warehouse, at Solitude Creek, to be one of the hubs for illegal-weapons traffic in Central California, and Santos of taking his own measures to shut them down and cover up the crime as the work of a psycho.

She remembered the sign she'd seen the day after the attack at Solitude Creek:

Remember your Passports for International trips!

She'd assigned Rey Carreneo to look into the matter. But he'd learned that Henderson *did* serve international routes, yes – but only to Canada. The owner didn't want to risk hijacking or robberies south of the border. No reason for Commissioner Santos to send a mercenary to destroy the company.

So who, she'd struggled to understand, was the unsub working for? Why was he killing people and filming it?

And then, finally.

A to B to Z . . .

Now another sweep of the so-very-handsome face.

'The violent websites on Stan Prescott's computer. That's your job, Andy. Yours and Chris Jenkins's. This wasn't about revenge or insurance or a psychotic serial killer. It was about you and your partner selling ultra-violent images of death to clients around the world. Custom ordered.'

Dance shook her head. 'I honestly wouldn't think there'd be that big a market for this sort of thing.'

Antioch March gave her an amused look. He remained silent but his eyes chastised, as if she was bluntly naïve. They said, Oh, Agent Dance. You'd be surprised.

CHAPTER 83

'You didn't kill Prescott because he drew attention to the murders in Monterey. It was because your website, Hand to Heart, was on his computer. He downloaded graphic images of corpses from it and re-posted them. You didn't have any pictures of Solitude Creek on your site, of course, but Prescott did on his. That made a connection between Heart to Hand and the roadhouse.'

Hand to Heart was the key to the men's operation. It *seemed* to be about humanitarian aid – and visitors could click through to tsunami relief or ending hunger sites. But most of Hand to Heart was pictures and videos of disasters, atrocities, death, dismemberment.

She speculated that the men noted who downloaded the most pictures and discreetly contacted them to see if they might be interested in something more . . . graphically violent. She was sure that, after sufficient vetting of both parties, and for the payment of a huge fee, clients could order specific types of videos or images. It answered the question they'd wondered about at the beginning of the case: why not just burn down Solitude Creek? Why not just shoot people at the Bay View? Because this particular client – whoever he was – wanted pictures of stampedes.

March tilted his head, brows dipping, and she had an idea what he was wondering. 'Oh, how we found you at TJ's? You used prepaid cells in the cameras and routed through proxies, but the video ended up at the Cedar Hills Inn server.'

Jon Boling had explained how the signals could be traced. She hadn't understood a word but kissed him in thanks.

'That just sent us to the hotel, not your room. But I correlated all the guests' names with anyone who'd rented a car in Los Angeles just after the panic at the theme park. Yours popped up. We hit the room at the inn and found a note with TJ's address.'

The same technology that was so integral to their perverse career had betrayed him.

He sat back, a clink of chain.

She was struck again by how handsome he was, resembling an actor whose name she couldn't summon. He had no physical appeal to her but objectively he was striking – dipping lids, careful lips that weren't too thick or too thin, noble cheekbones. And a cut, muscular physique. Even the shaved head worked.

'I want your cooperation, Andy. I want the names of your clients. Those in America, at least. And any of your – what would you call them? – competitors.'

The cases would be tough to put together, though she, Michael O'Neil and the FBI's Amy Grabe would try. But, in fact, what Dance wanted most was to understand this man's workings. He was unlike any other criminal she'd ever come up against; and, experience had taught her, if there was one with his proclivities toward the dark edge there'd be others.

'Before you answer, let me say one thing.'

'Yes?'

'Texas.'

His face gave a minuscule twitch. He knew what was coming.

'If you agree, I've spoken to the prosecutor here, and he'll accept a death penalty waiver.' She gazed at him steadily. 'And will guarantee no extradition to Texas. We subpoenaed your credit-card statements, Andy. You were in Fort Worth six months ago, finding clients for your website. The same time of the stampede at the Prairie Valley Club. You used that homeless man for your fall-guy there. But there'll be some forensics tying you to that incident, I'm sure. They'll go for capital murder. And they'll get it. The daughter of a state politician was killed in that stampede.'

The tip of his tongue eased against a lip and retreated. 'And here? I'll get life.'

'Maybe a little shorter. Depends.'

He said nothing.

'Or call your lawyer.'

March's eyes scanned her, from the top of her head to her

waist, leaving a chill repulsion in the wake of his gaze. 'You'll guarantee that?'

'Yes,' she told him.

'Personally.' He dragged the word out, almost seductively.

'Yes.'

'I have one condition.'

'What's that?'

'I can call you "Kathryn".'

'That's fine. Now, what's the condition?'

'That's it. You let me use your first name.'

He can call me whatever he wants. But he's asking my *permission* to use the name? The sensation of ice brushed the back of her neck.

She forced herself not to react. 'You can use my name, yes.'

'Thank you, Kathryn.'

She opened her notebook and uncapped a pen. 'Now. Tell me, Andy. How did you meet Chris Jenkins?'

CHAPTER **84**

The two men had become acquainted in one of the snuff forums online.

Dance recalled the websites that Jon Boling had found: they featured not only pictures that could be downloaded but forums where members could post messages and chat in real time.

Jenkins was former military. While on tour overseas, he'd taken a lot of pictures of battlefields, bodies, torture victims. He himself had had no interest in the images but he'd learned he could make good money selling them to news media or, even more lucrative, private collectors.

March explained, 'Every night I was online looking at this stuff. It was the only thing that kept the . . .'

'The what?' Dance asked.

A pause. 'Only thing that kept me calm,' he said. 'He had good-quality pictures and I bought a number of them. We got to know each other that way. Then he started running low on original material – he'd been out of the army for years. I asked if he'd be interesting in buying some from me – pictures he could resell. I didn't have much but I sent him a video I'd done of an accident during a bungee jump. I was the only one who'd gotten the actual death. It was . . . pretty graphic.

'Chris told me it was very good and he knew a collector who'd pay a lot for it as an exclusive. It would have to be private – if it was posted, a video lost its value. I got to work and started to send him material. After a few months we met in person and decided to start our business. He came up with the idea of a humanitarian website, with pictures of disasters. Sure, some people went online to give money. Mostly people downloaded the pictures. I took a lot of them myself, traveling overseas or to disaster areas. They were good, the video and the pictures. People liked them. I'm good at what I do.'

'Where did you get this material?'

A smile crossed his face. His eyes stroked her skin and she forced the cold away. He said, 'Next time you find yourself at any tragedy, a train or car crash, a race-car accident, a fire, a stampede.' His voice had fallen.

'Could you speak up, please?'

'Of course, Kathryn. Next time you're someplace like that, look around you.

'At the people who are staring at the bodies and the injured. The spectators. You'll see people helping the victims, praying for them, standing around numb. But you'll also see some people with their cameras, working hard to get the best shot. Maybe they're curious . . . but maybe they're collectors. Or maybe they're just like me – suppliers. "Farming", we call it. You can spot us. We'll be the ones angry at police lines keeping us back, disappointed there's not more blood, grimacing when we learn that no one died.'

Farming . . .

'You've always had this interest?'

'Well, since I was eleven.' His tongue wet his lip. 'And I killed my first victim. Serena. Her name was Serena. And I still picture her every day. Every single day.'

Kathryn Dance masked her shock – both at the idea of someone committing murder at that young age and at his wistful expression when he told her.

Eleven. One year older than Maggie, one younger than Wes.

'I was living with my parents, outside Minneapolis. A small town, suburban. Perfectly fine, nice. My father was a salesman, my mother worked in the hospital. Both busy. I had a lot of time to myself. Latch-key but that was fine. I didn't *want* too much involvement from them. I was a loner. I preferred that life. Oh, the weapon I used on Serena was an SMG.'

Lord, thought Dance. 'That's a machine-gun, isn't it? Where did you get it?'

Gazing off. 'I shot her five times and I can't describe the comfort I felt.' Another scan of her face. Down her arm. He focused on her hands. She was glad they were polish-free. She felt as if he'd touched her. 'Serena. Dark hair. Latina in appearance. I'd guess she was twenty-five. At eleven, I didn't know much about sex. But I felt *something* when I was watching Serena.'

Watching, Dance noted. That was what he liked.

Nostalgia had blossomed into pleasure at recalling the incident. Had he been caught? Done juvie time? Nothing had shown up on the NCIC crime database. But youthful offender records were often sealed.

'Oh, I felt guilty. Terribly guilty. I'd never do it again, I swore.' A faint laugh. 'But the next day I was back. And I killed her again.'

'I'm sorry? You killed . . .'

'Her, Serena. This time it was less of a whim. I wanted to kill her. I used twenty-shots. Reloaded and shot her twenty more times.'

Dance understood. 'It was a video game.'

He nodded. 'It was a first-person shooter game. You know those?'

'Yes.' You see the game from the point of view of a character, walking through the sets, usually with a gun or other weapon and killing opponents or creatures.

'Next day I was back again in the game world. And I kept coming back. I killed her over and over. And Troy and Gary, hundreds of others, hour after hour, stalking them and killing them. What started as just an impulse became a compulsion. It was the only way to keep the Get at bay.'

'The . . . ?'

He looked at her, a long moment. Debating. 'Since we're close now, you and me, I want to share. I started to say something before. I changed my mind.'

'I remember.'

It's the only thing that kept the . . . kept me calm . . .

'The Get,' he said. And explained. His expression for the irresistible urge to *get* something that satisfied you, stopped the itch, fed the hunger. In his case, that was watching death, injury, blood. He continued, 'The games . . . They took the edge off of what I was feeling. Gave me a high.'

Traditional cycle of addiction, Dance noted.

'More,' he whispered. 'More and more. I needed more. The games became my life. I got every one I could, all the platforms. PlayStation,

Nintendo, Xbox, everything.' He looked at her, his eyes damp; he was now gripped by emotion. He whispered, 'And there were so many of them. I'd ask for games for Christmas and my parents bought them all. They never paid any attention to the contents.'

His laundry list: Doom, Dead or Alive, Mortal Kombat, Call of Duty, Hitman, Gears of War. 'I learned all the blood codes – to make them as violent as possible. My favorite recently is Grand Theft Auto. You could fulfill missions or you could just walk around and kill people. Tase them and then, when they fell to the ground, shoot them or blow them up or burn them to death. Walk around Los Santos shooting prostitutes. Or go into a strip club and just start killing people.'

Recently Dance had been involved in a case in which a young man had lost himself in massive multiplayer online role-playing games, like World of Warcraft. She'd studied video games and had kept up with them, since she was the mother of two children raised in the online era.

A controversy existed in law enforcement, psychology and education as to whether violent games led to violent behavior.

'I think I always had the Get inside me. But it was the games that turned up the heat, you know. If it hadn't been for them, I might've . . . gone in a different direction. Found other ways to numb the Get. Anyway, you can't dispute the way my life went. As I got older, though, the games weren't enough.' He smiled. 'Gateway drug, you could say. I wanted more. I found movies – spatter films, gore, slasher, torture porn. *Cannibal Ferox*, *Last House on the Left*, *Wizard of Gore*. Then more sophisticated ones later. *Saw*, *Human Centipede*, *I Spit on Your Grave*, *Hostel* . . . hundreds of others.

'Then the websites, the one you found on Stan Prescott's computer, where you could see crime-scene pictures. And could buy fifteen-minute clips of actresses getting shot or stabbed.'

She said, 'And pretty soon even they weren't enough.'

He nodded, and there was some desperation in his voice as he said, 'Then something happened that changed everything.'

'What happened?'

'Jessica,' he whispered. And his eyes stroked her face and neck once more. 'Jessica.'

CHAPTER 85

'I was in my early teens. There was an accident. It was Route Thirty-five and Mockingbird Road. Minnesota countryside. I called the incident the Intersection. Upper case. It was that significant to me.

'I was driving with my parents, home from a family funeral.' He smiled. 'That was ironic. A funeral. Well, we were driving along and turned this corner in a hilly area and there was a truck in the Intersection right in front of us. My father hit the brakes . . .' He shrugged.

'An accident. Your family was killed?'

'What? Oh, no. They were fine. They're living in Florida now. Dad's still a salesman. Mom manages a bakery. I see them some.' A pallid chuckle. 'They're proud of the humanitarian work I do.'

'The Intersection,' Dance prompted.

'What happened was a pickup truck had run a stop sign and slammed into a sports car, a convertible. The car had been knocked off the road and down the hill a little ways. The driver of the BMW was dead, that was obvious. My parents told me to stay in the car and they ran to the man in the truck – he was the only one alive – to see what they could do.

'I stayed where I was, for a minute, but I'd seen something that intrigued me. I got out and walked down the hill, past the sports car and into the brush. There was a girl, about sixteen, seventeen, lying on her back. She'd been thrown free from the car and had tumbled down the hill.

'She – I found out later her name was Jessica – was bleeding real badly. Her neck had been cut, deep, her chest too – her blouse was open and there was a huge gash across her left breast. Her arm was shattered. She was so pretty. Green eyes. Intense green eyes.

'She kept saying, "Help me. Call the police, call somebody. Stop the bleeding, please."' He looked at Dance levelly. 'But I didn't. I couldn't. I pulled out my cell phone and I took pictures of her for the next five minutes. While she died.'

'You needed to take the next step. To a real death. Seeing it in real time. Not a game or a movie.'

'That's right. That's what I needed. When I did, with Jessica, the Get went away for a long time.'

'But then you took another step, didn't you? You had to. Because how often could you happen to stumble on a scene like Jessica's death?'

'Todd,' he said.

'Todd?'

'It was about four, five years ago. I wasn't doing well. The college failures, the boring job . . . And, no, the video games and movies weren't doing it for me any longer. I needed more. I was in upstate New York. Took a walk in the woods. I saw this bungee-jumping thing. It was illegal, not like it was a tourist attraction or anything. These people, kids mostly, just put on helmets and Go Pro cameras and jumped.'

'What you mentioned earlier? The tape you sold to Chris Jenkins.'

He nodded. 'I got talking to this one kid. His name was Todd.' March fell silent for a moment. 'Todd. Anyway, I just couldn't stop myself. He'd hooked his rope to the top of the rock and walked away to the edge to look over the jump. There was nobody around.'

'You detached it?'

'No. That would've been suspicious. I just lengthened it by about five feet. Then I went down to the ground. He jumped and hit the rocks below. I got it all on tape.' March shook his head. 'I can't tell you . . . the feeling.'

'The Get went away?'

'Uh-huh. From there, I knew where my life was going. I met Chris and I was the luckiest person in the world. I could make a living doing what I had to do. We started small. A single death here or there. A homeless man – poisoning him. A girl on a scooter, no helmet. I'd pour oil on a curve. But soon one or two deaths weren't enough. I needed more. The customers wanted more too. They were addicts, just like me.'

'So, you came up with the idea of stampedes.'

'The blood of all.'

He told her about a poem from ancient Rome, praising a gladiator for not retiring even though the emperor had granted him his freedom and the right to leave the games.

March's eyes actually sparkled as he recited:

> 'O Verus, you have fought forty contests and have
> Been offered the wooden Rudis of freedom
> Three times and yet declined the chance to retire.
> Soon we will gather to see the sword
> In your hand pierce the heart of your foes.
> Praise to you, who has chosen not to walk through
> The Gates of Life but to give us
> What we desire most, what we live for:
> The blood of all.

'That was two thousand years ago, Kathryn. And we're no different. Not a bit. Car races, downhill skiing, rugby, boxing, bungee-jumping, football, hockey, air shows – we're all secretly, or not so secretly, hoping for death or destruction. NASCAR? Hours of cars making left turns? Would anybody watch if there wasn't the chance of a spectacular fiery death? The Colosseum back then, Madison Square Garden last week. Not a lick of difference.'

She noted something else. 'The poem, the line about hand and heart . . . The name of your website. Sword in the hand piercing the heart. Little different from humanitarian aid.'

A shrug, and his eyes sparkled again.

'I'd like to know more about your clients. Are they mostly in the US?'

'No, overseas. Asia a lot. Russia too. And South America, though the clientele there isn't as rich. They couldn't pay for the big set-pieces.'

It would be a tricky case against many of these people – men, nearly all of them, Dance supposed. (She guessed the sexual component of the Get was high.) Intent would be an issue.

'The man who hired you for this job, in Monterey?'

'Japanese. He's been a good customer for some years.'

'Any particular grudge with this area?'

She was thinking of Nashima and the relocation center at Solitude Creek.

'No. He said pick anywhere. Chris Jenkins liked the inn in Carmel. So he sent me there. It has a good wine list. And comfortable beds. Nice TV too.'

She began to ask another question. But he was shaking his head.

'I'm tired now,' he said. 'Can we resume tomorrow? Or the next day?'

'Yes.'

She rose.

March said to her, 'Oh, Kathryn?'

'Yes?'

'It's so good to have a kindred soul to spend some time with.'

She didn't understand for a moment. Then realized he was speaking about her. The chill pinched once more.

He looked her up and down. 'Your Get and mine . . . So very similar. I'm glad we're in each other's lives now.' March whispered, 'Good night, Kathryn. I'll talk to you tomorrow. Good night.'

THE LAST DARE

TUESDAY, APRIL 11

CHAPTER 86

'Real, dude.'

Donnie and Nathan bumped fists. Wes nodded, looking around.

They were in the school yard, just hanging, on one of the picnic benches. There was Tiff; she looked his way and lifted an eyebrow. But that was it. No other reaction.

Some of the brothers, and there weren't many of them here, were hanging not far away. One gave him a thumbs-up. Probably for track. Donnie'd just led the T and F team to victory over Seaside Middle School, winning the 200 and 400 dash (though, fuck, he'd gotten the branch once he'd gotten back home because he was one second off his personal best on the 400).

That was Leon Williams doing the thumbing. Solid kid. Donnie nodded back. The funny thing was that Donnie didn't hate the blacks in the school at all, or any other blacks, for that matter. Which was one of the reasons that tagging black churches in the game was pretty fucked up. He disliked Jews a lot – or thought he did. That, too, was mostly from his dad, though. Donnie didn't know that he'd ever actually met somebody who was Jewish, aside from Goldshit.

Donnie looked at his phone. Nothing.

He said to Nathan and Wes, 'You heard from him? Vulcan?'

Vince had left right after class, saying he'd be back. It had seemed suspicious.

Nathan said, 'He texted.'

Donnie said, 'You, not me. Didn't have the balls to text me.'

'Yeah. Well. He said he'd be here. Just had something to do first and Mary might be coming by – you know her, the one with tits – and kept going on, all this shit. Which I think means he's not coming.'

'Fucker's out if he doesn't show.' There was a waiting list to get in the DARES crew. But then Donnie reflected: of course, for what was going down today, maybe better Vince the Pussy wasn't here. Because, yeah, this wasn't the Defend game at all. It was way past that. This was serious and he couldn't afford somebody to go, 'Yeah, I'm watching your back,' and then take off.

Wes asked, 'Just the three of us?'

'Looks like it, dude.'

Donnie glanced at his watch. It was a Casio and it had a nick in the corner, which he'd spent an hour trying to cover up with paint, so his dad wouldn't see it. The time was three thirty. They were only twenty minutes away from Goldshit's house.

'Plan? First, we get the bikes. Get into the garage. That's where they are,' he explained to Nathan. 'Here.'

'What's that?'

Donnie was shoving wads of blue latex into their hands.

'Gloves,' Wes said, understanding. 'For fingerprints.'

Nathan: 'So we get fingerprints on the bikes? We're taking 'em, aren't we?'

Donnie twisted his head, exasperated, studying Nathan. 'Dude, we gotta open the door or the window and get in, right?'

'Oh, yeah.' Nathan pulled the gloves on. 'They're tight.'

'Not now, bitch. Jesus.' Donnie was looking around. 'Somebody could see you.'

Fast, Nathan peeled them off. Shoved them into the pouch of his hoodie.

Wes was saying, 'We gotta be careful. I saw this show on TV once. A crime show, and my mom's friend Michael was over. And he's a deputy with the county. We were watching it together. And he was saying the killer was stupid because he threw his gloves away and the cops found them and his fingerprints were *inside* the gloves. We'll keep 'em and throw 'em out later, some-place nowhere near here.'

'Or burn them,' Nathan said. He seemed proud he'd thought of this. Then he was frowning. 'Anything else this guy would know, we should know? Your mom's friend? I mean, this is like breaking and entering. We gotta be serious.'

'Totally,' Wes said.

Nathan squinted. 'Maybe it's legal, doing this, you know. Like we're just retrieving stolen property.'

Wes laughed. 'Seriously? Dude, are you real? The bikes got perped during the commission of a crime, so don't count on that one.'

'What's "perped"?' Nathan asked.

'Bitch,' Donnie said. 'Stolen.'

'Oh.'

Donnie persisted, 'So? That cop, the friend of your mom's? What else'd he look for?'

Wes thought for a minute. 'Footprints. They can get our foot-prints with this machine. They can match them.'

'Fuck,' Nathan said. 'You mean the government has this big-ass file on everybody's footprint?'

But Wes explained that, no, they take the footprint, and if they catch you and it matches yours, it's evidence.

'*CSI*,' Donnie said. 'We'll walk on the driveway. Not the dirt.'

'They can still pick them up from concrete and asphalt.'

'Yeah?'

'Church.'

'Fuck. Okay. We leave our shoes in the bushes when we get there.'

Nathan was frowning, 'Can they take, like, sock prints?'

Wes told him he didn't think they could do that.

Nathan asked, 'That cop. Is he the guy I saw at your house, Jon?'

'No, he's into computers. He's my mom's friend.'

'She's got two boyfriends?'

Wes shrugged and didn't seem to want to talk about it.

Donnie said, 'So, I was saying: first, we get into the garage and get the bikes.'

Nathan said, 'Dude, I heard you say that before. "First". That means there's a second or something. After we get the bikes.'

Donnie smiled. He tapped his combat jacket. 'I brought a can.'

'Fuck,' Nathan said. 'This isn't the game. We're just helping you out, him and me.'

Wes was: 'Yeah! Dude, come on. Let's just get the bikes and get the hell out of here. That's what I'm on for. Tag him again? What's the point?'

'I'm tagging the *inside* of his house. Just to show the asshole.'

'Not me,' Wes said.

'You don't have to do anything, either of you bitches. Am I asking you to do anything? Either of you?'

'I'm just saying,' Nathan grumbled.

There was silence. They looked around the school yard, kids walking home, kids being picked up by parents, moms mostly, in a long line of cars in the driveway. Tiff looked their way again. Donnie brushed his hair out of his eyes, and when he smiled back, she'd turned away.

And she'd be interested why? he thought, sad.

Wes said, 'Hey, come on, Darth. We're with you. Whatever you want, tag or trash. We're there. I'll help you get the bikes but I'm not going inside.'

'All I'm asking. You two. Lookouts.'

'Fuck, amen,' the big kid said.

Nods all around.

'Roll?' Donnie asked.

A nod. They headed for the gate in the chain-link that led to the street.

Donnie and his crew. He didn't share with them what was really going down.

What he'd tapped inside his jacket wasn't a can of Krylon. It was his father's .38 Smith & Wesson pistol.

He'd made the decision last night – after the son of a bitch, his father, had pulled out the branch, tugged Donnie's pants down and wailed on him maybe because of the bike or maybe for some other reason or maybe for no fucking reason at all.

And when it was over, Donnie had staggered to his feet, avoided his mother's eyes and walked stiffly to his room, where he had stood for a while at his computer – his keyboard was on a high table 'cause there were plenty of times he couldn't sit down – playing Assassin's Creed, then Call of Duty, GTA 5, though he didn't shoot or jump good. You can't when your eyes are fucked up by tears. In Call of Duty, Federation soldiers kept him and the other Ghost elite special-ops unit pinned down and his guys had got fucked up because of him.

That was when he'd made the decision.

Donnie realized this life wasn't going to work any more. He had two ways to go. One was to go into his father's dresser, get the little gun and put a bullet in the man's head while he slept. And as good as that would feel – so good – it meant his brother and his mother's life'd be fucked for ever because Dad didn't treat them quite as bad as Donnie got treated, and he might've been a prick but at least he paid the rent and put food on the table.

So, it was number two.

He'd take his father's gun, go back to the Jew's house, with his crew. After they'd got the bikes – evidence – he'd have the others keep an eye out for cops and he'd go inside, tie the asshole up and get every penny the prick had in the house, watches, the wife's jewelry. He had to be rich. His dad said all Jews were.

He could get thousands, he was sure. Tens of thousands.

With the money, he'd leave. Head to San Francisco or LA. Maybe Hollister, where they made all the clothes. He'd get something on – and not selling ice or grass. Something real. He could sell the DARES game to somebody in Silicon Valley. It wasn't that far away; maybe Tiff would visit.

Life would be good. At last. Life would be good. Donnie could almost taste it.

CHAPTER 87

Charles Overby, a man who loved the sun, who just felt good with a ruddy complexion, now walked toward the Guzman Connection task-force room, deer-eye level in CBI headquarters, and wasn't pleased at what he saw.

It was late afternoon and the shade outside turned the glass to a dim mirror. He looked vampiric, which if it wasn't a word should be. Too stressed, too busy, too much shit. From Sacramento all the way to Mexico with their smarmy, law-breaking ally Commissioner Santos.

He stepped inside the room. Fisher and Lu, Steve and Steve Two were at one table, both on phones. DEA agent Carol Allerton sat at another, engrossed in her laptop. She seemed to prefer to play alone, Overby had noticed. She didn't even see him, so lost was she in the emails scrolling past on her Samsung.

'Greetings, all.'

Allerton glanced at him. 'Getting reports on that truck left Compton a day ago, the warehouse near the Four-oh-five. The Nazim brothers. May have twenty ki's. Meth.' This truck, Allerton explained, had been spotted on Highway One.

Lu asked, 'A semi? There? Jesus.'

The highway, between Santa Barbara and Half Moon, could be tricky to drive, even in a sports car. Narrow and winding.

'That's right. I want to follow it. No reason for 'em to be taking that route, unless they're going someplace connected with Pipeline.' Allerton said to Lu, 'You free?'

Lu nodded. 'Sure. Could use a hit of field.' The slim man rose and stretched.

Foster was lost in his phone conversation. 'Really?' Impatient, sarcastic, moving his hand in a circle. Get to the point. 'Let me be transparent. That's not going to work.' Foster hung up. A gesture to the phone. 'CIs. Jesus. There's gotta be a union.' He turned to Allerton and Lu. His moustache drooped asymmetrically. 'Where're you going?'

Allerton explained about the mysterious truck on Highway One.

'Contraband on One? Is there a transfer hub along that way we don't know about?' Foster seemed interested in this.

'That's what we're going to find out.'

'Hope that one pans out.'

Overby said to Foster, 'Can you and Al Stemple check out Pedro Escalanza?'

'Who?'

'The lead to Serrano. Tia Alonzo mentioned him, remember?'

Foster's frown said, no, he didn't. 'Where is this Escalanza?'

'Sandy Crest Motel.' Overby explained it was a cheap tourist spot, about five miles north of Monterey.

'I guess.'

'TJ ran Escalanza's sheet. Minor stuff but he's facing a couple in Lompac. We'll work with him on that if he gives up any info that gets us to Serrano.'

Foster muttered, 'A lead to a lead to a lead.'

'What's that?' Overby asked.

Foster didn't answer. He strode out of the door.

Outside CBI, Steve Foster looked over his new partner.

'Just for the record, I'm playing along with you because . . .' a slight pause '. . . the rest of the task force wanted it. I didn't.'

Kathryn Dance said pleasantly, 'It's your case, Steve. I'm still Civ Div. I just want the chance to interview Escalanza, that's all.'

He muttered, repeating, 'The rest of the task force.' Then looked her over as if he were about to tell her something important. Reveal a secret. But he said nothing.

She waved at Albert Stemple, plodding toward his pickup truck. His cowboy boots made gritty sounds on the asphalt. Stone-faced, he nodded back.

Stemple grumbled, 'So. That lead to Serrano?'

'That's it,' Foster said.

'I'll follow you. Brought the truck. Was *supposed* to be my day off.' Got inside, started the engine. It growled.

Dance and Foster got into the CBI cruiser. She was behind the wheel.

She punched the motel's address into her iPhone GPS and started the engine. They hit the highway, headed west. Soon the silence in the car seemed louder than the slipstream.

Foster, lost in his phone, read and sent some text messages. He didn't seem to mind that she was driving – some men would have made an issue of piloting. And he might have, given that Dance really wasn't a great driver. She didn't enjoy vehicles, didn't blend with the road the way Michael O'Neil did.

Thinking of him now, his arms around her at the stampede in Global Adventure World. And their fight after they'd returned.

Tapped that thought away fast. Concentrate.

She turned music on. Foster didn't seem to enjoy it but neither did the sound seem to bother him. She'd reflected that while everyone else in the task force had congratulated her on nailing the Solitude Creek unsub Foster had said nothing. It was as if he hadn't even been aware of the other case.

Twenty minutes later, she turned off the highway and made her way down a long, winding road, Stemple's truck bouncing along behind. From time to time they could see north and south – along the coast, misting away to Santa Cruz, the sky split by the incongruous power-plant smokestacks. A shame, those. The vista was one that Ansel Adams might have recorded, using his trademark small aperture to bring the whole scene into crystal detail.

Foster's hand slipped out and he turned down the volume.

So maybe he *was* a music-hater.

But that wasn't it at all. While the big man's eyes were on the vista, Foster said, 'I have a son.'

'Do you?' Dance asked.

'He's thirteen.' The man's tone was different now. A flipped switch.

'What's his name?'

'Embry.'

'Unusual. Nice.'

'Family name. My grandmother's maiden name. A few years ago I was with our LA office. We were living in the Valley.'

The nic for San Fernando. That complex, diverse region north of the Los Angeles Basin – everything from hovels to mansions.

'There was a drive-by. Pacoima Flats Boyz had pissed off the Cedros Bloods, who knows why?'

Dance could see what was coming. Oh, no. She asked, 'What happened, Steve?'

'He was hanging with some kids after school. There was crossfire.' Foster cleared his throat. 'Hit in the temple. Vegetative state.'

'I'm so sorry.'

'I know I'm a prick,' Foster said, his eyes on the road. 'Something like that happens . . .' He sighed.

'I can't even imagine.'

'No, you can't. And I don't mean that half as shitty as it sounds. I know I've been riding you. And I shouldn't. I just keep thinking, Serrano got away, and what if he takes out somebody else? He can fucking waste all of his own crew if he wants. But it's the kid in between the muzzle and the target that bothers me, keeps me up all night. And it's my fault as much as yours. I was there too, at the interview. I could've done something, could've asked some questions.'

'We'll get him,' Dance said sincerely. 'We'll get Serrano.'

Foster nodded. 'You should've told me I'm a dick.'

'I thought it.'

His silver mustache rose as he gave the first smile she'd seen since the task force had been put together.

Soon they arrived at the motel, which was in the hills about three miles east of the ocean. It was on the eastern side, so there was no view of the water. Now the place was shrouded in shade, surrounded by brush and scrub oak. The first thing that Dance thought of was the Solitude Creek roadhouse, a similar setting – some human-built structure surrounded by quiet, persistent California flora.

The inn had a main office and about two dozen separate cabins. She found the one they sought and parked two buildings away.

Stemple drove his truck into a space nearby. There was one car, an old Mazda sedan, faded blue, in front of the cabin. Dance consulted her phone, scrolled down the screen. 'That's his, Escalanza's.'

Stemple climbed out of his truck and, hand on his big gun, walked around the motel. He returned and nodded.

'Let's go talk to Señor Escalanza,' Foster said.

The two agents started forward, the wind tossing her hair. She heard a snap beside her. She saw a weapon in Foster's hand. He pulled the slide back and checked to see if a round was chambered. He eased the slide forward and holstered the gun. He nodded. They continued along the sand-swept sidewalk past yellowing grass and squatting succulents to the cabin registered in the name of Pedro Escalanza. Bugs flew and Dance wiped sweat. You didn't have to get far from the ocean for the heat to soar, even in springtime.

At the door they looked back at Al Stemple – a hundred feet away. He glanced at them. Gave a thumbs-up.

Dance and Foster looked at each other. She nodded. They stepped to either side of the door – procedure, not to mention common sense – and Foster knocked. 'Pedro Escalanza? Bureau of Investigation. We'd like to talk to you.'

No answer.

Another rap.

'Please open the door. We just want to talk. It'll be to your advantage.'

Nothing.

'Shit. Waste of time.'

Dance gripped the door. Locked. 'Try the back.'

The cottages had small decks, which were accessed by sliding doors. Lawn chairs and tables sat on the uneven brick. No barbecue grills, of course: one careless, smoldering briquette, and these hills would vanish in ten breaths. They walked around to the unit's deck and noted that the door was open, a frosty beer, half full, on the table. Foster, his hand on his weapon's grip, walked closer. 'Pedro.'

'Yeah?' a man's voice called. 'I was in the john. Come on in.'

They walked inside. And froze.

On the bathroom floor they could see two legs stretched out. Streak of blood on them. Puddling on the floor too.

Foster drew his gun and started to turn but the young man behind the curtain next to the sliding door quickly touched the agent's skull with his own gun.

He pulled Foster's Glock from his hand and shoved him forward, then closed the door.

They both turned to the lean Latino gazing at them with fierce eyes.

'Serrano,' Dance whispered.

CHAPTER **88**

They were back.

At last. Thank you, Lord.

The two boys from the other night. Except there were three of them at the moment.

Well, now that David Goldschmidt thought about it, there might've been three the other night. Only two bikes but, yes, there could have been another one then.

The other night.

The night of shame, he thought of it. His heart pounding even now, several days afterward. Palms sweating. Like *Kristallnacht*, the 'Night of Broken Glass', in 1938, when the Germans had rioted and destroyed a thousand Jewish homes and businesses throughout the country.

Goldschmidt was watching them on the video screen, which wasn't, as he'd told Officer Dance the other night, in the bedroom but in the den. They were moving closer now, all three. Looking around, furtive. Guilt on wheels.

True, he hadn't exactly gotten a look at them the other day, not their faces – that was why he'd asked Dance for more details: he didn't want to make a mistake. But this was surely them. He'd seen their posture, their clothes, as they'd fled, after obscenely defacing his house. Besides, who else would it be?

They'd returned for their precious bikes.

Coming after the bait.

Which was why he'd kept them.

Bait . . .

Now he was ready. He'd called his wife in Seattle and had her stay a few days longer with her sister. Made up some story that he himself wanted to come up for the weekend. Why didn't she stay and he'd join her? She'd bought it.

As the boys stole closer still, glancing around them, pausing from time to time, Goldschmidt looked up and watched them through the den window, the lace curtain.

One, the most intense, seemed to be the ringleader. He was wearing a combat jacket. Floppy hair. A second, a handsome teenager, was holding his phone, probably to record the theft. The third, big, dangerously big.

My God, they looked young. Younger than high school, Goldschmidt reckoned. But that didn't mean they weren't evil. They were probably the sons of neo-Nazis or some Aryan group. Such a shame they hadn't formed their own opinions before their racist fathers, mothers too probably, had got a hold of their malleable brains and turned them into monsters.

Evil . . .

And deadly. Deadly as all bigots were.

Which was why Goldschmidt was now holding his Beretta double-barrel shotgun, loaded with 00 buckshot, each pellet the diameter of a .33-caliber slug.

He closed the weapon with a soft click.

The law on self-defense in California is very clear . . .

It certainly was, Officer Dance. Once somebody was in your home and you had a reasonable fear for your safety, you could shoot them.

And for all Goldschmidt knew, they too were armed.

Because this country was America. Where guns were plentiful and reluctance to use them rare.

The boys paused on the corner. Surveilling the area. Noting that his car was gone – he'd parked it blocks away. That the lights were out. He wasn't home. Safe to come get your Schwinns.

The door's open, kids. Come on in.

Goldschmidt rose, thumbed off the safety and walked into the kitchen, where he opened the door to the garage. That location, he'd checked, was considered part of your home too. And all he had to do was convince the prosecutor he'd legitimately feared for his life.

He'd memorized the sentence, 'I used the minimum amount of force necessary under the circumstances to protect myself.'

He peered through the crack.

Come on, boys. Come on.

CHAPTER 89

'And you, Officer Dance. Your weapon too. Let's go.'

Without taking his eyes off them, the Latino tugged the curtain shut, a gauzy shield against passers-by.

'I'm not armed. Look, Serrano. Joaquin. Let's talk about—'

'Not armed.' A smile.

'Really. I'm not.'

'You say this, I say that.'

'Listen—' Foster began.

'Sssh, you. Now, Agent Dance. How about you just tug up that fancy jacket of yours, turn around like my niece does, pirouette? I think that's what it's called. She in ballet class. She's pretty good.'

Dance lifted her jacket and turned. Her eyes returned defiantly to his.

'Well, they don't trust you with guns, your bosses? My woman, she can shoot. She's good. You afraid of shooting. Too loud?'

Foster nodded toward the bathroom, where a man's legs were just visible. Crimson spatters covered the tiles. 'That's Escalanza?'

'The fuck're you to ask me questions?' the man sneered. 'Shut up.' He stepped to the windows and looked outside. Dance could see through the slit in the flyblown drapes. She saw no one other than Stemple, gazing out over the highway.

'Who's that big boy out there?'

Dance said, 'He's with us, the Bureau of Investigation.'

He returned. 'Hey, there, Officer . . . Or, no, it's *Agent*. Have to remember that. *Sí*, Agent Dance. I enjoyed our conversation in the room, that interrogation room there. Always like talking to a beautiful woman. Too bad no *cervezas*. You get more confessions you open a bar there. Patron, Herradura, a little rum. No, I know! Hire a *puta*. Give somebody head, they confess fast.'

Dance said evenly, 'You're in a bad situation here.'

He smiled.

Foster said impatiently, 'Look, Serrano, whatever you have in mind, nothing good's going to come from killing law.'

'That's your opinion, whoever you are. Were you one of those watching me in the goldfish bowl the other day?'

'Yes.'

'Fooled you pretty good, didn't I?' he gloated.

Dance said, 'Yes, you did. But my colleague's right. It's not going to work out how you want.'

The young man said evenly, 'You said nothing good comes from killing law. Well, you know what? I'm thinking a lot of good'll come of it. You been on my ass since Wednesday. I been hiding here, hiding there. That's a pain I don't need. So I think a lot of good is going to come from having you both fucking dead. Okay. Enough.'

Dance said, 'You shoot us and you think the agent out there won't hear? If he doesn't nail your ass, he'll keep you pinned down until a TAC team . . .'

Fishing in his back pocket, Serrano pulled a silencer out and screwed it onto the muzzle of his weapon. 'I like the way you say "ass".'

Dance glanced at Foster, whose expression remained placid.

'So. Here. I'm a religious man. You take a few seconds to make your peace. Pray. You have something you want to say? Somebody up there you want to say it to?'

Her voice ominous, Dance said defiantly, 'You're not thinking, Joaquin. Our boss knows we're here, a dozen others. I could get a call any minute. I don't pick up and there'll be a dozen TAC officers here in ten minutes, combing the area. Lockdown on the roads. You'll never get away.'

'Yeah, I think I take my chances.'

'Work with me and I can keep you alive. You walk out that door and you're a dead man.'

'Work with you?' He laughed. 'You got nothing. What they say in football, I mean soccer? Nil. You've got nil to offer.'

The gun was already racked. He lifted it toward Foster, who said, 'Lamont.'

The young man frowned. 'What?'

'Lamont Howard.'

A confused look. 'What're you saying?'

'Don't act stupid.' Foster shook his head.

'Fuck you saying to me, asshole?'

Foster seemed merely inconvenienced, not the least intimidated. Or scared. 'I'm saying to you, *asshole*, the name Lamont Howard.' When there was no response he continued, 'You know Lamont, right?'

The Latino's eyes scanned their faces uncertainly. Then: 'Lamont, the gang-banger run the Four Seven Bloods in Oakland. What about him?'

Dance said, 'Steve?'

Foster: 'You been to his house in Village Bottoms?'

A blink.

'West Oakland.'

'I know where the Bottoms is.'

Dance snapped, 'What's this all about, Steve?'

Foster waved her silent. Back to the young man. 'Okay, Serrano, here's the deal. You kill me, Lamont will kill you. Simple as that. And he'll kill everybody in your family. And then he'll go back to his steak dinner, because he likes his steak. I know that because I *have* been to his crib and had a steak dinner with him. A dozen of them, in fact.'

Dance turned to Foster. She whispered, '*What?*'

'Fuck you saying, man?'

'Are you catching on? I'm Lamont's inside man.'

Dance stared at him.

'No fucking way.'

'Yeah, well, Serrano, I can say yes and you can say no way until you have to take a crap. But wouldn't it make sense just to ask him? 'Cause if you don't and you take me out, Lamont and his crew lose their one connection to CBI and points beyond. DEA, Customs and Border, Homeland. And I wonder which dry well you and your mother and sister will be sleeping out eternity in.'

'Fuck. Wait. I hear something. A month ago. Some Oakland crew was getting solids from Sacramento.'

'That's me.' Foster seemed proud.

Dance looked out of the window. Stemple, still gazing away into the waving grass. She growled to Foster, 'You son of a bitch.'

He ignored her. 'So, call him.'

The Latino looked him over, not getting too close. Foster was much larger. 'I no got his number. You think him and me, we asshole buddies?'

Foster sighed. 'Look, I'm taking my phone out of my pocket. That's all. My phone.' He did. 'Ah, Kathryn, careful there.'

Her hand had dropped toward a table on which a heavy metal lamp sat.

'Serrano? Could you . . .'

The young man noted that Dance had been going for the lamp. He stepped forward and roughly pushed her against the wall, away from any potential weapons.

Foster made a call.

'Lamont, it's Steve.' He hit the speaker.

'Foster?'

'Yeah.'

'What you calling for?' The voice was wary.

'Got a situation here. Sorry, man. There's a hothead, from one of the Salinas crews, with a piece on me. He's out of the . . .' Foster lifted an eyebrow.

'Barrio Majados.'

'You hear that?'

Howard's voice: 'Yo, I know 'em, I work with 'em. What's this about? Who is he?'

'Serrano.'

'Joaquin? I know Serrano. He disappeared. There was heat on him.'

'He's surfaced. He doesn't know who I am. Just tell him we work together. Or he's going to park a slug in my head.'

'Fuck you doing, Serrano? Leave my boy Foster alone. You got that?'

'He with you?'

'The fuck I say?'

The gun didn't lower. 'Okay, only . . . any chance he undercover?'

'Well, he is, then he's the only undercover took out a Oakland cop.'

'No shit.'

Howard said, 'Asshole show up at my place unexpected. Foster, pop pop, took him down.'

'Steve, no!' Dance whispered, dismay in her voice.

Howard called, 'The fuck's that?'

'Another cop, works with Foster.'

'That's just fucking great.' The banger in Oakland sighed. 'You two take care of her. I got shit to do here.'

The call ended.

'Serrano,' Dance began, 'what I was saying before. You need to be smart. You—'

The Latino snapped, 'Shut up, Kathryn.'

With a cold smile, she said to Foster, 'The story you told me before. You don't have a son, do you? That was a lie.'

He turned to her, offering a nonchalant shrug. 'I didn't know what was going down. Needed you on my side.'

Dance sneered, 'You can't be running a network on your own. You're not that smart.'

Foster was indignant. 'Fuck you. I don't need anybody else.'

'How many people've died because of what you've done?'

'Oh, come on,' the man said gruffly. Then: 'Serrano, let's get this done. Do her, I'll get the asshole outside in here. We take him out. I'll tell the response team I got out the back and hid in the hills. I'll say it was somebody else here, not you. One of the crews from Tijuana.'

'Okay with me,' was the matter-of-fact response.

Then Foster was squinting. 'Wait.'

'What?'

'You . . . you said, "Kathryn". You called her "Kathryn".'

A shrug. 'I don't know. So?'

'I never used her first name here. And I was at the interview last week between you and her. She never said it either.'

I'm Agent Dance . . .

A grimace. The Latino accent was gone as the young man said, 'Yep, I screwed up on that. Sorry.' He was speaking to Kathryn Dance.

'No worries, José,' she said, smiling. 'We got everything we needed. You did great.'

Foster stared from one to the other. 'Oh, Jesus Christ.'

'Serrano' who was actually a Bakersfield detective named José Felipe-Santoval, aimed his weapon center-mass on Foster's chest, while Dance, relieved of her weapon but not her cuffs, ratcheted the bracelets on.

Adding to Foster's shock, the agent who'd been pretending to be the deceased Pedro Escalanza hopped to and dusted off his jeans, drawing his own weapon. He'd been lying face down, head hidden from the trio in the hotel room.

'Hey, TJ.'

'Boss. Good takedown. How's the blood?' He glanced at his legs, spattered red. 'I tried a new formula. Hershey's syrup and food coloring.'

'Big improvement,' she said, nodding at the tiles.

Foster gasped, 'A sting. The whole thing.'

Dance pulled out her cell phone. Hit speed-dial five as she glanced down and noticed her Aldo pumps had a scuff. Have to fix that. They were her favorite shoes for field work.

She heard, from the phone, Charles Overby's voice: 'Kathryn? And the verdict is?'

'Foster's our boy. It's all on tape. He's the only one.'

'Ah.'

'We'll be back in a half-hour. You want to be there, at the interrogation?'

'Wouldn't miss it for the world.'

CHAPTER **90**

Disgust overflowed in Foster's face as he looked from Al Stemple to Dance to Overby. They were in the same CBI interrogation rooms where Dance had held the phony interview of the phony Serrano last week.

TJ was elsewhere; the *faux* blood was good, yes, but it stained far more than he'd thought it would. He was presently scrubbing hands and ankles in one of the nearby men's rooms.

Foster snapped, 'Jesus, you wanted Kathryn unarmed and demoted to Civ Div but still talking her way onto the interviews with the suspect to track down Serrano. So I wouldn't feel threatened by her.'

Yep. Exactly.

Overby added, 'So you'd be free to cut a deal with Serrano when he pulled a gun on you.'

Dance told him: 'We made the case against the real Serrano ten days ago. Handed it over to the FBI, Amy Grabe in San Francisco. So you wouldn't get wind of it. She busted him. He rolled over on Guzman. They're both in isolation. The "Serrano" you saw was Bakersfield PD. José works undercover. He's good, don't you think?'

Not acting very professional. But she was in a mood.

'We got him because he looks like the real Serrano.'

Anger joined Foster's revulsion: 'Jesus. We were all suspects. And you faked the "leads" to Serrano – with Carol, the bungalow in Seaside. With Gomez, the houseboat. At the motel just now. You ran the same set, the same play at every one of them. TJ played the dead snitch. All I saw was the legs and torso. Not his face.'

Overby filled in, 'Except at the houseboat. That was Connie Ramirez, playing . . . What was her name again?'

Dance answered, 'Tia Alonzo.' She continued, 'It was a test we put together. The real traitor'd save himself. Those on the task force who were innocent? Well, I'm afraid they had a few bad moments when José turned his gun on them. But it had to be done. We needed to find who'd sold us out.'

In the first set, Carol Allerton had suicidally lunged at the fake Serrano, knocking a table of ceramic keepsakes to the floor. Gomez had sighed, resigned himself to death and said a prayer.

And Foster had played the OG card, invoking the name of Lamont Howard to save himself.

'If you'd passed the test, it would have meant Steve Lu was the one. Since you said you'd told Kathryn you were the only connection, he's clean.'

'You fucking set me up.'

Finally, quiet Al Stemple spoke: 'I think "set up" means more wrongly implicating an innocent person, 'stead of trapping a guilty asshole. Am I being transparent enough, Steve?' He gave a loud grunt, then sat back and crossed his arms, wide as tree trunks.

The Guzman Connection sting had been Dance's idea and she'd fought hard for it. All the way up to Sacramento.

She'd decided to put together the operation after a horrific drive-by shooting in Seaside, a mother killed and a child wounded. The woman had been a witness to one of the Pipeline hubs. But no one could have known about her – except for a leak inside the operation itself.

'I went through the files a hundred times and looked for any other instance of operations that could've been compromised. TJ and I spent weeks correlating the personnel. We narrowed it down to four people involved in all of them – and who knew that Maria Ioaconna was a witness. You, Carol, Steve Lu and Jimmy. We brought you here. And set up the operation.'

There'd been risks, of course. That the guilty party might wonder why Dance was apparently working on the Solitude Creek case but was officially barred from the Serrano pursuit.

(Overby had said, 'Can't you forget about Solitude Creek, stay home and, I don't know, plant flowers? You can still show up at the Serrano sets.'

'I'm working Solitude,' she'd answered bluntly.)

Risks to her physically too – as O'Neil had pointed out so vehemently: it was possible that their traitor would call someone like Lamont Howard, who'd show up at one of the sets with his crew and waste everybody present.

But there was nothing else to do: Dance was determined to find their betrayer.

Foster stared at the room's ugly gray floors, and the muscles in his face flickered.

Dance added, 'We never hoped for him directly. But getting Howard on the tape, ordering my hit?'

'Ah, that's righteous.' Overby beamed.

A word she didn't believe she'd ever heard Overby say. He seemed to mull the line over and was embarrassed.

But Dance smiled his way. He was right. It *was* righteous. And a lot more.

Overby looked at his watch. Golf? Or maybe he was considering with some dismay the call to Sacramento, the CBI chief, to tell them the traitor came from the hallowed halls of their own agency. 'Keep going, Kathryn. Convince him of the futility of his silence. Convince him of the shining path of confession. Whatever he says or doesn't, the media'll be here soon. You'll be at the podium with me, I hope?'

Charles Overby sharing a press conference?

'You've earned the limelight, Kathryn.'

'Think I'd rather pass, Charles. It's been a long day.' She nodded toward Foster. 'And this may take a while.'

'You're sure?'

'I am. Yes.' Dance turned to her prey.

CHAPTER 91

A shadow in her office doorway.

Michael O'Neil stood there. Somber. His dark eyes locked on hers. Brown, green. Then he looked away.

'Hey,' she said.

He nodded and sat down.

'You heard?'

'Foster. Yeah. Complete confession. Good job.'

'Gave up a dozen names. People we never would've found. Bangers in LA and Oakland. Bakersfield, Fresno too.' Dance looked away from her computer, on which she was typing notes from the Antioch March case. The promise of paperwork stretched out, long as the Golden Gate Bridge.

Documenting the Guzman Connection sting, part of Operation Pipeline, would be next, the arrest of Steve Foster.

She'd actually thought he was the least likely suspect, given his obnoxious nature. Kathryn Dance was accustomed to the apparent being the opposite of the real. Dance had suspected mostly Carol Allerton. What state cop didn't love bashing a fed? But now she felt guilty about that. The DEA agent had been a good ally after the first sting operation. And she was very pleased too that Jimmy Gomez, a friend, had not been the betrayer.

She now told Michael O'Neil about the finale of the sting. She, of course, didn't add that she believed she'd been right – that had she gone in armed, had she not maintained the sham of her suspension, Foster wouldn't have bought the scam.

Then she noted: O'Neil was listening but not listening. He regarded the photographs on her desk – the one of her with the children and the dog. The eight-by-ten of her with her husband, Bill. Whatever happened in her personal life, she was never going to put those pictures in an attic box. Displayed, always.

She fell silent for a moment, then asked, 'All right. What is it?'

'Something happened today. I have to tell you.' Then he turned his head, rose again and shut the door. As if he'd meant to do that when he walked in but had been so focused on what he wanted to say that any other thoughts had scattered, like dropped marbles.

Something happened . . .

'The hate crime I've been working?'

'Sure.' Had there been another defacing? Was it an actual attack this time? Hate crimes often escalated from words to blood. Dragging to death gays, shootings of blacks or Jews.

'Goldschmidt's house again.'

'The perps came back?'

'They did. But it seems Goldschmidt wasn't completely honest with us. Apparently he found their bikes and kept them. He wanted them to come back. He was using the bikes as bait.'

'So, they were bikers.'

'No, bicycles.'

'*Kids* were doing it?'

'That's right.'

She looked at him levelly. 'And what happened, Michael?'

'Goldschmidt had a shotgun. Didn't listen to you the other night.'

'Goddamnit! Did he shoot anybody?'

'He was *going* to,' O'Neil said. 'He denies it but – why else keep a loaded Beretta by the garage door?'

'"Going to"?'

'While they were on the street, getting closer, I got a call. It was from one of the perps, calling. He was warning me that something bad was going down. He was worried about weapons. I should get TAC and backup there immediately. *He* said TAC.'

'One of the kids? Called you? And said that?'

'Yep.' He took a breath. 'I called PG police and they had cars there in a minute or two. They secured everything. Kathryn, the one who called me was Wes.'

'Who?' Curious for a moment. And then the name settled. 'But you said one of the perps!'

'Wes, that's right. The others were Donnie, his friend, and another boy. Nathan.'

She whispered. 'A mistake. It has to be a mistake.'

He continued: 'It was Donnie tagging the houses. Wes was with him. Nathan and another friend were doing other things. Stealing traffic signs, shoplifting.'

'Impossible.'

O'Neil said, 'That game they were playing?'

'Defend and . . . I don't know.' Her mind was a whitewater rapid, swirling, out of control.

'Defend and Respond Expedition Service.'

'That's it. What about it?'

'It's an acronym. D-A-R-E-S. There were teams. Each one *dared* the other side to do things that could land them in jail.'

Dance gave a cold laugh. She'd been so pleased that the boys were playing a game with paper and pen and avoiding the violence of the computer world, which had seduced Antioch March and helped turn him into a killer. And now the analog life had proven just as destructive.

A game you played with paper and pen? How harmful could that be? . . .

'And Wes's team was dared to commit the hate crimes?'

'That's right. Donnie has some juvie time under his belt. Troubled kid. And tonight? He had a weapon. His father's gun. A thirty-eight.'

'My God.'

'He said at first he just brought it for protection but then he admitted he was going to rob Goldschmidt. Some dream of moving out of his home. I've spoken to his father. Frankly, hardly blame the boy. Whatever happens, he'll be better off out of that household. I think he confessed so he didn't have to go back home.'

Well, I'm not sure what to call you.

Mrs Dance . . .

'Wes actually wrote those horrible things on the buildings and houses?'

'No. He was just a lookout for Donnie.'

Still, that didn't absolve him. Even if he hadn't tagged the house himself he was a co-conspirator. An accessory. And with the gun? It could be conspiracy to commit armed robbery. And what if someone had been killed because of a stolen stop sign? Homicide.

'I'm just setting the stage, Kathryn. There's more.'

Seriously? How the hell much more bad can there be?

A cramp spidered through her right hand: she'd been gripping a pen furiously. She set it down. 'I was concentrating on Maggie, who was upset about singing a damn song, and here was Wes committing felonies! I didn't pay him any attention. His life could be over—'

'Kathryn. Here.' He set a mobile phone on her desk. And dug into his pocket and placed an envelope beside it.

She recognized the Samsung as Wes's. She looked up, frowning.

'There're videos on the phone. And this's a police report that Wes created.' He pushed the envelope toward her.

'A police report? What do you mean?'

'Unofficial.' O'Neil offered a rare smile. 'He's been working undercover for a month. That's how he put it.'

She picked up the envelope, opened it. Pages of computer printouts, a diary, detailing times and dates.

28 April, 6.45 p.m. in the evening, I personally observed subject Donald, a.k.a. Donnie, Verso paint on the south-west wall of the Latino Immigration Rights Center, at 1884 Alvarado Drive, with a Krylon spray can the words: 'Go back to Mexico you wetbacks.' The color of the paint was dark red.

O'Neil took the boy's phone and ran the camera app. He scrolled through until he found a video. It was shaking but it clearly showed Donnie tagging a building.

'And the other dares? The ones Donnie challenged the other team with? Wes documented those too. And the stolen street signs? Wes followed Nathan and some friend Vincent when they dug up the stop sign. He called nine one one right away to report it. And stayed at the intersection to make sure nobody was hurt.'

She stared at the video. In a quiet voiceover: '*I Wes Swenson am personally observing Donald Verso place graffiti on the Baptist New World Church . . .*'

O'Neil continued, 'A month or so ago a friend of Wes – I think his name was Rashiv – had a run-in with Donnie and Nathan and another one of Donnie's crew.'

Dance told him, 'That's right. Rashiv and Wes were friends. Then Wes just stopped seeing him. I don't know what happened.'

'Donnie and the others were bullying him, extorting money, beating him up. They stole a games console. Rashiv told Wes about it. There wasn't anything they could do themselves – you've seen Nathan?'

'Yes. Big.'

'He was the muscle in the crew. He'd do anything Donnie told him. Including hurting people badly. Wes'd heard that Donnie and his friends were into some illegal things – the DARES game was being talked about in school, though nobody knew exactly what it was. Wes decided to find out and – these were his words – "collar the bastard". He talked his way into the clique and finally got Donnie to trust him enough to let him play.

'He even set it up with Rashiv to meet "accidentally" and Wes'd pretend to steal a comic or something from him, threaten to hurt him. Donnie bought it all.'

'And today? At Goldschmidt's?'

'Wes'd noticed Donnie acting strange lately. More erratic. The night Donnie tagged Goldschmidt's house? Wes saw him pick up a rock. He was going to attack somebody who was approaching where they were hiding. Near Junipero Manor.'

Dance whispered, 'Me. That was me.'

O'Neil said only, 'I know.' He continued, 'Wes couldn't give himself away to Donnie that night but he turned his phone volume up and scrolled to ringtones. It played a sample, like he was getting a call. Donnie got spooked and took off.'

Dance closed her eyes and her head dipped. 'He saved me. Maybe saved my life.'

'Then tonight he caught a glimpse of something in Donnie's pocket and thought it might be a gun. So he decided, whatever evidence he had, enough was enough. It was time to call in the cavalry.'

'Why didn't he just report it in the first place? A month ago? Why play undercover?'

O'Neil's eyes swept her desk. 'I don't know. Maybe to make you proud of him.'

'I am.'

But even as Kathryn Dance said those words she wondered, Does he *know* it? Really know it?

Or, Dance suddenly thought of O'Neil, to make *you* proud of him.

Silence filled the room. Dance was thinking of the conversation she would have to have with the boy. Whatever the good motives, there were some minefields here. Dance had amassed capital in Monterey County with the prosecutor's office; she'd have to see how much, and how negotiable it was. And, she thought too, Donnie'll need help. Not just jail time. At that age, nobody was irredeemable. Kathryn Dance believed this. She'd do what she could to get him into treatment, whatever facility he was sent to.

Then she looked at O'Neil, to see that his expression and posture had changed dramatically. No kinesic subtlety here.

And everything she saw set off alarms within Kathryn Dance. She thought: As if what Michael just told me about Wes weren't enough. What was coming next?

He said, 'Look, as if what I just told you wasn't enough . . .'

Any other time she might have smiled; now her heart was racing.

'There's something else.' He glanced back to her door. Still shut.

'I can see that. What's it about?'

'Okay, it's about . . . I guess you could say, us.'

Dance's head rose and dipped slightly, a nod being one of the most ambiguous of gestures. It was often a defensive move, meaning: I need to buy some time and toughen up the heart.

Because she knew what was coming next. Michael and Anne were getting back together. It happened more than one might think, reconciliation. Once the divorce papers had been signed, a little cooling off, the ex-wife's lover turned into a creep or was duller than dull. Old hubby doesn't seem so bad after all. They'd decided to clean house, roll up their sleeves and try again.

Why else would Anne have been there the other day, at CBI, with the kids? Dressed like the perfect mom from Central Casting. O'Neil's comments: the sort-of babysitter, the plural pronoun about having plans the night of Maggie's show.

'So, here's the thing.'

Michael O'Neil's eyes were fixed on a thoroughly ugly yellow ceramic cat that Maggie had squeezed together in first grade.

Dance's eyes were unwaveringly on his.

CHAPTER 92

Her house beckoned.

The Victorian structure glowed, thanks to subdued sconces near the door and, from inside, light paled to old bone by the curtains. Dots of white Christmas lights around an occasional window or clustering on a plant added to the ambience of magic. The illumination was lopsided but no matter: Dance had never felt the need to be symmetrical.

Kathryn Dance shut off the SUV's engine but remained where she was, fingers enwrapping the wheel tightly. They trembled.

Wes . . .

Playing cop, Wes.

Lord, Lord . . . He might've been killed by Goldschmidt. A Beretta shotgun, O'Neil had reported. Those weapons are works of art, yes, but their purpose is to kill. And they do such a very fine job of it.

Releasing the wheel finally. Her palms cooled from the departing sweat.

Rehearsing what she'd say to her son. It was going to be a lengthy discussion.

Then, of course, her thoughts returned to what Michael O'Neil had said.

'Look, as if what I just told you wasn't enough . . .'

Well, isn't that always the case? The conversations you don't want to have, *can't* have, *refuse* to have . . . they happen on their own, and usually at the worst possible moments. She was still nearly paralyzed with dismay. A dozen slow breaths.

Dance finally now climbed out of the Pathfinder and walked onto the porch, key out.

She didn't need to do any unlatching, however. The door opened and Jon Boling stood before her, in jeans and a black polo shirt. She realized his hair was a little longer. It would have been that way for the past few days, of course, and she thought: Something else I missed. Missed completely.

Well, it had been one hell of a week.

'Hey,' he said.

They kissed and she walked inside.

A skitter of multiple feet behind her, claws that needed clipping. Some enthusiastic couch-jumping and a few good-to-see-you rolls on the back. Dance did the obligatory, but forever comforting to all involved, canine head rubs.

'Wine?'

Good diagnosis.

A smile, a nod. She sloughed off her jacket and hooked it. Too tired even to search for a hanger.

He returned with the glasses. White for both of them. It'd be an unoaked Chardonnay that they'd discovered recently. Michael liked red. It was all he drank.

'The kids?'

'In their rooms. Wes came home about an hour ago. Didn't want to look at a program I'd hacked together. And that's a little weird. He's in his bedroom now. Seemed kind of moody.'

Wonder why.

'Mags is in her room too. Been singing up a storm. Violin may be a thing of the past.'

'Not bad outside, the temperature. Shall we?'

They wandered out to the Deck, brushed curly yellow leaves off the cushions of a couple of uneven wooden chairs. The Monterey Peninsula wasn't like the Midwest, no seasons really. Leaves fell at their leisure.

Dance eased down and sat back. Fog wafted past, bringing with it the smell of damp mulch, like tobacco, and the spice of eucalyptus. She remembered the time Maggie had made a pitch for getting a koala-bear cub, citing the fact that there were plenty of leaves for it to eat in the neighborhood. 'Won't cost us a thing!'

Dance hadn't bothered to marshal arguments. 'No,' she'd said.

Boling zipped up his sweater. 'News did a story on March.'

Dance had heard about it; she'd declined to comment.

'Antioch March,' Boling mused. 'That's his real name?'

'Yep. Went by Andy mostly.'

'Are March's clients guilty of crimes?'

'I'm not sure where it falls. Conspiracy probably, if they actually ordered a killing. That's a wide net. According to March, though, a lot of the clients are overseas. Japan, Korea, South East Asia. We can't reach them and this isn't an extradition situation. TJ's going through the website's records now. I think we'll have some US citizens the Bureau'll talk to. March is cooperating. It was part of the deal.'

Another shiver.

I'm glad we're in each other's lives now . . .

Boling was saying, 'I've always worried about video games, the desensitizing. Kids, at least. They lose all filtering.'

In 2006 a young man arrested on suspicion of stealing a car wrested a gun away from an officer and shot his way out of the police station, killing three cops. He was a huge fan of the very game that March had mentioned, Grand Theft Auto.

Other youthful shooters – the Sandy Hook killer and the two Columbine students – were avid players of violent shooting games, she believed.

One side of the debate said there was no causal effect between games and the act of violence, asserting that youngsters naturally prone to bully, injure or kill were drawn to video games of that sort and would go on to commit crimes even without gaming. Others held that, given the developmental process of children, exposure to games did tend to shape behavior, far more than TV or movies, since they were immersive and took you into a different world, operating by different rules, far more than passive entertainment. She sipped her wine and let these thoughts slip away, replaced by the memory of Michael O'Neil's words an hour ago.

So, here's the thing . . .

A tight knot in her belly.

'Kathryn?'

She blinked and realized Boling had asked her something. 'Sorry?'

'Antioch. He was Greek?'

'Probably second or third generation. He didn't look Mediterranean. He looked like some hunky actor.'

'Antioch. That's a town, right?'

'I don't know.'

They watched a wraith of fog skim the house, urged on by a modest breeze. The temperature was cool but Dance needed that. Cleansing. So, too, was the noise of seals barking and of waves colliding with rock, the sounds comical and comforting respectively.

It was then, with a thud in her belly, that she noticed something sitting on the Deck floor, near Jon Boling's feet. A small bag. From By the Sea Jewelry in Carmel. She knew the place. Since Carmel was such a romantic getaway, the jewelry stores tended to specialize in engagement and wedding rings.

My God, she thought. Oh, my God.

The silence between them rolled up, thicker than the fog. And she realized that he'd been mulling something over. Of course, a rehearsed speech. Now he got to it.

'There's something I want to say.' He smiled. 'How's that for verbal uselessness? Obviously if I wanted to say something I'd just say it. So. I will.'

Dance administered a sip of wine. No, a gulp. Then she told herself: Keep your wits, girl. Something big's happening here. She set the glass down.

Boling inhaled, like a free diver about to test himself. 'We were talking about getting up to Napa, with the kids.'

The coming weekend. A little vineyard touring, a little shopping. On-demand TV in the inn. Pizza.

'But I'm thinking we shouldn't go.'

'No?'

So he had in mind a romantic getaway, just the two of them.

Then he was smiling. A different smile, though. A look in his eyes she hadn't seen before.

'Kathryn—'

Okay. He never used her name. Or rarely.

'I'm going to be leaving.'

'Now? It's not that late.'

'No, I mean moving.'

'You're . . .'

'There's a start-up in Seattle wants me. May be the new Microsoft. Oh, and how's this? It's a new tech company that's actually making money.'

'Wait, Jon. Wait. I—'

'Please?' He was so even, so gentle, so reasonable.

'Sure. Sorry.' A smile and she fell silent.

'I'm not going to use the clichés people throw around at times like this. Even though— Didn't you say clichés are clichés because they're true?'

A friend of hers, not she, but she didn't respond.

'What we've had is wonderful. Your kids are the best. Okay, maybe those *are* clichés. But they *are* the best. You're the best.'

She gave him infinite credit for not talking about the physical between them. That was wonderful and comfortable and fine, sometimes breathtaking. But it wasn't a spoke of this discussion's wheel.

'But you know what? I'm not the guy for you.' He laughed his soothing laugh. 'You *do* know what I'm talking about, right?'

Kathryn Dance did, yes.

'I've seen you and Michael together. That argument you had on the porch after you came back from Orange County. It wasn't petty, it wasn't sniping. It was real. It was the kind of clash that people who're totally connected have. A bit of flying fur but a lot of love. And I saw the way you worked together to figure out that the killer, the unsub, had done this for hire. Your minds jumping back and forth. Two minds but, you know, really one.'

He might have gone on, she sensed, but there was really no need for additional citation: it was a self-proving argument.

Tears prickled. Her breath was wobbly. She took his hand, which as always was warmer than hers. She remembered once, under the blanket, she'd slipped her fingers along his spine and felt him tense slightly from the chill. They'd both laughed.

'Now, I'm not matchmaking. All I can do is bow out gracefully and you take it from there.'

Her eyes strayed to the bag. He noticed.

'Oh, here.' He reached to the floor and retrieved it.

He handed it to her. And she reached inside. As she did, the tissue rustled and Patsy, the flat-coated retriever, thirty feet away, swung a silky head their way. Leftovers might loom. When she saw the humans' attention was not on food, she dozed once more.

The box, she noted, was larger than ring size.

'Don't get your hopes up. It's not really a present. Considering it was yours to start with.'

She opened the box and gave a laugh. 'Oh, Jon!'

It was her watch, the present from Lincoln Rhyme and Amelia Sachs, shattered in her enthusiasm to flop to the ground, adding credibility to the Serrano 'escape'. Clutching the Rolex, she flung her arms around him, inhaled his complex scents. Skin, shampoo, detergents, aftershave. Then she eased back.

In his face, sadness, yes, but not a degree of doubt, not a hint that he hoped for her to protest. He'd analyzed the situation and drawn conclusions that were as true as the speed of light and the binary numerical system. And as immutable.

'So, what I'm going to do now, so I can hold it together – because I really want to hold it together and I can't for very long – is to head home.'

He rose. 'Here's my plan and I think it's a good one. Come back every couple of weeks, keep an eye on my house, visit friends. Hack some code with Wes, come to some of Maggie's recitals. And – if you make the decision you ought to make – you and Michael can have me over to dinner. And – if I make the decisions I ought to make – I imagine I'll meet somebody and bring her along with me. And you can hire me to perform my cogent forensic analysis, though I have to say that the CBI's outside-vendor pay rate is pitiful.'

'Oh, Jon . . .'

She laughed through the tears.

They walked to the door and embraced.

'I do love you,' he said. And touched her lips with his finger, saving her from a stick-figure response. With a rub of Dylan's sleek muzzle, Jon Boling stepped through the front doorway and, to all intents and purposes, out of her life.

Dance returned to the Deck, sat back in the chair, enwrapped by the damp chill she hadn't been aware of earlier. Embraced too, far more strongly, by Jon Boling's absence. She slipped on the repaired watch and stared at the face while the second hand made full circuit, just visible in the amber light from a maritime sconce mounted on the wall above and behind her.

Then she closed her eyes and sat back, as Michael O'Neil's words, from forty minutes earlier, came back to her now.

'So, here's the thing. I've thought about this for months, and tried to figure out some other way to say it.'

Kathryn Dance had readied herself for ex-wife Anne's name to rear itself in the next sentence.

'I know you're with Jon now. He's a good guy and I've seen you both together. It clicks. The kids like him. That's important. Real important. He'll never hurt you.'

She'd wondered: Where is this going? These words, amounting to rambling from Michael O'Neil, were disorienting. Why was he justifying to her getting back together with his ex?

His eyes fixed on the ugly yellow ceramic cat, he'd continued, 'I was saying, months and months. But there's no way except meeting it head on. I don't think you're going to want to hear it but I've—'

'Michael.'

'I want to get married.'

Remarried to Anne? she'd thought. Why the hell ask my permission?

Then he added, 'You can say no. I'll understand. You can say Jon's in your life for ever. But I had to ask.'

Oh, my God. Me. He's proposing to *me*.

'I thought Anne was back,' she'd said. Well, stammered.

He'd blinked. 'Anne? Sort of, I guess. She and her boyfriend are getting a small place in the Valley. She knows she hasn't been the best mother. She's resolved to change that and's going to spend a lot more time with the kids. I was proud of her.' He'd given a shallow laugh. 'Anne has nothing to do with us. You and me.'

'Oh, my,' Dance had whispered. Her eyes, too, fell on the jaundiced feline sculpture squatting on her desk. It had never been examined as much as it had in the past three minutes.

Now, sitting on the chill Deck, she recalled perfectly O'Neil's next words: 'So there, I've said it. Will you marry me?' He looked her over closely. 'You know, I'm thinking, after all these years knowing you, working with you, I don't believe I've picked up a lick of kinesics. I have no idea what you're thinking.'

And Dance had risen from her office chair and walked around the desk to O'Neil. He, too, had stood up.

She said, 'Sometimes it's better to leave kinesics out of it. And stick with words. Well, one word.' She'd put her arms around him and, her mouth close to his ear, gripped him as tightly as she could. And answered his question. 'Yes,' Kathryn Dance said. 'Yes.'

Acknowledgments

With undying gratitude to: Will and Tina Anderson, Sophie Baker, Giovanna Canton, Sonya Cheuse, Jane Davis, Julie Deaver, Jenna Dolan, Kimberly Escobar, Jamie Hodder-Williams, Kerry Hood, Mitch Hoffman, Cathy Gleason, Emma Knight, Carolyn Mays, Claire Nozieres, Hazel Orme, Abby Parsons, Seba Pezzani, Michael Pietch, Jamie Raab, Betsy Robbins, Katy Rouse, Lindsey Rose, Marissa Sangiacomo, Roberto Santachiara, Deborah Schneider, Vivienne Schuster, Madelyn Warcholik. You're the best!

About the Author

A former journalist, folksinger and attorney, Jeffery Deaver is an international number-one bestselling author. His novels have appeared on bestseller lists around the world, including the *New York Times*, *The Times* of London, Italy's *Corriere della Sera*, the *Sydney Morning Herald* and the *Los Angeles Times*. His books are sold in 150 countries and translated into twenty-five languages.

The author of thirty-five novels, three collections of short stories and a non-fiction law book, and a lyricist of a country-western album, he's received or been shortlisted for dozens of awards. His *The Bodies Left Behind* was named Novel of the Year by the International Thriller Writers Association, and his Lincoln Rhyme thriller *The Broken Window* and a stand-alone, *Edge*, were also nominated for that prize. He has been awarded the Steel Dagger and the Short Story Dagger from the British Crime Writers' Association and the Nero Wolfe Award, and he is a three-time recipient of the Ellery Queen Readers Award for Best Short Story of the Year and a winner of the British Thumping Good Read Award. *The Cold Moon* was recently named the Book of the Year by the Mystery Writers Association of Japan, as well as by *Kono Mystery Wa Sugoi* magazine. In addition, the Japanese Adventure Fiction Association awarded *The Cold Moon* and *Carte Blanche* their annual Grand Prix award. His book *The Kill Room* was awarded the Political Thriller of the Year by Killer Nashville.

Deaver has been honored with the Lifetime Achievement Award by the Bouchercon World Mystery Conference. And recently he received another lifetime achievement recognition, the Raymond Chandler Award, in Italy.

He contributed to the anthology, *Books To Die For*, which won the Agatha Award and the Anthony.

His most recent novels are *The October List*, a thriller told in reverse, *The Skin Collector* and *The Kill Room*, Lincoln Rhyme novels, and *XO*, a Kathryn Dance thriller, for which he wrote an album of country-western songs, available on iTunes and as a CD; and before that, *Carte Blanche*, the latest James Bond continuation novel, a number-one international bestseller.

Deaver has been nominated for seven Edgar Awards from the Mystery Writers of America, an Anthony, a Shamus and a Gumshoe. He was recently shortlisted for the ITV3 Crime Thriller Award for Best International Author. *Roadside Crosses* was on the shortlist for the Prix Polar International 2013.

His book *A Maiden's Grave* was made into an HBO movie starring James Garner and Marlee Matlin, and his novel *The Bone Collector* was a feature release from Universal Pictures, starring Denzel Washington and Angelina Jolie. And, yes, the rumors are true: he did appear as a corrupt reporter on his favorite soap opera, *As the World Turns*. He was born outside Chicago and has a bachelor of journalism degree from the University of Missouri and a law degree from Fordham University.

Readers can visit his website at www.jefferydeaver.com.

In the best books, the ending often comes as a shock.
Not just because of that one last twist in the tale,
but because you have been so absorbed in their world,
that coming back to the harsh light of reality is a jolt.

If that describes you now, then perhaps you should track down
some new leads, and find new suspense in other worlds.

Join us at www.hodder.co.uk, or follow us on
Twitter @hodderbooks, and you can tap in to a
community of fellow thrill-seekers.

Whether you want to find out more about this book,
or a particular author, watch trailers and interviews, have
the chance to win early limited editions, or simply browse
our expert readers' selection of the very best books,
we think you'll find what you're looking for.

And if you don't, that's the place to tell us what's missing.

We love what we do, and we'd love you to be part of it.

www.hodder.co.uk

@hodderbooks

HodderBooks

HodderBooks